Shadow Dance

BLOOD LEGACY SERIES BOOK 5

ELISE HENNESSY

Flutterbye Trail Press
797 Sam Bass Road #2541
Round Rock, TX 78681

First edition

Editing by Red Loop Editing
Cover Design by FrostAlexis Arts
E-book Chapter Art by Real Life Design
Published by Flutterbye Trail Press

ISBN: 978-1-954582-00-2 (E-book)
ISBN: 978-1-954582-04-0 (Print)

Feedback: Encounter a problem with this book? Let us know at elisehennessyauthor@gmail.com

Books by Elise Hennessy

Books in the Altare World

GRYPHON RIDER ACADEMY
Second Chance
Chosen
Storm Front
Wild Flight

ROYAL SPY INSTITUTE
The Crown Heist
Five & Chance

Also by Elise Hennessy

BLOOD LEGACY SERIES
Dream Walker
The Winter Key
Queen's Return
Court of Illusions
Shadow Dance
Rule the Night
Dhampir's Wish

Blood Curse
Blood Legacy: The Complete Series

Shadow Dance

Blood Legacy Series Book 5

Elise Hennessy

Chapter 1
Sirius

Autumn leaves filtered through the air, following the swirling curlicues of playful gusts. An oak leaf as broad as a man's hand picked up a hasty breeze and smacked across the cheek of Blood Prince Sirius, the Dawn. It clung to his skin, limp and musty.

Considering that Sirius was approaching a fae he needed to impress, he wasn't too happy that the other man's first glimpse of him was seeing him sputter and peel away the offending greenery. When the fae laughed, Sirius locked his jaw to keep a growl from escaping.

Though anger churned in his gut, the ringmaster of the circus around them was not the cause of his ire. He was perched on a spare box in the rest area of the fairgrounds, far from the largest tent, where Sirius had viewed the first show of the day. Other off-duty performers sprawled on an eclectic assortment of mismatched chairs and more boxes.

"There is nothing to see back here, sir." The ringmaster's voice was just as rich and deep as the velvet vest he had unbuttoned and waving in the breeze. Its plum color offset the orange of his fiery skin, cutting a distinct figure even from a distance. He drew on the end of a pipe, blowing a ring of smoke toward Sirius.

Deep breath, he reminded himself.

His inner beast wanted to bear its fangs, seeing the drifting smoke ring as an insult. *Here's your entertainment.*

The beast misread many things, and Sirius was determined not to let it ruin this conversation before it began. "I'm not here for entertainment," he said in a low voice. Despite his best efforts, his words were tinged with the growl of the magic within him. As a shapeshifting vampire, his burden was magic bonded to his instincts and deepest, darkest thoughts. It had a mind of its own, and sometimes, it was the one in charge.

The fae man considered him with eyes of white flame similar to the butterfly-shaped fire that flowed from his back as wings. Like many beings in Faerie, he was unlike anything naturally born on Earth. Humanity didn't come in loud colors.

"What are you here for, human-born?"

Sirius turned a grimace into a smile, fangs and all. Most fae didn't know exactly what he was, since vampires didn't just walk into Faerie. But with eyes an unnatural shade of dried blood and the kind of muscle that put bodybuilders to shame, it was obvious he was something more than human. So, he was referred to as "human-born" or "flat-skinned" around here, the latter of which was supposedly an insult.

"I want to join your circus." Sirius had cornered another performer to know who to ask, and this man was it. Ringmaster and owner of Cloman's Own, Variety Show and Circus.

The fae's brows furrowed as he took another look over Sirius.

"I'm a dancer," Sirius continued. A bold lie, but how hard could it be? He was sure he could pass any test by using the other-worldly grace of the beast within him.

"Are you really?" The ringmaster breathed another laugh.

Except this test. His beast's anger stirred, urging him to get into the fae's space and force him to accept Sirius rather than embrace any doubt.

He'd stripped down to a white undershirt and a dark pair of pants for this, leaving most of his gear behind in the saddlebags of his elk. He was ready to go, needing no extra time to overthink this decision. When this circus packed up, he would be amongst the crew leaving to the next destination.

The fae pointed his pipe toward the one thing Sirius wouldn't part with, even while pretending to need work. "What dancer needs a sword?" he asked with a raised brow.

Considering how deadly iron was to fae, Sirius figured his weapon was a prime target for theft or destruction. He cursed under his breath. Maybe he should've hidden it behind one of the tents before approaching this man.

He pulled his gaze away from the worn grip of his weapon. "Look, I want to come with you. Let me prove I can be an asset," he stated.

The fae tilted his head. A chortle told Sirius that they were gaining an audience as bored carnies listened in and edged closer to this little post-performance sideshow.

It seemed he wasn't the only one who noticed, as the ring-master hopped off his perch and pulled at the wrinkles in his vest. "Come along, then, and tell me about yourself. This is a first. I've never had a human-born interested in joining my humble show."

He and Sirius stepped onto a grassy path trampled down to the earth. They were on part of the front garden of Ironhold Keep, home of the Unseelie Queen Kalimea. Considering what he'd gleaned of fae, the moment these tents came up and the circus wagons trundled away, a small army of druids would descend upon this area, and within hours, there would be no sign of the massive crowd it'd hosted. Most fae had a great and abiding love for nature. Full garbage bins were posted indiscreetly next to wood frame kiosks lining the path and still smelling like fried foods.

Everything was abandoned like a ghost town, save for a handful of carnies already tearing down tents and dragging away props. There were a masquerade and feast to be had in the palace at this time, and everyone who was someone was already inside.

Sirius knew he was a nobody, despite his fancy titles. He'd been asleep for a thousand years, and the world had moved on without him. Humans didn't even know that vampires existed, let alone that the first generation of them had saved Earth from ravenous monsters.

He was a prince to air, his original kingdom drowned and

then exploded into dust. So, why not join the circus? Why not turn his well-honed warrior's body to the task of flips and contortions for the entertainment of others?

Stupid, his beast snarled.

It spoke up just in time to confirm his other thought. If he couldn't get the magic inside him under control, he was nothing more than a beast himself. He'd alienated his friends and family one by one until the only logical way forward was to leave. To pursue a different path.

He was chasing a woman, a performer at this circus, whose touch filled his beast with peace.

Talina, he and his beast sighed at the same time. The only thing they agreed on.

The ringmaster stopped at the biggest tent, drawing the fabric aside. Within, the magic that produced stadium seating into the earth was gone, revealing an empty stage. Wooden supports extended into the darkness of falling evening, the very top in shadow. As the fabric slid behind them, shadows cast a gloom over a place that had been full of energy and color only hours ago.

Sirius preferred it, naturally. One of his unique abilities as a vampire was the ability to walk through the day without harm, but he still desired the cool darkness of night.

His beast wanted to hiss when the fae beside him clapped his hands, igniting a pair of spotlights to shine down on the stage. "Quiet, broody type, hmm?" he asked Sirius.

He spared the other man a confused grunt.

The ringmaster put a hand to his chest. "Name's Cloman, as you may have figured out. Who might you be?"

Oh. "Sirius," he answered. Well, Cloman had already noticed his sword, he might as well not keep secrets. "Blood Prince Sirius, second only to my brother, the King of Vampires."

Was Adrius still King of Vampires when he was a dragon shifter now? He didn't have an answer. They'd parted ways right after Adrius had put a new crown on his head. Maybe if Sirius twisted his beast back under control, he'd get a chance to ask.

Cloman's eyebrows rose up to his hairline. "Blood Prince...a Fell Hunter? Who wants to be a...dancer?"

"That's right," he muttered, his scowl inviting the other man to ditch any extra questions.

A grin split the ringmaster's face as he held up a finger and ducked behind the stage. Sirius rolled his shoulders, cracking his neck as he waited with barely leashed patience. His frown deepened when Cloman returned with a thin rapier in hand. The fancy velvet he'd worn was gone, the ringmaster stripped to his undershirt.

"I know your type, sir. Let's take some aggression out, and then we can talk," Cloman said, falling into a ready stance.

"I may kill you, sir," Sirius echoed him as his beast rose, its claws raking the air.

Fight, it howled. It didn't call for this fae's life only because they didn't know the other man. But that he would challenge Sirius showed he had no idea who he was up against.

"Let's stop just short of that, shall we?" Cloman was still grinning, his bared teeth calling to the aggressive side of Sirius's beast.

He'd have his fight all right. Drawing his sword soundlessly, Sirius closed the distance between them in a heartbeat. He would break that flimsy twig the fae called a weapon and end this duel before the beast drove him to seriously injure his opponent. Cloman had offered this duel out of ignorance, after all...

Except Cloman's rapier flashed up and parried Sirius's strike with enough force to send their weapons ringing.

Fae had a title for those of their kind who'd mastered martial magic and channeled it through their weapon of choice. They were called Blades, and every Blade he'd had the fortune to meet were masters of swordplay. Now Sirius understood Cloman's excitement. Maybe they were more equal than he'd first realized.

"Not bad," the fae sneered.

He likely wanted to make him see red, but that's where he underestimated Sirius. With his adrenaline up and his eyes narrowed to animal slits, man and beast alike were in agreement. They would win this duel, no matter what magic Cloman possessed.

They moved in the kind of dance Sirius recognized, swords flashing and sparking. His beast offered him the kind of boneless grace only an animal could possess, twisting out of the way of strikes that would skewer a common man. In return, Cloman's weapon withstood the force of a Blood Prince's swing despite its thin construction.

"I've never seen a human-born move like you," Cloman said. Their duel continued as the night fell around them, the darkness enclosing their world down to the boards of the stage.

"You've never met a human-born like me," Sirius replied.

A claw of pain ripped his front as Cloman found a weakness in his stance, opening a shallow wound. It healed quickly, but the blood remained and chilled on his skin.

"Isn't that true?" Too busy talking, the ringmaster took a nick of Sirius's blade in response. His wound smoked, and he hissed in pain as his flesh cauterized from iron exposure.

He faltered for a moment too long. Sirius pressed the tip of his weapon close to Cloman's neck, securing his victory. They parted with the fae laughing while Sirius's beast grumbled. It'd been too brief and bloodless.

Too easy.

"You could be your own act," Cloman said as he placed the rapier aside on the stage. He rubbed his injured shoulder with a wince.

"I want to be a dancer," Sirius said firmly.

Cloman tilted his head, his fiery eyes flickering. "You could also run security for the circus. Don't think I don't recognize you."

Sirius paused, confused. His adrenaline was still up, and thus, he drew a blank for when they'd met before.

"You're the man who saved us when mutated animals attacked our camp. You and a redheaded human-born burst out of nowhere and saved us when we didn't have our magic," Cloman said, referring to Neala. She was his sister by convoluted family ties, but many battles together had cemented that bond.

Neala was also the only person who could effectively bring Sirius to heel. He didn't appreciate the reminder of the last time they'd worked together, just to part on the worst circumstances days later. Her words still stung his hide.

"I lost several good fae during that mishap," Cloman said, his expression sober. "So, we could use a fighter like you. If you have your heart set on dancing, prove it to our lead choreographer on the road. We are leaving as soon as we tear down."

"That is fair," Sirius said, his beast perking its ears. Maybe they would have more fights. Maybe *Talina* was the lead choreographer. Either way, he got what he wanted. He was a carnie now.

Chapter 2

Talina

What a day.

Talina knew she should be packing her things. Cloman had drawn everyone together and made it clear that they weren't paying respects to Queen Kalimea. No one was to attend the masquerade or the feast. Once the Unseelie Queen was finished with her revelries, she'd come outside to realize that Cloman's Own didn't appreciate being left in the cold for several days.

For what it was worth, Talina believed that Kalimea had been in a coma all that time. It was too bizarre not to be real. Too many weird things had been happening lately, one after another.

She sat in the shadowy recesses of the biggest tent, hidden as the sun set. She could've nodded off up there if it weren't for the headdress squeezing her temples, the heavy thing slowly slipping down her head. Eventually, she yanked it off and winced as its clasps pulled a few navy strands of her hair free along with it.

The carnies would eventually need to tear down this tent, but until then, she rested her aching feet and kept her swollen ankle elevated in the most literal way possible. It rested on a cushion of wind magic she'd woven. She'd overdone it today, chasing after that human-born man who'd saved her life and then performing her heart out for the enjoyment of Ironhold's citizens.

Did she regret it? No.

Except that man...that *vampire*. He was the one.

"Here for a spell and soon to wander," she murmured.

Her familiar, a Pullin's Island hummingbird, stirred in her fingers. His name was Gem, after the iridescent pink of his feathers, plus the tiny white throat that she liked to tickle with her fingertip. He spoke to her in her mind, as was the way of familiars. *"Overthinking again?"*

She frowned and rubbed his back with a gentle finger. "Who says that?" she whispered. "Who talks like that? No one talks like that."

"It was just a coincidence," he said firmly.

"I think it was the trigger phrase. You know, for my prophecy," she said, a sick twist of nerves in her belly.

"You don't have *a prophecy,"* he argued before flipping his wings and turning abruptly in her hand. She glanced the same way, seeing a triangle of light as two people entered the tent. Masculine voices drifted up toward her.

She tucked her limbs and cloud-like wings into the darkness, stiffening as she recognized Cloman and a distinctly human-shaped man approaching the stage. She was too far up to hear what they were saying, but Cloman activated the spotlights. Those two would be here for a while.

"Want me to see what they're talking about?" Gem offered.

"Sure. But be careful," she responded in kind. Since she didn't have skill in Mind-aligned magic, the only being in the whole of Faerie she could communicate with mentally was her sweet, little familiar.

Gem nuzzled against her thumb and flittered away.

She carefully twisted her body so she could see what was going on below. They were...fighting?

She shook her head, suppressing a sigh. *Men.* They were always hitting each other.

"So, like I was saying. He said the trigger phrase of the prophecy." She was sure of it.

Any fae of consequence was given a prophecy at birth. The more expensive the seer, the more accurate the prophecy, considering how difficult a craft it was to view the future. Her mother had had a prophecy made for her, but it was lost to time.

Talina's prophecy was spoken by the wind instead. Its touch caressed her even here in the stuffiest spot amongst the rafters. It found her anywhere she went, though it didn't always speak.

"Just because you hear things doesn't mean they're prophetic," her familiar answered stubbornly.

She wanted to believe him, because, well...

She didn't have her journal with her, but she'd recorded every phrase and whisper carried on the breeze. At some point, she'd realized she was the only one who could hear the caressing whispers of the wind. That awareness had come hand in hand with the understanding that everyone around her thought she was at least a touch crazed. She kept this particular part of her secret now, glad to be amongst a new crowd that had no idea of her past.

"The vampire wants to join the circus as a dancer," Gem reported.

"No!" she gasped. *"Cloman wouldn't actually take him on as a dancer, would he? Completely, totally, absolutely the worst possible idea ever."*

Gem paused for a moment. She felt his amusement flicker over their shared bond. *"How bad an idea?"* he teased.

"The most awful one."

"He's more muscle than brain. I doubt Cloman will assign him to you," Gem said.

She was watching the fight, though. Cloman sometimes bragged about the very expensive, very exclusive ring he wore that gave him extra-strong Blade magic. She thought it was cheating every time she watched him trounce another person relying on their natural talents and magic. But the vampire he fought was something else. He made fighting Cloman look like a stroll through the park.

He's the one, she thought again, rubbing her belly as it grew queasy.

The moment she had her journal, she'd confirm it. As it was, she remembered a few lines of her prophecy, burned into her mind like a brand.

He will come for you from another world.
Your mate, unlike you've seen.

He will lead your soul to change.

The vampire took a strike across the chest. She flinched at the splash of red across his undershirt, but he finished the duel moments later. A strange tension melted away from her lower back. Now, Cloman would tell him to take a hike, and she wouldn't have to worry about what context the wind meant by her soul *changing.*

Fae only referred to soul changes as cataclysmic, life-shaking events. It changed their true names, staining their immortal existences forever. She wanted nothing to do with that. Absolutely, positively, unquestioningly zero interest.

The two men conversed quietly. She shifted impatiently until Gem finally told her what was decided. Her heart dropped somewhere into the vicinity of her knees. *"Did he really say the big vampire might be a dancer if he proves himself to me?"* she asked in a nervous squeak.

Gem fluttered up to perch on her thumb. *"Yup."*

The tent went dark as the two men left. She let her head thump back onto the wood as she took deep breaths to calm her racing heart.

"What's the matter?" Gem asked, cocking his head in the gloom. *"Just tell him no."*

She thought of her only face-to-face discussion with Sirius. How his blood-red gaze had spoken of deep intensity. He wasn't the kind of man to take no for an answer.

Chapter 3
Sirius

"Who is the lead choreographer anyway?" Sirius had asked.

"She's my best dancer, Talina. I'll introduce you soon," Cloman promised.

That was hours ago. His skin still sparked from the lightning bolt of that knowledge; fate had put him back on track to meet his lifemate again. He had a second chance to speak to her and ask why she'd spooked so quickly during their last conversation.

He rode his elk in the back of the caravan of wagons, watching as the moon peeked above the horizon. His beast wanted to bask in the dim light of the near-full disk. Unlike most vampires, his talents waxed and waned with the moon, and his beast was at its most vicious and uncontrollable when it was full and high in the sky. Just the sight of it gave him extra energy, which was fortunate, seeing as he'd agreed to several hours of watch duty.

Cloman wanted to make significant progress away from the city before daybreak. Sirius wondered what the hurry was, though it suited him just fine. He didn't have to tell Neala that she was right.

He *was* selfish. He'd rather turn his back to his duties and pursue his lifemate. A demonic invasion was looming, but he figured he would be useless against it if he lost the last threads of his discipline and his beast assumed full control. No one knew how close he was to that precipice. He'd kept his mouth closed about it, because he had at least one "ally" that would chain him like an animal rather than help him.

Sometime during the slow journey, he realized he didn't recognize the path despite having traveled it to Ironhold. Called Plunder Road, in the typical contrarian nature of Unseelie, it had been a barren wasteland as he and his small group had raced along it with a terribly injured Neala. There had been a mysterious dead zone placed over the land at the time, making magic impossible to use.

Now that that dead zone was lifted, so was the illusion of emptiness. They passed villages and townships gone dark with the passing evening. Insects sang in autumn-bronzed grass. The air was sweet, laden with the distant scents of ripening fruit and wizening leaves.

Two other guards rode behind the caravan with him. They whispered together, but neither mustered the nerve to address Sirius. He could feel their attention turn to him occasionally and kept his expression flat and scowling. The less these fae knew about him, the better. All that mattered was Talina.

Talina, his beast sighed. It was of the opinion that once the caravan made camp, he should find her, sling her over his shoulder, and disappear with her.

Tempting. Except he was a beast, not a monster. He would have her consent before any attempted faenapping. He had to know if Talina could accept and love him even in the depths of his struggles. Her fleeting touch had been the only thing to silence his inner voice, to tame the magic. That split second had changed his life. Man and beast alike craved another brush of her fingertips, desired another smile to light her delicate face.

He didn't know Talina, but he would do anything for her. Including walk away. It had been his second instinct—to not drop his burdens on her slight shoulders. He would not ruin a beautiful bond, even if it was supposed to be his.

Mine, the beast keened.

He would see her again in good time. He reminded himself of

that even as they made camp and he bedded down at the very edge, where no one would disturb him.

Sirius didn't sleep for even a moment. His gaze kept finding the moon, tracing its path across the sky until it disappeared to graciously allow the sun to rise. Manic energy buzzed under his skin.

The beast was pacing. Was he going to see Talina today? What would she say when she learned Sirius had followed her?

Sometime around daybreak, he abandoned the pretense of rest and tucked his sheathed sword deep within his bedroll. He smoothed over the fabric so it looked flat. At this point, he barely cared if someone stole the weapon—he had to get away.

The beast loved three things: running, fighting, and killing. And maybe Talina, though Sirius rated her at a fascination at present. He wouldn't approach her with that kind of energy. So, he spent it on a run, discovering rabbit trails off the main path as he ducked and weaved through the surrounding oaks. If anyone asked, he decided he was "running surveillance."

"Surveillance" took a long time. He jogged up and down a stretch of Plunder Road for a straight shot before the camp even stirred, loping like a wolf coming in for a kill. As soon as fatigue touched his awareness, he knew it would be a long day, because the camp was just waking up as he stopped, drenched in sweat. Thankfully, he'd spotted a stream not far from there while his beast picked up the smell of sizzling fat as breakfast was prepared.

He took his time washing up since he didn't actually need food for sustenance. By the time he returned to camp, scrubbed and in a new set of comfortable clothing, most of his new fae companions were clustered together. Dozens of eyes turned his way, and he felt like a sideshow yet again. How many had witnessed his early morning jog?

"Sirius!" It was Cloman, waving him over to the fire pit. A set of lesser fae was tending the fire and roasting the hearty breakfast

Sirius's beast rumbled to taste. One offered him a plate piled high with blackened sausage and pan-fried eggs, its thin arms betraying a tremble as the ceramic rattled in its hold.

"Thank you," he said, offering a closed-lip smile as he accepted the offering and a fork.

Cloman clapped him on the shoulder. "Where'd you disappear off to?" he asked, steering Sirius into the crowd of carnies.

"Surveillance," he grunted. His keen gaze roved the faces around them, moving on when they weren't the woman he was looking for.

His skin crawled, his beast going alert. Cloman's hold on his shoulder was chafing. "Before we move on, I wanted to introduce you to Talina. She can assess whether you would be a good fit as a performer."

Sirius didn't hear much past her name, finally spotting her at the corner of the camp. She was perched on a spare box, a plate of cut fruit in her lap. The moment their gazes met, Sirius lit head to toe with awareness, his gaze narrowing down to her and her alone.

Vampires knew their one and only on sight. Sirius had watched others fall to their knees for their beloveds. His brother's mate was his moon and stars, and he'd personally witnessed how Adrius's night turned despondent black when he'd thought her dead. Could this woman be the same for him?

Her gaze widened when they made eye contact, before darting about in search of an escape route.

"Talina, this is Sirius. I want you to see if you can use him in your acts," Cloman was saying.

She forced an overwide smile. "O-of course! We've met," she responded. Sirius gave himself a shake. Her body language screamed discomfort. Her slight shoulders were lifted defensively, and her overlarge eyes flooded with clouds like an overcast day within her thoughts.

Oh no.

She was *afraid* of him, he realized.

What had he done wrong? What did he say?

Steal her. Make her yours, his beast whispered unhelpfully.

Shut up, he snarled back. He turned to Cloman and nodded curtly. Unfortunately, he had experience with frightened women. He'd saved his share of scared people in his Fell hunting days. Maybe it wasn't so different to now.

He started by lowering himself to the ground, averting his gaze. His meal awaited, growing cold by the moment. Much as he wanted to set it aside and focus on Talina, he speared a link of sausage and bit it in half. His skin itched to look at her again.

She was an aether fae, one of the prettiest women he'd ever seen. From this vantage, he could see her blue calves. She was barefoot, her feet slim and fine-boned, toes painted purple with a sprinkling of white dots. Bandages wrapped one ankle.

The goal was for her to speak first, even though he wanted to demand to know how she'd gotten hurt. He gave her the power here, making himself as small and nonthreatening as possible.

The minute of silence between them after Cloman walked away felt like the longest vigil of his life. But eventually, she asked in a quiet voice, "Why are you really here?"

He glanced up with relief. She'd tilted her plate, letting the pink hummingbird perched on her hand dip its beak into the juice accumulating under the fruit. Her face was creased with more curiosity than suspicion, though he read both emotions clear as day off of her.

"Would you believe I rediscovered a passion for entertaining others?" he asked, keeping his voice low and gentle.

Her lips pursed. "Not really," she answered just as softly.

"Then you have your answer." He waited a moment, watching her turn those words over. "You seem quite attached to that bird."

Her eyelids fluttered at the change of topic. Without a visible pupil, he had to guess that she took a glance to the hummingbird and back to him. "Vampires don't have familiars, do they?"

"No. What is a familiar?" he asked, soaking in the hint of her smile as she stroked the bird's back with her fingertip. It was a peek at the cheerful personality he'd seen yesterday, before he'd spooked her somehow.

She tilted her head and so did the hummingbird, echoing her.

"Almost every fae has a familiar. They're like..." Her eyes tilted skyward as she thought. "Like a reflection of who the fae is."

"So, you're a little bird on the inside," he said. He could see it clearly.

She giggled for a moment. "No! I mean, yes. But no. We trade a little piece of magic to make a familiar bond. Gem represents precision, especially with wind magic and flight, so he gave me a little extra when we bonded. In return, he lives as long as I do."

He shoved another bite of food into his mouth. All he could think about was her earlier performance, when she'd defied gravity with a ballet midair, each movement sharp and sure. She put a new word to it, *precision*. "All that from a little bird?" He couldn't help a chuckle.

Gem fluffed into a pink puffball. If birds could glare, he had the feeling that's what the hummingbird was doing.

Talina stiffened too. "Yes. He helps me a lot," she said, sounding defensive.

Lifting his hands, Sirius assumed a submissive posture again. "Have I done something to offend you?" he asked. "If so, I sincerely apologize."

Her brows drifted closer together as she took him in, her gaze darting to Gem as he peeped. Was there some silent exchange going on there?

Before she could answer, though, a third person sat next to him, crossing her ankles and beaming. "I found you, Dad!" she said brightly.

The words were clearly aimed at him. His jaw dropped, and he gawked at Cossette like she'd lost her mind. Maybe the girl-Ancient finally had, right in front of his lifemate.

Talina brightened immediately. "You have a daughter?"

Chapter 4
Talina

"I sure...do." Sirius shoved a piece of egg into his mouth, chewing like a starving man as his pupils turned to animal-like slits.

"Hi!" The cherub waved, smiling wide enough to show dimples. "I'm Cossette." She wore a pastel dress that matched the sky-colored ribbon tying her hair into a high tail. Someone had done it up with care, giving her white crown of hair a bow like a little present. She couldn't be more than seven or eight years old, with solemn, red eyes that clearly came from her father.

"Aren't you a doll?" Talina gushed. "We haven't had a kiddo in the camp since our last strongwoman had her twins."

Sirius looked downright sheepish, a huge change from the diamond-hard intensity he'd turned on her when they made eye contact. *You have your answer.* Had he really been ashamed to admit he'd been looking for a job to provide for himself and his daughter?

"Thank you," Cossette answered, sugar-sweet. "You're really pretty, miss."

Talina giggled, her shoulders sagging with relief. *"It really was a coincidence,"* she said privately to Gem, who she knew would be gloating later. *"He's not my heartsong. I was just jumping to conclusions."*

Despite that, distrust thrummed through her familiar as he kept a leery eye on the two human-born.

"Well, when you're ready, let's see if you can follow a routine. Cloman gives generous bonuses if we can advertise new talent. Generates more sales, you know?" she said, determined to discover whatever dancing skill was hiding within Sirius's hulking body. From how he fought, she figured it wouldn't be hard to find.

"Of course," he said through a tight smile.

Despite her just stating she was *not* a little bird on the inside, the moment he stood, her heart leapt to double time. He was a good foot taller than her, maybe more. He moved with easy grace, flowing to his feet and following her with long strides as they went to a quieter side of camp.

"How old is she?" she asked.

"Pardon?"

She giggled. "Your daughter."

Sirius scratched the back of his head. "Ten?"

"You don't sound so certain."

"The years just blend together." His heavy gaze was now on the girl smiling brightly beside him.

She shrugged to herself and only stopped when they were in the shadow of one of the wagons. It was as private as they could get in a camp so large. She glanced to Gem, humming. *"Why don't you let the girl hold you while I see if he can dance?"* she suggested.

Her familiar puffed with discomfort, turning his beak up at the thought.

"Please? You know how the kids love you," she wheedled. *"I'll give you your favorite flowers."*

She sensed rather than felt him sigh at her. With a flutter of his wings, he hovered over to Cossette, releasing a friendly peep. Her lips parted with wonder as he landed on her hand.

Sirius's hooded eyes flicked from her to Talina. He gestured for her to speak first.

"So, you told Cloman you want to be a dancer. Do you have experience with that? Maybe from a different circus...?" she asked.

"I don't. But I assure you, I can learn," he stated. His voice hit a low register that did something to her insides. Either he was tying her nerves into knots, or something else.

"Okay. What dances do you know?"

He named a few foreign-sounding waltzes and other formal dances. Her brow crinkled with confusion. This man was for real all right. She had a sinking feeling he knew nothing about being a performer.

"Did you watch my performance yesterday and say to yourself, 'I can do that'?" she ventured. Because he certainly couldn't. She'd devoted herself to her craft—mind, body, magic, and soul. Her twinging ankle reminded her of the cost of such things as she shifted in the grass.

"Certainly not. I could never dance like you do," he said quickly.

She stifled a sigh. "Okay, how about this. I'll walk you through some steps, and we'll see how you do." That was her job, after all. She'd taught a few promising dancers herself, when Cloman had picked them up off the road. The ringmaster had an eye for talent.

It was just...he was obviously *different*. Cloman hadn't scouted him as an apt novice. Sirius had come forth out of seemingly nowhere and volunteered. She could work with anyone and actually loved the challenge of a new member to her crew. But where would she put a human-born man in any of the old routines?

Sirius was a quick study, too, watching her every move and echoing it back to her with the kind of fluidity that would make her old trainers weep. He could make his big, muscle-bound body appear as weightless as a leaf on the breeze. It was hard not to be impressed, even when he was simply aping her.

He was something else impersonating a dancer. She already knew it; she'd seen him fight with the same mastery of motion.

"You don't think this is weird?" Gem ventured. His unease was starting to filter into her headspace, dampening her enthusiasm.

Despite the kiddo sitting in the grass, watching them perform,

Talina knew he was right. Sirius had the kind of talent that didn't need a circus. She needed some time to think, sans vampire. "Are you sure this is what you want?" she asked him.

His maroon gaze was fixed on her. "Yes."

"But you're not a dancer," she said, uncertainty pulling at her.

"Have I not proven myself to you?" he asked quietly.

"You could be the best dancer. A *premier danseur*, if you wanted and spent time at a proper ballet academy."

He'd grown very still. "What did you say?"

She stiffened too, some little instinct lifting every little hair on the back of her neck. "Y-you could be..."

"*Premier danseur*," he repeated, the words rolling off his tongue naturally. "First dancer?"

She relaxed when he did. "That's what it means, yes. Most ballet terms are from your world. From a place called France."

Unexpectedly, his face creased with amusement. "Yes, the mystical France."

"Have you been?" She clasped her hands. It was the one place on Earth she wanted to visit if she ever had an opportunity to go. Faerie had adopted ballet when it was at its height of popularity, borrowed first by a troupe of fae who'd pretended to be French ballerinas.

"Long ago, I hailed from the Kingdom of France. But the place you're referring to and the one from my past are likely very different," he said, the humor leaving his bearing. For a moment, he'd been nearly approachable, but that left swiftly.

She cleared her throat, unsure of how to respond. "So, like I was saying...you have talent. I'll add you to the routines."

He breathed a sigh. It sounded a lot like relief to her. "Outstanding."

"And I'll let Cloman know that you have a new job. He'll likely want you to run security for a while longer." She knew Cloman would have mixed feelings about Sirius's reassignment. Someone so strong was a natural for guard duty, but the next time they rolled into a city to perform, they could advertise their newest addition.

Fae would pay good coin to see a vampire like Sirius dance.

"That's no bother," he rumbled. "I can do both."

"I don't think Cloman will pay you extra for that. And we'd have less time to practice," she ventured.

He lifted a shoulder. "I don't like to be idle." Unexpectedly, he reached out and grasped her hand. Bending his head, he brushed his lips over her fingertips. She flushed head to toe with tingling warmth, like the first rush of static from an oncoming storm.

"It will be an honor to learn from the best," he said.

A horn blared from the camp, and she jolted away, knowing what it meant. His hand was still there in midair, lingering, until he rose with a soft growl in his throat.

He reminded her of some kind of graceful animal, fangs and all. A chuff slipped past his lips when she explained the horn was the call to return to the wagons. "We're running behind," she said as they went their separate ways, seeing the annoyance that flickered over his features.

"Of course. After so long in Ironhold," he said, watching the camp bustle with activity. "When shall I see you again?"

"I'll come find you," she promised.

She meant to turn and hop into the wagon with the rest of her little troupe, but the wind chose that moment to blow past. Her navy hair lifted with the caress of the breeze. Inhaling deeply, she raised her arms to feel it eddy over her skin.

It brought with it one of its secret messages, flowing into her pointed ears with a whispering breath. *"You've found him at last."*

She froze, her eyes flashing open. But the zephyr was gone, her hair settling in a limp screen over her face.

"Gods above," she muttered, using her control of the wind to lift her feet in her haste to reach her wagon. She greeted the gaggle of fae ladies she performed with, diving for her journal before they rolled out.

"Weren't you just with that hunky human?" Wisteria asked.

"What was he like?" called another dancer from the side of the wagon.

Giggles filled the space as curious eyes turned her way. She hugged the leather-bound journal to her chest, rubbing its weathered spine out of old habit. "In a word? Intense," she answered.

The more they asked, the more she realized she'd barely learned anything about the vampire, save for his talent. He'd be the third male dancer she'd ever trained with in the circus and the only one on hand at present. Talk about standing out.

Well down the road, the other dancers finally got tired of her "I don't know" answers and turned to safer topics. She cracked open her journal, scanning the contents with a sigh.

Flipping to the last page with writing on it, she jotted the wind's newest whisper on the next line. She'd ordered her prophecy as best she could, but this was a new development that deserved its own space. Hundreds of lines lay within the pages.

She scanned those scribbles and the arrows reordering and grouping together different lines, delivered out of order on the whims of the breeze. *I'm not crazy*, she thought.

Tell that to the girls who made her life miserable.

Amongst the lines of her prophecy, she'd immortalized the words that had cemented her path to this wagon rather than a different set of stages as a graceful ballerina.

Crazy freak was the kindest insult.

She snapped the journal shut, tears pricking at the corners of her eyes. Why did she write down what those girls said about her? She could've just let them fade to the background to be forgotten.

A little part of her worried that they were right.

No one else could hear the wind talking to them, nor did it tell them that they'd found someone who would lead their soul to change. A bead of sweat made its way down her spine as she opened up the journal again, her finger finding the line she'd circled and underlined as the very first.

Just here for a spell and soon to wander. Spoken word-for-word from Sirius's lips. No one had ever said it to her before. It was the trigger for the rest, she was sure of it.

She followed an arrow to the next line: *One day, you shall dance in the wind, with shadows.*

And she'd still not figured out what that meant. She danced with the wind all the time, but shadows?

Maybe she and Sirius would figure that one out together.

Chapter 5
Sirius

"So, you're my daughter now," Sirius began to the girl seated before him on his elk. He rode out of earshot of the other guards, his gaze swimming with barely leashed fury.

Cossette was no girl, but a woman of nearly nine hundred years trapped in a young frame. She'd slid in and manipulated Talina so thoroughly he worried how the fae would react when she learned Cossette's true identity and how he'd unwillingly played into it.

His beast snarled, even more worked up than usual because of who the offending party was. He had a code, and right atop it was how he would never hurt a child. The beast within him always played by that rule. Cossette was skilled enough in appearing and acting like a kid that she had it fooled. His anger had nowhere to go.

"For now," she answered cheerfully, glancing up at him. "I'm here to help."

"I don't need your help," he snapped.

She giggled girlishly. "Sure."

A few minutes passed before he breathed a sigh. "Tell me why you're here, then." Though faulty, Cossette possessed the rare ability to see the future. Those overwide albino eyes turned solemn and clear when she spoke as an adult, sharing bits and snatches of incoming fate. After spending extended time with

Izell, who pinched the girl-Ancient anytime she regressed back to her giggly, girlish side, Cossette was more lucid than he'd ever seen her.

"I'm your guide," she said, a self-important smile crossing her face. "Izell took me to Faerie and promised I'd get what I came here for if I helped lead you to your goal."

Now she definitely had his attention. "A deal of mutual benefit, then."

"Mostly for you. You need a lot more work than I do," she said flippantly.

"I'll kick you off this elk," he grumbled.

"You wouldn't really do that, would you?" She flashed an innocent smile. "Dad?"

He muttered uncharitably under his breath. Damn her for twisting his arm like this. Talina probably thought he was already mated.

"For the record, I'm eight. Next time someone asks," she continued like she didn't hear him. "You look like a bad dad if you don't know that right off."

Great, now Talina thought he was mated *and* a deadbeat.

"Anything else?" he demanded.

She hummed and started ticking off on her fingers with each sentence. "Talina thinks you're weird. Lucia's not dead. Neala's worried about you."

He worked his jaw. "Weird how?"

"That's the one you're asking about?"

He glared with the kind of look that could make grown men piss their pants.

"I know you're not going to hurt me, Dad." She muffled another giggle even as he growled his displeasure. Irritation sparked under his skin.

Run. Fight. Kill. His beast's favorites were all off the table. He'd have to sit on this elk and take this unique torture.

"Weird like, c'mon. You're a prince." She reached up and poked his cheek. "Where's the charm? You can't stare at her and expect her to fall at your feet."

Had he been staring? He scratched the back of his head,

feeling his lips take a sheepish twist. "I haven't charmed a woman since..." Brow furrowing, he turned back time in his mind. Far, far back.

Cossette waited patiently, her little hands folded under her chin.

"Since none of your business. Too busy for women," he grumbled, forced to acknowledge just how long it'd been since he'd known a woman's intimate touch.

She considered for a few moments, finally lifting a shoulder. "To be fair, it's not just you making it weird right now."

Talina's sudden fear of him came to mind. "Tell me more," he said, wanting to shake her for more information. Enough of the bits and snatches. He wanted the full puzzle, every piece in place.

"Not my place to say it. But if I may offer a word of advice instead?" She waited until he nodded. "You should be honest about who you are and where your powers come from. The weirdest thing about you, to her, is how you've come out of nowhere with an abundance of talent."

"How is that weird?"

When her eyes glazed over and she smiled vacantly, he ground his teeth in frustration. End of the line. He had to admit she'd done well holding an adult conversation, and he'd wasted some of it.

He should've asked about Neala.

You inflict your anger on others and expect them to deal with it.

Truth. He sighed, scrubbing his face. In quiet moments like this, he could admit that he'd alienated the only friends he had. No wonder he was alone now, his "guide" notwithstanding.

I know what your problem really is. You're selfish.

His beast hissed. *No, it couldn't be.*

He uncoiled his fist, revealing inch-long claws and the punctures he'd made in his palms. If Neala was right, he'd turned his back on everything he used to be: a Fell Hunter, a hero, a champion of mankind.

Now, he was the kind of man who made his prospective lifemate feel *weird*. Who was he now, and how could he turn back time to return to the person he wanted to be?

"What's wrong, Mister Fabron?" Cossette asked with childish innocence. "Do you want to play a game to pass the time?"

Her words hit him unexpectedly hard, cracking his heart like dropped ceramic. She reminded him that he wasn't the only one with deep flaws under the skin. If the person who'd tortured her psyche was still alive, he swore they'd know true agony and death by the time he was through with them.

"Stop that," he murmured. Retracting his claws, he pinched the soft flesh of her upper arm. She shook off the juvenile countenance, her expression clearing. *If it works for Izell, it will work for me too*, he thought.

By the time Sirius found his bedroll again, exhaustion finally pulled his discordant thoughts under a blanket of rest. He entered a foggy dream state through a funnel of darkness. In the junction where reality met fantasy, he recognized where he was. A warehouse. New York. Modern times.

Had it only been a few months since he was here? Boxes and pallets were stacked nearly to the ceiling, making a maze. Magic hung heavy in the air like oppressive humidity, making his inner beast snarl and curl into a furious ball within him as its presence faded to a whisper.

Silence.

"Sirius," a voice sing-songed. "I know you're here." The maze and the magic, it was all a prison for one person in the heart of it all, shackled to a concrete wall with golden nephilim chains.

Lucia, as she'd once been. Before the corruption and insanity. Her wrists strung up above her, her thick, black hair hanging limp over her shoulders. She raised her head and smiled, her lips still scarlet against moon-pale skin. Clear of darkness, her silver eyes sparkled even in low light.

"You're always here for me," she crooned.

Sirius came here countless times while everyone else was

busy with their own affairs. It was a bubble in time, one that had burst the second Lucia died and came back with hellfire still singeing her skin.

Dreams were strange that way, picking just the right moment before an irrevocable change. Sirius didn't have his animosity nor his beast here, just the same question he always asked her.

"Why?" This time, it came out as a demand.

"Oh, it's good to see you too," she said. The way her mouth lifted at the corner sardonically was out of the norm. She usually bowed her head again in exhaustion. "Always back to the beginning, no matter what dream we walk together."

His brow furrowed. This wasn't how he remembered his visits.

"Why did I betray you?" She tilted her head. "I didn't betray *you*, dear Sirius. You could've stayed in Nyixa a thousand years ago. Maybe it would've been better for both of us if I'd crowned you king rather than let you leave the island."

"Attacking my brother was attacking me," he stated.

Her expression shaded with deep boredom, every line of her face digging in. "He was supposed to die."

"He was," Sirius agreed. The dream threatened to flicker out and show him Adrius, but she lifted a shackled hand. His thoughts went blank, spine rigid.

"It's no matter anymore. Time marches forward without us."

"As it always will," he sighed. He saw double, his vision twisting around as wakefulness rose and then settled them both in a different scene.

He remembered this night, over a thousand years ago. The crescent moon burning through Nyixa's darkness, causing the white-stone palace to glow like a beacon. Frothy light filtered through the windows, casting an alluring angle over Lucia's nude form.

"Come to me," she whispered, beckoning with soft hands.

His body went still with a hard inhale. *No.* His beast built up to a roar, beating on the cage of his mind. *No. No! Kill her! KILL HER!*

"What's the matter? Shy?" Her smile formed a blood-red

bow. "It's been a thousand years, but surely you're as lonely as I..."

His lips pulled back from his teeth. He advanced one heavy step, his world narrowing in a scarlet haze. "You're defenseless. I'll make you wear your blood instead," he growled.

When the island was at peace, his brother newly married and blissful, Lucia had tried to seduce him in exactly this fashion. Sirius had been drunk on the nectar of life, of surviving a bloody war. He'd had eternity before him as an immortal hero.

But he'd refused to sleep with Lucia. He still remembered her as an old, bent-over crone before drinking the blood of the Fell Emperor. No veneer of fine beauty could change his associations. She hadn't tried beckoning him back to her bed, instead swearing that he would regret scorning her.

Lucia had killed Adrius for the first time and banished Nyah only a week later. He was eternally grateful he'd never touched Lucia intimately, since she became his eternal enemy from that moment onward.

"I need your soul, Sirius," she sang, her silver eyes feverish. "What do you prefer? Do you want this instead?"

In a blink, she was Nyah seated primly at the foot of the bed, golden and glowing with a nephilim's light. The only thing she wore was Nyixa's moonstone crown on her brow.

Sirius recoiled, his expression twisting with horror.

Kill her! the beast screamed.

"No? I guess not." She stood, prowling over toward him. Lucia had caught the predatory ease in her gait, a new trait from Nyah's wolf side. But those eyes were wrong, too dark and crazed.

Sirius backed up, hitting the wall. "Don't come any closer," he demanded, his heart threatening to beat out of his chest.

"Why not? Is there someone else?" she asked, tilting her head. Sirius said nothing, but her lips pulled up anyway. "I can see her in your mind."

In a blink, she sized down into Talina, wearing the leotard she performed in last. "You have a lifemate now," she said, her voice shading into Talina's higher register. "Oh, Sirius. Now I have you."

"Sirius? Wake up. Sirius!"

Light poured into his corneas. He was awake in moments, his face inches from Talina's. She startled away when he sat up.

"You overslept," she said, releasing a soft giggle.

His brows drew together as her voice echoed in the groggy fog of his mind.

"Just a bad dream," he murmured, feeling it already fading away. The only thing that remained was the fierce ache of his beast craving violence to the highest degree.

Chapter 6
Talina

Despite having slept through breakfast, Sirius had bruise-like shadows beneath his eyes. *"He looks dead,"* Gem commented from his perch on her shoulder.

"Don't be rude." But if Gem was saying it, she was thinking it. *"Maybe it's a vampire thing. He could be sick."*

"Are we moving?" Sirius was already on his feet, rolling up his supplies and securing his sword at his side.

"Pretty soon. Cossette's riding with my troupe, by the way." When his brow furrowed, she rushed to add, "She's going to have a lot of fun! My girls love children. You'll find most of us do."

Shrugging, he slug his bedroll over his shoulder. "Fine."

She followed as he went to his elk where it milled in the grass placidly. The beast lifted its head, trotting up to him and closing its eyes as he stroked its snout.

"There's my girl," he murmured. Turning, his eyes widened upon seeing Talina still standing behind him. Maybe he expected her to flutter off like a frightened bird.

She was all too aware of Gem over their bond, urging her to do just that. Some of the color had returned to Sirius's face, but he was still the man from her prophecy. *"I'll handle it,"* she assured her familiar.

"I have a few questions." Her voice came out less certain than she liked. She earned a solemn nod from Sirius, as if he was expecting this.

"Would you like to ride with me?" he offered.

"No need. Cloman wants me to get you into an act as fast as possible, by the way." She smiled brightly for him and Cossette. Surely that would be good news for a man wanting a fresh start with his daughter. Unease tickled her belly when he barely nodded.

Maybe he wasn't a morning person? Now that made sense for a vampire.

"We're almost to the city of Terisz. We've missed our engagement here by..." She tilted her head back and forth as she considered. "...at least four days. But we're going to take an extra day to rest up and spread some excitement that we finally arrived."

He stroked his elk's neck idly, turning so his gaze oversaw the camp as stragglers boarded their wagons. "Will I be expected to perform in a couple days, then?" he asked.

"If you look good doing it," she answered, nearly startling at the low rumble from him. It rolled into a single, rusty laugh, one side of his lips lifting. She caught a glimpse of pearly teeth, a sharp upper canine amongst them.

The horn to move out sounded, and the caravan rolled into the road. Sirius's mirth faded as quickly as it came. He swung onto his steed's back, offering her a hand up when she didn't move. She shook her head, rolling her shoulders so her cloud-formed wings stretched behind her. With a single flap, she hovered a foot off the ground.

Sirius raised a brow. "Won't you get tired?"

"You'll see." She giggled, lifting her face to the morning breeze as it eddied over them.

"*Daughter,*" it whispered today.

That's right, she was an aether fae, a daughter of the wind. She felt more at home in her body with her feet off the ground. She flew by Sirius's side as the back of the caravan started moving, glad to be afforded some privacy as the other guards avoided getting too close.

"Before you ask your questions, I have a confession," he said, taking a long look around before turning to her. Her head bobbed at his eye level, dipping in a graceful arc with every slow glide of her wings.

Her heart, meanwhile, took an inelegant dive somewhere alongside her knees. Suddenly, she didn't really want to know why he was the one the wind spoke of.

"I thought you said you were handling it," Gem snarked.

She cracked a nervous smile and listened, hoping Sirius answered some of her uncertainties upfront.

"I did watch you perform a few days ago and said to myself, 'I can do that too,'" he began. "But if I truly can, it's not because I have any talent I've worked hard to earn."

"Are you not a highly trained swordsman? You beat Cloman," she nearly blurted. He fought the exact same way he danced, as far as she'd seen. One did not wake up with a body like his, not without an abundance of time and effort.

Another of his rare smiles made an appearance. He was alluring in an odd sort of way, since he had a human face. His beard had quickly grown from a shadow on his jaw to the kind of scruff she wanted to touch and know the texture of. Instead of porcelain-perfect fae skin, there was texture to his pale cheeks, his brow and cheekbones set differently than she was used to.

And she was staring. She flicked her gaze up to the sky before he noticed. The sun was screened by broad, orange leaves from the trees above, but many branches were stripped bare as the seasons changed. She wouldn't be surprised if they saw snow in the coming fortnight.

"Cloman has loose lips," Sirius said, drawing her attention back to him.

Actually, she figured the ringmaster was mortified that he lost, but she didn't want to admit to having had the best seat in the house to watch their duel. "He was undefeated." She affected a shrug. "You must be something special, since he cheats."

He stilled, frowning. "What do you mean, cheats?"

"Well, he wears a ring that makes him the best swordsman." She tilted her head. "Second-best swordsman. Catch him drunk.

He brags about how it cost him more than employing the whole circus for a month."

Sirius was quiet several uncomfortable seconds too long. His eyes were narrowed to cat-like slits, and she wondered what it meant when they contracted that way. "He has a Fell Key," he rumbled.

"A what?"

"A ring of power." He clutched his forehead. "I can't believe I didn't notice him wearing it. But...that circles back to what I wanted to tell you."

It did? Right, he was confessing, and she'd gotten him distracted.

"Like Cloman putting on that ring, I've inherited a lot of power as well. It was overnight for me." He scratched the back of his head. "I know this will seem hard to believe, but I'm over a thousand years old."

"Oh, sure," she nodded. Many greater fae lived that long or longer under the peaceful rule of King Orin and Queen Kalimea.

"I seem a thousand years old to you?" he asked, sounding puzzled.

"You can act whatever age you want in Faerie," she said cheerfully.

His expression shaded harder into confusion. "I was hoping I didn't seem that old. I'm really only about fifty."

"I'm thirty-four," she volunteered, hoping that might make him feel less self-conscious.

"And I've been asleep for a thousand years."

"Oh!" she gasped. "Were you cursed?"

"Apparently, I took in a huge dose of something called languor dust."

She nodded along, feeling her eyes round with sympathy.

His lips quirked. "And the way vampire abilities work is that they grow stronger the longer you're alive." His maroon gaze met hers, shadows dancing in the dark color. "Upon waking up, I've been able to do things most dream of, because I'm a shapeshifter. I used to be limited to animal forms, but now, I can borrow traits from any animal in a split second."

"Like a druid?" she asked, naming the profession that maintained the world's balance, flora and fauna alike. Nature's blessings often included shapeshifting magic.

He shrugged. "If a druid can do what I can, maybe I am not as unique as I thought. Can a druid give themselves hollow bones like a bird and the grace of a striking snake at the same time?"

She recoiled at the idea of somehow hollowing out one's bones, even with magic. That sounded like a great way to break something with a mistimed fall. "I don't think so."

"Well, that is how I dance. Without magic, I would be a stumbling oaf." He flashed a grimace.

If she didn't know better, she'd say he was nervous. A part of her was tickled that this big, human-born man was already so invested in what she thought of him. He was surrounded by fae just as talented as her, yet he sought her out.

There was no doubt in her that he'd joined Cloman's Own for any other reason than her. He fixed her with a serious look and said, "I have to ask a burning question. What did I say that scared you so?"

The fizzy feeling in her belly soured to ice droplets. Her smile fell off her face, clouds undoubtedly skidding over the clear skies reflected in her eyes. Did she dare tell him about the prophecy?

"Just here for a spell and soon to wander," she echoed his offhanded comment, the phrase she'd never heard other than from a sigh on the wind. "It told me that—"

She choked on saying it like her nerves tied themselves around her throat. Sirius tilted his head, clearly not seeing how fateful his words were.

C'mon, you can say it, she told herself. *He joined the circus for you.* He clearly wasn't interested in money, even with a young daughter to support. One didn't develop a sudden abiding love for something they'd never done, as he'd confessed. He had to already know.

Still, it felt like letting a djinni out of its bottle.

"It told me that you're my true mate," she admitted quietly. "And I'm just not ready for that."

As she expected, he showed no shock over their potential

connection. "Do you want me to go?" he offered. "I would never put undue pressure on you."

If he did leave before anything happened between them, the prophecy would be off. She wouldn't have to worry about experiencing something that'd change her very soul.

She didn't hesitate as she answered, "No. Stay."

How fundamentally broken was the man beside her that his immediate offer was to give up? She'd seen through his tough, human-born face: he didn't think he measured up for some reason. He didn't know her, though. Most men would take a second and third look at themselves for any attraction toward her if they saw the scribble-scrabble of a journal she kept. If they knew she talked to the wind and could swear that, sometimes, it answered her.

I'm not crazy.

But the problem was...she might be. Sirius had no idea what he was getting into, but the smile he gave her could've melted the clouds of an overcast day and let the sun shine through.

He offered his hand, and this time, she took it. Tingles ran up her arm, turning into a flutter of butterflies through her chest as he brushed his lips over her fingertips, his hooded eyes fixed on her, brighter than ever with warm intent. She felt this was how he declared his interest, a gentleman of old at his core.

Chapter 7
Sirius

It wasn't until after Talina left that Sirius wondered how, exactly, an offhand statement had clued her in on their budding connection. He'd been so blinded by the way she'd smiled and told him to stay, some of her bubbly personality shining through the cracks of the fear she'd erected as armor.

Cossette was right. Telling the truth about himself was the best option. He could share his gifts without adding what they cost him, how he couldn't truly control a thousand years of shapeshifting magic with only a paltry amount of practice.

Talina, his beast sighed. He wished she'd chosen to ride with him, but the moment after he'd kissed her hand, she'd decided that was enough private time and flown off to one of the wagons.

Even her blush was pretty, though. Her skin had flushed purple. Now that he thought of it, it made sense for red blood to turn her skin that shade, but it was still exotic on a woman born in a different world.

With that line of thinking, he dug in his saddlebags during the noonday break and pulled out a sealed case. Cold mist drifted into the air as he opened it and withdrew a silver-plated vial.

Izell, the fae that'd brought him to Faerie in the first place, had given him this case and likely set the enchantments over it personally.

"You can never drink fae blood. Do you understand?" she'd demanded before the trip had even begun. If he hadn't agreed and sworn an oath on his blood, she wouldn't have brought him.

For the chance to find his self-control again, he'd have pledged to far worse, though the cold, magically preserved blood was akin to hospital food for mortals. He held the frosty vial while he traveled, but magic was what made it chilled. No amount of time would warm it up.

Grumbling, he popped the seal on it and took a sip. His beast growled, wanting to kill something and feast on its flesh instead.

Shut up, he sighed, watching the world scroll by. The blood had almost no taste, but it would keep him going, and that would suffice.

Maybe if he saw Neala again, he'd ask what fae blood tasted like. He knew she was nibbling on that new mate of hers, the half-fae Cedric.

I wonder how they're doing.

He should've said goodbye, at least. It was stupid to get heated with Neala and not bid her a proper farewell. If there was any wisdom he'd carved from his experiences, it was that any farewell could unexpectedly be the last.

Neala would be fine, though. And so would he, right? So, why was he worrying?

Thoughts of Neala's mate brought him back to his own. Life-mates were a rare glimmer of light in the night of a vampire's world. They were either equals or opposites, usually the latter in Sirius's experience. Neala had bonded to an opposite so comically different from her it was a wonder nature had shaped such a man. Gentle, sensitive, and upbeat compared to his sister's stark warrior attitude. They were good together.

He figured he and Talina were equally extreme as opposites. He just had to look at how delicate she was, spun of sky and fleecy clouds. As she'd flown beside him, he'd wanted to bury his face in her wings to see if they were as soft as they looked.

Those thoughts were *not* his beast talking, either, though it wasn't opposed to anything that involved touching her again.

They set up camp earlier than expected, coming to a grassy ridge overlooking another fae city. Sirius heard that this was Terisz, the next major settlement west of Ironhold. To his surprise, carnies started popping tents and other attractions with speed and efficiency. He stood aside from the bustle, wondering if he should be helping.

"You're Sirius, right?" A terran fae had slid to his side, eyeing him through her lashes. She was tall and willowy, like many of the fae he'd met, her eyes like shining emeralds set in the earthy tone of her face. She was still a head shorter than him, something he'd gotten used to since he was a practical giant even by comparison to normal vampires.

He recognized the coy tilt of her head. Though she was lovely, she wasn't the fae he wanted to see. "That's right," he replied in a wary grumble.

"I'm Wisteria, one of the troupe! The girls and I have been waiting so patiently to meet you." She curled a length of lavender hair around her fingers.

He forced a small smile. "Where is Talina?" He didn't need to know her troupe. A collection of women was drama, in his experience, like crabs in a bucket waiting to claw at the single woman he was interested in lifting away from them.

Wisteria's pout told him that was exactly what was waiting for Talina unless he made it very clear his interest was unwavering. "She's making sure we get a few hours with the stage for practice."

"So, she is with Cloman?"

Wisteria nodded and took him to the front of a tent, where Talina and another fae were deep in argument while Cloman stood back and listened.

"I don't *care*. The dancers are always hogging the stage," snarled the man nearly in Talina's face.

"And your people can still practice out in the grass!" Her voice was shrill as she gestured in irritation. "We need the stage!"

Sirius growled low in his throat, coming up behind Talina. He projected some of his power, eyes narrowing and starting to glow as his fangs descended. "Is there a problem here?" he rumbled.

Fear scented the air, his beast rolling in it with relish. He was the apex predator here—they should be scared. Talina's anger extinguished with a surprised sound, while the fae she'd been arguing with backed away.

"Y-you must be the human-born she was talking about," he said, putting his hands up. "My guys can practice in there later, I guess."

"Good decision." Sirius stared until the other man disappeared behind a group of carnies lugging a rolled-up tent.

Only then did he turn and point to Cloman. "Duel?" he asked, grinning with the lethal points of his fangs on full display. More than one fae heard the invitation and stopped to look.

Cloman glanced around, his lips pursing. With the power of a Fell Key on his finger, surely he never backed down from a challenge. "We'll use the stage. And if you're not cut to ribbons, then you can clean it and use it for your practice," he answered.

Word traveled quickly, all hands turning to erecting the main tent and setting up its stage. Talina cut him a wide-eyed glance in the midst of its preparation while he stretched fluidly and made a big showing of preparing. He knew he had to sell this well.

"Why?" she asked simply.

"If he commands a Fell Key, I have to see what he can do," he said.

She shook her head slowly, her hair shifting to the side like a navy flag as the wind combed past them. "But you've already defeated him privately. Isn't that enough?"

"How many people do you think he's told about that?" His budding plan wouldn't work if everyone already knew about their first duel.

"No one," she murmured. "I just...I was there for the first time."

"Where?" He breathed a chuckle. Hopefully, she wouldn't tell another soul.

She lifted her hand. A pink blur buzzed past her fingers, and she giggled. He savored the sound of her glee as Gem zipped laps around her head and shoulders. "Aw, Gem! You're back," she said loudly, turning away.

As a Seelie, she couldn't tell a lie, so he figured there was some secret she didn't want to share. He allowed the distraction as she lifted the hummingbird cupped in one hand. Now that he was still, Sirius spotted a mini red ribbon tied around the bird's neck. "And someone gave him a tiny bow. Did you have fun with Cossette?"

That must've been Cossette's cue, as she appeared next to Talina in a blink. Her hair was in a complicated braid, crowned by a colorful ring of flowers. Wearing a showy little dress and makeup, it looked like a bored troupe of fae had spent significant time turning her into a living doll.

Sirius flashed a smile like a fond father would. She *was* cute, but it was so hard to act like the girl was anything other than a venerated vampiress playing pretend. "We had a lot of fun," she said, her red eyes sober and gleaming up at him. "The ladies are sure interested in you, Dad."

"Great," he muttered. He knelt down to adjusted her flower crown and spoke at a near-inaudible level. "Do you think my plan will work?"

She giggled and tugged at his hand, beckoning he bow his head further to whisper in his ear. Just a girl sharing a secret with her father. "It's a better shot than just asking for it," she told him.

He nodded, patting her shoulder in acknowledgement. That was about what he thought too. Rising to his feet, he waited until everyone was ready. And by everyone...he thought the whole circus was in attendance as he climbed onto the newly erected stage and stood opposite of Cloman. He stripped his shirt off, not wanting to damage it.

A rippling, feminine sigh sounded to his beast's advanced hearing. Cursing, he reminded himself that he was putting on a show for more than just Cloman. The light caught the fae's ring as he, not to be outdone on his turf, stripped off his shirt and vest as well. The Key's stone glimmered a steely color.

The beast was pleased to hear fewer sighs when Cloman bared his chest.

Sirius took a deep breath, reminding his beast not to take this personally, then gave everyone what they came for; a good show.

But in the end, he pretended to mistime one stroke of his sword, and the crowd cheered as Cloman claimed victory in their duel.

The fae grinned. "Guess the first time was a fluke, hmm?"

"We'll have to do best two out of three." His beast growled, the sound echoing deep in his throat. It made the job of looking like a sore loser that much easier.

Chapter 8
Talina

"AM I STILL PURPLE?" SHE ASKED GEM AS SHE MILLED WITH her troupe, waiting for the stage to dry. Sirius had offered to mop up any errant blood and made sure it was spotless for their practice session.

All while not wearing a shirt. Gods above, the man had muscle definition. He'd been so focused on the simple task of scrubbing that she'd gotten a less-than-discrete eyeful of his perfectly shaped abs and the hint of a sculpted v-line interrupted by the line of his pants. He was almost as pale as a curse fae, which she understood to be an unusual complexion amongst humans. Not that she'd met any other than him.

He kept flicking a shaggy mane of black hair out of his face as it hung loosely when he bent over. While he worked, her gaze kept catching on one flaw: a crescent of scar tissue marking the curve where his right arm and shoulder met. What had happened to permanently mark him?

She'd glanced up from her last perusal just to meet his gaze. He'd flashed a knowing smile and melted her insides with a lingering smolder. Maybe her blush would never ease. It certainly felt like it, to be caught admiring him so openly.

"You resemble a lavender cluster," Gem answered. As a hummingbird, he saw color better than she did. They'd learned pretty quickly that he had names for shades she'd never be able to

see, so he just referenced various flowers to compare. And anything in purple tints meant she hadn't mastered herself yet.

Her familiar cocked his head. *"Isn't it good to be attracted to your mate?"*

"He's *not my mate yet*," she protested privately, making the switch because her dancers were milling about impatiently to begin as well. Everyone wanted to see Sirius dance after his duel with Cloman. He'd used the same boneless grace as the last match between them, but this time, he'd lost. It niggled on her mind. How could he possibly have lost when he'd obviously been more than a match for Cloman during their first duel?

"Thank the fates for that," Gem muttered. She shot a surprised look down at where he perched on her wrist. *"Sorry. I don't trust that guy at all."*

"Why not?"

"He's keeping secrets, Talina. That whole bit about his magic? I think it was just scratching the surface. He's awfully awkward around his so-called daughter." She sensed some hesitance before he added, *"There's something off about her as well. She doesn't act like a little girl unless she's with someone else."*

Her eyebrows raised. *"What does she act like when no one else is around?"*

Gem tilted his head the other way, considering. *"Still. Silent. Not for five seconds, like the average kid. Hours, just content doing nothing."*

She rubbed a flare of goosebumps off her arms. Gem was a good familiar. He rarely lied except to spare her feelings. While others scoffed at her accepting a familiar too small to do anything "useful," they overlooked how he could go unnoticed despite his bright coloring.

"You're right, that's weird." She would need to think on it and what it could mean. But in the meantime, she took to the stage with her ladies, leaving Sirius—who'd thankfully donned his shirt again—to sit and wait. It was easier to refresh everyone else on a semi-dated routine first. It'd been a couple years since their last male dancer quit. He'd been a whirlwind of drama anyway, so the only loss was that Cloman didn't

permit her to choreograph a routine with a woman in a male role.

If this were a proper ballet company, not only would they have enough men to perform any dance they wanted to, but she wouldn't have a boss hovering about and reminding her about concerns over "optics." Alas, she'd left that life behind to bring a hint of style to a variety show. She could make a huge, human-born man look more natural than a woman dancing a male role if the dance was choreographed right, but it wouldn't be ballet.

For now, she reminded everyone of a routine that had a small part for a man and then called Sirius up to teach him. Ordinarily, having a new person on board was a bore, but every lady lay around on the edge of the stage or amongst the first row of seats to watch him mimic and acclimate to her steps.

The soft whispers of clustering women faded the more Talina leaned into the routine. Though Sirius's part was brief, it was stunning and expressive when done right. She'd adapted this dance from a longer ballet telling the story of a man going to war and not returning. Sirius danced the farewell piece of the soldier to his wife while the troupe gestured with grand swoons and sweeping sighs, creating a visual spectacle with three layers of movement—above, behind, and center stage.

Tingles broke over her hips when she instructed him to grasp them, the solid wall of his body inches away. She wet her lips, suddenly aware of him for different reasons. "Nearly done. Have you done a stage kiss before?"

His gaze dropped to her mouth. "Can't say I have."

Gods above, he was smoldering again. Heat tickled her cheeks until she glanced away. "It's pretty easy. Dip, kiss, done. The curtain falls, and we clear out for the next act."

"Dip, kiss, done," he echoed with his rumbling laugh. Her insides tied themselves up at the low sound.

She walked him through positioning them both so his back was to the stage. A stage kiss would look real if their faces weren't really visible. He dipped her with ease, the two of them moving as if they'd done this dozens of times. He leaned down, his breath skating over her neck.

"Like this?" he asked.

She felt him watching her neck and the flickering pulse there. "A little higher," she managed to gasp.

He placed her back on her feet, his strong arms flexing. She knew he'd never drop her if they were dancing together. She turned and beckoned to another dancer. "Now, let's see you dance with Wisteria. She's going to be your partner tomorrow."

Sirius's gaze flicked to the purple-haired fae, then back to her. Lips quirking, he hesitated before taking her hand and offered a dip of his chin in greeting. The short spell over Talina was at its end, as she was suddenly hyperaware of her troupe and their admiring eyes. As she drilled Sirius through his part, now with Wisteria, she realized she was doing the same thing. Appreciating the lines of his body as he sold his part, even if his expression remained as passionless as carved granite.

When he dipped Wisteria, she rubbed a pang of jealousy off her chest. She never danced on the ground in any routine. Her unique talents made her a hog of center stage. As talented as Sirius was, he couldn't perform his part midair.

The whole troupe ran through the act multiple times before Talina called it for the evening and sent them to dinner. Watching the performance of Sirius and Wisteria had stolen her appetite. "Don't be foolish," she muttered to herself as she ducked her head and carried Gem toward their wagon, where her things were in a locked chest.

"Dancing is a team sport," she told her familiar as she ducked into the wagon and opened her chest. Her journal laid on top of her personal belongings. "It's completely normal for him to dance with someone else."

"*Uh-huh,*" the bird twittered back.

"Totally, absolutely, completely normal," she sighed. Taking the journal, she locked her things up again and peered outside.

She fretted with the leather spine as she glanced around, making sure the coast was clear. She didn't want to talk to anyone. Not the troupe, and not Sirius either. "I'm being a weirdo, aren't I? Tell it to me true, Gem."

"*Slightly weirder than normal.*"

Sighing, she climbed out of the wagon and returned to the main tent. The wind blew ever so gently, its whispers out of reach for now, though she could hear its distant words as it spiraled up and away from her pointed ears.

Gem tilted his head when they slipped past the canvas and into the quiet tent. They'd arrived before anyone else claimed the stage to practice before night fell. She flew up to the tallest beam, curling her legs so they would be nearly impossible to spot from the shadowy nook.

"You already like him, don't you?" Gem asked.

She switched to mental speech again, not wanting anyone else to know about her favorite hiding spot. *"I guess I do."* And that was supposed to be completely normal. Absolutely, positively, a hundred percent expected. Fae didn't recognize their true mates on sight like vampires did, but they grew attachments so quickly that it was obvious when a match was met.

Seeing Sirius's hands on Wisteria, watching him in the soldier's role, bidding goodbye to her like a beloved wife...

Well, Talina hated it. A lot.

"So, dance with him instead," Gem interjected.

"That's not how it's supposed to go."

She opened her journal, eyeing its contents in the low light. Shadows spilled over the ink, making the prophecy even harder to make out than usual. She searched for any kind of answer, even though she knew it wasn't there.

Her eyes lit on a single line, caught by the word "beast." A word that suited Sirius well with his mastery over many animal forms.

Never run from a beast.

She put her finger next to it, skimming for any connection. Hadn't she just run from him? The lines preceding it seemed to have new meaning as well: *Take his hand. Show the way.*

The way to perform that dance?

"I don't think this is the way to figure yourself out," Gem ventured. *"You read these words over and over and over."*

"Every time, they get new meaning."

The tiny bird nudged a page over with his beak, making it flop halfway over her handiwork. *"Exactly. You give them meaning. They're words, ink and paper, but you're the one that gives them power."*

She leaned back, tapping her head against the wooden beam behind her. Breathing a sigh, she closed the journal and set it aside. It was getting too dark to read anyway. *"You like him. So, go talk to him,"* her familiar urged.

"Gem," she murmured. She could tell him the truth, at least. He knew everything else about her. *"I've never felt like this before."*

"That's completely normal," he said gently.

"Is it? Because all I can think about is his touch," she admitted. *"I don't want to talk to him. I want him to touch me again."*

"No wonder you're jealous of Wisteria," he twittered.

She nodded in agreement, already thinking about how best to switch jobs with Wisteria. The other fae wouldn't be happy. Neither would the rest of the troupe, because it would be blaringly obvious Talina did it so Sirius danced with her instead. Many of them already thought her an attention hog, showing off with her wind magic and making herself center of most of their routines.

Too bad. She was the choreographer here and...she'd figure out how to sell this without causing a catfight. Hopefully.

Chapter 9
Talina

Voices drifted up from below. She must've dozed off, because she'd missed when the two people on the stage arrived. No one else had used the tent, which she assumed was because of Sirius's intimidating stare. Word traveled fast, especially when everyone had gathered to watch him fighting Cloman.

Speak of the man, though. His deep growl was one of the voices, the other belonging to Cossette as she giggled. Gem was fast asleep in Talina's hands, favoring sleeping there, where he felt warm and safe. She closed her eyes and focused, trying to make out what they were saying.

"You're sure fae dance the same way?" she heard Sirius faintly.

Cossette replied to the affirmative. "Like hugging someone without your fingertips touching. That's first position for your arms." Though she knew it was Cossette replying, the child spoke like an adult. Clear, crisp, and as serious as a little girl could sound.

Talina leaned over, watching in disbelief as Cossette posed her arms and led him through doing the same. He followed her lead, mimicking every move she made as they practiced...the very basics of traditional ballet. No barre, no mirrors, just a girl telling an adult how to dance like a practiced instructor. They'd brought a few lamps and set them on the stage, so Talina could see their movements clearly.

Gods above. What was going on?

Cossette taught him to *plié*, or to bend his knees with flat feet. Then to *relevé*, lifting to his toes. They spent more time focusing on a perfect *sauté* because he kept jumping too far in the air. Cossette wanted what Talina would want, a short jump with good form.

Sirius learned unnaturally fast. Talina would've never taught anyone so much in a couple hours, but she saw that he could handle it quite clearly, moving like a breeze with the kind of body control her twelve-year-old self would've sold her wings for.

She was stuck watching it happen, too, because both of them would've noticed her flying out of the tent. They didn't know she was there, in the shadows where the lamplight didn't reach. Her head filled with questions, especially about Cossette.

She rested Gem's sleeping form atop her journal when Cossette finally left. Sirius continued to practice without her, muttering to himself through the various positions as his strong body shifted into each.

Except he kept getting one wrong now that his young instructor was gone. Talina cut a glance to her journal and bit her lip. Gem was right about one thing—she wouldn't get all the answers she wanted by reviewing the same words over and over. She drew a deep breath and floated down from her perch, letting a gentle swirl of wind magic catch her for a graceful landing.

Sirius whipped around to face her.

"Good evening," he said, transitioning to a fluid bow. She curtseyed back.

"I have questions," she murmured.

He offered his hand, an invitation she sorely wanted to accept. She wanted him to touch her, for them to move together. Just the two of them in this bubble of lamplight.

"That girl. Is she a thousand years old too?" she asked, keeping her hands folded. He didn't budge, instead tilting his head. If she wasn't mistaken, his red-tinged eyes were glowing faintly, independent of the reflection of the ambient light.

"How long were you watching us?"

"Long enough," she admitted.

"She is unique. An adult in a child's body," he said, slow and reluctant.

Her brows furrowed in confusion. She'd never heard of something like that before. "Was she cursed?"

"Close enough," Sirius rumbled, his eyes narrowing like a cat's. "She stopped growing because another messed with her while turning her into a vampire."

He read her expression and blew out a curse, dragging a hand down his face. "Since you caught us, you might as well know it all. She's about nine hundred years old and not related to me. I imagine she lied to protect everyone from the truth of her real nature."

She didn't know where to start on this revelation, taking a step away. If she lied to keep others from understanding what horror had been inflicted on her, then this man went with it to protect her. "It...sort of makes sense," she murmured.

"Talina, please." He echoed her step with one forward, trying to coax her closer. His calloused hand was inches away, ready to sweep her up like he'd practiced. Palm itching, she finally rested it overtop his own.

They danced. He, a soldier going to war, and she, the wife he was leaving behind.

"Why can't you be my partner tomorrow?" he breathed, bending deftly to whisper in her ear. A swift *plié*, she realized as his feet moved to the next step without a stumble.

"We don't have enough time to change the routine."

He dipped her, their faces a breath apart. The embers in his eyes danced as he read her face. She suddenly wanted him to close the distance between them more than anything. "We have all night, do we not?" he asked, setting her back on her feet instead. He didn't let her go this time, tucking her into a hug.

The tingles along her skin turned to comfortable warmth. She rested her palms on his chest, feeling the contours of his muscles through his shirt. "You don't want to sleep?" she asked, feeling more alive in those few moments than she had all day. The same feeling she always had while moving her body midair, embracing her wind-born heritage rather than a man.

His lips twitched, spreading into a genuine smile. He was finally at ease for her eyes alone. "If I may only hold you this way in the middle of the night, I hope the sun will never rise again."

The back of his knuckles grazed her cheek, her lips parting from the gentle touch. "I can be myself with you," he continued quietly. "The magic in my head is quiet when we touch. The beast wants for nothing."

She didn't say anything for a long moment, wondering if he felt the same tingles as her or if that was just attraction. "Beast," she echoed. *Never run from a beast.* The prophecy referred to him yet again.

"It's hard to explain," he murmured.

"Fae have it too, mostly druids. It's just a part of having shapeshifting magic." She'd learned enough about it in school, since young druids could be dangerous before they learned to control their magic.

Sirius hummed. His gaze was on her wings as they flicked idly. His arms were through them, but when he lifted a hand to touch the inner curve of one, she bit her lip from the explosion of sensation. Her toes curled, and she tensed, wondering if he'd do it again. "They *are* soft," he marveled. "What magic do you have, Talina?"

"Wind magic," she said, breathless.

"Of course. But what else? Don't all fae have at least three kinds of magic at their disposal?" His fingertips dipped into her wing, which gave to his touch like water vapor. They were just magic, capable of going through most things and only vulnerable to the cut of magic-treated iron. But to touch them so casually was reserved for lovers, for obvious reasons.

Distracted, she fluttered her eyelashes until she remembered what they were talking about. "I'm what's called mono-talented. I can only do wind magic things like summon and manipulate wind and lightning, but I have more skill at it than even a Sorcerer. Thus my special dancing skills."

He nodded, watching her face as his thumb traced the wispy edge of her wing.

"S-Sirius," she said on a gasp.

His smile widened, but he stopped, dropping his hold to take her hands in both of his. "I take exception that your magic is called mono-talented. I've only seen you dance midair once, and that was real talent. Teach me, Talina. Make me a partner you're willing to stay on the ground for." The sincerity in his voice grabbed her more than anything and had her nodding slowly.

Her heart fluttered as she envisioned a future with a dance partner just as invested as she. "There's a lot to learn."

If he hesitated, she'd know this was a flight of fancy, something to win her over on this quiet night. But there was no trace of doubt in him as he said, "One step at a time, then."

Chapter 10
Sirius

"ARE YOU READY?" TALINA ASKED THE NEXT EVENING. THEY waited behind the curtain off stage in front of a gaggle of dancers, watching Cloman on stage with the spotlight aimed at him.

The ringmaster narrated the dance to come as the story of lovers. They were some new lines, not that Sirius would know. Talina had mentioned that he was giving the audience context, just in case they didn't understand what they were seeing in the motion of the performance.

Neither of them had slept. He'd expected be tired by this point, but he was wired to a thick rush of adrenaline. The crowd's murmuring and shuffling filled his ears. Performing for an audience was different than helping Talina improvise something for them to add to the performance.

"I had better be ready," he answered her, hearing their cue. As Cloman left the stage, darkness descended long enough for him and Talina to rush into position. The magical spotlights reignited, the light blinding him to just how many faces watched them.

Music drifted up from an orchestral pit before the stage. That feature hadn't been there yesterday. Someone with magic had expanded the inside of the tent, sloping the ground to make tiered seating as well. He didn't understand how it happened or why it could be reversed easily once the tent was broken down.

All he knew was that Talina was posed before him, her arms in a graceful arc. She'd donned a new leotard with a flowing skirt that would lift and roll with her movements. It was a deep royal purple studded through the bodice with polished amethysts, just like the hairnet she wore that made her crown sparkle all the way to the tight bun she'd tied her hair into.

The light contoured her face, and she smiled up at him with the kind of excitement only borne by someone in their element. Her eyes were most brilliant of all, warm and blue, clear as a summer's day.

He nearly missed the first step, admiring her so. But once they were in motion, there were no mistakes. The crowd cheering and calling only fed to his adrenaline high, made his movements that much crisper. Talina was the star anyway, weaving and twirling.

Her idea was simple: before the rest of the troupe came to dance the farewell between their characters, they'd have a duet. She didn't use her wind magic today, even though she'd taught him how to lift and spin her midair and around his body in a technique she called an aerial.

Before he knew it, their duet was done. They held each other, panting lightly, as the rest of the group filed in. He knew the layers of movement were quite a spectacle as the lady dancers swooned and sighed, acrobats doing the same while hanging from their toes. The performance sped to its conclusion, the crowd screaming, and Sirius didn't want it to be over. Even as he grasped Talina's hips and moved to dip her, he wanted more.

Heart throbbing, breath heavy with excitement, he watched Talina giggle, giddy triumph marking her face. They were both high off the performance, the uproar of the unseen crowd better than any midnight practice.

He didn't even hesitate, kissing her soundly at the apex of the dip. The lights went out, and the curtains shadowed them. He swallowed Talina's gasp, felt her freeze in surprise. For a moment, his insides iced, wondering if he'd overstepped her boundaries. He'd had the hardest time *pretending* to kiss her.

Her fingers dug in a heartbeat later, and she kissed him back clumsily before slipping away and tugging on his hands. "We have to get off the stage," she whispered.

Of course. There was another act already coming in, with Cloman's smooth voice giving narration. He followed her bobbing bun and emerged into the night air behind the tent, feeling lingering static over his skin from the brush of her lips. To kiss a lifemate for the first time was supposed to be electrifying, but he'd expected more of a kick. Maybe they needed to try again.

Meanwhile, Talina's face and neck were nearly the same color as her leotard. "Ladies and, uh, gent. That was great! Did you hear how they loved us?" she said to the group. The dancers clustered in a gaggle, whispering and laughing.

"I think they loved you two," Wisteria sighed, inspecting her nails.

Talina turned away from her, her expression scrunching and then turning back into her stage smile. "Why don't we go into town, find a nice inn?" she suggested, coaxing the group to agree once they had a chance to change. They were doing two nights of performing, with one show this evening and two over the course of the next day, before Cloman's Own would be rolling to its next destination. Sirius imagined getting to spend the night in a bed on such a schedule would be a blessing.

He didn't need to change, so he waited uncomfortably in the shadows of a wagon as the troupe took their sweet old time picking outfits or whatever a group of ladies did while holding up his lifemate. Talina emerged last, talking quietly with Wisteria. She'd changed into a soft pink dress, its waves of fabric kissing her ankles as she walked. Gem perched on her hair like an accessory.

She glanced his way, and lavender tinged her cheekbones before she turned away, loosely surrounded by her dancers as they walked out of the fairgrounds. Well, obviously, he'd pushed her too far. His beast whined as he stuck to the back of the group, barely listening to a pair of dancers as they bracketed him and chattered.

Talina had kissed him back. But after they passed the gates into Terisz, he wondered if he'd get another glance from her tonight. His feet dragged, the high of performance absent as he wondered how to broach her discomfort before it festered.

The group branched out, mingling with the local Unseelie and catching a handful of merchants who hadn't yet packed up for the night. When Sirius had first arrived in the Unseelie capital, he'd expected the dark fae to live in squalor and dress richly, as befitted their paradoxical nature. Now that he'd taken a peek inside of Ironhold and walked the streets of Terisz, he realized he'd let his biases take over.

The streets were cleaner than any place a human stepped foot in, the buildings sided with freshly cured pine that drew the attention of his beast and pulled a reluctant purr, distracted from its low over Talina. A purple-skinned death fae passed by, arm in arm with an aether fae, both dressed comfortably against the chill lowering in with the setting sun. If he looked more carefully, more mismatched pairings dotted the crowd, Seelie with Unseelie, or Unseelie with lesser fae.

"Sirius?"

He nearly walked into Talina, his neck craned around as he scanned faces. She'd stopped before a two-story building that looked exactly like a pinewood lodge to him, transplanted straight from the mountains. A couple of their fellow dancers were halfway up the stairs.

Here was his chance, a moment alone with her. A single cloud drifted over one of her eyes, which lacked the storms that raged inside when she was uncomfortable. Did he really know her well enough to say that she wasn't upset?

"Do you have money for the night?" she asked.

He muttered a curse and patted down his flat pockets. He'd barely been on Cloman's payroll, so he had no coin or whatever fae paid in. "Guess I'm sleeping outside," he muttered.

"No way! I'll buy you a room." When his brows raised, she hurried to add, "Your own room. By yourself. You'll pay me back when you can."

He bit his tongue. *Don't laugh. Don't startle her.* "Of course."

"Of course," she echoed.

"About earlier, I—" he began.

At the same time, she said, "I wasn't really expecting—"

They paused, and she gave a nervous titter.

"Go on," he said.

"No, it's fine, what were you saying?"

He fought a losing battle with the amused smile threatening his lips. "You talk, I'll listen."

Her cheeks shimmered with a dusting of color. "Oh, ah. Maybe warn me next time? That kiss felt like a lightning bolt from the gods above."

Perking up, his beast purred more deeply. Talina *and* pine. It was in bliss.

"A good kind of lightning bolt?" he pressed.

"Um, yeah. Not wrathful angry lightning. Good...lightning?" she stammered. "Electric, dynamic...nice stuff. Yeah. It's late?" She hooked a thumb over her shoulder, backing up in a swift retreat from her own tongue until her heel met the first step up to the lodge. Hissing in pain, she pinwheeled her arms and fell backward.

Sirius was there in a flash, catching her shoulder and hip before she could bash her head on the stairs. "Ow. Heck." She sighed a few more half-hearted curses as he centered her gravity. She began limping up the stairs. "That was dumb, wow."

"Are you all right?" He hovered behind her in concern, watching her favor one leg.

"Yeah. Old injury."

Sure, an old one, when he'd seen her bandaged ankle only days ago. Sighing, he scooped her off her feet to cross into the lodge in a few long strides. She weighed about as much as the clouds on her back. "Sirius," she complained. "I can walk!"

He scanned the entryway lined with hunting trophies, spotting the nearest employee of the establishment a stone's throw away. The fae man was handing off a pair of keys to an antlered lesser fae, the creature looking more like the prey on the wall rather than the fae dining to their left or getting a drink at the bar.

The man Sirius assumed was the lodge's owner took one glance up, his lips parted in a surprised "o." He was a teal-tinged curse fae, an Unseelie with a backward tongue like the rest of his fellows. Sirius knew Unseelie only spoke lies unless their words fell in the gray area of a question or command. He thought it was the strangest thing, but he was also a human-born in the middle of fantastical Faerie.

"Do you have a medical kit?" Sirius demanded.

"This is really not necessary. I'm fine," Talina protested even as the Unseelie ducked into another room behind his counter.

He noticed she wasn't trying to get out of his hold, her arms folded and eyes rolling like this was a minor inconvenience. "So, the kiss was electric?" Maybe it was unfair to bring it back up, but she couldn't injure herself again because of the topic.

Her eyelashes fluttered. "Are you really fishing right now? Yeah, it was amazing. Probably the best first kiss a girl can ask for."

A throat being cleared drew a sharp glance from him. It was the Unseelie man, offering a tray piled high with medical equipment. Sirius found a chair and lowered Talina onto it gently, the tray on the ground next to him as he knelt before her. He spared the other fae a nod before slipping off her sandals.

"Your first ever?" he asked, eyeing her ankles. The right one was starting to swell and turn purplish. "I didn't think you'd twisted your ankle this badly."

"It doesn't take much," she sighed. "It just needs a compression bandage."

"It's already bruising. You may need a healer," he hedged, already unrolling linen from the supplies.

"No, really. It's an over-healing injury."

His brow furrowed. "Over-healing. Like, healed multiple times?"

She tilted her eyes skyward as she nodded. "I guess vampires don't have to worry about it. But a fae can only have the same place healed so many times in a short time period before it doesn't work anymore."

"You've broken this ankle?"

"Multiple times," she sighed.

Setting the bandages aside, he leaned forward earnestly. "Who harmed you? Who do I need to kill?"

Chapter 11
Talina

Sirius's eyes practically glowed with intensity. She had no doubt that he was sincere. If someone had truly hurt her in her past, he'd drag them out back by their hair and take care of it.

Her heart gave a little flutter. He was like her storybook knight, except the only monster he needed to slay was a twisted ankle. It hadn't healed from earlier, and she'd gone and aggravated it again.

She looked away, heat licking her cheeks. "It wasn't a person. Really, it's embarrassing. I hurt myself a lot in ballet school."

"To the point your ankles were healed multiple times in a row?" he asked in disbelief.

His hands, roughened with calluses, were ever so gentle in turning her foot and positioning it just right. Cool linen slid over her skin, starting higher up her calf than she'd usually do for herself.

"Have you done this before?" she deflected.

He blew out an animal-like chuff, his nose wrinkling ever so subtly in frustration. "Countless times. You have to be good at doing it quickly on the battlefield. Stitches too, though my brother used to hate how crooked mine were."

"I didn't know you had a brother," she ventured, getting the sense this was just scratching the surface of his life.

"Have. He's still around." His fingers slowed as he started

wrapping her ankle directly, testing the pressure and watching her face. He loosened it when she winced. "He and I have a difficult relationship. Not because we hate each other, but because we've been through a lot. More than any pair of brothers should ever go through."

"Do you want to talk about it?" she offered, her teeth set against the rush of pain as he wrapped her swollen ankle firmly, the pressure just right.

He stopped and considered her. "Too tight?"

"No, it's fine. I'm just a baby about pain." She felt lame even saying it. "Sorry. It must seem bad, with you talking about battlefields and stitches."

He shrugged, wrapping her heel and to the middle of her foot before finishing the bandage with a bow. She wanted to protest that it wasn't necessary to cover most of her leg, but the last touch was cute. He turned to Gem, who was watching this first aid with an attentive eye from the tray of medical supplies. "Look good to you?" he asked the bird in a light tone.

Gem peeped in the affirmative. He also fluttered away when the vampire reached out to pet him.

Sirius stood and cracked his neck with a sigh. "I'll tell you about Adrius if you tell me what happened in ballet school." He made the offer over his shoulder while carrying the supplies back to the lodge's owner, who was also watching the two of them from a safer distance. They spoke quietly, so Sirius completely missed Talina's face.

The very last thing she wanted to do was crack open her past. It would be awfully hard to tell him about her injuries and not reopen the book on her prophecy, how it related to him, and how it'd gotten her mercilessly bullied by the other girls when she hasn't had a sensible adult around to warn her not to talk about her...quirks.

But she also wanted to know everything about the man now demanding a floor-level room for her. Adrius had to be his brother's name. What did he mean by "difficult"?

"Don't you think he deserves to know about the prophecy?" Gem fluttered to her hand, perching there with his head cocked.

He was privy to all her inner turmoil but picked at the one spot she was terrified of.

"Yes, but..."

What if he thought she was crazy too? Was a future rejection the warning of her prophecy, the reason he would cause a soul change in her? Even now, with her lips still tingling from the memory of his kiss, she knew it would hurt like two broken ankles if he left her. Add in every injury she'd put her body through learning to dance, and that would equal the sight of Sirius's turned back.

"It will only get worse the more you put it off." Gem flew up on her shoulder, nuzzling her cheek. She pet him with one finger, wishing he was bigger so she had something to snuggle to her chest for comfort.

He was right, and she hated it. Absolutely, positively, truly despised that she was weighing her options for the best case scenario to hold on to Sirius's affections for as long as she could without also causing herself too much heartache when he left.

The man himself was coming back to her, keyrings dangling from his fingers. "He says you can pay tomorrow." He offered her one of the keys before lifting her again, nodding to a fae heading into the dining room like carrying her was a completely normal thing.

"I can walk, you know," she said, feeling the edge of embarrassment returning as they caught more attention passing by couples and guests having their evening meals or a drink. Turning a corner, they approached a hall lined with doorways.

"You also need to rest that ankle. Especially if you intend to perform tomorrow," he rumbled, his eyes narrowing to catlike slits between the dim fairy lights hanging in the hall.

"Gosh darn it. I forgot about tomorrow," she sighed. "And we're performing twice, too."

"We can sit it out? Spend the day here," he suggested. Though he kept his expression stonily neutral, she sensed him glance toward her with a measure of heat.

She shook her head quickly. "We'd lose our jobs. Especially

since Cloman's probably raking in good ticket money for folks to see you dance again."

"You're injured."

"It doesn't matter." It never had. In school, she'd pushed past injuries all the time. Either she said "yes" to a part, or she was overlooked for a season. She'd learned that the hard way as well.

His brows drew, but he was quiet as she unlocked the door to her room for the night. She stifled a gasp when she realized this was a family suite, one of the corner rooms.

"Don't worry. I convinced him to give you a good price," he said. "Bed or...?"

She had him place her on the couch since there was a small seating area with wood-frame furniture and a solid table of fused pine. She wondered if the owner of the lodge was a druid to have such a fine piece of wood casually placed in one of the rooms. Weaving a cushion of air, she elevated her hurt leg atop it.

She patted the seat next to her. "Won't you stay for a little while?"

Sirius was already turning to leave. His gaze snapped up, dark red eyes glowing like faint embers in the shadows cast over his face. Surprise had him by the throat, she thought. Like it was a shock someone wanted to spend more time with him.

"I thought you wanted to hear about my schooling," she ventured. His stance relaxed, and he nodded, sliding onto the cushion close to hers. A few inches separated their thighs, a charge of static between them.

Despite this, she kept her hands folded, her heart flickering against her ribs like a caged bird. She knew why women invited men to stay with them overnight—and she wasn't like that. She'd built high walls around herself because she knew she was different. Her heartsong and her soul were tied up in that prophecy, and she'd hoped to never find the man who made the wind whisper to her.

Talina wanted to be *normal*. But that meant she couldn't have a man like Sirius. As he relaxed beside her, looking expectant, she realized that she wanted two things at the same time: to be like everyone else, but with Sirius. Let him be anyone else.

Anyone at all. Just not the man who'd lead her to a soul change.

"It's a lot," she said quietly. "And not the happiest story."

"If it were joyful, you wouldn't be so reluctant to speak of it. I will keep your confidence," he promised.

She opened her mouth, then hesitated. "Um...where to even start? I had a lot of wind magic in me, even as a kid. When my mom was alive, we lived in the Outer Reaches, where the air was thin and the wind danced with us." Pressing her fingers to her lips, she hid their trembling. Her mother was this larger-than-life shade of her past, full of wonder and whimsy.

"How did you lose her?" Sirius asked. A concerned frown starting to form around his lips.

"I don't know if you know this, but in Faerie, we have illnesses that can't be healed with magic. Either we recover from them or...we die. And one of them got my mom when I was ten." She'd been lucky not to catch it too. "We lived a few miles from the nearest village, so it took a while for anyone to check on us. I was quarantined while the villagers called the crown officials to come pick me up."

"What of your father?" He was shading toward a scowl.

"I didn't know him. My mom always promised she'd introduce me someday when I was older, but..." she shrugged, her gaze flicking toward the floor. "I got taken to Ironhold instead."

She smiled for one part of this, at least. "Queen Kalimea herself came to pick me up since she's a Sorceress. You should've seen her, scolding out the village elders for keeping me isolated after I'd been alone with just..." Her mother's corpse. But she didn't want to dwell on that or bring up those memories any longer than she had to.

"That woman." Sirius shook his head, loosing a quiet laugh.

She brightened. "You know her?"

"We've met. I'm more acquainted with her sister." He rolled his eyes.

"Well, Queen Kalimea swooped in and saved me, but it completely upended my life," she said, remembering her brief time in Ironhold Keep and being spoiled with food and toys from the queen. "She runs an orphanage, but she moved me on from it pretty quickly once I felt better. She paid for me to go to a premier ballet school for Seelie fae. My mom had taught me a lot already... She was an incredible dancer. She moved with the wind with such grace, letting it be her partner. She would let it pick her up and twirl her like she didn't weigh anything at all, and I desperately wanted to learn how to do that too."

"I'm not sure I like where this is going," he said, reaching out to close the gap between them. He rested his hand over hers, the static lingering over them giving her a quick jolt. Something about him was simply electric, she decided. Her heart fluttered harder as she turned her palm and laced their fingers together.

"A young girl going off to school alone. What could possibly go wrong?" she asked with a sad kind of laugh.

Here was the moment. She felt Gem's mental nudge, her familiar listening in somewhere above them. Probably perched on a fairy light, his body so slight that the magic wouldn't even notice him.

She took a deep breath, clutching Sirius's hand tighter. "I, uh, learned I could do something in my first couple years there," she started slowly, like she could steel her nerve if she focused hard enough. "The instructors thought I was just a weird kid and tried to tell me it wasn't possible but...it was real no matter how much they denied it. The other kids weren't so kind..."

"Deep breath. Just say it," Gem encouraged.

She took a long breath and sighed it out. Sirius had his head tilted, a line between his brows as he waited. "I, um... The wind speaks to me."

"Oh?" He seemed more puzzled than anything.

"Not, like, full conversations or something. That would be weird." She tittered nervously. "It talks at me, more like. Tells me what's to come. At first, it was little things, like what would be for dinner that night or to go inside right before it rained. But then it started talking about a prophecy and repeating itself constantly. I started writing it down, trying to make sense of it."

She stopped and read his face for any sign of disbelief, hoping to pin the moment he turned from her like everyone else who knew her secret.

"So, you possess future sight?" he asked, serious and intent on her. How he usually looked.

"No. Future *sight* has a visual element, and I failed all the tests for it." She blew out another sigh. "It's something else."

He chuffed quietly. "Have you taken these tests more than once? Or as an adult?" She shook her head. "You obviously have some element of the future in your magic."

"It's not really...my magic?" She pressed her lips together. Why was she arguing him away from a reasonable assumption about this? "No one can really figure out how it works. Just that it does. And it's caused me nothing but problems!

"I would give it away, if only I could. Because it's built up this one prophecy for years and years. It's not even done giving me the pieces to it yet! About a man from another world...my match. *You!*" She pointed straight at him, glad for a moment that it was out in the open at last, that it'd left her shoulders with heated relief.

His eyes were retracted to slits, a growl rumbling from his throat. It was deep, the kind of sound a predator made before it sank its fangs into its prey's throat.

He spoke in a low hiss. "And what does the wind have to say of me?"

Recoiling, she folded her hands to her chest. "That..." Gods above, she should've never told him. Her vision swam at the edges. She dreaded sharing anything more and knew he'd demand it. His roughened hands closed around her cheeks, centering her gaze up at him.

He'd stopped snarling. But that didn't mean his expression was anything but a banked fire, ready to rise up again with the right fuel. "What does it say?" he repeated more gently. She gulped on a dry throat, knowing her eyes were filled with skittering clouds. "I'm not mad at you, Talina. But if it pertains to me, I want to know."

"I-It calls you a beast," she said. The better she knew him, the more accurate she realized it was. "And...that you will lead me to a soul change."

"A soul change?" he murmured.

"It's another fae thing. When something traumatic happens to us, it changes our souls and true names. That event is called a... a soul change..." she drifted off as she felt it, palpable in the air. He was *furious*.

"So, you think I am going to hurt you?" He was deathly still. In the moment, she knew that he could. His hands had fallen away from her face; he could lash out in an instant. But...

"Not intentionally," she said in a frightened squeak.

"Let me get this straight." His breathing was haggard, chest heaving, expression twisting.

He was...afraid, she realized.

"A soul change can't be considered a good thing? Your soul can't have this happen if it's something..." He gestured vaguely. "Nice?"

She shrugged weakly. "I don't know. I don't know what's going to happen."

"I can't believe this...written in the future. That I'm going to hurt you." He stood, backing away. "Talina, that's the last thing I want to do. I know I'm not a saint, but I would never..." He bit off a curse, turning away.

She clutched the front of her dress, paralyzed. "Sirius...don't go," she whispered.

"I will not be a danger to my lifemate. I refuse to let hurting you be my legacy," he snarled, a wounded note in his tone.

He unlatched the door, throwing it open, pausing there. Someone else stood at the threshold, her wide, red eyes solemn as she craned her neck up at him. "Come with me," Cossette said. She leaned around his legs, waving to Talina. "It's okay, Miss Talina! I'll bring him back!"

Chapter 12
Sirius

Cossette pulled him out of the room with all the vampiric strength in her little body. He took a few paces from the door and rounded on her.

"What are you doing?" they demanded at the same time.

"Saving you from doing something stupid, *Dad*," she grumbled.

Heartache and anger warred within him. His beast screamed, no, *howled*. If only he could cut his magic loose, let it go somewhere else, then he wouldn't be a prophesied threat to the woman he was destined for.

"I'm going to save her life," he growled.

She propped her fists on her hips. "You don't even know the whole story!"

"I know enough. I'm not going to subject her to my presence any longer." He chuffed, most furious with himself for thinking he could handle his beastly rage around her. The kernel of hope that she could be the key to his control flicked out of reach. Clearly, it was untrue.

She didn't think he would hurt her intentionally, but clearly, it was in the cards. The wind itself warned her...of him.

"And you haven't considered asking your seer daughter about what's to come?" Cossette put a hand to her chest, her eyes wide with hurt. Fake or not, he couldn't tell.

"I hadn't. What is the soul change?" he asked through gritted teeth. "Why is the wind speaking to her?" Not a moment of doubt had filled him from Talina's tale. He figured she was a seer too, as magic moved in strange ways. The fae here didn't seem open enough to the idea of magic behaving *differently*, but as a vampire, he'd seen it a lot. His people were magic, just not in the traditional fae way.

He hung on her every word after Cossette considered. "I don't know for certain," she said slowly. "All I know is that it's big."

"Will she die?" His worst nightmare given form.

"No. But you might." She pulled the punch of those words with a girlish giggle.

"What do you mean?" he demanded. She giggled again, so he got down on one knee and pinched her. "In what context?"

Her expression sobered. "Hmm?"

"Why might I die?" His voice had pitched to a low growl.

"Who says you're going to die? I don't think it'll happen." She smiled reassuringly. "You're on a good path, Mister Fabron. A hard one. But you'll be all the better for it."

He stifled a frustrated snarl. "Why does everyone keep mentioning my *path* but not what's going to happen on it?"

Her eyes twinkled. "You have to see for yourself. Now...you scared her." She jerked a thumb over her shoulder. "I don't think you meant to do that, either."

Ah, shit. He really hadn't, but now, all he could see in his mind's eye were her big, frightened eyes full of skittish clouds. It was like a douse of cold water over his head.

"Really fucked that one up, didn't I?" he muttered. He wouldn't be surprised if she told him to leave her alone for good after an outburst like that.

Cossette tilted her head. "It'll be much worse if you don't go back in there and apologize."

"I'll grovel if I have to." He drew to his feet, stepping past her.

Something possessed him to stop and turn. She watched him

with quiet sympathy. He'd never expect that sort of emotion from Cossette...for him. "Thank you," he said. For saving a situation again? For understanding?

Why not both?

She bobbed her head, eyes crinkling at the corners. In that instant, she was young...no, actually. She'd smiled like that despite being an Ancient, happy for him. "Let me sleep in your room." She pointed at the keyring he'd placed in his pocket. Shrugging, he tossed it to her and practically tiptoed back into Talina's room.

She glanced up and over her shoulder from the couch, her eyes red-rimmed and full of storm clouds.

"I'm sorry," he said immediately. "This was supposed to be your moment to confide in me, and I blew it."

Though he'd closed the door, he didn't move inside. She didn't twitch, either, frozen in place. He had maybe two sentences of time before she told him to leave, he thought.

But she spoke up, her lips forming quivering words. "You were already afraid you'd hurt me. Why?"

Why indeed? The question he often asked himself about his life.

"I can barely control my inner beast. My magic." His hands balled into fists. "It craves to act like an animal, to feed and fff—" He bit his lip. "—Find a mate. And fight. Anything that could be my equal, it wants to fight."

Despite his admission, his beast was oddly silent, lying somewhere despondently in the corner of his mind.

"I came to Faerie hoping to learn control. And...I haven't yet. That doesn't stop me from trying, then failing. Now, I'm here to try again."

He bowed his head, a submissive beast. "If you want me to leave, I will. I am truly sorry."

"Sirius," she whispered. "It's okay. Please don't leave like that again."

"May I sit with you again?" he asked, glancing up through his lashes.

She gestured him over, and he sat so tantalizingly close to her. No, he couldn't do it. He wrapped his arms around her middle, drawing her carefully into an embrace. She melted into him with a sigh, closing her eyes.

"Have you tried meditation? It helps," she offered.

"No."

"I'll teach you."

His lips twitched. "Still teaching me, hmm?" he teased.

She huffed. "Close your eyes," she said in her firmer, instructor manner. He complied.

She talked him through imagining a box. All his worries, fears, and even thoughts get locked in there. And then they breathed together, with her counting up and down from five to start with. His adrenaline eased, but it probably had more to do with her sweet scent filling his nostrils and her soft presence than the breathing exercises.

They meditated for longer than strictly necessary, but he didn't move, sensing a change in her. Her voice faded into a murmur and then to nonsense as she dosed straight to sleep from how relaxed she'd become. He was nearly jealous that it'd been that easy for her, but then again, they'd danced all through last night. Fatigue gripped him closely as well.

Before anything else, he tucked her into the voluminous bed in the suite and fell asleep on the couch, a pillow from the bed clutched to his chest.

Talina was peeved to see him early the next morning, in her room. "I can walk just fine, thank you," was the last thing she'd said before they made their way back to the fairgrounds separately. Gem had seemed to glare, tweeting loudly at him on her way by.

His beast flopped about, whining. It knew she was close and wanted to go to her, but he kept it quiet and sat around polishing his sword and armor while watching the sun travel ever so slowly across the sky. Talina needed some space, he thought. And since

Cossette had disappeared, he had no one to talk to except his magic, and it only spoke in one to two-word fragments at most.

What he wouldn't do to have Neala, or maybe even Ash, around to smack him over the head for being an idiot. Maybe they would have some advice. There had to be some sweet spot in between "don't go" and "I can walk just fine" that he was missing.

One of the dancers came to get him before the first performance of the day. "It's time to warm up," she said, looking up at him with a giggle. He hadn't had this much female attention in his life, and here he was, stony faced and disinterested. The only one he wanted was Talina, and he went a while longer before finally spotting her behind the stage soon before they were to perform. She'd wrapped her other leg to match the right one, and the bandages glittered with the same sort of body paint that gleamed up her bare thighs and over a sequined gold leotard.

He admired how her face glittered like a sunrise with gold makeup and paint. A shy sort of smile graced her lips.

"Is your ankle feeling better?" he asked. Surely it wasn't good for an injury to decorate the bandages, but something told him Talina knew how to compensate for it.

Annoyance flickered through her whole bearing. "I'll be okay."

Maybe he was more worried than she was, remembering all too well that she had several pirouettes to balance on her right foot in the routine. Not to mention the leaps and aerials.

She seemed just fine for the first performance. They waited together in between, sitting close but not too close. She spoke to the other dancers, cutting him glances occasionally. Something was on her mind.

During the second performance, she mumbled his name just below the sound of the music. Her footwork was different, masking a stumble midway through. Eyes widening under a bright stage smile, they improvised new steps and turned the other way so she could spin on her left leg.

When the lights dimmed and they were finished, a stage kiss amount of space between them, it was she who closed the gap this time. It was a short, sweet brush of their mouths, a sigh of gratitude there before he carried her off stage.

He tingled head to toe, though concern mixed with the adrenaline high of a finished performance. She confirmed that she didn't need the healer as he checked and rewrapped her ankle with new, clean linen. In those moments, he realized she'd never finished her story of how this injury had happened in the first place.

"They're going to tear down tonight, so we'll be leaving early tomorrow," she said while he worked. "But we could still rest at the inn, if you'll actually use the room I paid for."

"Sorry. I let Cossette have the other room," he said.

"I know. Everyone knows." A purplish blush took over her face. "You and I were seen leaving the room together."

"And this...upsets you?" he asked, baffled.

"I mean. It's not that..." She shifted her balance, and realization struck him.

She was embarrassed. If she'd just had her first kiss yesterday...

He coaxed her into sitting next to him on one of the mixmatched benches in the rest area. Leaning over, he whispered into the shell of her ear, "Are you untouched?" He was tempted to lick the pointed tip, especially when it turned as purple as the rest of her.

Do it, the beast whispered. He didn't, because that seemed like the exact thing that would make her most uncomfortable.

A part of him was infinitely pleased when she nodded, studiously avoiding looking at him. His lifemate, untouched by another man. She was too sweet for him.

But that was also the problem, wasn't it? He didn't want to hurt so delicate a woman as her. The possibility was there.

"I stayed in your room last night to protect you," he said quietly. "It's old habit. If anyone thought to burst through the door, they'd have to go through me to get to you."

Her brows drew in. "Were you expecting...?"

"I'm always anticipating the worst." He jerked his chin to the right, toward a fae man. "He's been staring in your direction for five minutes. There's another fae here with at least three daggers on his person."

He kept listing threats that had casually walked by, her eyes widening until he stopped for her benefit. "None of them pose a direct threat to you right now, but they could."

She shook her head slowly. "Fine, there are armed people all around us. But I've lived this long around, apparently, a lot of armed people, and nothing's happened. You don't *have* to protect me."

He snorted, eyeing her askance. "That's like telling me that I don't have to breathe."

She threw her hands up. "We've kissed all of twice. You barely know me. But everyone thinks we're sneaking off together and doing, um..."

"Relations?" he offered.

"Yeah. And I told you I wasn't ready for this yet," she finished. Her wide eyes were gently clouded. It was hard to look at her so vulnerable and fragile and not close the gap between them.

Sirius had some emotional intelligence jammed up in his head beside his beast. He tried to push his instincts aside, which were screaming that he needed to hold and protect his mate.

No, she's uncomfortable because this is new, he thought. He shouldn't feel offended that she was embarrassed. He *wasn't*, though his beast was the more he thought about it.

Instinct told him that she was his and that she should be proud of and desire his protection. However, she wasn't a beast like him; she was a reasonable person who needed him to back off.

But not too far. They were still courting.

Women are complicated, his beast grumbled.

Now that, he could agree with. "If you need space, I'll give you space," he promised. But if she needed him to punch someone in the face, he'd more than gladly do that too.

God. He needed some new hobbies.

"But at least let me carry you back to your room?" he added.

"All the way across town? I don't want to be a bother... I could walk. Or fly."

He ended up carrying her back to the lodge. Instead of a kiss, he left her with a dramatic bow and a flower he'd picked along the way, a pretty pastel bloom that had flourished despite the chill in the air. As they went their separate ways, he glanced over his shoulder. She stood there a few moments longer with the flower tucked to her chest, the sunniest smile across her delicate face.

Chapter 13
Sirius

If Sirius had to describe the next couple weeks in one word, he'd call them "content." It wasn't like his beast to ever consider being content, but he was finally keeping it at bay.

He'd taken up woodworking again, finding he could focus on it in those long hours on the road at the end of the caravan. Like a magpie, he'd swoop up decent pieces of wood to work on, plus anything shiny for decoration, or pretty flowers to give to Talina.

He'd enjoyed woodworking a lifetime ago. During a part of his earlier life, he'd had the concentration to make miniatures, mimicking the fine details of faces or the texture of fur and feather and scale. Now, he relearned that patience one piece at a time, often discarding his mistakes with a frustrated growl to try again on new wood.

He looked forward to the evenings, where he'd learn to dance with Talina or sit and chat as the moon rose. They stuck to the safe topics. He actually did most of the talking, since he had so much to share about his past.

Nothing too bloody, not to affect her sensibilities as a lady. But he talked about his family, about Nyixa as it used to be, about his position and duties as a Blood Prince. She listened with a wistful smile when he finally shared about Adrius and his devotion for Nyah, how they had a child and... After hesitating, he'd shared that they had one on the way. He'd learned through Cossette, but he doubted she'd lied about something like that.

Sometimes, he thought he bored her, because she often went to sleep resting against him, his arm around her companionably. Apparently, she'd learned the skill to sleep anywhere and often did—which alarmed every protective instinct in him. He made sure to tuck her somewhere comfortable every time it happened.

As for him, he rarely slept. His beast was uneasy every time fatigue approached, trying to curl its fingers around him to drag him into darkness. If he did sleep, he woke angry, craving the blood of Lucia on his claws. Since sleep stood in the way of his perfect routine, he simply went without.

Not that Talina liked that. Nor did she approve of his daily challenges of Cloman, watching him manipulate the fights so he just barely won or lost each one. As they rolled into the next stop, she flew next to his elk and tried to get him to drink a cup full of green goop. Herbs floated at the top for extra texture.

"It'll help you," she was saying. "I had Mags make it special."

Magdalena, or just Mags, was the sole healer amongst the circus. He'd met her a couple times. Tough as nails and grumpy as an elder.

"It certainly seems *special*," he said, squinting suspiciously as he tilted the cup and its contents oozed to the side like thick honey. His nose wrinkled.

"Please take it? She said it'd guarantee you a good night's sleep tonight." Talina turned a look of sunshine and pity up at him, her wide eyes pleading and clear, bracketed by concerned brows.

Well, damn. Now he had to take it. He grumbled about flavor as he tipped it back before a pear-sweet taste coated his tongue. *Huh. Not bad.*

"When are we performing next?" he asked, handing the empty cup back to her.

"Oh, one of my favorite places! Cordaria, the city of druids," she exclaimed, face creasing with delight. "It's a totally awesome, wonderful, outdoorsy kind of place."

"Totally, completely, utterly?" he teased, chin propped on his fist. The more she relaxed around him, the more he heard that particular quirk.

"Exactly," she said. "You'll love it. You're always sniffing wood."

He snorted, nearly doing a double take. "Huh?"

"Like for your carving." She gestured toward the half-formed duck he'd tucked in front of him. Taking it up, he tossed it over his shoulder after a quick inspection.

"Hey!" She whirled on her wings and caught it, turning it over in her hands. "You never keep these."

"I only scent wood to make sure it's not rotting. And I cut the bill too short on that one."

"So? Why don't you finish the rest of the carving?"

"It would look goofy." And he didn't do goofy.

"Well, if you only carve the whole thing if you don't make a mistake... What if you mess up the feathers or the little feets or its eyes? Do you throw it away too?" she asked.

His lip twitched. "'Feets'?"

"It's a thing humans say," she said brightly.

Considering some of the humans and young vampires he'd met recently, he didn't doubt it. "And yes, I would. It has to be perfect."

"But you're not going to practice all the little detail stuff if you don't get over the beak thing."

He raised a brow. "Do you want me to finish the duck for you?"

She handed it back to him with a bob of her head. "It's good to finish things," she said.

"Thank you for your wisdom." Chuckling, he turned the piece of wood over with renewed interest. Maybe he could save it after all. "Are we staying in Cordaria long?"

He certainly hoped so. They spent the most time together when the caravan stopped, all too brief with how backed up the circus's schedule still was.

"Cloman wants to have a big bash! Really advertise our new dance." She wiggled her shoulders, her whole body bouncing from a jaunty snap of her wings. "It's going to be huge! Maybe three days, or four."

"Thank god," he murmured. "Sleeping in a real bed." Now that he'd finally been paid, he could afford some luxury.

"Right?" She sighed.

"Tell me about Cordaria?" he invited.

"Oh! It's beautiful, for one thing," she said with a smile. "It's right on the ocean, so you get those fresh breezes."

"By fresh, you mean salty?"

"Salty and fresh breezes," she amended. "Druids take care of familiars, which start out as really smart animals. So, there are sweet creatures everywhere that will let you pet them. It's where I met Gem."

Said hummingbird was perched on her back as she flew, still glaring at him. They usually ignored each other unless the bird was twittering loudly in complaint when Sirius tried to touch him. Apparently, he was protective of Talina...but he was still just a tiny bird.

"Plus, nature. All those druids in one place means you see some cool things. And they cultivate plants that last year-round."

"Are there rules against picking flowers?" He mused over the wisdom of doing so. Though he hadn't shared with her about Adrun—fae were odd about shifters, thinking them cursed—he'd met the druids there. They'd worn clothes completely fashioned of leaves, blooms, and roots but were fiercely protective of the lands they tended. He wouldn't have dared touch their greenery unless invited.

She considered his question for a long while. "I don't think so," she finally said. "I mean, half of them get eaten. That's just nature."

Great. He'd find her a whole bouquet, then. As they rolled closer to the location, his beast became oddly awake, rising to the surface of his thoughts and tugging for control. "Are we close to a place of power?" he asked between gritted teeth from the effort of holding his beast's urges back.

Run. Fight. Kill.

She glanced over curiously. "The Druidic Sanctum, maybe? Why?"

A Sanctum. He'd felt this same energy from his beast in the Sanctum of Adrun, where the spirits of deceased fae dwelled, creating a font of power. But this was Faerie—if it served the same purpose, it had to be even stronger than the one in Adrun by the sheer number of souls within it.

So, perhaps he felt it from farther away.

"The druids live close to it. It's Getana's seat of power," she said. When his brow furrowed, she added, "You know, the Lady of Life? Goddess of Earth?"

He muttered a curse. "I've heard your people believe in four gods, but we might be close to one? Is it possible we would see her?"

"Oh! No. Most fae never see the gods. Getana loves her druids. So, she invited them to live close to her. At most, they feel her smile when the sun rises and the flowers bloom. I think the Archdruids are the only ones that actually meet her." She seemed wistful as she sighed. "Can you imagine actually meeting one of the gods? Especially the Lady of Life. They move and shape Faerie constantly. They're too important to talk to any one person."

"I can't," he said. His beast quavered at the thought. The only beasts guaranteed to be more powerful than him were the four dragon gods of Faerie. He knew it from even the brush of energy from Getana's Sanctum home.

"I wish I was important enough to talk to a god. Just once," she admitted. "I want to know what they really look like."

"If you have fae who've met them, surely you all know what they look like."

She shook her head, sending navy strands of hair rippling behind her. "They don't appear in the same form to everyone. They're the elements themselves...and all elements have their variations. Like how fire can be different heat levels. Or how the seasons change."

"Fascinating," he said, doubting either of them would even see a god. So, why speculate?

He knew they were coming upon Cordaria as forest gave way to pasture on one side of the road. Animals of all kinds watched the caravan roll by. Some were immediately identifiable, like the horses and zebra cropping grass and keeping a careful eye out. Other creatures occupied the same space, though he didn't know what to make of them with their extra limbs or odd colors. On Earth, they wouldn't all live together, but he assumed they were thriving under druidic care.

Talina floated upward to peek over the wagons. "Oh, we're going straight in!" She rolled midair, an excited twirl, grabbing on to the roof of the wagon at the end of the caravan to watch what was coming.

When Sirius finally saw what she did, his beast scented the air with a pleased purr. The road snaked through an artificial tunnel of flower-laden trellises, each bloom vibrant with health. Bees and hummingbirds buzzed amongst the greenery, though the latter flocked over to Talina with a flurry of excited squeaks. He smiled, watching her giggle and beam as the tiny birds danced for her.

Once they'd passed through the blossoms, a wooden gate awaited, thrown open for them. The timbers that made up the high wall surrounding the city shone like they'd just been painted with lacquer, but he didn't smell anything except the concentrated perfume of flowers and pollen.

Above the gate was a massive sign that read "Welcome to Cordaria!" Some jokester had attached two crooked boards right underneath it, faded paint adding the message: "Pets Welcome."

Chapter 14
Sirius

THE CITY ITSELF WAS MASSIVE AND SPRAWLING, NATURE overgrowing most buildings with vines of ivy or trees directly supporting structures. The fae here had made most buildings as far as a block apart, save for a cluster of housing he saw far in the distance. Animals and fae existed here side by side. Though there were few roads and paths to traverse with grass threatening to overtake even the cobblestones, no one had trouble stepping aside and waving to the incoming circus.

Sirius took a deep breath, savoring how clear the air was, with only a tinge of salt. His beast wondered if they'd entered Heaven. It was noticeably warmer once they traveled past the city gates, like a temperate spring day.

When Talina and her flock of hummingbirds returned to his side, it was a brief visit, the lot of them darting about. "I should talk to Cloman real quick," she said over her shoulder. "I think our troupe is up for advertising duty."

She returned a short time later to herd him onto a platform on wheels that looked like the bottom of a dismantled wagon. "Just smile and wave," she whispered before disappearing again with the ladies.

He shrugged and waited until the dancers returned dressed in their leotards and sequins. Talina squeezed in next to him, Gem atop her head and her colorful flock dotting her shoulders and arms. He wondered how many leotards she had, as this was another one new to him. Forest green, molding to the slim curves of her body, with a sequined skirt split in four sections to leave little of her legs to the imagination.

"Wait for me!" A giggling Cossette chased the platform as a pair of elk started to pull them slowly down the main street. The ladies helped her up, a team of hands passing her over to him. Right, he was supposed to be her father still. He hoisted her onto his shoulders as they made four rows, so he was back-to-back with a slim fae as they faced different directions.

He saw now. They were waving to the locals, inviting them on the platform too. A second platform carrying a group of musicians playing jaunty tunes followed them. He caught the groove of Talina's hips as she moved to the music, and soon, the whole group was dancing in place and having a miniature party as they spread the word of Cloman's Own being in town.

Just as Sirius admitted to himself that this was fun, he made eye contact with a familiar face in the crowd. The druid gasped, transforming into a hawk to fly into Sirius's chest and startling the rest of the dancers on his side of the platform. Many of Talina's hummingbirds fled with a flurry of alarmed twitters.

"Great going," he muttered, lifting his wrist where the druid had clamped onto.

"Could say the same of you," the hawk replied, clearly enunciating despite his beak. "We need to talk. Care to hop off?"

Sighing, he passed Cossette to Talina and muttered, "I'll catch up with you."

"So, you joined the circus, huh?" Once he had space, the druid transformed back into himself. Sirius's beast hissed, wanting to back off from this man. It recognized their mirror, a fae with a powerful reserve of shapeshifting magic. He was a terran fae, crowned by long and unruly evergreen hair studded with leaves, white feathers, and a few beads carved with fae symbols. Though he was obviously male, he had mischievous, elfin features.

Despite being an Archdruid, Theron Shadestone dressed plainly and looked as disheveled as he'd been the other time they'd crossed paths. Unlike the druids of Adrun, he wore leather. His skin was the color of earth, blending in like camouflage in a druidic city like Cordaria. Curiously, he was the only fae Sirius had met who had pupils—just slits hiding in the glowing green of his eyes. He cocked a sideways grin full of gleaming, white teeth. "Let me guess what your act is. Name an animal, any animal. And in a flash, I will become"—he became a silver hummingbird and squeaked—"that animal!"

"Sure," Sirius scoffed. In a heartbeat, he was his old self, scowling sullenly. After weeks of being the biggest, strongest man around and showered with applause, the first thing a person from his old life did was mock him.

Theron transformed back with a sigh. Sirius wanted whatever enchantment was on his leather—he went naked after changing fully into an animal and back, but Theron's leather remained in place without any fuss. "Look, shit's going down, and you disappeared," the Archdruid said.

"You all were better off without me," he muttered, crossing his arms.

The smile left Theron's face. He raised a brow. "Are you sure about that?"

"Positive."

"So, you don't want to know about Lucia attacking Queen Kalimea?" Sirius's anger spiked to hear the demon's name again.

Kill her! his beast screamed. This close to the surface of his thoughts, his nails lengthened to claws reflexively with the whims of the beast.

Theron's gaze dipped. "Nor that Kalimea has called a wild hunt for Lucia's head and any whereabouts of Izell?"

He cut to the chase, knowing he'd only be teased with hints of what he'd missed unless he asked. "What of Neala?"

The Archdruid smiled. "Enjoying her new position as Kalimea's Blade. It's purely a ceremonial position, but considering how she saved our queen's life, she's set." He led Sirius to a bench hidden under the low branches of a tree, where they could have some privacy. Then, he explained everything that Sirius had missed.

Neala had used the Mind Key to help Kalimea turn Lucia's plan on its head and expose the demon at the masquerade. There'd been a big production of helping Lucia's converts purge the demon blood from their systems and rejoin fae society while the Unseelie Queen herself put a huge bounty out for anyone who could sever Lucia's head from its shoulders.

"But why is she hunting Izell as well?" Sirius asked. While he was glad for his sister, he couldn't even imagining being so content.

"I'm not privy to that." Theron shrugged. "Izell made a misstep anyway. She was revealed as a *mort loci* at the masquerade. Most folks assume Kalimea wants to make sure she goes and guards a portal like a good little cursed fae."

That didn't sit well with him, considering how he'd seen Kalimea embrace Izell in all her golden-scaled glory. The Unseelie Queen already knew that Izell was a dragon shifter, so why make a big deal of it across her kingdom?

"Kalimea also executed Lucia with hellfire, so it's unlike her to believe the demon is even still alive," Theron continued. "But since Lucia apparently survived that, that's a threat we're all on high alert for. Yet you're out here partying. Why?"

He pinched the bridge of his nose. *Why indeed?*

"I followed my lifemate," he murmured, feeling all the shame of his first night amongst the circus over again. He had abandoned his responsibilities, and that wasn't what a warrior...what a *Blood Prince* did.

"I didn't know Cloman's Own had any vampire performers," Theron remarked.

"It has me."

The Archdruid laughed. "Fine, besides you! What vampiress caught your eye?"

"My lifemate is an aether fae. I like her very much." He felt his lips lift at the thought of Talina. To say he liked her was an understatement, but he'd promised he wouldn't go too quickly with their relationship.

Theron's lips parted in disbelief. "Full aether fae?" he asked.

"I assume so?" He didn't like the expression on the Archdruid's face. Maybe he was some sort of purist who thought human-born and fae shouldn't mix. His hands balled into fists, world narrowing as his beast stoked him up for a fight.

Theron raised his hands slowly. "Sirius," he said in the kind of gentle tone reserved for speaking to an unruly animal. "It's impossible for a pure fae and human-born to have a bond like that."

Definitely a purist, then. Sirius would rearrange his beliefs with force. "I know what I feel," he rumbled.

"You were born on different planets. Separated by a barrier of magic. Think about it." Theron spoke quickly. "Vampire life-mates are determined by proximity and personality. Fae heart-songs are found by harmonizing the songs of our souls. We're different species. Any exceptions are very rare."

"What exceptions?" he growled. He started one of the breathing exercises he did with Talina, trying to calm his racing heart and the furious beast pacing back and forth inside his consciousness. It didn't relax but a fraction, not as empowered as it felt so close to Faerie's Sanctum.

"I'd have to inspect your magic for a fatecross mark. It's the third and last way two people can be bonded before they meet. Are you going to be around for long?" Theron asked, flashing his sparkling smile again. "Kalimea fired me from being a diplomat. Said I was 'unsuitable.'" He put on exaggerated air quotes. "Can you believe it? Oh well, more time to do what I do best. Help broody guys like you."

Sirius muffled an uncharitable curse under a growl. His beast didn't want to cooperate either, screaming that they needed to go and run far from this place.

Chapter 15
Talina

"*Daughter*," the wind whispered, embracing her as she danced in the large hole left in Sirius's absence.

Ever since their fright at his reaction to the prophecy, she'd clammed up about the wind and how it continued giving her bits and snatches about what the future held for her.

"*Fear lurks behind. The little old one knows,*" it told her.

She was side by side with "the little old one," or the girl who pretended not to be an elder immortal. Talina knew why she'd lied about her age and relationship with Sirius, but she still avoided Cossette and the too-old eyes in her young face now that she knew the truth.

If she listened to the words filtering in on the breeze, the girl now waving at the front of the dancers knew something...about fear? Something else?

As afternoon shaded to evening and the sun set, their advertising duties were at an end. The girl came to her, tugging on her fingers. "C'mon, Miss Talina. This way." They walked through a meadow, startling a cluster of dragonflies.

"Where are we going?" she asked.

"I figured you had questions." The girl that looked up at her was completely serious, lines of concern etching deeper in her chubby cheeks as the evening rays caught the side of her face.

"Well, I am wondering where Sirius is," she admitted. "And... maybe about you as well."

"I'm right here, Miss Talina. And I'm taking you to him now." She skipped a few steps with a girlish giggle before giving her head a vicious shake. She pinched her own thigh and resumed a more dignified walk.

What an odd soul, she thought.

"What do you know?" she asked quietly.

"The future," Cossette said. "Never run from a beast. That's the most important thing for you right now."

Her breath caught to hear that line from another set of vocal cords. "Do I have future sight like you?" she practically demanded, wanting to grab the girl's shoulders in her eagerness.

"No. It's something else."

Talina's shoulders lowered as she sighed. "But you're also not crazy, so that's nice, right?" Cossette continued.

"Can you give me *some* answer?" she asked, feeling frustration bubble in her belly as she questioned the girl rapid-fire. "What does 'fear lurks behind' mean? What do you know that I'm supposed to ask about?"

Cossette waited patiently, walking with her hands clasped behind her back. "I told you, I know the future." She tilted her head. "Much of it, I can't speak of. I can no more talk about it than you can tell a lie."

"But...why?" she whispered.

"You'll get your answers soon. I promise. I'm here to help you where I can," she said, offering a smile. "Please don't be afraid of me, Miss Talina."

"It's not that... How could I be afraid of you? You've been nothing but sweet," Talina protested. "I just feel bad. Have you really been this small for many years?"

"Nine hundred of them, yes," Cossette sighed.

"Is there anything I can do to help you?" Fae didn't believe in taking and taking of a generous soul's help. When something was given, it was expected to mirror it with a gift in return.

Cossette shook her head, scattering her head of styled, white curls. Talina knew that Wisteria in particular enjoyed dolling her up on the regular. "Not yet, so don't even worry about it," she said. "You should be concerned for Sirius right now. Fear lurks behind *him*."

They were coming up on a temple, one of the only stone structures in this nature-loving city. It loomed up two stories high, carved with symbols for the four elements. A druidic temple. They were still amongst its garden, with Cossette offering her hands up to a curious doe cropping down some of the flowers, when Sirius's form burst from the front. "You won't catch him," the girl said as the deer bolted, its white tail flipping up in warning as it bounded away.

Sirius turned, his blazing maroon eyes pinning onto Talina across the distance. He was furious, an animal's snarl fixed across his lips. She faltered a step, recognizing the same anger level as when she'd tried to open up about her prophecy. For a moment, she thought he might not recognize her, but then he lifted a hand, palm out. He shook his head. Then, he pivoted away and took off at a run.

"What fear caused *that*?" she whispered, stuck in place as her heart fluttered in her chest.

"Be careful, Miss Talina. I'll see you tomorrow, okay?" Cossette reached up and gave her hand a squeeze.

She knelt and hugged the girl with a sigh. "Thank you for the wisdom you could share," she murmured into her white hair.

A cluster of druids was just now coming out of the temple, looking for Sirius. As she and Cossette parted ways, she approached them. "Um, excuse me?" She wavered when she saw an Archdruid at the lead of the group, his visible pupils a telltale sign of Getana's blessing.

"Hello, little lady. Did you happen to see a giant brute of a human-born man run by?" he asked with far more flippancy than she'd expect of one of the venerated Archdruids.

"I think he went this way, sir!" one of the other druids called, pointing out a footprint in the grass.

"What did you guys do to anger him so much?" she asked, watching two druids peel off from the group and follow the trail Sirius had left behind.

The Archdruid eyed her up and down, humming. "Would you happen to be his fated mate?" At her cautious nod, he introduced himself as Theron Shadestone and invited her inside the temple. The entry hall was lined with more carvings, hung with the symbols and a few traditional depictions of the gods at the four corners of the room. Instead of a stone floor, the druids had built on grass and flowers and kept it flourishing. He took her to the right, where there was a small dining area.

She knew most temples housed druids and their guests, keeping a cozy space for everyone who wanted to come pay respects to the gods. She'd never expected to visit one with an Archdruid and have him buy her a cup of tea, seated in a private booth. "I have a few questions for you, Miss...?"

"Talina."

"Miss Talina. Have you ever had your magic tested?"

She blinked, puzzled. "How does this relate to Sirius getting all angry?"

He blew on the rim of his mug, earthy steam rising from his own drink. "I tried to test his magic, and he lost control of himself. Since I was looking for something in particular, I was wondering if you'd allow me to look for it in your own magic."

"Well, you won't find anything. I'm a hundred percent wind magic." So she knew, because her magic was tested several times for any hint of the future sight virtue manifesting in her.

He braced his chin on one hand, his pinky tracing a path back and forth over his lower lip. "That's interesting, actually. Ever hear of a fatecrossed match?"

It sounded familiar. Wracking her brain, she eventually snapped her fingers. "When the gods pair a man and a woman?" Her eyes rounded. "Is that...real?"

"Let me put it this way... I've never met anyone fatecrossed before. The gods have put their hands up when it comes to forcing fae together." He lifted his own palms for emphasis. "But anyone with a fatecross will have a mark of it in their magic."

"Wait. Do you think he and I have a mark like that?" she asked in disbelief.

"There's only one way to tell. May I?" He held out his hand.

She let him take her arm, flipping it so it rested palm-up on the table. The air shifted as he gestured and swirled his hands through a complicated spell, his fingertips dragging green light as the symbols he drew remained suspended in midair. He eventually clapped, drawing all those symbols in to smash together and fill his fingers with a green glow.

Holding his hands over her wrist, he spread them again. The sheet of magic that stretched between his palms turned a silvery-gray, glowing intensely with the concentration of her wind magic. "Ah," he said, clenching his jaw to hide some reaction.

With a jerk of his chin, Theron summoned a young fae whose wings hadn't grown in yet. He held the spell until the youngling returned, offering up parchment and a charcoal pencil. Taking one last look at her magical reading, he ended the spell by reaching for the items. He quickly sketched something out and lifted it up to her.

"Do you know what this means?" he asked, stabbing a finger at the heart of the drawing. It resembled a swirling funnel, a twisting column of a tall tornado.

"No?" She glanced between it and him, knowing her eyes were clouding over with concern.

"Well, that's a problem." Theron turned the parchment to look at it again.

"So, it's not a fatecross mark?"

"Actually..." He bit his lip. "I think it is. Since they're so rare, it bears some research. I don't want to give you anything definitive until we know more."

She nodded slowly. "How does this help Sirius, then?"

Theron frowned and told her about the conversation he'd just had with Sirius, getting a dumbfounded look from Talina. She had no idea that a pure human-born and pure fae couldn't be matched. "Maybe I'm not pure fae?" she suggested. "I never knew my father. Perhaps he was a halfling of some sort."

"Anything is possible." He pulled at his face with a sigh. "I'm not sure how much you've seen of it, but Sirius has...a problem."

Much as she hated hearing it from an outsider, she knew. His anger was on a short leash, and it scared him. It was the thing he feared the most, losing his head at the wrong moment. "He has it mostly under control."

Theron muffled a sarcastic laugh. "Do we know the same Sirius?"

Her gaze narrowed. "I'm starting to think that we don't."

"I wanted to test him for something else while he was here, but..." he shrugged. "You see how well that's going for me. He may be a good candidate for druidic rage therapy. He has literally every sign of having rage fever, except he's not a fae nor a druid."

She shifted uncomfortably. "Well, he's a shapeshifter. Maybe he is a druid too."

Theron clicked his fingers and pointed toward her. "Exactly. So, when he relaxes, I'm hoping we can do the tests. Get him some real help." He pushed up from the booth, taking his mug with him. "Do you have a place to spend the night, Talina? I would like to offer you a bed here free of charge for your help this evening."

She was glad to pounce on that offer. "We'll come get you if we can get Sirius to return," Theron continued, walking her to the guest wing of the temple. "In the meantime, I need to send an urgent message to the Unseelie Queen."

Chapter 16
Sirius

He was being hunted. He turned his narrowed gaze behind his back, sensing the two druids keeping pace with him. This was their turf, but he wasn't going with them. Not when aggression rolled under his skin like a living thing.

Run. Fight. Kill! his beast screamed.

Kill her! KILL HER!

He'd seen Talina for only a few moments, but the beast had clearly lost its mind. They would not be laying a single finger on her until he got it under control. It was the blasted Sanctum, empowering the beast to the point that he could barely tell who was in charge between the two of them. As night fell and he slipped through the city, approaching the gates he'd entered through, it became increasingly obvious.

The beast was in control. He was simply steering it, promising it a reward if they got as far from the Sanctum—and Talina—as possible before they had to sleep. He had to get a grip before it turned him around and sank its fangs and claws into her tiny body.

The fuck is wrong with you? he hissed at his beast. Just today, they'd entered under these trellises overflowing with flowers and watched her laugh and play with a flock of hummingbirds. He'd been content then, enjoying the cute moment for what it was.

Now, his beast wanted to murder her in cold blood. The only

thing that'd happened in between was Theron finding him and telling him everyone was fine.

Including Lucia.

Heat poured from his skin at even the thought of *her*. If she encountered him in this state, he'd dismember her and leave no evidence with which to claim her bounty.

Get away. Stay away.

He couldn't make Talina's prophecy come true. He would never hurt her.

Only when the moon's silvery rays hit him did he finally succumb to his exhaustion. What felt like a lifetime ago, he'd taken the pear-tasting green goop to sleep well this night. His beast screeched and thrashed, but the medicine had its hold on him. He collapsed in a pile of leaves and closed his eyes.

No! NO! NOOO! The beast raked its claws through the darkness they descended into.

"Good evening, Sirius."

He whirled around. He was now standing in the exact same spot he'd fallen, face to face with Lucia. A broad grin pinned her pale face as the rising moon emphasized the beauty of her old Sorceress self.

"Are you ready? I've waited so eagerly for this night," she purred.

Snarling, he lunged toward her, hand going to his sword hilt. She stepped backward onto the path sloping toward Cordaria. "Sleepwalking. I've never actually gotten another to do it before," she said conversationally as she scooped something off the ground. "Oh, why do I bother trying to talk to you at night? You always forget it all."

She wound up and threw a ball of ink into his face. It exploded into dark vapors, blinding him. "Come and get me!" she taunted, her voice retreating as he roared in fury. "Chase, you stupid beast!"

He stumbled after her, breathing in the dark smoke and choking as it rolled down his throat. The moment he could see, he rushed at her, sword out. She ran as fast as she could, but she could never hope to outpace him. With a single swipe, he cut her clean in half.

Her body began to slide apart, but instead of bleeding, it wavered at the edges and disappeared. An illusion. He cursed and cast a glance around, getting pelted along the cheek by another ball of ink for his efforts. This time, Lucia took the form of her borrowed body. A sea serpent shifter. He'd heard what it looked like from Theron, but this was his first time seeing it. Unmistakable, with glittering, teal scales that caught the moonlight.

"I need your soul," she cackled. Her voice still rose from the new form.

He ended this illusion's life as well, loping after her like a wolf on the hunt.

Kill her! Bathe in her blood! his beast screamed.

"You want it, bitch? Come and take it," he shouted, cutting through her illusions one by one. She was toying with him, like she always did. Too much a coward to fight directly, knowing he'd scythe through her just as easily as he destroyed her illusions.

The next person he saw just stood in the road, pinning him with doe eyes watering with hurt. "You really think I'm a bitch?" Talina asked.

He faltered for a split second. "Talina," he whispered.

No! Imposter!

His beast pushed him, swinging the sword for him. Talina shattered into pieces, just another illusion.

"Don't you dare impersonate her," he snarled, seeing red when the next illusion was his fated match once again.

And the next as well. "Don't hurt me, Sirius," she whimpered.

When it was gone, he inevitably chased the next. "Jealous?" He scoffed, grabbing this next version of Talina by the throat and turning her around. "Are you bitter, Lucia? You realize she's everything you're not?"

Lucia dropped the innocent act, grinning viciously in a way he recognized. "Why would I be jealous? I don't go for second best," she hissed. The illusion exploded into dark vapors, which he swept aside and kept going through. His legs felt like putty all of a sudden, and he listed to one side as he choked on a cough.

"Always in Adrius's shadow. Ever the prince, never the king." The next version of Talina hurled Lucia's spiteful words right in front of him, her delicate head cocked. She pressed a finger into her cheek. "Does it sting that everyone loves him and hates you?"

With a scream of rage, he launched himself at her, cutting that coy mouth before it said another word. "I am not second best to *Adrius*," he shouted.

Something struck his forehead. Not shadows. When he checked, his fingers came away wet. A second cold droplet plinked off his cheek before an unexpected storm opened overhead with a distant roll of thunder. Clouds rapidly rolled over the moon, leaving him in pitch darkness.

His beast automatically adjusted with night vision, chasing Lucia through the shadows. His boots slipped in the mud, and he fell into a bank of darkness, his head striking a rock.

With a groan, his eyes cracked open. His vision swam double as he breathed within an inky cloud of mist. Rain pelted his face in icy, unforgiving lashes while his inner beast was still in charge and screaming for him to *kill her!*

Lucia's Sorceress face appeared over the lip of the bank, her lips quirked. "You're awake. How unfortunate."

With a roar, he grabbed the hilt of his sword and jackknifed to his feet. He launched toward her, but she was no longer there. A portal snapped shut inches from the edge of his sword. She was gone.

No! his beast screamed in denial. The rain washed away any hopes of scenting her, except...

She was running from him. He caught the edge of movement as her wet clothes flapped awkwardly behind her. Forcing his wobbly legs to move, he pursued as quickly as he dared, recognizing the treacherous footing in this fae forest with the moon shadowed by clouds.

Lightning flicked across the sky, highlighting another portal as it closed. She was jumping ahead of him, he realized, because otherwise, he'd catch her in minutes. He tried something different and tossed his sword the moment he spotted her again, nailing her through the shoulder.

Her body exploded into dust motes. He snarled a curse. *An illusion!*

His beast rumbled with impatience, like it could've told him that.

"Oh, Sirius!" Lucia's voice sang over the hiss of falling rain. She spoke from Talina's vocal cords, wearing her green leotard. This illusion was much faster than the last, running swiftly past the now-familiar trellises of flowers until he struck her down right beside one. His sword cut into the wood frame, sending it toppling with a wet crash. The illusion screamed shrilly moments before it disappeared.

"You'll have to pay for that," Lucia taunted, another copy of Talina standing there at the wide-open gates. Early morning light struggled through the clouds to limn her wet, navy-dark hair. Her voice shaded higher. "Why are you such a monster, Sirius?" she asked in Talina's voice.

His vision swam with fury. He might've exploded with it rather than bursting into motion, though his momentum was stolen as he slipped in a patch of mud and crashed into the last trellis, sending half of it collapsing atop him.

He roared curses at Lucia the moment he was back on his feet, careening after her once he checked a lurch to the side. He coughed and choked on more unsavory language, the double vision back. Even as he caught up to Lucia's newest taunting illusion, he swiped at air rapid-fire as he tried to figure out which version of her was just his vision playing tricks. He was slowing, his limbs feeling like they weighed hundreds of pounds. But man and beast agreed: he was going to get her before he collapsed. The real her. He would dance in her blood.

No other death would be so satisfying.

Kill her! His beast saw the opening, and they finally skewered the illusion with a victorious scream.

He didn't know where he was. The illusion had led him up and down Cordaria, and it was still just a whim of magic from the real Lucia. She'd make a new one within moments. The seconds ticked by as he waited, catching his breath raggedly.

He could hear Lucia's voice faintly. *"Remember, you will always be second best."*

"Sirius?" Talina asked faintly.

There the trick was, behind him. He turned a furious look on this copy of Talina wearing a night robe just beginning to soak with water. Her eyes were wide and cloudy, fear etched across her face. He bared his teeth in a snarl and prepared to take her down, too.

Chapter 17
Talina

The rain and wind pattered outside, and Talina slept soundly, cocooned by the sounds of the storm. That was, until the wind shrieked. She sat straight up in bed, her heart beating wildly as she wondered what that was. It sounded like the cry of a distant, shrill creature or the awful sound nails on a chalkboard made, but magnified tenfold.

"*Come!*" the wind called through the stone walls, disguised in a howling gale.

She'd fallen asleep in the fur night robe a druid had offered her upon seeing her leotard and lack of luggage. She belted it more carefully to cover her up to her collarbone and rushed out of the little room she'd rested in. It was still early morning, and...

Gods above, what was that sound? Like the roar of a huge predator. The wind called again, so she reluctantly went outside into the rain to feel its embrace more directly. A funnel of wind surrounded her, cool against her skin as it dampened.

Sirius's wet form stood several yards away, his back to her. His shoulders rose and fell as he breathed heavily. What looked like the silhouette of a woman stood next to him, made entirely of shadowy ink. That strange being glanced her way, its eyes flashing silver, before cupping its hand to whisper into his ear like a conspirator.

Goosebumps raised all over Talina's body. She glanced inside the temple, where a young fae was closing the front door against the rain. Making eye contact, she gestured for him to go get help.

She had a terrible feeling. Maybe it was nothing, but she was about to find out for herself. "Sirius?" she asked, uncertain.

The moment he turned, she realized she'd made a terrible mistake. His face was wrinkled in an animal's snarl, forehead blackened by a mix of blood and mud. Glowing out from his face were eyes like twin coals, zeroing in on her with nearly no pupil from how dilated they were. Dark shadows haloed him. She hadn't noticed them tangling in his soaked hair of the same color, but against the tenor of his skin, they circled in mist-like clumps around his torso and limbs.

He faced her, lifting his sword. Alarm screamed through her as he muttered someone else's name and lunged with another animalistic roar. The stones of the temple rattled with the force of the noise, and she quavered, frozen, watching his attack come for her in surreal slow motion.

The wind around her unfurled, becoming a howling gale that picked him up and slammed him into the side of the temple with a dull smack. She gasped, backing away in horror. What was happening?

"S-Sirius?" she stammered.

The same breeze that'd saved her now pushed back against her as she tried to turn and run. "*Never run from a beast,*" it reminded her in a whisper.

Groaning, the vampire rolled back to his feet, coughing hard. New blood streamed down his cheek from where he'd been flung headlong into the stone. That didn't stop his gaze from meeting hers with a new blaze of hostility.

If she couldn't run, what did the wind want her to do? Snapping her wings out, she lifted skyward, rolling away from a swing of his sword just in time. The deadly, iron edge whistled by her arm, giving her heart a hard jolt. She had to get away! Encountering no resistance midair, she drew on the might of her magic, buoying herself up to the top of the temple roof two stories up. It was built of stone, with a slight raise in the middle to draw rainwater downward.

There, she thought. He couldn't follow her up here.

Except that shadowy creature was back, whispering to him again. His neck was craned upward, every iota of his focus on where she'd landed.

"Fear lurks behind, right?" she asked to the sky, hoping the wind had some answer for her. Trepidation filled her as Sirius clasped the middle of his sword in his mouth and started to scale the stone.

If ever she needed a prophecy, it was now. She held her heart in her throat as cold wind settled over her skin. Shivering, she strained her ears to hear.

"To your hand alone, the beast submits," it whispered.

Sirius reached the stone lip of the roof, hoisting himself up. He spat his sword aside, catching it as he rolled a few feet from her. There weren't many options up here. No druidic help would arrive in the space of a sword swing. The shadows swirled all the heavier around him. Talina wondered if they implied mind control by that creature that hovered up belatedly, standing behind Sirius and watching with the flash of a smirk in its amorphous face.

If she dove, he could jump after her. If she flew, he still had a chance to strike her.

The wind's wisdom faded from her mind as she spread her fingers. "Sirius, forgive me," she whispered. Static danced between her fingertips as she took aim and fired a bolt of lightning before he could take that swing and kill her.

She hated this side of her magic. Wind was harmless and sometimes sweet, but lightning killed. And her lightning was always too strong, burning a bright white streak through her vision. Unclenching her eyes, she witnessed him taking the last of the voltage, his whole body twitching and sparking with arcs over his wet skin.

His deadly iron sword clattered on the stone, tipping over the edge. And with a spasm of his muscles, Sirius dropped face down on the roof.

The shadow creature stopped smiling. It eyed Talina anew and disappeared in a burst of smoke. "Cheap...shot...Lucia..."

Sirius muttered, disjointed, as his form continued to quiver with electricity.

A blast of wind forced Talina a step forward. She took a knee next to him, reaching out to take back the voltage still tormenting his body. His head snapped up a moment before she could make contact, half his face sparking with a lightning-shaped wound.

Her attack hadn't even stopped him—she screamed in alarm as he grabbed her wrist and rolled off the roof, pulling her down with him. Her ankle caught the lip of the roof, twisting with a sharp snap of agony as gravity took over.

Once freed, his other hand curled around her throat. She wheezed, choking as the world narrowed to his maddened face. This was it, then. Her soul change...her death. She hadn't expected it to come so quickly for her, but she couldn't fight him.

Sparks danced around her throat, the same electric touch that happened every time they touched. Sirius's pupils ballooned, and his angry snarl went slack a split second before his fingers left her neck. The ground rushed up, jolting her whole body. She clenched her eyes closed, expecting more pain.

All she heard was a ragged breath. A pair of arms surrounded her middle, and when she finally opened her eyes, she realized Sirius had cradled her and taken the brunt of impact. Pink spittle hit the grass as he coughed and twitched.

"Talina," he rasped. "I didn't...did I..." He hiccupped a wet hack, his whole form convulsing. With her electricity fading, it had to be something else. "Ta...lina...I would...never..."

Shouts drowned out what he was trying to say. A druid woman pulled her away from him, giving her a glimpse of the fae pouring out of the temple and clustering around Sirius like an impenetrable wall.

The woman coaxed Talina into the temple, conferring briefly with Theron as the Archdruid stopped a headlong rush at the sight of her. He looked more disheveled than ever, his eyes glazed with shock.

"Gods above," he muttered. "Send another message to Queen Kalimea. We will need extra help."

She nursed a tepid cup of hot chocolate from a comfortable seat plopped in front of her by a rushing druid. It'd taken a team of them to roll Sirius's body onto a litter and carry him to the biggest room in the temple—the inner sanctum, otherwise known as the shrine. Usually, its wooden doors were flung wide open for worshipers to come in and pay their respects, but they were shut tightly after the initial stream of healers and assistants.

Numbly, she watched pages fetch bandages, boxes full of herbs and other medical supplies, and, finally, a set of thick wooden manacles fashioned of some sort of root. They were etched with symbols up every loop and whorl.

No one had time to speak to her after making sure she was alive and dry and ready to wait. A kind druid has wrapped her ankle, but it wasn't the perfect job Sirius would do.

The Archdruid had listened to her accounting of what happened, his lips thinning when she mentioned the shadowy creature whispering to Sirius.

"Do you believe it was mind control?" she'd asked.

"Quite possibly. But it will be a while until we know what exactly happened," he warned, clapping her on the shoulder. "Will you be willing to wait?"

She was willing, and so here she was. There was a performance this evening, and she didn't budge as the minutes ticked on, knowing her troupe had to be wondering where the two of them were. Unless the locals had seen him rampaging around. She'd caught whispers that he'd damaged some structures in addition to attacking her.

Attacking her. Why was she even here, with concern holding her heart in a vice? She twisted the cup back and forth in her hold, worry making her queasy. The man had held her throat in his fist, murder in his eyes.

But the touch of her skin had brought him to his senses. She still felt the lingering warmth on her throat and wrist. Sirius had meant to kill her—right until they touched. Surely he wasn't in control of himself. He'd never been so violent before.

So, she waited with lingering fright. She'd get some answers if she was patient enough to earn them with her time.

She knew when Sirius was awake, because that's when the roaring began. Sirius sounded more like a wounded animal than a man, scuffing and screeching echoing from the shrine. Talina retracted in on herself. What could possibly do this to him? It just wasn't normal, or right.

After what felt like an eternity, a new person arrived, drawing Talina's attention immediately by her sheer presence. Another human-born with her head lifted high, her red eyes and larger stature marking her as a vampire much like Sirius. She wore metal armor and a sword strapped to her waist, her expression set like she was heading to war.

This woman's hair was swept back in a copper ponytail, leaving little of her face to the imagination. A thick scar cut across the side of her mouth, permanently tugging her lip into a half-frown. Her gaze cut to Talina, and she dipped her head in greeting before throwing the inner sanctum's door open and stomping inside.

Muffled, the woman's surprisingly melodic voice lifted through the barrier of wood. "Release him! Can't you see you're making it worse?"

Talina's breath caught. What if Sirius attacked this woman too? They were obviously restraining him for everyone's safety.

She was so preoccupied with her cup, her ears straining to hear the muffled conversation past the door, that she didn't notice another person sitting on the stone floor beside her until he spoke up with a hello. She jerked, nearly dropping her cocoa.

"Hey, it's okay." The newcomer laughed, holding up his hands. He was a half-fae of some sort, bearing pointed ears and a starry, narrow face with human eyes and a dazzling smile. Dressed in a peacock-blue suit, he'd come equipped with a lute, which he tuned up and strummed. The silvery note that raised from the instrument drew a sigh from Talina, her shoulders relaxing a fraction. "Waiting's a bummer, so let's wait together. Who might you be? I'm Cedric."

HE WOKE IN CHAINS. SIRIUS UNDERSTOOD THIS WAS THE END for him in a split second of seeing the wooden shackles wrapped around his wrists and ankles, glowing with fae runes. He'd behaved like a beast. Out of control. Rabid. So, now he was to be restrained like one.

Still, the part of him that was still more animal than human screamed and thrashed, trying desperately to pull free. Panic seized him when the manacles didn't bulge, cutting further into his circulation instead.

Voices surrounded him. Hands on his body.

They tried to press fabric to his wounds. Fingers attempted to clasp his jaw to force medicine down his throat.

He lunged at those fingers, trying to bite. He jerked his head away when a bandage approached. Animal panic set in.

Escape, his beast cried.

It considered biting off their wrists. He'd never tried to regenerate a whole hand, but it didn't matter right now. The only thing he cared about was getting away before he lost all of his strength. Before he became a beast in a cage, an oddity to stare at. Something too strong and too wild to release back into polite company.

"Release him! Can't you see you're making it worse?"

He knew that voice. His slitted gaze slid closed, the world spinning the moment he relaxed even a fraction. Someone took advantage of his momentary calm, and a prick of pain touched his neck, followed by the murky darkness of dreamless sleep.

THE FIRST THING HE HEARD WAS THE WOMAN'S MELODIC voice. "I understand."

"There's very little we can do for him. We've never seen anything quite like this," a male voice responded.

"Unfortunately, we have, with his brother," she said. "He drank the blood of the strongest Fell and immediately went into convulsions from having too much power."

There was an uncomfortable murmur of several voices and shuffling feet. "How did you save his life?" the man asked.

Sirius pictured the scene in his mind's eye, knowing exactly what they were talking about. His brother had thought he could take every dark power the Fell Emperor held—but it was a foolish notion. He'd overflowed with magic, dying because of it.

They'd just barely conquered Nyixa and routed the Fell that lived upon the island. Countless vampires had died, leaving Sirius and a handful of others to help Adrius by biting him and draining some of his overflowing magic into themselves.

Sirius had been first. He'd gained his inner beast from that moment forward, sparing his brother from having to carry such powerful magic.

He cracked his eyes open slowly. The woman who narrated this history lesson stood a few paces away, her red gaze fixed over Theron's shoulder as he held his palms a foot apart. A thin sheet of blackened magic sparked between his hands, showing something they were both reading.

Neala had taken the power of illusions from Adrius, sparing him yet another powerful ability that she went on to master. However, she never used it on herself if she could help it, showing the world her scarred face with all the blunt honesty of her warrior nature. He could hardly believe it was really her there, weeks after they'd parted so sourly.

"There's only one problem right now. We have no vampires

with which to share his magic," Theron pointed out once she was done speaking. "I assume you are at capacity."

"As was Sirius," she said, frowning severely.

"Far over capacity, based on his rage fever," the Archdruid murmured.

Her red gaze lit on Sirius's face. Pressing her lips together, she then glanced around the room. "I require a moment alone with him."

No one argued, a set of shuffling footsteps following her announcement. Neala loomed over him, her arms crossed. "Are you in your right mind?" she asked quietly.

His best response was a pained grunt. He was still getting his bearings, not recognizing where they were. It was a stone room built from marble-like rock fae used, paving the walls in smooth, shiny blocks. The roof was what he was most acquainted with, each block engraved with a fae rune, creating a swirling display of multicolored light that illuminated the whole room gently.

"Come to laugh?" he asked, choking on a cough as his sore lungs spasmed in complaint. "Come...to gloat?" A scowl slashed across Neala's face as he struggled. "Selfish cur...getting what he deserves..."

Her lips pursed, and he knew what that look meant. He'd been verbally eviscerated by this woman enough times.

"I wish I'd realized how bad it was. How long have you been suffering?" she said, instead. "Theron showed me that you're developing fourteen new powers at once. Your body can't handle it, Sirius."

He blinked, sluggish. Was that pity in her tone? Neala didn't spare sympathy for anyone...except him, it seemed. "I'm dying?" he whispered.

"Theron is searching for options. We're not going to let you go that easy," she said fiercely.

He let his head fall back, wheezing a little laugh. "Just...let me go... Wouldn't that be easier?" Talina's terrified face flashed in his mind's eye, his hand moments away from crushing her windpipe. "I...I hurt her... I don't deserve..."

Neala blew out a curse as she watched him struggle. "I couldn't kill Lucia... She was so close..." he rasped.

Neala's voice grew hard, and her armor protested as she made two fists. "An eyewitness spoke of a shadowy figure whispering in your ear as you were having your...moment. Whatever's happening, it's an attack from Lucia. She's waiting for you to die right this moment." She leaned forward, her eyes blazing with conviction. "You're *not* going to die, Sirius. She cannot have your soul."

I need your soul. How many times had he heard those words disguised in a dream? In this delirious moment, he realized Lucia had said it many times, laughing each time he forgot.

Come and take it, bitch, he heard himself responding.

Like always, she attacked indirectly. Put him in a situation where his shame and limitations made him want to give up and hand her what she wanted on a silver platter.

You really think I'm a bitch?

She'd asked with Talina's face. Talina's voice.

He muttered viciously, struggling against the chains binding him. "Let me go... Let me at her..." His voice was slurred, the world muddy shades as he fought to keep his eyes open. At the edge of his life, he knew it was Lucia that'd tricked his beast, making him see her when it was really Talina. He'd nearly murdered her.

Logically, he would've taken his life the moment he realized what happened. Lucia waited to sweep up his soul and take it to Hell for whatever her purposes were. Yet another twisted plan on her part, but bolder than he'd usually expect.

Neala's strong hands took hold of his shoulders, pushing him back onto the cold stone slab beneath him. "Stop. She's not here." She countered his struggles until he lay limp in his restraints. "You're going to get her, just not right now."

He must've passed out, as the next thing he knew, more noise filled his ears. Voices he couldn't understand. Decisions he could barely hear. His beast was ever aware of the restraints, but he was tired. So tired. He had no fight left to escape, knowing the end loomed whether he was bound in chains or lying in a field.

Eventually, a jolt of magic on his neck had his eyes springing wide open. Looming in and out of focus was Theron's face. He was saying something. Sirius squinted, seeing the word "consent" purse the fae man's lips.

His brows puckered. White noise stole everything away, and the world was fuzzy at the edges. Adrius's brush with too much power had spelled for a violent near-end, but Sirius could feel himself slowly fading by comparison. Maybe it was the last mercy these druids could spare him.

The Archdruid gave up speaking aloud, switching to a voice in his head. *"I need your consent for a dangerous ritual. We are going to attempt a Convocation of the Elements and beseech the gods for help."*

Anything involving gods seemed deadly to him, but what did he have to lose? He dipped his chin in a nod. "Oh...kay," he rasped.

Theron patted his cheek, withdrawing from his line of sight. The wood binding his wrists and ankles went slack, dropping his limbs like iron weights. Sirius groaned as his body ached all over, pins and needles reminding him of his continued existence past a head full of ringing noise.

The cold edge of a glass touched his lips, tipping back thin, bitter liquid. Before he could spit it up, a firm set of fingertips caught his throat and made him swallow.

His eyes closed, and he drifted slowly into darkness, hearing Theron's voice as a distant murmur.

<h1 style="text-align:center">Chapter 19
Talina</h1>

CEDRIC LISTENED PATIENTLY AS TALINA EXPLAINED WHAT'D happened down to every excruciating detail. He'd cycled through several songs in the interim, discovering that she loved upbeat melodies she could bounce her head to. "Am I stupid? To wait for him?" she asked, worrying her hands. She sensed Gem was somewhere else, taking shelter from the rain with his kin in a tree. Her familiar was an angry little presence in the back of her mind, practically begging her to abandon Sirius and return to their old life in the circus.

As evening approached and the storm continued to lash the earth, she knew she was choosing Sirius over her job. Cloman would be none too pleased, maybe even toy with the idea of firing her and promoting one of the dancers to head choreographer. A few of the women had been in the circus for as long as Talina—they knew the routines and could take it all in a new direction. They might even be happy to be free of her and her oddities.

"I don't think you're being stupid at all. In fact, could you be..." Cedric said, bringing her out of her thoughts. He played a single, jaunty high note. "...in love?"

Her cheeks lit up purple. "Uh. I mean..."

Judging by how she yearned to go to his side, there was a tiny possibility. She loved a lot of things. Gem, ballet, the smell of fresh wind and morning dew. She'd even loved her mother, though the thought of her was tinged with sadness at her abrupt departure from this world.

If Talina felt that way for Sirius, a part of her worried events would color it with sorrow as a young druid approached and placed a potted lily in front of her with a bow. She blanched.

"What's wrong?" Cedric asked, glancing between her and the flower.

She was a little surprised he didn't know. "It's tradition," she murmured, placing the pot right beside her chair as she smiled to the druid, who moved into the inner sanctum. Now that Sirius had relaxed, it was as silent as a tomb in there.

"Tradition for what?" Cedric asked nervously as, an hour later, she had five more flowerpots beside her.

She picked up the most recent gift, a diminutive clay pot decorated with white swirls. It was full to the brim with inch-long wildflowers. Sighing, she touched the soft edge of a tiny, white petal. "It's a druidic condolence. It means that—" Her breath caught as she fought off watery eyes. "—things aren't going so well in there."

He whistled low. "I'm sorry."

"Me too. I'm the one who hit him with lightning," she said, regretting only the necessity of it. "Earth magic is all about life and death, you know? The flowers are a reminder that there's still life to live."

He was starting to frown at the connotations of that when a portal opened up just feet from them. A pair of women walked through. Talina stood carefully, keeping her foot elevated on a cushion of air. Cedric followed suit with a crack of his knees. "Damn, getting old already," he murmured, bending down to rub one.

He was surprisingly irreverent in front of the Queen of Faerie.

Talina bowed her head respectfully, watching Kalimea through her eyelashes. The woman was hardly changed from when she'd rescued Talina from a remote village's quarantine. Petite for a fae, she wore cool colors to offset the auburn ringlets of her hair and her bright, destruction fae eyes, twin pits of orange-red fire that matched the regal halo of flaming wings on her back.

Behind her was another destruction fae, a tall and lean woman wearing leather and a bandolier of daggers. Her snowy white hair and scowl announced who she was by sheer reputation: Princess Ashaela, the queen's sister and closest bodyguard.

Kalimea stopped short. Her fingers felt hot after so long in this drafty hallway, lifting Talina's chin with gentle pressure. Those fiery eyes searched her face, her other hand tapping her chin.

"Ah, Talina. How could I think to forget that face?" she said at last.

She felt warm all over, a pleasant little jig going on in her belly that the ultra-important Unseelie Queen remembered her. She nodded, flashing a shy smile, and let the other woman draw her into a brief hug. Over her shoulder, she saw Cedric chucking Ash on the shoulder as they shared a laugh over something.

"Are you still working with"—the queen's nose wrinkled delicately—"that sideshow that snubbed me a few weeks ago?"

"That's the one." Oops. If Kalimea wanted to have words with someone about that, Cloman's Own was in the same city as her.

"Your talents are wasted there, my dear." She looped her arm around Talina's shoulders, tugging her along as her heels clicked on the stone.

They headed straight for the inner sanctum. "Um, I don't think I'm invited..." she protested weakly.

"Nonsense." The queen marched her inside, their presence causing a small stir as the druids were slow to notice Kalimea's presence. Most were spellcasting, creating a half-circle of bodies around the shrine in the center of the room. Someone had moved the offering plates to the four corners of the room, which were each decorated to honor one of the gods of Faerie. Amongst this many druids, the earth corner was the most cramped, overflowing with beads and baubles sacrificed to the Lady of Life.

Kalimea went straight to the two people standing out of the way of the ongoing druidic spellcasting. Well, Theron was still casting but was mid-conversation as his fingers wove green symbols with methodical care. The giant redheaded woman was next to him, her scowl drawing deep lines in her face.

"'Bout time, woman," Theron greeted Kalimea.

Talina's mouth dropped open in shock.

"You're lucky I like you," the queen responded. "I'll let Ash rearrange your innards later."

"Looking forward to it," he said, jerking his head toward the woman still standing behind Kalimea. "Can you control some of the shadow magic he's leaking?"

Leaking? Talina edged to the side, craning her neck to look over a druid's shoulder. Sirius's prone form lay over the stone altar, his arms strung up with glowing, wooden manacles attached to hanging creepers grown from the ceiling while his legs hung more loosely. The stone itself glowed with green magic, a slow roll of druidic runes surrounding him in a protective bubble. A collection of hardy plants and weeds flourished along the stone floor, soil actively terraforming from the sheer pulse of life magic filling the air.

Sirius was indeed losing shadows, though, dripping from his body like a dark fog. Ash lifted a hand and flicked her wrist, gathering up a fistful of shadowy magic as it rolled in her direction like mist in a breeze. "Hmm. What do you want me to do with it?" she asked.

"Destroy it," he deadpanned, the two of them sharing a nod before the Unseelie went to work. He turned back to Kalimea. "We need four powerful souls to call a Convocation."

"Are things so dire?" she asked.

"The demon lurks, waiting to grab his soul if we can't keep him alive. If ever we needed a godly miracle, it's now," he said gravely. Talina stifled a gasp. Things were so much worse than she thought, waiting uselessly outside this room.

Talina's heart lurched. She saw the serious tones painted between them both and asked, "What is a Convocation? And can I help with it?"

Theron's gaze slipped her way, doing a double take as if noticing her for the first time. "As a matter of fact, yes. And...do you think having Fell blood qualifies a vampire to stand it for water?" he asked Kalimea. "It helps if all four know the petitioner."

She bubbled with impatience as the queen considered and nodded slowly. "Neala, you shall be water. Cyranos will take it as an insult, but we don't have the time to find a Water-aligned fae who knows Sirius."

"Fine," the redhead replied. Her voice was practically melodic, even in that one word. Had they met under better circumstances, Talina would've asked her to sing.

"Let it be done, then." At Kalimea's words, Theron launched into motion. He cleared out the other druids, sending a few for vials of some semi-transparent potions. Talina watched as the Archdruid spoke to Sirius quietly and freed his limbs, earning a low moan from the man.

Kalimea put her arm around Talina again, offering the warmth of her side while they waited. "A Convocation of the Elements is a ritual to bend the gods' attention toward one person or group." It sounded incredibly dangerous to her without needing any further explanation. She regretted wishing she could meet a god only a day ago—it was reserved for the most powerful fae for good reason. "Only a fae who already has the favor of a god may attempt to call a full Convocation. I remain in good standing with Raenith, so Theron undoubtedly will want me to lead the call."

Quiet awe lit over her shoulders. "You've met her?"

"I've met all four, my dear. An experience in humility all fae should experience." Kalimea laughed without humor. She went on to explain that they'd take a potion to experience a heightened dream state as their souls visited a higher plane where the four gods could all attend at the same time. They would have a representative of the four elements to call to the individual gods, though Neala was certainly stretching it.

"Cyranos will leave, if I know him. He *hates* anything that reminds him of the Fell. However, three of four gods can still be considered a Convocation. I will share the words of the ritual with you as it unfolds." Kalimea accepted a vial of potion as she spoke, as did Talina.

They had to go quickly. Without the magic around Sirius, his coughing had returned. His skin was paling, turning him into a black and white shade on that altar. She knocked back her potion in one gulp.

Gods above, please make this work.

She didn't know what she'd do with herself if Sirius died tonight.

Chapter 20
Sirius

Sirius dreamt of a black void, standing in the middle of it as a passive observer.

"Mind. Body. Soul. Magic." Theron stood next to him, hands clasped.

With each of the Archdruid's words, a different corner of the void erupted into light. Blue, silver, red, and green, divided by clear lines to claim an equal share of territory. The color defined the space around him, revealing that he was in some sort of magical box as big as a bedroom.

A woman's form appeared on his opposite side. His eyes widened to behold Queen Kalimea herself, the strong-willed destruction fae's burning eyes fixed straight ahead as she recited, "Fire, water, air, and earth. The sacred elements decided at the birth of the world." The colors swirled with motes of their chosen elements.

Finally, a third and fourth person entered this void. Talina spoke hesitantly, her voice a high squeak compared to the confident tones of the other two. "And we keep your balance to this day. Four are your number, and four do we call." Much as Sirius's heart lurched to see her again, he could not move or speak. He stood paralyzed, struggling to catch a glimpse of her blue skin out of the corner of his eye. She wasn't looking his way.

"So may it be," Neala added, glancing around with obvious discomfort.

"I call a Convocation of the Elements," Kalimea intoned.

Magic flared, a blinding glare that could've melted most vampires and exploded them into ash like the lash of an unforgiving sun. Sirius squinted his eyes closed, opening them to see his four companions facing the four corners and their respective magic.

Power poured over him from all directions. He'd say his beast was cowed, but there was no inner beast here. Just Sirius, a slate of numbness as a literal miracle unfolded around him.

"I protest being called by a *vampire*," hissed a voice like rising steam. In the blue corner was a winding, serpentine form made of pure sapphire water. It had to be a miniature manifestation, as it couldn't be longer than Sirius's arms fingertip to fingertip. Still, the serpent coiled in hostility as it caught its bearings.

"Cyranos, please. Show some decorum." The creature of wood spoke more primly from her druidic-green corner. "Who is our petitioner?"

Kalimea gestured over her shoulder toward Sirius. "This human-born man. I have called you in haste, so I have not confirmed his true name."

The goddess lifted her head. "Well, what is it, then?" She was a dragon, but not the kind he'd expected. She looked a lot like the fire dragon Keegan kept as a familiar, but a skeletal version. Her face was one carved piece of wood, resembling a fire dragon's skull with green fire animating the empty pits of its eyes. If he looked closely, he could spot the individual finger bones amongst her talons and her ribcage. Obscuring those details was flourishing life, flowers and grasses in her forelegs, moss and trees lining her spine and woven lovingly between the bones of her wings like sinews.

Getana, the Lady of Life. She was the only one of the four he'd heard named directly.

He felt he could finally move now that he was addressed. "I'm afraid my people don't have a concept of a 'true name.'" As the words came from his mouth, he noticed the three fae around him turning in confusion. The ever-present tingle of translation magic was gone from his tongue, so perhaps he'd spoken in the thick accent of his native language.

"Just your name, then, please." Getana seemed amused, at least, as Cyranos slithered within the confines of his corner with an impatient hiss.

He opted for the full name rather than any fancy titles. Something told him the Gods of Faerie wouldn't be impressed. "Sirius Raphael Fabron."

"And what is your petition?" asked the Goddess of Earth.

Kalimea held up a hand, answering for him. "Sirius is afflicted by an influx of magic his body can't handle. A measured attack from a demoness who wishes to drag his soul to Hell for her own purposes."

A loud warble sounded from Cyranos. His arrow-shaped head fixed on Sirius, watery eyes slanted in hatred. "Your entry into Faerie has brought this upon you. You shall earn no assistance from me." His body disintegrated into a puddle, the blue light emanating from his corner dimming to black.

"Not entirely unexpected," spoke a voice like crackling flames and burning timbers. The Goddess of Fire sat on her haunches, her tail tip twitching. She was hard to look at directly, the miniature of her form made of white-hot flame that transitioned to blue in her eyes and talons. She had the general shape of a fire dragon; four strong limbs, a long neck, and two massive wings meant to propel all that bulk in flight.

"Can we count on your assistance, Lady Raenith?" Kalimea asked.

"That will entirely depend. His soul yearns for the freedom of wind's touch, wouldn't you say, Zalice?" The fiery dragon turned to the last corner, where a bird-like form of gray wind magic made him nearly blend in with the silver light that surrounded him.

Zalice didn't speak, per se, but a light breeze carried his words past Sirius's ears. *"I see no reason not to test his memories. Let us see if we can save his life."*

Talina's back went rigid the moment the God of Wind spoke.

Sirius cut a glance her way, wondering if she finally had an answer for why "the wind" carried lines of prophecy to her ears.

Trepidation gripped him as he thought over what the god had just said. "My memories?" he echoed.

Part of Adrius's redemption had come at the claws of a fire dragon ghost, who had tested Adrius by scraping out every scrap of memory from his skull and spreading it out in a split second to study and gain insight from. Zerenth had eventually found him worthy and forged a connection between them, making them a dragon shifter. Unfortunately, his guide had witnessed all of his memories through the magic of the ceremony. Said guide was also Adrius's daughter, Celeste, a moment branded in Sirius's memory from sheer secondhand embarrassment for his brother.

In his brief time in Adrun, he'd heard that shifters were born of a twisting of the familiar bond. A person tied to the spirit of a deceased animal rather than partnered with a living one. The shifters borrowed and adjusted existing fae rituals to make their own work.

Was he about to experience the same as it was meant to be done? All of his memories spread out for his companions to see?

Zalice answered his thoughts in a whisper of wind. *"That's right."*

"Please, not everything." He was ready to beg. There was so much he didn't want Talina to see. The others three could witness him at his very worst, but not his delicate fated match. He knew he had to be moments from losing her forever if she had just one more reason to fear him.

"Let us not waste time," Raenith said. With a gesture of her talons, red light surrounded and drew him into her corner. The rest of the room faded in the background, leaving his world awash in shades of crimson and flame.

Heat coiled, the impact making his eyes roll back.

Images flickered by. Not *everything*, but he recognized many moments of his life he'd rather never talk about again. He re-remembered how hot Fell blood tasted as it slid down his throat—simultaneously filth and honey, power burning in his veins. It was addictive.

In this space, he was aware of a giant claw shifting through his mind and only one other presence. It was Kalimea, watching him with burning eyes, and presumably his memories as well. "Don't worry. I don't care what I see, and Raenith will not look through everything," she told him. "Neala will see nothing, as Cyranos is not here to search your mind."

"I just don't want Talina to..." He drifted off when she raised her hand again.

"You came here with no magic, so I can't understand you. But I presume my own translation magic is working?" she asked, continuing after he nodded, grumbling at this particular irritation. "Talina is stronger than you think. She can handle whatever she sees. But if you're worried about Theron..." She flashed a grin. "He'll just tease you mercilessly if it's embarrassing."

He let off an exaggerated sigh to show how he felt about that.

In the meantime, he re-experienced the battles of his past. Vicious Fell cutting down his fellows all around him but dying like beasts for their efforts.

"Raenith is the Lady of Passion. She only cares about your moments of highest emotion and anything that's transpired in Faerie that she doesn't already know about," Kalimea explained.

Raenith stopped and really analyzed a moment he found hard to forget.

They plunged into the depths of the memory, bringing it to focus and forcing Sirius to relive it like it'd just happened yesterday. An older woman, fragile in her unique way, had her hand resting on his arm. He treated her with care, doting on her like she was his own mother.

There was no anger here for her. Not yet. Lady Gwendolyn Firetree had been through Hell and back, losing her nephilim powers and her youth one day at a time as she struggled to adjust to the necessities of vampirehood. She struggled with arthritis and other aches and pains, immortalized at the onset of such things.

She was a strict taskmaster, ardently focused on her faith to get them all past the horrors of the Fell Crisis. A thousand years ago, her wielding of burning light had saved his life countless times. Adrius hadn't been willing to let her die when it'd been her time. Had Sirius been presented with the choice, he'd have turned her too.

That was the depths of his loyalty.

She had betrayed *him*.

He escorted her to the after-party of a wedding, a disastrous affair that showed how deeply Lucia's evil was entwined with his family. After seizing power by killing Adrius for the first time, and presumably Nyah as well, the only way to keep Nyixa's peace was to marry her to his brother upon his return to the dark island's shores.

Gwendolyn had supplied the wine. Sirius and the rest of the Blood Princes were in attendance to swear fealty to the newly united royal family, which was the perfect moment to strike them all down with a sleeping tonic. They were meant to die together as the island sank, forced underwater when Lucia was plunged into a coma.

As he drank, he witnessed the flicker of regret on Gwendolyn's face. Her sadness was the last thing he remembered before waking up a thousand years later with Adrius and the surviving Blood Princes.

She was still alive, swearing that she'd done it to contain Lucia and Fell Madness. But she'd shoved a dagger into their backs, and for Sirius, the wound was exceptionally slow to heal.

"You hate her," Raenith remarked, drawing him back from the hallucination.

Without the beast screaming, he was stony and numb in the void of the gods' magic. "Why wouldn't I? I respected her. I honored her." He gritted his teeth, his hands balling to fists. "And she condemned me to *die*."

"But you are not dead." Already, he could feel the goddess moving on, jumping to the incredible peak of rage he and his beast had shared upon realizing he'd lost a thousand years of life. How he'd woken up a stranger in his body, a forgotten shade in a modern world.

The months that followed were hard for him to see again. He could feel Kalimea's attention on it all. The broken screams, the fits of fury that left his surroundings crushed to splinters and dust.

Faces new and old turning away.

His stay in a white-walled hospital, clinging to life even with Jaromir's healing. How he'd nearly been dismembered by Adrius's brush with Fell madness.

Him leaving his brother. "The strongest vampire in the world has the weakest will," he'd said with venom, intending to leave his brother at last to survive on his own merits.

Adrius never apologizing.

For *anything*.

He clutched his head, praying the onslaught would stop soon. Raenith paused, flipping back the pages of his memories as if he were a book.

"Your brother," she mused.

Unlike a book, his riled memories showed him Adrius in a thousand different ways at the same time.

Adrius with Nyah on their wedding day, glowing with love.

A heartbroken Adrius begging for the death his Fell Key prevented.

Adrius, who went out of control without his wife's golden purifying potions, lunging at mortals, intending to eat them despite his better judgment.

Adrius dead. Freed from his Fell madness. Ready to start again.

Twenty years. Sirius had lived with this for twenty years, forcing his brother to continue on and not succumb to his despair and transform into an undefeatable monster.

"Please. No more," he whispered.

The memories shattered, his ears ringing as his awareness returned to the colorful void, his four companions looking at him. Kalimea's gray skin had paled further, her expression betraying intense shock.

Chapter 21
Talina

While Sirius disappeared with Raenith, Getana's gentle voice tickled her mind. *"Daughter of the wind: Attend me."*

She imagined she disappeared too, sinking into the green corner of the Lady of Life's druidic fold. To come face to face with a goddess was incredible, though she'd always been a little queasy when viewing depictions of Getana's true form. The implication of her appearance was clear, showing how life grew from death, forever intertwined.

But when it came to the goddess who nurtured the land and those within it, she expected something she could hug. A mother figure.

"Perhaps I can entertain the idea," Getana said, startling her. "Your thoughts are loud, young one."

She felt her cheeks heat, mortified that she'd been caught critiquing the goddess's chosen form. "I have a request for you," Getana continued. "As you well know, all magic we perform has a price. You are in the unique position to pay for my contribution when we heal your fatecrossed match."

"You're going to—" she began to blurt before veering toward a different thought. "He's really...? Which of you has crossed his path with mine?"

Getana's eye sockets blazed brightly. "All of us. But it is not my place to explain."

She paused, thoughtful. Talina was ready to jump out of her skin and beg to know more. "Would you accept debt for Sirius? After what happened?" Getana asked. "I beseech you for mercy for another."

Before Talina could ask, their perspective shifted, revealing a memory. They were out on an ocean together, standing on a bobbing raft as a sea serpent went zipping past. The memory was so real she could feel the splash of salty mist on her face.

The serpent was a beautiful creature, its many coils teal with an edging of white fins. It rose up, pointing its snout to the sky and releasing a splash of water. Balancing atop the mini geyser, she realized, was an astral fae woman, soaked and laughing.

"Meet Lyana," Getana whispered, her skeletal form watching with her. "And the kin which used to live with Cyranos."

At the mention of the sea serpent god, she realized they weren't on a raft at all, but the scaly side of a massive serpent resting in the shallows, watching the two play. Another form cut through the water, a second teal dragon launching at the first and sending Lyana toppling, still laughing. She tucked her legs and landed in the water with a splash.

"Why are you showing me this?" Talina asked quietly. She had a bad feeling—Cyranos seemed too unhappy in the Convocation for this to be his reality now.

"Because a great injustice happened to this family. Those two serpents are Cyranos's sons," Getana said, her voice heavy with regret. "And Fell devoured them both. Lyana managed to survive, but she took the spirit of her familiar into herself. She is a *mort loci*."

Death speaker. Talina bit her knuckle, still emotional from the toll of nearly losing Sirius. The woman seemed so happy, rolling through the water with her serpent. Anyone who paired with one of the great dragons of Faerie was a powerful magic user in their own right—but to earn the attention of a direct descendant of a god meant Lyana must have the power of Cyranos flowing through her fingertips.

"Because she was unable to let go, she was bound to one of the standing portals between Faerie and Earth as a Guardian. It is through this portal that your future mate traveled."

The scene shifted as the goddess spoke. Now, Talina saw a cave and a cluster of people, recognizing some of their faces—Sirius, Ash, Neala, and Cedric. But it was another *mort loci* fae that drew her attention, someone wearing the golden scales of a fire dragon.

Getana focused on her too, showing her and a half-serpent Lyana together in a different scene, making Talina blink rapidly at the sudden changes to her perception.

Lyana was gesturing toward a block of stone etched with fae runes. "Izell Firebrand freed her," Getana narrated as the golden fae breathed fire over the block, melting off the magic and turning it to slag. "Afterward, Lyana went to the human world, and our vision clouds. She returned to Faerie only a couple days later... different."

Getana explained how the gods saw through to the demon possessing her, Lucia, the same one tormenting Sirius. But before Lucia had laid her claws on him, she sought to build a power base of her own, just to be thwarted mere weeks ago and forced to try a new plan.

"What a terrible, good for nothing, awful person," she murmured.

"Cyranos agrees. He is furious, as you can imagine." Getana turned to her. "If Lucia is to be slain, the sword would go into Lyana's heart. There are many futures where this occurs."

She saw a few glimpses of it, with one of three different men in each. Sirius, or two other human-born she didn't recognize. Their blades would end Lyana's life in the same moment as Lucia's unlife.

"Oh, gods above." Talina wept, turning away from the visions of death as her stomach somersaulted.

"However, there are two alternatives for Lyana." Getana waved away the visions, replacing them with two more, side by side. In one, Izell held up her arm and peeled back the scales from it, showing a black tattoo of unfamiliar runes on the back of her arm like a sleeve.

The other vision showed her own memory. A shadowy figure standing behind Sirius, whispering in his ear.

"If you can see her, you can do something about her," Getana said. "You will have an opportunity to give Cyranos a gift and save the last of his kin. I ask you act to spare her when Lucia is to be killed, if you can. In exchange, I will give Sirius a boon."

Her heart raced, adrenaline peaking from even the sight of that whispering shade. "What if I can't save her?" Since the demon was able to turn even Sirius's intentions, what hope did she have against such a powerful foe?

"You have it in you," Getana said gently. "I just need you to agree."

"Then...I agree." The magic of a sealed deal settled over her, and in a blink, she was back with the others.

Sirius had returned too, his skin waxy and pale while the hollows under his eyes were more pronounced. He still spoke in his strange native language, his head turned toward the last god, Zalice.

"It would be a mercy to your body if we finished this quickly," whispered Zalice's wind. Goosebumps thrilled up her arms at the familiar sound of, well, *the* wind as it enveloped her and Sirius alike.

The vampire glanced around, his eyes widening in panic. They were surrounded by wind magic, suspended in a vortex as Zalice continued the process of sorting through Sirius's memories.

And as he relived them, she saw them too. His nightmares. Time and again, that *woman* impersonating Talina, trying to get into Sirius's space and seduce him.

Blushing fiercely, she trembled with unexpected anger. "She had no right," she railed, raising her fist. Sirius briefly turned to her, the ghost of a smile on his tormented face.

"The beast saved you," Zalice said to Sirius.

The "beast" inside Sirius had a voice, savage and guttural. *Kill her! Bathe in her blood!*

It screamed no matter what form or strategy Lucia took, ending nightmares and even keeping Sirius awake to avoid her. The play-by-play of his nights was a broken record. But it formed an association between Lucia's viciousness and Talina's face.

"So, that's what happened," she murmured. They'd suspected as much, but to see it confirmed...

Well, she couldn't hold Sirius accountable for that. When he tried to reach out, brush his thumb past her hand, a punishing pulse of electricity hit them both, and they recoiled.

"*This is not the time,*" Zalice's wind sighed. "*We have confirmed many things from your memories, Sirius. This insect has attacked you and the other human-born you've taken to us for this Convocation. She scrabbles desperately to hold a human-born's soul.*"

"But why?" Talina breathed.

She felt the god's attention shift to her, warm and electric, soothing after that hard zap they'd taken. "*It can be assumed she needs a soul to take her place in Hell if she wishes to continue walking free from her eternal punishment.* "

Sirius muttered a clear curse.

"*There is one other thing you need to see.*" The god directed them back to Sirius's nightmares.

Lucia used shadow magic on him, throwing it in his face, forcing him to inhale it. The last nightmare had been the most blatant usage.

"*You know that magic is never destroyed. Only recycled,*" Zalice said. "*And recently, your brother released the burden of his magic by becoming a* mort loci. *His magic was not lost.*"

Sirius stabbed a finger toward his chest. Though a little lost—when had Sirius mentioned his brother was paired with a deceased familiar's spirit?—Talina had a sinking feeling that this was nothing good, judging by the horror on his face.

"*That is correct. Lucia knows how it works all too well and was able to funnel his lost magic into you, considering that Adrun lies within the territory of Faerie.*"

Sirius's expression gave way to fury. Not a snarl like an

animal, but a deep, hateful expression that was somehow far more frightening than his usual growls and rumbles.

"That is where we come in. There is a solution...and a price. Getana asks her boon from Talina, Raenith still considers, and I have a requirement from you both."

"What is it?" Talina asked, uncertain. Getana's price was not so bad, in her estimation. But this already sounded different, more serious.

"You both shall come to me, physically. The Lord of Storms calls your name. Do you answer?"

Sirius opened his mouth, but he popped out of existence a split second later. Talina and Zalice's magic hung there, alone.

She waited, but so did the god, moments ticking by until she finally spoke up. "Have you been giving me my prophecy this whole time?"

"Not a prophecy, little one. Instructions." Wind combed through her hair, a brief caress. *"If you want answers, you will visit me."*

With that, they were no longer alone. Zalice's wind coiled back into a bird-like shape, and Sirius clutched his knees, breathing raggedly.

The lightshow around them was dimming, the three gods coming together in a cluster. Their heads were nearly touching, and for a split second, Talina worried that Getana would be set ablaze by Raenith's flaming muzzle. No such thing occurred, and instead, the fire dragon spoke for them. "This Convocation of the Elements comes to a close. We have decided what to offer the petitioner. But first...my Chosen. It is time the former Fell Lands was raised from the ocean and reinstated as a part of Faerie. It is our will that we meet our lost kin residing in the secret nation of Adrun."

Kalimea bowed. "It shall be done," she said, crisp.

"You may go." As Raenith spoke, Kalimea disappeared from the void of magic. "As may you, Neala Applewhite. Your presence is an honor to the petitioner, even if our godly counterpart did not agree." Neala was abruptly gone when the gods dismissed her as well.

"May I hear the verdict?" Theron asked, clasping his hands when Raenith's burning gaze turned to him next.

"If this goes well, you shall see it soon." It was Getana who answered, casting him out of the Convocation with a flick of her wooden claws.

Sirius and Talina exchanged a glance. She reached for his hand, relieved when she felt his warm skin rather than a bolt of electricity. The back of her hand lit up with something new, and she stifled a gasp. Etched in her blue skin was a white outline of the cyclone-like symbol Theron had found amongst her magic.

She turned their hands over, inspecting Sirius's. He had a mark as well, nearly the same color as his blanched skin. It was mostly horizontal lines, with sharp edges toward his thumb like a punishing gale hitting a solid object.

Her mouth dried out as she glanced up, meeting Sirius's maroon gaze. He inspected their marks and then her face, his lips parted to speak before he thought better of it. Instead, he tipped her head up and pressed a gentle kiss to her forehead.

"I forgive you," she whispered, wishing they didn't have such a powerful audience in that moment.

She leaned up on her tiptoes, the two of them coming in for a tender kiss. Fire crackled, and Raenith's amused voice cut between them. "You can do this later." A breath away from their mouths meeting, Talina jerked awake in her own body. She squeezed her eyes shut, groaning in frustration.

Chapter 22
Sirius

Alone with the gaze of three gods upon him, Sirius clenched his glowing hand into a fist the moment Talina disappeared. That was cruel. His body ached, weariness setting in on a level that went deeper than the flesh.

He reeled with the knowledge that Adrius's magic festered within him even now. In releasing himself from the shackles of his dark magic, his brother had laid down the trap that was now around Sirius's throat.

Typical, he thought, scoffing bitterly.

"Sirius Raphael Fabron. We wish to assist you," Raenith said. "Our offers are independent boons, but they harmonize best when you accept them all."

"Our magic works like a more advanced deal. If you uphold your side of things, you will keep your boon. However, should you fail or quit, our magic will withdraw and leave you right where you are now," Zalice added. Without the backdrop of silvery magic, he was a gray shade in the darkness of the void. Not quite a bird, Sirius realized, but a type of dragon he'd never seen before, with a flexible muzzle shaped like a bird's beak and a long tail of feathers designed for distance travel.

He shifted, fighting off the edge of impatience. They wanted to help him, after all. "I understand. I'm waiting to hear what you would like to offer."

"I offer you a sigil of protection," Raenith began. "While it burns within you, no one will be able to walk in your dreams without your knowledge. As a campfire warms all around them, your presence will ward others of the same fate."

Sirius started to nod eagerly, wanting safety in his own dreams now that he saw how quickly and viciously Lucia had attacked him at night.

"In return, you will speak with and offer true forgiveness to your brother and Gwendolyn Firetree. Confront them, rail at them, but find it in yourself to move on before your grudges destroy you."

He froze, dismay stealing away any excitement at the offer. "How will I do that?" he asked. "They are a world away. Adrius rules a new nation. And Gwendolyn...I don't even know what she is doing."

Raenith cocked her head. "I wouldn't ask an impossible task of you. We shall visit them when you're ready."

A cold sweat beaded down his spine. She was as serious as a heart attack. "Fine," he grumbled. He'd enjoy the boon while he could, then, because he had to have time before she expected him to pay up on such a tall request. Her burning gaze had witnessed a lot of his life; she had to know what she was asking.

"Talina has already paid for your boon from me," Getana said as the fire dragon nodded. "I would have your overflowing magic, Sirius, and any shadows that linger in Faerie, waiting to latch on to you. There are pockets in Faerie where even the most stubborn of magic cannot escape. I will bury your burdens deep in the earth and fuse your inner beast to you so you will have an easier time controlling it."

"Yes," he blurted. "Do it right now." The dragon's skull tilted, the green flames in her eyes flickering. Did that mean he'd offended her? He backtracked quickly. "Please."

"Her offer and mine come together," Zalice whispered. *"Even if she took everything from you, your body will not easily recover from the trauma it's experienced. You already know my price, and you decide for yourself and Talina alike."*

Sirius tensed. He may have her forgiveness, but did she

approve of the idea of visiting Zalice directly? They'd banished her before he could...attempt to ask, considering the language barrier that hung over him.

"In exchange for you both walking the Path of Imagination, I offer you the biggest boon: I will make you part fae."

Raenith crackled, and Getana rustled, the two of them turning toward him with astonishment. "Very generous," the earth goddess murmured.

"Consider it, Sirius," Raenith said. "You would be truly unique and free of the irons that hold you down. A vampire, shapeshifter, and fae, all in one."

Sirius wet his lips, wanting to be sure he made the right decision. "What is the Path of Imagination?" he asked.

"There are many paths to my mountain home," Zalice answered. *"Everyone who wishes to see me in person must undergo their own trials to reach me. But the rewards are great... especially for you."* He extended a set of wicked-sharp talons, showing the glint of a ring there. Sirius's eyes widened, frozen. That had to be a Fell Key.

"I will not agree to anything that will harm Talina. She fears a soul change." He eyed the gods before him, hoping for some hint as to what that was.

Raenith tilted her head. "Ah, but souls change all the time. If you agree to our boons, your soul, too, will bear a new true name. All your former blood oaths will be at an end." She considered, spreading her talons as she made a gesture. "You may drink fae blood."

"Without fear of gaining too much magic from it," Getana added.

Was that why Izell had restricted him in the first place? Knowing her, she must've somehow known this godly meeting would happen. *Would it have really troubled her to give me a warning?* He sighed to himself.

"I will not say the path is without danger. It is a hard one to walk," Zalice said.

Sirius was ready to twitch. There was his "path" again. "I accept," he said, thinking he could do this. "I accept your deals and promise I will make the attempt to uphold them." He was looking to Raenith as he said it, watching her head shake minutely, as if an attempt wasn't enough for her.

Getana extended her claws. "Put your hand in mine. I can allow you to keep maybe one of the many abilities you've inherited. Here are your options—"

"I want the shadow mastery," Sirius interrupted.

Her wooden jaws clacked. "You did not hear the options."

"If the shadows are an option, I want them." Sirius knew exactly what they did, having witnessed Adrius wield shadows like physical whips or shrouding a whole group of vampires with them. They'd been like an extra limb, and, well, his brother had to be missing them. He'd be able to face Adrius again while wielding his brother's former prized power, and that was going to feel *amazing*.

Getana's laugh was like the rustle of greenery. "Very well. The shadows it is. I shall grant and shape your powers so you are more like a druid. You will always be a little bit animal, but..." Her claws glowed with green magic as she affected a shrug.

"Good luck, Sirius. This Convocation is at an end," Raenith proclaimed. The three gods disappeared, though their magic lingered within him as he passed into the black tide of unconsciousness.

Chapter 23
Sirius

T‍he first thing Sirius noticed was the heat simmering in his chest. Raenith's blessing kindled to life right next to his heart, circulating warmth through his veins. His fingers twitched, toes curling, as sensation returned in sluggish increments.

Softness pillowed his body. For a moment, he imagined he was waking from a particularly vivid fever dream. The alternative was that he'd really succumbed to his beast, nearly died, and met the four elemental gods of Faerie.

He opened his eyes. He was tucked into bed in an unfamiliar room, soft fur brushing his arm as he lifted it and realized he was wearing a lined robe. Was this a corner of the druidic temple? There was a chair by his bedside, currently unoccupied. The bedside table had a bowl of water and a washcloth. His nostrils filled with the faint scents of multiple people hanging over the seat, so several someones hadn't forgotten about him at the very least.

A dim fairy light showed that there wasn't much more to his surroundings. His scuffed armor was hanging in a tiny closet hidden by a thin wooden screen, but there was no sign of his sword. *Damn.* The weapon was the most valuable thing he owned.

He noticed the changes in himself slowly with the absence of a mirror. His nails were thicker, each ending in a wicked point. Brailing his face, he felt that someone had tamed his beard. He'd been meaning to shave that off anyway. While his features didn't feel much different, he paused as he traced the shape of one ear. It was pointed. The rasp of his calluses on the shell of it felt overly loud, so he flinched away from inspecting further without the help of a reflective surface.

Checking that his robe was secure, he stepped into the hallway. He expected pain as he walked, but there was none. He also expected that it would be hard to find a familiar face when the area outside his room was full of them. Wan evening light flooded in from the windows overhead, mixing with the lazy plucking of a lute as Cedric leaned his head against Neala's shoulder, dozing.

Kalimea was bracketed by two officials in palace livery, while Ash stood propped against the stone wall, one foot braced against it casually. A cluster of druids waited as well, their faces semifamiliar in the haze of Sirius's treatment.

A scent like a cool breeze tickled his nostrils. *Talina*. So, he still had an inner beast, but its wistful sigh was his own. It simmered under the surface of his skin, ready to run, fight, and kill, like always, but no longer slamming against the edges of his control to go do those things right that moment.

His little blue fae nearly walked right by him, preoccupied with balancing a half dozen pots and planters. She glanced up, a gasp stealing her breath. "Sirius! You're awake!" The others stirred from their tired vigils, multiple sets of eyes fixed on him. He didn't care, only giving her a few moments to place her burden aside before sweeping her up.

Their lips collided as he spun her around, holding her tight even as she automatically wrapped her arms around his shoulders and her legs around his middle. He kissed her with sheer relief wrapped in elation. They were alive, they were together, and that's all that mattered.

A woman sighed. "Makes me miss my mate," Kalimea whispered.

"Mine too. At least yours is still in Faerie," Theron grumbled back under his breath. Sirius's newly sharpened hearing picked up every murmur around them, but he didn't care. The moment belonged to Talina. He brought his forehead to hers, drinking in the scent of woodlands on her clothes and hints of freshly turned dirt on her fingers.

He was reluctant to let her go, instead burying his hand in a fistful of her clothes. "This is new." She was wearing a fur-trimmed cloak over fleece-like material that held her body heat.

"Yeah, um..." Her gaze turned downward. "They're very new."

Something had happened his absence. He knew it the moment her lips quirked. "You'll need new clothes too," she said, gesturing to him. "Have you...seen...?"

"Myself? There were no mirrors in my room." He wondered if there was something wrong with his face with how some of the druids were staring. Talina tugged out of his hold, pulling him along by his hand.

The attention followed them, drilling into his back. "Return him quickly. I need him to express some gratitude," Kalimea called after them.

Talina lifted her free hand. The room she took him to was larger than his and smelled strongly of her; plus, it had a dresser.

The mirror's reflective surface cast a silvery puddle, a triangle of illumination from the shine of a bright fairy light. He closed his eyes as he let her guide him to stand there, seized by sudden and intense nerves. Though he'd allowed the gods to fiddle with his magic and make him "part fae," he realized he didn't know what the end result would be, physically.

Fell blood mutated humans into the vampires, and he'd drunk more of it than most of his kind. He and the other Blood Princes were forever transformed by the brush of liquid power, because the changes didn't stop at a pair of fangs and a set of shadowy magic powers. Fell blood enhanced their abilities and made them taller, stronger, and thicker. He'd practically demanded Getana take away said abilities.

When he finally looked, he confirmed his theory. Less power, less of that Fell-borne change. He was smaller, no longer dwarfing petite Talina by a solid foot, and leaner, more of a dancer than a brute. He was now closer to six feet tall in his estimation. He glanced over at her, considering that that might not be such a bad thing if it made her easier to kiss.

He still had strong features, his face mostly untouched save for the eyes, which had shaded to a bright ruby rather than Blood Prince maroon. It was how they'd looked when he first turned, before getting a deep taste of Fell. A clear sign that he had less vampire in him. He was unbothered with the knowledge; it was truly for the best if he contained only the power he could control.

His pupils shifted as he inspected them, dilating back and forth like an animal's might at every minute shift of lighting. Not that he noticed in his own vision, but it might take others some getting used to if it were a constant thing.

Pulling his lips back, he recoiled at the first glimpse of his fangs. They were fully elongated, so it was a wonder he hadn't scraped his tongue across the edge of one. He tried to retract them, but they wouldn't budge, the sharp points longer and thicker, less like needles and more like a predator's canines. He had a bottom pair as well, less prominent but still ready to inflict some damage.

"No wonder they were staring," he muttered.

His ears didn't seem like such a big deal anymore when he had the kind of fangs that could tear a man's throat out. Turning his head, he lifted the dark locks covering his decidedly fae-shaped ears.

Talina gasped quietly. "Oh, I didn't see those," she said, breathing a little giggle. "Did you notice the, um..."

He glanced over at her, confused. "The what?"

"The wings?"

He'd been so preoccupied with hoping he still had a decently attractive face that he hadn't even glanced behind him. "Well, I guess they're not technically wings, but they're something," Talina continued as he inspected the waves of darkness he could see. Dark curls of mist fell behind him, moving with him like an elongated shadow. He turned his back toward the mirror and tried to get a better look over his shoulder.

"Huh. Can you feel your wings? Are they like limbs?" he asked. Hers were wide and meant for flying, while he couldn't even feel that anything was attached to him. The mist curled through his fingers like water vapor when he reached to hold a handful.

"Yes, they're exactly like an extra pair of arms," she said, her head tilting in fascination.

"When I said I wanted my brother's shadow magic, this isn't what I meant," he remarked. What was he going to do with this?

"Maybe they'll gain their shape with some time," she suggested. Her own wings batted the air while she gained a thoughtful look. "Some fae have that problem at first. Wings are like our overflow magic. We're not considered of age or at full power until they grow in."

He blew out a sigh. "I sure hope they gain some shape. This is too strange. Well, this and..." He beckoned, taking her hand. The same pair of symbols from before glowed on the back of their hands.

A purple tinge lit her cheeks. "We're fatecrossed."

He leaned in, breathing her wind-touched scent and his beast sighed, placid from the barest touch and smell of her. If he were truly a beast, she was his mistress.

"But what does it mean?" he asked, tugging her closer.

"I don't know much about it," she admitted. "But the gods decided we would be a good match and somehow made sure our paths would cross. You know, crossed by fate? Fatecrossed. I think Theron knows more about it."

He tucked her back to his chest, resting his chin on her glossy, navy hair. She fit perfectly in his hold, soft and slight. Now that he thought to look, he watched her wings turn to mist and spin over his biceps rather than pass through him like they did her clothes.

"It doesn't matter right now," he murmured. He wouldn't question a good thing or the peace her touch brought.

She met his gaze in the mirror, her eyes flashing with uncertain clouds. "Sirius...the circus left without us."

"Hmm." No big loss there. He played with a lock of her silky hair.

"They took all our things with them. And Cossette," she said more firmly.

He stilled and considered. His vials of blood and camping supplies from Earth were amongst his possessions. Plus the elk he'd bonded with. He rumbled with displeasure. "Did they think we wouldn't come for all that? Cossette will keep it all safe for us."

"I think Cloman felt we abandoned the circus. He's done this before," she admitted.

He pulled some of her hair back, bending to nose along the point of her ear. Her blush was back, twin to a quiver up her spine. "We can worry about Cloman tomorrow." His warm breath washed over her, and at her sensitive twitch, he noticed his own predatory smile reflected back in the mirror.

Too sweet. He could just eat her up. The swanlike curve of her neck called, his mouth watering in answer. He wondered if she would taste as she smelled, fresh as a wind-touched forest. Pressing kisses to her cheek and jaw, he coaxed her into turning her head.

He'd sworn to Izell he wouldn't drink fae blood, but she must've seen this possible future. Alone with Talina, his blood supply swiftly leaving. Thirst nipped at him. All blood oaths had a warning, some resistance to warn that he was on the verge of breaking his word.

Except he'd had a "soul change," and the gods had specifically mentioned tasting from a fae. They *were* suspiciously interested in his relationship.

Did he care? Maybe the tiniest bit, not enough for it to distract him. For as often as he and Talina talked and practiced and danced, they'd never quite been this alone. Her mouth was parted, eyes lidded, and he watched her expression in their reflections.

He kissed her neck, hands tightening possessively on her hips. Her lips widened into an "o" of surprise as his fangs slipped past her skin.

Bliss etched across her face as she arched into him. The first taste of her blood was like a bolt of lightning, liquid static pouring into his veins and sharpening every sense. He couldn't get close enough, a soft growl in his throat as her fine new clothes served as a barrier between them. Her head fell back, and she breathed a soft moan that nearly unmade him on the spot.

Reluctantly, he released her neck and licked the little punctures marring her soft skin. Their ragged breathing filled the room as he pulled away, resting his head against the wall. The scent of her arousal stung his nostrils, the ultimate siren's call.

"Sirius?" She sounded shaky, uncertain. He pictured himself how she must see him, biting her without invitation and then flinging himself away just as quickly.

His beast was just as confused. Here it was, the perfect opportunity to claim and mark his mate, and he was ruining it.

It's not the right time, he told himself, taking a moment to breathe. He still wore naked lust as he shifted back to Talina. Whatever ambiguity that lay between them was erased as her throat clicked with a dry swallow. Still, she didn't run. But she also didn't move, frozen like a doe facing a dangerous beast.

Not completely still, actually. Her gaze drifted down the line of his body.

"Like what you see?" He cocked a grin. "It's yours. I've realized I belong to you, sweetheart."

She glanced away, shy. He knew he was too much for an inexperienced woman. "U-uh. Your friends are waiting for us," she stammered.

"I know. You deserve better than a quick drop as your first time," he said more gently. "Go. I'll be out once I calm down."

She didn't leave in the hurry he expected. With her hand on the doorknob, she glanced over her shoulder, taking him in one last time as she bit her lip. She *did* like what she saw.

If she hesitated a second longer, he might've lost his tenuous self-control. But she left, and the tension unwound the moment there was a solid wall between them.

He buried his face in a palm, groaning when it still smelled of her. "I will have her," he muttered.

Not while a group of friends that had literally saved him from death were waiting to see his new face, though. He counted up and down from five, cycling through all the breathing exercises Talina had taught him.

Talina, his beast sighed.

He had a lot to teach her, too.

Chapter 24
Jaromir

Meanwhile, in a quiet library, Blood Prince Jaromir, the Mender, contemplated the contents of a passage without comprehending it. Dim light filtered in from the bay windows before him. Night's fall triggered a sudden influx of light as braziers heaped with floating fairy lights leapt to their brightest setting.

The Library of Faerie was open at all hours, a fact he occasionally took advantage of as he engaged in the monumental task of understanding an ancient magical ritual performed thousands of years ago. A lot hinged on his study, because he was the only one stopping to plan out how exactly he and his allies were going to successfully create a second Dark Eye of Worlds. They had to re-tether the mystical barrier separating Earth and Faerie from the eternal war waged between angels and demons, else said war would roll through everything and decimate countless lives.

The deadline was coming soon. The yoke of worry around his neck weighed more heavily every day while his friends and allies were off doing other things. Izell popped in on the rare occasion to tell him tidbits. Neala and Cedric were officially mated. Lucia had nearly died a permanent death by the demonic fire summonable by a destruction fae...but she'd gotten away *again*. Sirius had met his true mate.

Jaromir huffed a sigh. Who needed a mate when the apocalypse was looming over their shoulder?

As he set his book aside with a bookmark securing his spot, one of his two companions raised her head and gave a hopeful whine. The tan-furred pup spent half of her time in his lap, the other half staring out the window while she chewed on a toy and gazed longingly at the specks of fae passing by the library some four stories down. Jaromir and the library staff did their best to walk, feed, and entertain her, but the puppy was still an oddity in the largest repository of knowledge within Seelie lands.

Jaromir had Izell to thank for the pup, of course. She'd pushed her into his hands at the end of their last meeting. If he could call a quick kiss on the cheek, a wink, and "You're doing a great job!" as a meeting.

"Here, you need a companion while I'm not around," she'd also said.

So, now he had a dog, whom he'd named Sofia. He had to admit he loved watching her roll around and frolic. She was a good listener as well, perking her ears any time he read parts of passages aloud, hoping that hearing them would bring new insight. Maybe Izell had given him exactly what he needed.

He glanced to his other companion and shook his head slowly. Alaku was asleep again, using the middle of an open book as a holder for his face. The boy was his library-assigned "research assistant" since Jaromir spent so much time here.

Alaku was part of a race of lesser fae that claimed nearly every position in the library, from cleaning staff to librarian. Called terrix, they were a cross between owl and human. Jaromir had learned that they were created through magical means for the purpose of being great scholars and keepers of knowledge.

He was tired of magic. Maybe *exhausted* was the right word. Day in, day out, magic, magic, magic. Izell was the Archfae. She should've been here along with him, picking through all these tomes on King Oberon's life and works, plus extra books on magical theory and the art of altering unique spells into different incantations. Instead, he was basically alone.

He bent down and shook Alaku awake. The youngling

popped his head back with a startled chirp, the single feather drooping over his forehead whipping wildly as he took in his surroundings. He had an owl's moon-like set of yellow eyes, fixing up at him as his brows drew in obvious regret. "Sorry, Prince Jaromir." His voice was in the squeaky adolescent phase, breaking to a high note in the middle of Jaromir's name.

Alaku had a set of blunt-tipped wings resting over his back in a shape akin to a heart. When viewed from behind, the brown wings and the feathers mixed in with his hair would suggest he was more owl than boy. But when viewed from the front, he was a gawky teen who just so happened to have a line of down-like feathers trailing up his arms and thin, humanoid legs that ended with politely filed talons that would otherwise hook over his toes. Alaku had kicked off his shoes again.

"Let's go home. It's been a long day," Jaromir responded, gently tugging the book free from the terrix's chin and smoothing creases in the paper.

Ever since hearing his full title, Alaku had puffed up with excitement to serve a "real prince from a human place." That eagerness to please remained despite Jaromir trying to explain that it was just a title. Alaku scrabbled up and fretted with the feathers along his forearm as Jaromir stacked their books and set them aside for the night. "Am I taking anything home tonight to study for you, sir?"

Jaromir shook his head. "You've spent enough time with your beak in a book today." He'd meant it as a joke, but the boy's tanned skin flushed brightly. Alaku had a mostly human face, sporting a hooked nose like a miniature beak and a thin mouth. His chubby cheeks gave his head a rounded shape, which reminded Jaromir the most of his owl side.

"S-sorry. I couldn't focus," he stammered quickly.

The librarian who'd lent Alaku's services had scoffed when she pushed him to Jaromir's side. She'd warned him of the boy's dyslexia as if describing a lost cause. The concept of "dyslexia" was new to him and quite a fascinating side conversation when he'd learned that Alaku struggled to read because his mind switched letters around.

Considering that terrix culture, as far as he understood, revolved around the sanctity of knowledge in written form, he'd had to talk Alaku into casting a "cheating" spell to have books read themselves aloud to him. Alaku was still reading his first book for Jaromir, *The Legacy of Primal Magic,* one painstaking page at a time.

Research assistants, Jaromir had learned, were unpaid interns who came here to perform extra study duties and learn as much as possible. Considering how greater fae of all stripes were usually accompanied by a small flock of teenage terrix, Jaromir knew there was some bias going on in regards to the library staff helping him with his research.

Oh well. He helped Alaku up and offered the youngling his backpack, which sagged with the weight of several texts and workbooks. Homework awaited the glum teen once he made it home and had a late dinner.

Movement caught Jaromir's eye over Alaku's shoulder. A flash of gold in the stacks. "I'll just be a moment, young man." He patted the terrix reassuringly. In truth, he had a lot of sympathy for him and his plight of being constantly forced into a task he struggled with.

Not that Jaromir could truly help him, though. Truth be told, for someone titled "the Mender," he needed some fixing himself. Few knew this better than the woman standing right behind a bookshelf, casually covering up her golden dragon scales with a glamor to change her appearance into that of a generic astral fae.

Izell Firebrand, in the flesh. He stopped short and inspected her face, recognizing some features even though she'd magically superimposed a different person's skin over them. Her eyes were over-bright, nearly feverish as she smiled with all her teeth.

He felt his brows start to draw in concern. "Iz—"

She clapped her hand over his mouth. "Shh, I'm a secret."

Honestly, not the weirdest thing she'd said to him. He still fixed her a look of disbelief until she released him.

"How are you?" he asked in what his friends labeled his "doctor's tone": concerned, soft-spoken, but firm. Those three descriptors matched him well, he thought.

She waved dismissively. "Terrible, thanks for asking. Look, I can't stay for long. I just wanted to tell you that things aren't going as planned, and I can't figure out why and..." She paused for air. "...I'm looking into it. But for now, we can't be seen together. You don't know me. All right?"

With a flourish, she produced a scroll she'd fastened to her belt and offered it to him. "Wanted: any information on the whereabouts of the *mort loci*, Izell Firebrand. By royal decree," he murmured aloud as the fae words blurred in front his tired eyes before reforming into something he could read. A spot-on likeness of her true form was sketched out, including the scaled and taloned arms she often crossed over her chest. He rolled it back up and waved it. "What is this?"

Her wide smile shaded to a grimace. "Kalimea is on to me too early. This shouldn't have happened."

He shifted uncomfortably, sensing something was definitely off about her. This wasn't the confident woman who'd grabbed him by the neck a month ago and invited him to make out in the stacks. She had a manic energy and a nearly reptilian blankness to her expression. The dusky-eyed looks through her lashes were gone, as was the way she used to slow herself down to speak quietly with him on the deeper topics.

Well, he couldn't blame her. No one really found him interesting for long. He'd grown too used to being a loner, the platonic friend who had an extra-strong healing Gift. Except he'd lost it, so he wasn't even good for that anymore. He was boring. But he could tell the shift wasn't just about him—something had changed about her as well.

"What, exactly, are you worried about her being 'on to you' about?" he asked with air quotes.

"My plan, of course," she said with another wave.

He fought off the urge to sigh. "Which is...?"

For a moment, she hesitated. Usually, she offered a tidbit of what was to come and where his hard work would lead them. But today, he saw the tightening of her lips, the way she moved to turn away and leave him emptyhanded.

"Wait. Please." His hand closed around her wrist before she

could summon a portal and disappear again. Her cross look came with a blast of heat close to his face, a reminder that she was still a fearsome dragon shifter under her constantly shifting glamors. "I've come a long way in understanding the spell that made the Eyes of Worlds. And I have a question for you."

She made an impatient gesture with her free hand, as he didn't release her wrist, too afraid she'd bolt the moment he did. "Who dies?" he murmured.

Her head tilted with a leery look. "My last visions of the future are no longer accurate. I'm not sure who will die."

"Specifically, who dies to make the new Dark Eye?" he amended, watching her put on a blank poker face rather than show any reaction to his question. He knew he was on to something, his heart dropping. "Izell...every account of King Oberon's spell talks about one thing. It was his 'greatest work' spell. He poured every ounce of his power into it. Body, mind, soul, and magic, the holy number four of your culture."

He leaned in, taking in the wood smoke and wind smell of her. "Who dies for this new spell, Izell?" he asked, growing more sure as she ducked her head rather than meeting his gaze head-on.

She yanked her arm from his grip. "I'm sorry, I need to go," she said, replacing the warmth of her skin with a leather bag in his palm.

"Izell," he protested a split second before she opened a portal and disappeared through it, slamming it closed before he could follow.

His shoulders dropped as exhaustion settled into the wake of her absence. In fleeing his question, she'd answered it, and he hated that she hadn't trusted him enough to say it aloud.

Izell was planning on dying. And there was nothing he could do about it. Just another person he failed to save added to the long list of specters lining his past. *The great healer, Jaromir,* he mocked, fist tightening around her little parting gift. It squished in his hold with a sound like rustling grass.

Jaw tight, he pulled the drawstring and realized she'd given him the pouch that held her bitter leaves. She chomped on them after meals like they were mints. Hard trepidation seized him in an iron fist, but he wasn't quite sure why. What were the leaves a remedy for?

Standing there with yet another piece of Izell's puzzle, Jaromir felt the need to curl into a ball. "Why doesn't she trust me?" he murmured. It wasn't about attraction or affection. He'd put his trust in her and believed that, through all their stay in Faerie, she had a plan. And so far, it'd led to the betterment of his fellow Blood Princes, if her spotty reports about them were to be believed.

He walked back toward his little nook before the bay windows, numbness stealing over him. What if she'd made sure everyone she'd brought along to Faerie had their lives improved in some way? She *had* promised she'd find a way to return his Gift.

It could be her way of saying farewell. He gusted out a sigh, swearing that he'd find a way to help her, too. And that...definitely was relating to attraction, his quiet crush on a woman who'd brought vibrancy to his night-touched world.

Glancing up, he realized there was someone else occupying his chair, an astral fae man who lounged casually and chatted with Alaku. The young terrix stood straight in his "eager to please" pose despite Sofia pawing at his leg for attention. "Oh, there he is! Prince Jaromir, come quick. Mister Arus is in town," Alaku chirped.

Said fae stood and offered his hand. "Alaku was just telling me he was acting as research assistant for a human-born prince." He flashed a brilliant, white smile, made all the brighter against his dark-as-night complexion. Like midnight in the light-polluted Earth, the stars that were supposed to speckle this fae's skin were as distant as faded pinpricks. "I'm Sondus Arus."

"Jaromir. Not a prince, sorry." He still shook the other man's hand, hiding a spark of shock, as most greater fae either stared or ignored him within the hallowed halls of the Library of Faerie. "How do you know Alaku?"

Sondus flashed a fond smile over at the teen. "I taught a few classes at his school when he was younger."

He nodded, biting his lip so he wouldn't yawn. That would be dreadfully rude. "Well, it is nice to meet you. I should get

Alaku home. It's looking like another long night of research for me." Izell had given him another thing to look up for his peace of mind before he could seek out some rest.

"You're going to keep going?" Alaku asked, his owlish eyes widening. The sun had fully set by this point, usually the time they called it quits together.

"Ah. If you like, my wife can walk him home," Sondus offered. "Her shift ends in a few minutes."

Jaromir waited to get a look at the woman first, a little surprised to see a terrix woman dressed in warm colors come over about a minute later. She shared a quick kiss with Sondus and leaned against his side companionably. It seemed that there were no taboos between cross-species pairs here, because they weren't the only mismatched couple he'd seen in his stay in Faerie. Sondus introduced him to Zizi, a librarian who ran the rare and arcane texts section. Her gray eyes were shaped by a set of horn-rimmed glasses, giving her a more severe expression than her kind voice and smile suggested.

"Come home soon, honey," she bade Sondus, waving and ushering Alaku away when Jaromir was satisfied that she seemed safe.

"Right behind you, dear." The fae blew her a kiss before turning to Jaromir. "So, what are you researching?"

"You're not going with her?" How odd.

Sondus shrugged. "I have a few things to look up for my boss first. She can be quite demanding. Perhaps I can help you find something, though, since it seems Alaku was your only assistant. The boy is dear but a little young to be interning here."

Jaromir nodded in agreement, hesitating as he flipped the drawstring of Izell's pouch through his fingers. "Know of any guides that can help me identify a plant like this?" He opened it and showed its contents to Sondus, who plucked out a dark leaf and turned it over in his fingers. He held it to his nose, brows drawing.

"Certainly. I'd be happy to help you with this." Sondus flashed a smile before pocketing the leaf.

Chapter 25
Talina

The next day, Talina avoided a flurry of motion surrounding Sirius in getting him fitted with new equipment and clothing to match his change in stature. She saw an opportunity to be alone and took it, wandering Cordaria with her arms full of old clay pots the druids weren't worried about losing. Electricity crackled between her fingertips while she lined up several pots on a damp fence.

A colorful flock of hummingbirds watched her from the safety of a raspberry bush. Unlike in the wild, these potential familiars liked the company of other hummingbirds, all of them following Gem and helping him scold her for not leaving to chase the circus.

"We're getting answers soon," she told them all before starting her target practice.

She'd embraced her wind since she was very small, but the dangerous side of Wind-aligned magic was the lightning. It sprung from her hands in thick bolts, branching outward the farther she threw it. *Too strong*. Her mentors hadn't been equipped to teach her how to control it, except to separate her wind from her lightning and lock the latter down tightly. A good ballerina didn't shock her fellow dancers.

Any time she released her hold on the power, it suffused her.

Wind made her feel alive, but lightning made her feel *strong*, its excess energy crackling over her skin and darkening her puffy cloud wings.

She pointed, shattering the first pot waiting on the fence. "I want answers very badly," she said, turning her head skyward. Inviting the wind to brush past her face.

"*Come to me,*" the wind whispered faintly on a gust. A beautiful, clear day lay overhead, barely a cloud skating across the sky.

"To think that all this time, it was you talking to me." She spoke upward, wondering if the Lord of Storms would continue to linger. He'd answered her so quickly.

Cool wind caressed her pointed ears. "*I have much to say, but few listen.*"

"But why me?" she asked faintly. "Why make me look crazy? Why give me a prophecy? Sorry...directions." No one else spoke to the wind or heard its directions whispered past their ears.

For a few moments, she thought he wouldn't answer.

"*Come to me,*" he finally echoed. Just like always, repeating himself until she had the message.

She stomped her foot in a fit of pique, shooting more lightning. The pots on the fence exploded one by one. It didn't make her feel better. "I need some explanation. Something. Are you singling me out? Why? *Why?*"

The wind's answer was a sharper gust. It nearly lifted her off her feet and blew a few hummingbirds skyward, to a chorus of tiny complaints. It swirled around her shoulders in a familiar way. "And you protected me, too," she murmured, remembering the sudden blast of wind that had sent Sirius flying after coiling up around her body.

"*Always,*" the wind answered.

Gem fluttered back to her a minute later, hovering in front of her face for attention. "*I heard strangers say your name,*" he said.

Brow furrowed, she followed her familiar until he alighted on the hanging branches of a willow tree not far from her practice spot. Multiple limbs braided together to create a screen, a semi-common sight dotted around Cordaria to hide benches meant for private moments. She hunched down, hearing a familiar voice drifting out from the bench.

"Did you do your research?" Queen Kalimea was mere feet away from her. The willow benches were supposed to have a privacy spell over them—but this one didn't.

"Promptly, Your Majesty," an unfamiliar man's voice answered her. "And I made contact with the last Blood Prince as well. The perfect opportunity presented itself."

Silence took over between them. Talina shifted uncomfortably as the moments ticked by.

"I trust you were careful?" Kalimea finally asked.

"Of course. I believe he will be key to apprehending Izell," he responded. The scowling *mort loci* who wore a fire dragon's golden scales flashed through her mind. "How long can you be here before Ash panics at your absence?"

"Long enough. Tell me everything."

"As to the matter of fatecrossed pairings, I have discovered that the practice is tied to those with a god's favor. It seems that your ward is exactly who you think she is."

Silence fell for a few long moments. Talina put a hand over her mouth, muffling a gasp. *"Gem, you did such a good job,"* she praised, impressed that he'd caught wind of this conversation.

"The moment I saw her face, I knew," the queen murmured.

"With how our gods have retreated from polite society over time, we've had fewer and fewer pairings. The gods have had a history of bringing together two fae not a hundred percent suited for each other but able to do greater things together because of each other's support. Many of our heroes and legends came about because of a fatecrossed pair, did you know that? It is said you and King Orin are such a pair, too." He chuckled at the thought.

Kalimea scoffed. "If only. It would've made selling our 'whirlwind romance' more palatable to the average fae."

"As for how a human-born and a pureblooded fae could both have the marks, it is possible to carry both a mark for yourself and one destined for another. Skin contact and a trigger of sorts are all it would take to give the mark to their fated match. I felt that was the most likely explanation. Except..." Wind lifted tendrils of willow branches, and Talina flattened herself to the ground, desperate to hear more.

Kalimea didn't seem to appreciate his pause. "Except?" she echoed sharply.

"They should have mated by this point. The average time from marked to mated is about a week. And it's been far longer since the night of your masquerade," he continued. A sound of knuckles rapping against a book's cover drifted from the willow. "Unlike a lifemate or even a heartsong, it's not a suggestion. It's a 'you will choose this person.' I have a theory about this as well."

"Of course," Kalimea remarked.

"You shared that there were three deals struck between Prince Sirius and the gods. Did Lady Raenith share what they were?"

The Unseelie Queen recited them, and Talina perked up to hear what else was said once she was forced to leave the Convocation of Elements. Kalimea explained her deal with Getana as a "personal favor for Cyranos," but the rest sounded more specific.

"Ah-hah. Part fae, hmm," the man interrupted.

"Significant to your theory?"

"The gods don't care about a single human-born man unless it fits their master plan."

"They weren't about to empower the demoness that attacked me," she hissed.

"Prince Sirius didn't need *three* boons to avoid that fate." He snapped his fingers. "He was reshaped for the purpose of becoming Talina's mate. We're about to see the first pureblood fae and vampire pair in Faerie's history."

Wind and blood rushed through Talina's ears. She felt her whole self flush purple in sheer embarrassment. Why were they discussing her relationship like it was some kind of spectacle?

At the same time, she remembered his smoldering gaze in the mirror, her belly quivering in memory of the explosion of pleasure that'd been his bite. *I belong to you, sweetheart.*

He'd acted like parting from her was the hardest thing he'd ever done, telling her to go. And...it'd been just as hard for her to leave, if she were honest. He'd awoken from the Convocation, and they'd been all over each other.

"...I'm not worried," Kalimea's voice interrupted her thoughts. "I presume the gods have chosen him based off of more than his good looks. We will not interfere with what will be, Sondus. In fact, once we know which Path of Imagination they are walking, we will move soldiers and bounty hunters that way as well. Lucia has already received warning to be in the Outer Reaches if she wants to gain a powerful soul..."

Another silence stretched out between them, long enough to become uncomfortable. Talina started shifting backward, not wanting to be caught this close to them once they were finished talking. Gem twittered loudly, calling his flock of kin. Their bird-song covered the sound of her retreating footsteps.

Except Sondus's next statement re-captured her attention instantly. "Izell has been taking an herb to suppress demonic influence." Talina froze and tilted her ear back toward their conversation. *Demonic influence? How horrifying!*

"What!" Kalimea exclaimed.

"I will need more time with Prince Jaromir to learn more. He had a bag full of the herb last night, but it's unknown how long it's been in his possession."

"It's imperative that you learn more," she replied.

"Yes, Your Majesty," he said crisply.

"You also might be interested to hear that Sorsha owes him a great debt. Ash shared that he lost his healing magic protecting her from being infected with the Fell disease." As she spoke, a surprised gasp sounded from the man.

"Sorsha wasn't able to repay him?"

"The only thing he wants is his magical Gift back." There was a shrug to her tone.

Sondus hummed. "I have an idea."

"Of course," she said, muffling a chuckle. "And I should be heading back to Ironhold."

Talina took that as her cue to actually leave, sneaking back from the willow tree and finding a path to meander down. It went this way and that, eventually looping around to the druidic temple that'd become a temporary home. Along the way, Gem and his little flock returned to her, covering her arms, shoulders, and hair like multicolored decorations.

"Does this mean you've forgiven me?" she asked Gem, who rested on her hand.

He inspected her fatecross mark and lifted his wings. *"It's not like you had a choice."*

Though made offhandedly, his comment speared into the center of her uncertainties. She went inside for a late lunch and a serving of sugar water for the hummingbirds, her thoughts full. Gem was right. Being fatecrossed to another person wasn't a choice; it was a decree by the gods. Human-born and fae weren't even compatible in such a way.

Would Sirius have ever given her a second glance if it weren't for the marks on their hands? The man she knew wanted to be in control of every aspect of his life.

Her heart sank as she envisioned having another conversation as doomed as her telling him about her fears of a soul change. It would be so much worse this time, though. He'd have to do something drastic to avoid the fatecrossed match between them.

She was poking glumly at her salad when he walked in, his sheer presence drawing her to sit up straight and take note. He was dressed in the kind of leather armor druids wore, shiny-new and a dark brown to help him blend into the night. He wore the fae style of a low-slung belt, the cut emphasizing the masculine V-shape at his waist.

That wasn't what she admired most about the view, though. He'd gone clean shaven and trimmed his hair in a short comb over, exposing his newly pointed ears. He cleaned up well, she decided.

"Gods above. Don't start drooling over there," Gem interrupted her perusal. She snapped her mouth shut as Sirius's gaze roved over the small café, heading over the moment he spotted her.

His ruby-red gaze flashed to her salad. "That seems mighty boring. Can I interest you in something better?" A teasing smile lit his face.

"Better food, or better something else?" That expression definitely didn't look food related.

He offered his hand. "Just better. Let's go on a date. Get away a while...just the two of us. What do you say?" His gaze was soft, hopeful. Like he could think of no better way to pass the time than to be by her side.

She didn't overthink it. She put her hand in his.

Chapter 26
Talina

He led her into Cordaria, pausing only to buy a towel at the local market. It took her far too long to remember what day it was and why there were already clusters of couples and families waiting on their own towels in a sloped meadow facing the sea.

Someone must've given Sirius the hint that it was Veltaun's Day, honoring one of the first Archdruids. It was supposed to be celebrated in the evening, but already, there was a stage set up on the other side of the meadow, where nature met the cobbled path up toward the city. A cluster of musicians was tuning their instruments up there, Cedric included. Neala's red hair gleamed in the sun as she sat on the stage's edge, waiting for him.

Talina nestled into Sirius's side, relaxing from his warm presence. For once, she wasn't worried about the circus who had most of their things, nor the fact that they needed to discuss what a fatecross actually meant for their relationship.

Her wings tingled to even acknowledge that she was in a relationship. She felt like a teen again, with effervescent bubbles in her belly. Sirius held her around the waist, casually tracing his thumb over her hip bone. Despite the beautiful view, he had eyes only for her.

Could there be a more peaceful moment?

She worried she'd ruin it if she spoke. There were so many heavy topics looming over them. She wanted to keep the right now sacred, where her feelings told her things weren't as complicated as she thought they were.

Gem lit atop her head, chattering in birdsong. Sirius stirred, his brows raising. "We're going tomorrow," he said to some unanswered question. "And I intend to kick his ass."

"Huh?" She glanced around, wondering who he was talking to.

Gem's determined feelings flashed through her familiar bond as he continued to twitter.

"Sorry. I think you and I agree on a lot of things, though," Sirius said, his quiet voice hitting the low register that did silly things to her insides.

"Are you talking to Gem?" she asked, realization and quiet awe kicking in. Familiars could speak to their master's mate. But... she and Sirius weren't mated quite yet. So...

He seemed just as puzzled as she felt. "I've been hearing small voices all day. Gem would like me to apologize for my language, but I really am going to kick Cloman around for stealing our things. Tomorrow. Kalimea plans to give us a portal to the circus's next stop because I promised her a show."

Gem hopped up and down on her head and twittered. "She's heard me say worse," Sirius chuckled.

She reached up and snagged her hummingbird, who was puffed up to twice his size. "This is amazing," she said, stroking Gem with a fingertip to relax all his bright feathers. "You're a druid! A vampire druid. I didn't know that could happen."

"I've met one." Sirius tilted his head, considering a moment. "In Adrun. I suppose you know about it now."

"The place full of *mort loci* which used to be the Fell Lands? Sort of. Queen Kalimea's been talking about it a lot. We all have," she admitted.

"Shifters. *Mort loci* seems derogatory." His gaze flashed toward the stage, where Cedric strummed his lute and Neala sang a melodic scale. The half-fae made noises of applause and strange, metallic clicks with just his tongue. Considering how she'd been around to hear him sheepishly admit to Kalimea that he was a lyrebird "shifter," she already knew a lot about Adrun because he'd come clean about its existence and the thriving of its people despite living in a place of eternal darkness.

"My brother," he admitted softly, "is the king there. He's a dragon shifter now."

She perked up. He hadn't opened this part of himself up often. "So, that's the real reason you're a prince?"

"No. I have a title. Air." He made a dismissive gesture. "His lifemate settled and ruled Adrun in the interim while Adrius and I slept for a thousand years. He married her again, gaining a crown and a real throne."

She felt there was more to that sentence that went unsaid. That somehow, Adrius had left Sirius with less than what he expected. "You don't have air. You have the wind," she said, wanting to see him smile. She spun a playful curl of magic, ruffling their hair with a gust that circled them alone.

He sighed and held her closer. "You're right. All I need is you," he murmured. His warm breath skated over her ear.

She shivered, feeling little tingles down her back in the wake of his stroking hand. Tilting her head up, she met his lips halfway for a slow, lingering kiss. His fingertips traced her cheek and neck, a tender touch to match the way he looked at her in that moment.

Foreheads brushing, he whispered for her ears only, "Be my mate, Talina."

It was a yes or no invitation. So, of course, she overthought it. Shouldn't she mention the fatecross and the gods' hands in this moment? Maybe everything else she'd overheard?

But she wanted to say yes right away. Why? Was it the mark on her hand, or how she felt for him?

The word stuck in her throat, but he waited, his thumb stroking the sensitive patch of skin right below her ear.

Instead of a yes, her mouth blurted for her, "Are you sure?" She regretted the question the moment it left, but Sirius didn't flinch.

He wound her hair around his hand and pulled her into his mouth. Her toes curled as she read every intent from his passion, deep and intense like the brush of his tongue against hers. For him, there were no questions, just the need he expertly stoked in her before their lips parted.

Breathless, she flushed, smoothing the electric tingles off her. They were literal, zipping over her blue skin in tiny, white arcs. "Did I shock you?" she asked, wondering why he'd even stopped otherwise. Her heart fluttered like a hummingbird in her chest.

"Seems we both have our oddities today," he said. He touched one of the racing electric arcs, and it dissipated against his claw. He flashed a wry grin. "I prefer this to the last time you showed me your lightning."

"I'm really sorry—"

"Don't be," he interrupted. "You have to hit harder if you're ever in danger again. Not from me, though. I swear I'll kill myself if I ever become a threat to you again."

"Sirius," she gasped. Here he was, bringing in clouds on their moment.

He shrugged, playing with a lock of her hair. She could tell he wasn't about to take that promise back, no matter how shocking it was to hear aloud. "Should I worry about getting zapped if I kiss you again?" he asked, his tone shading to playful.

"Why don't you try and see?" She just wanted him to kiss her like that again, even though she jolted him on purpose as a little charge built between them with every brush of their lips. He laughed, holding her despite the electricity.

She only realized she'd never answered his question as the band began to play and he stood, hand extended in invitation for a dance. The music didn't match anything they'd practiced, so they danced to their own rhythm with Neala's soaring vocals in the background. The first song was slow and meaningful.

Sirius held her close throughout. Their breath mingled as she rode a cushion of air to keep her weak ankle elevated on the uneven grass. Now that they were in motion, she could've danced like this for the rest of the day and night.

"You know what you never told me?" Sirius murmured.

A yes or a no? She was ready to answer, but he veered away from that. "What happened in ballet school," he supplied.

"Oh!" She tittered.

Most of her nerves centering around that time were completely gone. "My ankle. Right. There's not much to tell anymore, now that we know who has been whispering to me," she admitted. "I wanted to emulate my mom and how she always danced with the wind as her partner. So...when I was still a kid, I tried summoning wind powerful enough to dance with."

She'd seen it done with such grace and skill, so why not? "I missed her so badly," she whispered, hiding her face in the warm leather covering his chest. "It's embarrassing. I thought I could do it too, so outside of school hours, I would practice. My wind was strong even then, but fickle. It would throw me around and drop me at the wrong moments. Over the years, I broke my legs, my kneecaps, my ankles, some of the bones in my feet. All from falling."

He tugged on her locks, his expression creased with concern. "You didn't think to stop?"

"No," she said immediately, lifting her chin. "I *knew* I had it in me. And the school had the best healers, who got me back up and dancing within days. Until..."

Her lips quirked. The nasty words and emotions of that time came roaring back now that she dwelled on it. "The wind spoke to me a lot around that time. Warning me of small dangers or just looking after me so I wouldn't get wet without my raincoat, that kind of thing. I had no one to talk to, so I shared it with the other girls, thinking maybe the wind talked to them too. It was a terrible idea."

He nodded slowly, frowning. "They didn't understand."

"They really didn't. The teachers thought I was making things up for attention, and the girls said plenty of terrible things." She sighed, shaking her head. "If my mom had been around, she'd have told me not to talk about it. But I learned the hard way instead. I didn't have any friends in ballet school, but I showed enough talent to be considered for prima ballerina roles. I mean, to be the lead role. Center stage. By the time my wings grew in, I had the same teachers who scoffed at me all trying to become my mentor. Except for one."

She saw Madame Bencor in her mind's eye: pinch-faced and

disapproving of anything that had to do with Talina. "She was already mentoring my rival, her daughter. I was better than her." She only spoke facts, though she knew what it sounded like. "I used to be the best."

A low rumble sounded in Sirius's throat. "What did she do?"

"I was recovering from an ankle injury," she said, forcing a swallow as her throat grew thick. It was her fault for being injured in the first place, struggling to dance without the wind she'd become accustomed to. "She snuck into the infirmary and..." she made a small "tich" sound and twisted her hand. "Told me it was for my own good and that a woman of my mental capacity wouldn't make it as a prima ballerina."

Anger made his eyes brighter. "Where is this person now? I think she and I need to have a *conversation*."

"She passed away soon after," she said, feeling a little thrill rather than a flutter of fear. If only she'd met Sirius sooner. Her life would've been much different with a protector. "But the healers couldn't mend my ankle fully. You may already know that fae are made of magic. When we get too much healing magic in one place, our bodies get all confused. So, that area's always weak."

"And it can't be fixed, even by traditional means?" he asked, gritting his teeth and forcing his eyes closed. He breathed more slowly to tame the anger that leapt up so easily within him.

"Are you talking about human medicine?" she asked. She'd heard human practices were barbaric, relying on cutting skin to expose and fix injuries within. Cool sweat slicked her back at the thought.

He tilted his head. "Like re-breaking it and setting it to where it should be. Letting it heal without assistance."

"*Re-breaking?*" she squeaked. He was completely serious.

"Perhaps it wouldn't work for your very magical body," he teased, putting a hand up. "But I know a doctor you can trust, if you want to give it a try."

"Maybe someday," she hedged. Soon, the slow song was done, and he dipped her, sharing another static-filled kiss. They didn't stop as the band transitioned to a new piece, enjoying the moment and a reason to move together.

The sun tracked across the sky. It felt natural to spend the day in his arms, no matter what the future held. There was a change in him as night fell and they finally took a break, enjoying fried skewers of meat and squares of quivering cake. Something troubled him, turbulence rolling behind his eyes despite still holding her like the most precious thing he owned.

"What's wrong?" she asked quietly, dusting powdered sugar off her fingertips.

He shook his head. "Just...what's coming next." He inspected her for a long moment. "How many of my memories did you see?"

"I saw your nightmares. All those times Lucia came in and messed with you." She rubbed a chill off her arm in remembrance. "Why?"

He sighed, weary. "It occurred to me that there's some things you should know about me before you consider me as mate material. I'm glad you didn't see more memories. It means I can explain myself."

Her brows drew together. "I don't think you need to explain anything," she said gently. "Because...if you ask again, I'll say yes. I want to be your mate."

He smiled tenderly, bundling her into his lap for a full hug. His warmth enveloped her just like last night, the two of them fitting together comfortably. She rested her head back on his shoulder, realizing he was pensive, like they hadn't just made a big step together.

"You've seen the good and bad sides of me," he murmured, his eyes full of shadow in the evening. "Let me tell you about the ugly and see if you will stand by that decision."

Chapter 27

Sirius

What was he doing? His inner beast snarled to be quiet. They'd had a perfect day... Now he wanted to talk about Adrius?

"I'm supposed to forgive two people to keep one of my boons from the gods," he found himself saying. "If we meet them...you should probably know why there is bad blood there."

The last thing she needed was to regret choosing him as a mate. He'd been careful not to talk about his past in too many specifics, sure that she was better off not knowing all the sordid details. But he couldn't avoid introducing her to the rest of his family forever.

He told her the story between fireworks. Fae didn't use gunpowder, she told him, but colored fire magic to create and shape the explosions of light. Each created a series of pops and booms that shook the ground, followed by cheers and whoops amongst the druids and their families.

It was easier to watch the lights than her face, though he did both, sure he was going to see judgment on her features. He started by speaking of Lucia's betrayal and her master stroke to take Nyixa's throne by banishing Nyah to what would become Adrun and poisoning Adrius so he would die for the first time.

"Adrius took the Shield Key when he wed Nyah and had it

bound to him as a sign of devotion. It became a curse...because he couldn't die," he sighed.

"Shield magic isn't supposed to be infinite..." she said uncertainly.

"When it's contained within a Fell Key, it is." And thus began the grim truth of his story. "Nyah was the reason he got out of bed every morning. To think that she was gone and he had to continue on..." An explosion of blue light haloed her face and her glossy hair, her bright eyes gently clouded in concern.

"I didn't really understand. I didn't have a mate, or really any woman I was close to." But he did now, and for the first time, he held a glimmer of new sympathy for his brother. "He never moved on. Instead...he died a little inside each day. But he was still the rightful king of the vampire nation. By staying away from Nyixa, he forfeited his title for twenty years."

Twenty years of Hell for them both. "We relocated far from the island. It was me, Adrius, and our friend Korin. Korin dove straight into a bottle of moonshine." He scoffed, his nose stinging from the memory of the fumes coming off his best friend's home-made swill. Regular alcohol wasn't strong enough for a vampire, and Korin was the largest Blood Prince of them all. His escape from reality was a difficult one.

"So, it was basically Adrius and me," he said, blowing out a sigh. "A huge side effect to his resurrections was that Adrius would continue to bleed from the wound that killed him last. It healed so slowly. He would go crazy with bloodlust or court madness waking up just one more night without his mate by his side."

Talina's hand circled his, her eyes depthless pools of the daytime sky. He held her like an anchor as his riled memories threatened to drag him under. "The only way to stop him was to kill him before he could do something he regretted," he whispered. "I had to do it. He would wake up a few days later, the darkness in him gone. Resigned for more mindless existence until it built up in him again."

"Gods above. That's terrible," she murmured.

He nodded slowly. She probably spared her pity for Adrius,

as everyone did. "We lied to make it a little easier on him. He thought it was Korin who dealt the blows, but most of the time, it was me. Korin could barely raise his sword most days." He blew out a sigh.

"I fed him from my own veins and made sure he didn't become a monster. We did small things, like selling our swords to a local company, for survival money. When Adrius stumbled, I picked him back up."

"For twenty years," she murmured.

He gritted his teeth. "Yes. And I grew very tired of both my friend and brother. Adrius never tried to be better...and I realize now that he was suffering from depression. But after a while, all I felt was that I was his punching bag. The one who did the dirty work.

"After twenty years, I saw a glimmer of the old Adrius when we returned to Nyixa. All he had to do was kill Lucia and put the crown back on his head. He couldn't do it. He refused to consider evacuating the island and putting her to the sword, since in those times, if Lucia died, the island sank. He was forced to marry her instead." He dragged his hand down his face, muffling a frustrated groan. "It's not like it was consummated. We were put into our coma and slept a thousand years starting that night. But just the thought of it makes me so angry. He could've ended our problems there instead of having her continue to taunt and torment us a thousand years later."

"There's a lot there," she said, venturing a touch of his jaw. A tingle followed her soft fingers over his late evening stubble. He turned to kiss her palm.

"If you want to hear all my dinosaur history, we can talk about all the politics later," he promised. She wasn't looking at him any differently, so there was hope she'd stay with him through what remained of his story. "When we woke up, my brother opened his eyes already defeated. It re-broke his spirit that we were betrayed so deeply by someone we trusted. The second person I'm supposed to forgive, Gwendolyn, is the one who put us to sleep in the first place. We loved and cherished her as Nyah's mother and...she meant for us to die, not to sleep. I find it hard to look the other way from that, no matter her reasons."

"Well, of course," she murmured.

He forced out the rest before he could hold it back. "I gave up on Adrius not long ago. He turned on me." He drew his hand along the crescent-shaped scar that remained after Jaromir had reattached his arm to his shoulder.

Closing his eyes, he narrated the scene. Adrius had succumbed to Fell Madness, embracing its darkness and hatred. He'd been tormented by the demon who was Lucia's predecessor, Jazrach, finally snapping when someone suggested his long-lost wife may still be alive. When Sirius and Korin had arrived to stop Adrius from going on a bloody rampage amongst mortal kind, he'd turned and attacked them instead.

For as strong as Sirius was, he paled in comparison to Adrius at his peak, as the King of Vampires. "As I lay in the hospital, healing, I knew two things: that it wasn't fully Adrius's fault that he'd had a break with reality but that I was done with him either way. He woke up from death not remembering everything. He didn't know how close he'd come to killing me, and he'd forgotten Nyah."

The moment Adrius had looked at him with bewilderment at her name was burned into the back of his eyeballs. "He forgot *Nyah.* Just like that. The reason he'd put us both through Hell and back. The reason he nearly tore me apart. I just...couldn't take it anymore. I left him." He flushed with angry heat. "I told him he was weak, and I left him. And without me, he went on to impress a dragon, become a mythical savior of Adrun, and remarry Nyah, gaining a throne he did next to nothing to earn."

He looked into Talina's concerned face and told her the truth. "I'm a selfish bastard," he growled. "I should be happy for him, but all I can focus on when I think of him on that throne is that he never apologized or tried to make amends for what we've been through. I've tried to get over it." He pulled at his face, finding it hard to speak. "I don't hate him. But what we've been through... it's unique."

"No kidding," she whispered. The towel whispered as she

shifted. The boom of yet another firework blinded him for a moment, so all he felt was her arms slipping around his middle. She held him tightly. "I don't think you're selfish, if that's what you're worried about."

He was frozen for a moment, hoping he hadn't misheard her.

"If anyone else does, they don't really understand what you've been through," she continued, a sad, little smile crossing her face. "I bet you came to Faerie to make something new for your life. Not to just find control of your inner beast."

"Yes. That's exactly right. I didn't expect to find a mate, but here you are. If you still want me now that you know this about me..." He would never let her go.

But before he could circle his arms around her again, she released him and shifted to the side. Her cool fingertips brushed through his hair, rubbing away some of the tension gathered there. As her nails glided after her touch, he groaned low in his throat. "I think we need to relax," she said, turning him to putty with just her fingertips. "We used to have a dancer who gave the best scalp massages. They're great, right?"

He practically purred in response.

"I think I agree with Raenith, though," she said, taking him by surprise. His eyes flew open even while she worked her magic. "It's not healthy for you to have so much you haven't expressed to your brother. And, maybe, a lot he hasn't said either."

"I suppose," he murmured.

"It's probably not macho to talk about your feelings, especially with your brother." She shrugged, her gaze earnest. "But you already acknowledge that the way you feel about him is not the best...so now, you have an opportunity to change it."

Confront them, rail at them, but find it in yourself to move on before your grudges destroy you. If Talina agreed, he knew there was wisdom there that he should heed.

"I will try," he promised. It was all he could offer to her and Raenith.

She lifted her gaze as another cluster of lights bloomed in the sky. "Oh, the four-leaf clovers." She giggled, her fingers digging into his skin and finding the perfect pressure by accident. "That means it's all over." Rapid-fire, the sky bloomed with multiple clovers, coming alive in a dazzling display of shamrock green. The magic fell into the sea like shining rain, letting the brilliant night sky take its place a few moments later.

Talina didn't stop rubbing his head until Cedric and Neala came over to say their goodbyes and walk them back to the temple.

"Time to head home," he caught himself saying.

"Home? What is that?" Talina laughed without venom. She smoothed over his hair and tittered with surprise when he picked her up to carry back.

"A place we're going to make together," he murmured in her ear as she settled in his hold. A little blush touched her cheeks, shining lilac in the halo of the hanging fairy lights they passed. He noticed Neala shooting a glance to Cedric, her brows rising. Something passed between them in hand gestures, which he tried to ignore.

"Are you two betting on us or something?" Talina asked for him.

"Noooo. Why would we do that?" Cedric elongated his vowels, his eyes darting to Neala, who grinned.

"I'm winning," she stated.

"Wish we could come with you two. I'd write your relationship into a song." Cedric plucked his lute in the dark, twanging out a few notes. Apparently, he never put that thing away.

Sirius turned to him, expression serious. "If you ever write a song about me, it better be more epic than Adrius's."

The half-fae stood straight and attentive, nodding along. Then, he cracked up. "Of course! And when Adrius asks why you got the better song, I'll write him an even grander song. Until I keel over at the ends of my awesomeness."

Talina tittered a giggle, which eventually broke Sirius's resolve. He released a single laugh. Cedric darted over to cling to Neala's side, pointing. "Did you hear that? He does laugh!"

"Sometimes."

"Oh, please. He does all the time," Talina said, rolling her eyes.

The other couple exchanged another glance. "Have a good night." Neala pulled Cedric toward the room they were sharing the moment they reached the temple.

He looked to Talina, who tweezed her lip between her teeth, considering him. After that decidedly unsexy retelling of his past, he figured he was out of luck, especially when she muffled a yawn in the next moment.

"Would you hold me tonight?" she offered, kicking a foot and glancing away shyly.

His beast perked up, seeing opportunity there. And progress. "Your room or mine?"

They chose her room, as it was slightly larger. He finally changed into something more comfortable amongst the new sets of clothing and armor he'd been given, ending up in a warm robe while she changed to a pair of fluffy pajamas. "What?" she asked, glancing down at herself when he'd stopped in the doorway to admire her sleepwear.

"Did you pick those out for yourself?" Amusement crept into his tone. Little, fluffy cloud shapes were dyed in the gray material, some with stylized yellow threads of electricity shooting from them. "It's very you."

Laughing, she let him in. *Don't mess this up,* he told himself even as he reached out to stroke the side of the material that covered her. Soft, also like her.

His fingers itched to grab a fistful of her clothing and haul her in for a kiss. It nearly killed him to acknowledge that she needed to make the first move, and she was already lying down with another yawn.

"This is okay, right?" she asked, shifting to make room in the bed for him. She sighed happily when he spooned her, her fluffy wings within kissing range. Would she notice that? She only seemed to shiver from surface-level touches; otherwise, her wings turned to mist between his fingers.

She glanced over her shoulder, sleepy but trusting. Here he was wondering how to get her out of her clothes when this was the limit between them for the moment. "Just fine," he murmured. He snuck a quick kiss, promising himself that tomorrow was their day.

With a tap of her palms, the fairy lights in the room dimmed. Her breathing evened out, proving yet again that she could sleep anywhere. Until he heard her murmur his name. "Sirius? Does your brother really have a song?" she asked sleepily.

Off-key, he serenaded her to "The Dragon of Adrun" or whatever Cedric was calling it. He knew every word by heart. He secretly loved the stupid thing.

She fell asleep murmuring, "Your song will be bett..."

Better, he finished for her, closing his eyes with a sigh as he nuzzled into her hair. *I sure hope so.*

Chapter 28
Sirius

AND BECAUSE NOTHING COULD LEAVE HIM WELL ENOUGH alone lately, he dreamed. He was distinctly aware of walking through a nebulous darkness, every millimeter of his body primed for another attack from Lucia.

A feminine voice made itself known to him, but it didn't belong to the woman he expected. "It is easier once you rip those old memories open."

From the mist ignited a dragon's shape, formed of white-hot flames. Raenith was taller than him now, seven feet at the shoulder. Her power poured off her in waves, forcing his inner beast to bow its head to the superior predator. He averted his eyes out of necessity, otherwise risking having them blinded by her sheer radiance.

"Lady Raenith. This is a surprise." He tried for a respectful tone as nerves formed a waltz in his stomach.

She snorted, blowing a wave of heat over him. "Please. Save your formality for the Lord of Storms. Do you know why you're here tonight?"

He licked his lips, unsure of what tone this all-powerful goddess wanted. He was about to shrug when he noticed what they were walking past. Mortals liked these things called movies, and that's what the moving images reminded him of. Except instead of fiction, they reflected back moments from his life. He stopped at one, extending a hand with a wistful twist in his gut. When his fingertips made contact, his senses attuned to the moment he was seeing.

"Adrius has a crush?" asked a young version of Korin, before Fell blood turned him into a juggernaut nearly as tall as this version of Raenith. His bearded face split with a wide grin as he turned toward Adrius, who sat a table away, picking at rations.

Sirius's memory turned back to Korin. He knew the conspiratorial smile they'd shared. It was the best news they'd heard in months of hard marches and bleak landscapes wiped clean by Fell fangs.

"With flowing, golden hair," he said, echoing his memory's voice. "And the kind of body you can squeeze."

"A woman! Here!" Korin crowed.

"Would you two stop?" Adrius hollered, a touch of red across his cheeks.

Sirius turned away, forcing a grit of his teeth. The memory faded to where it belonged. "Back when he had shame," he muttered.

"Oh, indeed. That's exactly what you were just thinking," Raenith said behind him.

"Like you can read my thoughts."

He regretted saying it immediately as she responded, "Can't I? Go ahead, lie to a goddess and say you weren't thinking about how you missed having that kind of rapport with both of them."

He ground his teeth, cursing quietly instead. "Apologies, Lady Raenith. That's the truth," he said.

"That's better." Her bright form lingered at the corner of his sight. She stopped and lifted a talon. "How about this one?"

He turned, resigned to watch whatever she wanted him to see. He was surprised to be greeted by Adrius's furious young face.

"What are you doing here?" he hissed. It was dark, and Sirius couldn't see well. He was human in this memory, he realized. Raenith had dug far back to find a moment where Adrius was a newly turned vampire, flashing his fangs like a green fledgling as he gestured angrily.

"The last thing we need is my kid brother getting underfoot," he continued.

"Wait, please. I can be useful," Sirius murmured, barely scratching the passion of his fifteen-year-old self as his newly monstrous brother tried to leave him behind.

Adrius leaned in. "Look at me. Those creatures damned me." His ruby-red eyes glimmered with fear as he lifted his lips, properly showing the twin fangs that unsheathed from behind his eyeteeth. "If you really want to fight them...the same will happen to you."

"I don't care. I want to come with you and Korin." It'd been an unfair twist of fate, that the two men closest to him would be stricken in battle while he assisted his father on the farm.

He blinked slowly, shutting the memory out. "God," he muttered.

When Raenith gestured again, he knew what he'd see. The same young Adrius, grimly offering him a bleeding wound after he'd followed the nascent Fell Hunter army regardless of what Adrius had said. His first encounter with a Fell was stained with pain and blood, a bitter defeat dashing his hopes of being a hero like his big brother.

At fifteen, he'd been the youngest vampire around, turned at an age where he continued to grow and age despite the cursed blood in his veins.

The goddess at his back helped him remember it all. Reluctantly, he walked the progression of his youngest years. The early evenings spent squaring off with Adrius, Korin, or even Gabriel Legion, their commander. He practiced until his hands bled. He improved until he was face to face with another Fell, but this time, he won, watching its pitch-black eyes grow dull.

"I get it," he sighed, back in his current mind again. "There was a time when Adrius supported me."

"You mean to say that was the same support you gave him?" her crackling voice asked as the scenes they passed changed. He tried not to look, recognizing the pleading, broken tone in Adrius's voice on the edge of his awareness. "You cannot balance the suffering you both experienced on a scale and expect there to be a winner and loser."

He whirled around, heat rising over his skin as he snarled. "Then what is the point? All you're doing is making it worse for me. I don't want to dwell on any of this!"

Her pointed snout tilted, those eyes of blue flame narrowing shrewdly. "Let's change tactics, then. If you could say anything to him right now, what would it be?"

Sirius muttered uncharitably.

"A little louder?" she said, her laugh like the snap of burning branches. "Close your eyes. Pretend I'm Adrius. You have a chance to express how you feel, so what do you say?"

"I would say..." He clamped his eyes shut, still seeing the after-images of her white form. This was stupid. Did this fire lizard just want to torment him?

The words stuck in his throat. It was unexpectedly hard to form how he *felt*. He was a warrior; he didn't deal with feelings except by hitting things harder. This was the one thing he couldn't wrestle and punch into submission.

"I would say that I realize life isn't some fairytale, where things are all magically solved in the end. But I feel like he stepped on my face to climb up to where he is now. He's had one, two...*three* chances to be a king, and he'd better not mess this one up, I swear to God." His hands balled into fists. "Everyone sympathizes with him. Boo-hoo, so depressed. Who was it that got him this far? Who carried his dead body back to a safe place every time it had to happen? Who put his life on hold for twenty years going on a thousand just so *Adrius* could have his happy ending?"

He blew out a scoff. "And people wonder why I have a problem. He gets to be the big hero and kill the demon, while he left me outside, unconscious. He gets to nearly kill me, and everyone still loves him. I'm tired of the double standards. I'm tired of sitting in his shadow, waiting to be asked why I'm so fucking *angry* all the time and why I can't be more forgiving and stoic like my brother. The same man who wasted the magic he was blessed with so Lucia could use what he *threw away* to nearly kill me. All my problems trace back to fucking Adrius. When I said I was done letting him ruin my life, I meant it. He obviously doesn't need me."

He took a deep breath before he could cut into his palms further with his sharpened fingernails. "He doesn't need me anymore," he repeated to himself. "And while I prefer it, I don't know what to do with myself. How do I dig out of the hole I've made with everyone else now that he's become the man he's supposed to be? Who am I supposed to be? I don't even know what I am anymore or where my purpose lies."

"That's the beauty of starting again, isn't it?" The quiet voice was Adrius's. Sirius startled and opened his eyes. He was standing in a lazy river, its water lapping at his upper calves. Turning, he realized Raenith was gone, leaving him alone with this version of Adrius. He was without his shifter features, casually tossing aside a fly rod.

It really was just like his brother to be fly fishing in his dream. Sirius shook his head in denial as Adrius asked, "Is that really how you feel about me?"

That damn dragon tricked him. Sirius knew he'd somehow been transplanted into his brother's dream space, thousands of miles and a barrier of magic away in the land of Adrun. "How much of that did you hear?" he replied.

Adrius shrugged as he waded to shore. "All of it, I think."

In a blink of the eye, he was already sitting on a rocky outcropping with his legs dangling over the river. Adrius sat by his side. Dream logic? *Probably*, he thought. Who knew what either of them would remember about this meeting. "Yes," he said, ready to own up. "That's how I feel."

"Would it help to punch me?" He tilted his head, patting his strong jaw. "Right here. Go ahead."

"No," Sirius growled. "I'm supposed to forgive you, damn it, not beat you up."

His brows lifted in surprise, but he sat back, getting comfortable. "It's fortunate you've come here, actually," he murmured. "I've been worried about you."

Sirius crossed his arms. "Why?" he grumbled. He could take care of himself without any worry on Adrius's part.

"Oh, I don't know. Izell coming up to me one day and saying, 'I'm taking your hothead brother to Faerie before he murders you in your sleep. Say goodbye now, or it'll be a while' does something to a man." He shook his head with a little, wry laugh. "I thought she was exaggerating, but it really sounded like you could wring my neck right now and have good reason for it."

"I'm not going to hurt you, for God's sake," Sirius said, his voice rising angrily. "I'm not going to punch you, or break your neck, or murder you in your sleep!"

Adrius eyed him askance. "I'm really convinced."

Sirius covered his face with his palm. This wasn't going how he expected at all.

"Look—" they both said at the same time.

Adrius rushed to be first after they paused from the coincidence. "I never wanted you to feel used. In fact, I seem to recall begging you to leave my miserable ass to die."

"Not like you *can* die." And this drew a soft laugh from Sirius, cutting through the tension lining his shoulders. "Do you ever miss being normal?"

"All the time," his brother sighed. "I watch how carefree mortals seem, with their technology boxes—"

"Phones?" Sirius guessed.

"I think so. And I envy them. If you really want to be a king, maybe you should reconsider. I know nothing about Adrun, and I have thousands of shifters thinking that I'm some sort of legend come to life." Adrius brushed a hand through his hair. It was growing long around his ears, the same shaggy and unkempt style Sirius had just tamed on himself. His brother really was his mirror in appearance without Zerenth's additions. "But I want you to know I'm trying damn hard to be impressive and worthy of my second chance."

"Good."

They both waited as the word hung between them. It really encapsulated Sirius's thoughts on his brother's growth. Any improvement and effort was a good thing. He had Nyah by his side to mentor him, but now, neither she nor Sirius would pick him up and carry him through the worst moments. He had to stand on his own two feet.

Adrius smiled uncertainly. "And how is Faerie treating you? What did you mean, about my magic...?"

"One of the very first things we learned about fae magic. Nothing's destroyed, only recycled." He frowned into the middle distance, not wanting to see familiar regret on Adrius's features. "I guess it's not your fault, but it was your magic. What you shed when you became a shifter was weaponized and forced into my body. It took an intervention of Faerie's gods to save my life, and now, I'm paying for it."

He told the story of Lucia's nightmares, which led to more questions. Who was Talina? What did he mean, Neala was attacked too? He unpacked his adventures one answer at a time, saving his hopefully soon-to-be mate for very last as Adrius reeled.

"First, I'm sorry she used my magic against you like that. I thought it was lost." Adrius shook his head. "Just letting you down again."

Something in him softened to hear an apology at last. "Like I said, not really something you expected," Sirius murmured.

"But who is Talina?" he asked again, elbowing his side. He read something in Sirius's expression, grinning.

"A pretty lady fae—" was about as far as he got before Adrius slapped his back with a guffaw, nearly sending him into the water below.

"A woman! Finally." Adrius laughed harder, and it sounded like sheer relief. "Is she your equal or opposite?"

"Opposite," he said immediately.

"Since you called her pretty, she'd have to be."

Sirius shoved him into the river, rolling his eyes. The dream blipped, and Adrius was back at his side, cheerful and soaking wet. "What is she like? Is she *serious,* or is that why she's your opposite?"

His nostrils flared in a hard exhale. How could he forget his brother punned his name with that trait? They were pronounced the same, so it was low-hanging fruit. "You think you're clever?"

"Sometimes. Usually, no." Adrius offered a shrug.

"She's amazing, though. And completely unexpected." Talina was perhaps the one subject he wanted to talk about, so Adrius heard all about her. The joy she took in dancing, the way her puffy cloud wings waggled when she considered something she liked. Their impossible connection, which he was finding harder to ignore with each passing hour by her side. Not a life-mate, nor a heartsong, but a fatecross. Something new and unique to explore.

"...And I have to take her to see the God of Wind in person. They call him Zalice, the Lord of Storms. Taking her into danger is the ultimate price I will pay for this." He traced the sharp point of his fae-like ear.

"I was wondering," Adrius murmured. "And you took my shadows, too?" He grabbed a handful of the shadowy mist that still ebbed off Sirius's back, unburdened by a form and no closer to being wing-shaped like the fae were expecting.

"They've been useless. But yes," he said.

Adrius leaned back on his hands, looking thoughtful, then breathed a slow sigh, mustering himself. "Do you want a lesson in using them? I have thought about...what you were yelling about when you came here. How I could possibly repay you for what you've done for me."

His gaze was sincere as he turned to Sirius. "I can't go back and fix it. But I can try to be what you need, going forward." He wet his lips, uncertain yet again. "So...I decided to send Korin to Faerie behind you, too. You need his help more than I do right now."

He blinked in surprise. "You did?"

"Yeah, with a few other friends. I hope that's okay. They're using his blood tracking to find you and the others, but if you're as spread out as it sounds, Korin's going to go to find you first. I'm still trying to look after you." He chucked Sirius's shoulder.

Sirius smiled slowly. *Maybe I haven't given Adrius enough credit.* He seemed to sincerely want to improve and maintain where recent events had gotten him.

But did he forgive his brother?

"Can't wait to see them. Also, I'll take that shadow lesson," he said.

Yes, he thought. Yes, he did forgive Adrius. Maybe he begrudged the miracles that Adrius rode to success, but he acknowledged that envy was an ugly look. He'd find his own success, with his own woman and his own way.

The sun came out, gracing his head with warmth. He glanced up, just now noticing the black dragon prowling toward the opposite shore and laying out with a contented huff. Sirius was struck for a moment by the true form of the massive predator, each polished scale gleaming like onyx in the light.

Adrius smiled, standing. "Look at that lazy thing." The moment he turned away, already talking about shadow magic, light and heat coalesced into a draconic form behind Zerenth. His bony face creased with pleasure as she nuzzled behind his ears.

Raenith's fiery gaze met his. She inclined her head in approval.

Chapter 29
Talina

Talina stirred from a deep sleep, comfortably groggy and secure. A strong arm was still encircling her waist, and she slowly realized Sirius's warm presence had given her the gift of comfort through the whole night.

He fidgeted with her hair, running it through his fingers. She felt him catch an ebb of her cloudy wing, playing with the soft magic until it dissipated. Shifting, she caught his content smile and sleep-darkened eyes. "Good morning, sweetheart." His deep voice tied her insides up just right.

Something about him was different. Lighter. She couldn't put her finger on what, though.

"Hi," she replied, suddenly hyperaware of him. Every plane of him, especially his thigh, which she'd parted her legs for. Their bodies fit perfectly.

She turned around, pressing her lips to his, inviting more. He hooked a hand under her knee as the heat between them grew, showing that there was another way they fit together like two puzzle pieces. "Is your answer still yes?" he asked when they came up for breath.

Talina nodded eagerly. She didn't think of the gods or the fatecross that had made sure they stayed together. Her whole self responded to him, wanting to belong to him.

"Let me hear you say it," he rumbled. His lips traced a path down her jaw.

She gasped as he found her pulse, his kiss coming with the sharp touch of fangs. "Yes," she said, grabbing hold of his shoulders to brace herself. "I still want to be your mate."

He groaned quietly. His bite hit her with a wave of bliss, shocking static between them at every touch. And that was the least of the pleasures he showed her that morning.

Yet try as they might—and they tried several times before an impatient Ash came knocking—they were unable to secure a mating bond. It was supposed to come naturally—a moment of intimacy when their souls united to the same rhythm.

It was the only thing interrupting the cloud of joy she took into the day. What had gone wrong? She'd sung her heart's song and everything, but he hadn't been able to form a bond with her over it. And their private fun hadn't built a connection, even though she could fleetingly sense the offer being extended.

We just have to try again, she thought, resting a hand over the warmth still curled in her belly.

Kalimea was waiting for them as soon as she had her meager possessions packed up. "Remember that you owe me a show," she said to Sirius, who held two duffle bags and wore an irritated expression that hadn't abated since they'd been interrupted.

"Yeah, yeah," he grumbled.

He'd finally been reunited with his sword, belted at his waist with the druidic leather on rather than his old suit of armor, which he was leaving behind. The shadows of his "wings" were tamer today, forming a dark sheet down his back like a cloak.

Kalimea nodded, holding her occultarus and gesturing. A portal ripped into being, showing fairgrounds swarming with carnies. Talina swallowed in a dry click. It wasn't just the three of them going through—Ash, Neala, and Cedric also crowded through, sure to turn the confrontation to come into a huge spectacle. Despite her hurt that her former employer had dropped her like yesterday's trash, she just wanted to get her things and go rather than face her former peers.

Warmth encircled her waist. Sirius shifted his bags to hold her instead, and he leaned down to brush a kiss over her forehead. "We'll be quick," he promised. She brightened a few moments under his tender gaze. The second he turned from her, his expression twisted back to anger. She saw it for what it was now, a mask. The carnies had spotted them at this point, whispering behind their hands as she and Sirius rejoined them by the side of the Unseelie Queen herself.

"You," Sirius barked, beckoning sharply to one of the smaller lesser fae, a cat-like creature with spotted fur and dexterous paws. It scampered over. "Tell the camp I demand a duel with Cloman for his slight against me."

"A duel!" it squeaked, its whiskers going stiff in shock. It turned to another of its fellows, repeating the message. The two of them rushed into the maze of half-raised tents.

"There. He'll be the last to hear it," he muttered. "Queen Kalimea, if I lose, you should know that he possesses a Fell Key and I need it."

She smiled with her fangs. "Is that so? Which one?"

"Combat."

Ash rolled her eyes. "Maybe I should challenge him next?"

"The man wouldn't bet on a Key in the first place," Kalimea said, her head tilted thoughtfully.

Sirius shrugged. "We'll have to see." He seemed quite confident, and Talina realized this must've been part of his plan all along. Cloman had to think he was nearly on par with Sirius's swordplay after they'd dueled so much, but Sirius had held himself back each time.

That was also before the Convocation. Sirius had lost muscle mass and height—was he still a match for someone with the Combat Key?

She was worrying her lip when a blur of white stopped before them. Cossette waved, hopping and smiling with joy. "You're back! You're here!" She launched herself at Sirius, who released Talina to catch the girl-Ancient. "Don't worry too much. I made sure they didn't sell your elk," she whispered loudly behind her hand.

"Thank god," he murmured. "Any advice?"

"No, but I did find some friends," she chirped.

She directed them to the big top, where he placed her and his things aside gently before rushing into a backslapping hug with one of the people waiting beside the structure. Talina watched in astonishment, exchanging a glance with Cedric, who played a confused twang on his lute.

"That's Korin. But what's he doing here?" Neala mused.

Kalimea's nose wrinkled with displeasure. "Another group from Earth." She turned to Ash, gesturing. "Do you know these human-born?"

The other Unseelie sighed, naming them as they approached but didn't mingle with the other group. Beside Blood Prince Korin, the Bane, was a human man she identified as Gabriel, an angelic warrior. He was tall and blond, fairly ordinary-looking in casual human clothes, except he had a sword at his side as well. The sight of both men's faces chilled Talina's blood.

Getana had shown them to her as potential killers of Lyana while executing the demonic spirit possessing her. In the vision, Gabriel had worn brilliant silver armor outlined in light-filled runes, bird-shaped wings of golden magic flowing behind him as he wielded a sword like a crystal spire. She recognized the pommel of that same sword as the one he wore now. He was most assuredly a warrior trying to blend in.

The angel was arm in arm with an older woman wrinkled with age despite a severe bun and aristocratic features. She shifted slightly behind Gabriel as Ash identified her as Gwendolyn, and Talina gasped. The second person Sirius said he needed to forgive—and definitely shying away from the moment he noticed she was there.

Rounding out their group was a man Ash sneered at. "Bryant Collins, certainly worth mentioning," she said dismissively.

"Why's that?" Kalimea frowned.

The pudgy vampire didn't seem like too much to Talina,

dressed plainly in brown with his gaze on the ground. He wore his shoulders low and sloped, the picture of a troubled mind.

As Ash opened her mouth, Sirius called Talina over with a big smile for introductions. She cracked her neck looking up to say hello to Korin. And she'd thought Sirius was tall! She took a step back and floated on her wings to talk to him more properly. Korin was built like a wall, broad and hard with muscle. His face was roughly hewn with a solid jaw covered in scruff and squinty eyes of Blood Prince maroon.

He spoke and gestured slowly, as if he had all the time in the world. "A pleasure to meet one who captivates Sirius's heart," he rumbled. His deeper register didn't hit her just right, though. That was something that belonged to her mate-to-be.

Said man had finally turned toward the others in Korin's group. His smile froze as a growl escaped his lips. "Korin," he muttered, expression shading quickly. "Why is Gwendolyn here?"

"Where Gabriel goes, so does his wife," the other Blood Prince sighed. He clasped Sirius's forearm with both hands and pulled him away, inclining his head with knightly formality to Talina. "Excuse us."

Meanwhile, Gwendolyn and Gabriel were both hugging Neala. The elderly woman covered her mouth and wept quietly. Sirius and Korin stopped out of earshot, and Sirius leaned in, his fists clenched as he snarled something at the other man.

Talina clasped her hands, feeling awkward. Thankfully, Cossette found her and tugged one of her hands free to hold it instead, beaming up at her. "Want to see a secret?" she asked brightly.

"I guess so?" she said, letting the girl-Ancient whisk her off to a familiar cart. Her troupe was gone from it, except for Wisteria, who froze upon seeing Talina and Cossette.

"We took care of her, promise," Wisteria blurted. The purple-haired dancer had a book in hand, leaning against the cart as she paged through it quickly. Talina recognized it—a manual on choreography and dances.

"I'm glad. Thank you," she said, knowing Cossette could care for herself. "Does this mean you're lead choreographer now?"

"Yes, but—how do you do it all?" The other fae clapped the book closed with a sigh. "I didn't realize your job was so hard."

Talina considered her and offered a little smile. "I can give you some pointers. But first, Cossette was going to show me a secret."

It turned out, the secret was...her things. The dancers had locked her chest of clothes and knick-knacks, hiding it when Cloman came around demanding they sell her possessions when it was clear they were moving on without her. "Someone special visited," Cossette continued as Wisteria unlocked the box and offered its contents to her.

"Her name is Izell Firebrand, and she had a good giggle over your journal," the girl continued. The leather-bound book was what she swept up first, realizing someone else's handwriting was now within it. She gasped, stamping her foot when she saw cross marks and x's, lines and diagrams. "It's a good thing! She wanted to help you."

"She read my journal. That's completely awful, terrible, and a breach of my privacy," Talina muttered. She tossed it in disgust and set aside her performing leotards, offering all of them to Wisteria. Something told her she wouldn't need them anymore. She kept only her favorite, a lilac number with a glittery front and two layers, the first a leotard to keep her covered, and the second layer a flirty skirt that fell to her ankles but lifted to her hips when she twirled. It had puffy, little bell sleeves and was the most comfortable thing she performed in, so she folded it to be stuffed in with the rest of her new belongings.

She took her money, jewelry case, and other small items too, as well as the journal after confirming that it wasn't a trick—someone really had written all over her "prophecy" and destroyed what she'd spent years interpreting. A sick feeling formed in the pit of her stomach despite Cossette's cheerfulness about it.

She'd deal with it later. She sat with Wisteria on the lip of the wagon and quickly gave her tips from what she'd learned as lead choreographer. There wasn't much time before Cloman had to respond in some way to Sirius charging in and demanding a duel, and it came as little surprise when Gem reported on it, *"They're going to fight on stage in front of everyone."*

Talina reached over and gave Wisteria's hand a squeeze. "You're going to do great," she said.

"We're going to miss you," the other dancer murmured as she squeezed back. They walked with Cossette to the big top, where Wisteria peeled off to sit with the dancers toward the front of the seating. A few beckoned to Talina, calling out to her, but she smiled and waved a "no" before going to the front, where Kalimea's distinctive wings were in place front and center. There was a spot next to her, which she gestured Talina into, leaving her bracketed between the queen and Korin.

"We meet again," the vampire said.

She glanced up at him in concern. "Was Sirius okay?" He was not in sight, the stage currently empty except for the glare of the spotlights.

"As he ever is." He offered a shrug. "They didn't speak yet." He glanced to the side. Gwendolyn and Gabriel were seated several spots to his left, so he simply lowered his voice. "Did Sirius tell you why he dislikes her?"

"I think so," she whispered back. "She's the one who sent him into his thousand-year coma, and it was actually meant to kill him. It's a deep grudge."

"Indeed." Korin released a weary sigh. His face brightened a moment later as a pink blur settled on his finger. Talina's jaw dropped. The big man held Gem up to his face, his eyes nearly crossed while inspecting the hummingbird. "Pretty, tiny bird," he cooed, venturing a gentle touch of the bird's wing.

"Gem? Why?" Her familiar rarely perched on another person.

Her familiar twittered and leaned into Korin's fingertip. *"I like him."*

She shook her head in disbelief. He hadn't even let Sirius touch him yet, and he was nearly her mate. *"Still don't like that one. He's too angry,"* Gem added, sensing where her thoughts were going.

"He has it under control." She knew that despite seeing the

fury on Sirius's face when he finally stepped on stage, his armor replaced by just a ratty, old pair of pants. Cloman entered opposite of him, dressed much the same way. There were no feminine sighs this time, tension raising the hair on the back of Talina's neck. Nearly everyone had shown up to watch.

"Ladies and gentlemen, you are about to see the duel of a lifetime," Cloman announced, his smooth voice and cocky smile showing he was unbothered by this challenge.

Kalimea lifted her hand, a crackle of magic raising from it. When she spoke, her voice was loud enough to broadcast. "Less theatrics, if you would. What is the wager between you?"

Murmurs rose in the wake of her voice. Cloman shifted and swallowed, glancing blindly into the crowd. With all the lights on, he wouldn't be able to see who was watching him. "Your Majesty." He bowed deeply. "If he is to win, I have promised the ring of power which helps me protect my people." He lifted his hand, the silvery Combat Key shining. "And if I win, he has pledged to serve in my circus until he earns me the same amount the ring cost me."

Talina muffled a gasp, knowing exactly how expensive it was. Had Sirius really agreed to that? But of course he had. He'd set up Cloman for this moment, pretending to lose night after night. Cloman was sure he was about to win, but so was Sirius.

"Why does he look different?" Korin asked her quietly.

"That's a long story," she admitted. Neala, sitting on Korin's other side, nodded in agreement.

Sirius raised his voice into a shout. "This man has threatened to tarnish my honor, stealing from me and my woman," he announced. "He will lose for his audacity."

"And this vampire should know that the circus stops for no one, especially those who think they can abandon us. Right before a performance we hyped him for!" Cloman shouted, shaking his fist. The audience murmured harder, a few cheering in agreement.

"Like two strutting cocks," Kalimea muttered. Ash snickered in agreement.

"We've agreed that first blood will win. Otherwise, we may

kill each other," Sirius told the crowd. Though, from his tone, Talina knew he was really saying: *I might kill him.*

First blood, though? That meant Cloman only had to get lucky once.

Talina nibbled on her lower lip nervously as the two men finally launched at one another. Their swords met with a screech before Sirius leaned his weight backward, letting a second swipe from Cloman sail over his head.

The two exchanged words, too low to be heard from the audience. Korin started rumbling a deep belly laugh as Cloman jabbed and swiped and struck, just for Sirius to gracefully dodge and parry each time. He didn't attack in return.

Talina's eyes widened in astonishment as she watched Cloman's face redden with anger or effort. Perhaps both. She cut her gaze to Korin. She recognized that Sirius described this man both as an alcoholic in the past and his best friend in the here and now. He seemed sober and deeply amused as he glanced back at her.

"Don't worry, little lady," he said. "I think most of us could eat this fire fairy for lunch in a duel."

Neala cupped a hand over her lips. "It's fae. You might insult someone around here if you call them a fairy."

Korin laughed. "Says the one who got a magic fairy princess voice." He continued chortling even when she punched his shoulder. By the sound of it, that wasn't a gentle hit. He didn't seem to notice the force, though. "Where we're from, it's a spit in the face to let someone exhaust themselves like this," he told Talina.

As the duel stretched on, she saw why. Cloman couldn't hit Sirius, no matter what he did. She started to feel secondhand embarrassment for him, here in front of all of his employees and the Queen of Faerie, who watched with an approving smile. Just as she was hoping it would end, Sirius turned his sword and cut Cloman's arm, raising the edge of the blade to show everyone the red that coated its side as the fae hissed in pain.

The audience cheered and screamed, but Talina strained to hear what the men on the stage were saying. She mostly read their lips.

"That's what your audacity deserves," Sirius growled.

"You didn't send word! You and one of my best dancers left us out to dry," Cloman shouted, holding the sizzling cut. "I refuse—"

"To give it to me? Too bad." Sirius's low voice still carried to the front row. "We shook on a deal." He held his hand out for the ring.

"Aren't you a liar, though?" Cloman grumbled. "Pretending to let me win. Dishonorable."

"For the record…" Sirius glared as he waggled his fingers, demanding his prize. "I wasn't able to dance for the circus those nights. I was fucking dying. Did you ever send anyone to look for me and Talina? You could've easily found out for yourself." He snatched the Combat Key as Cloman's jaw dropped, turning sharply and marching off the stage. As he reached the curtains and their shade fell upon his face, his gaze found Talina amongst the crowd. He smiled briefly, flashing a wink.

Korin started to laugh again. "He's got it bad, doesn't he?" he asked Neala.

"As bad as I have it for Cedric." She flashed the half-fae a fond look.

He elbowed her. "Send you lot to Faerie, you all fall in love with fairies. Did Jaromir do that too?"

She considered, shrugging. "Does Izell count?"

Korin grinned. "Okay, so where's mine?"

Talina couldn't help rolling her eyes alongside a giggle. She could see why Sirius was friends with this man.

Chapter 30
Sirius

Once Sirius was re-dressed in his leather armor, he chafed to leave. A few people assembled with Queen Kalimea to see them off. Familiar faces like Neala, Cedric, and Ash were staying with the Unseelie Queen for her continued protection while there was a demon with a history of coveting her crown loose in Faerie.

Which meant, by a twist of fate, he was taking all of the newcomers with him. They'd volunteered, using Korin to speak for the group since he refused to acknowledge Gwendolyn, which meant her companions—Gabriel and Collins—also felt his cold shoulder. Cossette wanted to come too, and he wasn't about to begrudge his "daughter" what she wanted, considering that he owed her greatly.

He held the reins of his elk after thanking the creature in her language for putting up with him. She wasn't the smartest animal, sadly, but she'd put her head in his chest and accepted rubs along her thick neck. Cossette had made sure she wasn't sold, even though her saddlebags had been ransacked.

He still burned with fury that his bags were empty except for the half-carved duck. All the supplies he'd brought from Earth, gone. They'd even sold the case of magically chilled blood. What a fae would do with that...he didn't want to know.

Cloman deserved what he'd gotten and more. Sirius had only held back because he knew Talina was in the audience.

"The Path of Imagination takes many forms," Kalimea said as their group split in two. Those who were accompanying Sirius and Talina stood behind them as the queen gave them instructions. "I can only teleport you so close to Lord Zalice's peak. There's a set of stone arches you will pass under, and up to three paths will become known to you once you do. Each will be difficult in different ways, but you will not know what those challenges are until you choose one path to walk."

Sirius's hackles threatened to rise. There was that idea again: his path. Echoed so much he knew this moment was meant to be by the guiding hand of fate.

Raenith had also known he would see Gwendolyn again, forcing him to consider how he was going to forgive her for her betrayal when he still ached from the repercussions of her actions.

"You will be unable to fly." Kalimea glanced to Talina and then over her shoulder to Gabriel. "The Path of Imagination is a trial for the worthy. There are three similar rituals to undergo if you want an audience in person with the other gods. Most undertake them out of necessity when a god demands it. The gods do not manifest anywhere but their place of power. Some will say that to look upon a god's true face is to invite madness, but the true reason is that our gods are too powerful a presence to wander amongst us without purpose. They can destabilize our weather or atmosphere with just a glance."

She took Talina's hands, pressing a bundle into them. "So, be careful," she murmured. "The Lord of Storms is unpredictable, but he has good reason for wanting to see you. This should cover the travel costs."

"Why does he want to see us?" Talina asked. She glanced inside the pouch, the light catching the glint of gold coins within.

Kalimea lifted her shoulder. "When you find out, do tell me. Everyone's journey to Lord Zalice's home is different, but you will face challenges along the way. You will know he's found you worthy when you see his home in the distance—the highest peak ringed by an eternal storm. You may be blessed with the ability to fly again once you see it."

"Based off of the god's whim?" Sirius grumbled. He distrusted the necessity of most of this. Let them find the god and be done with it, not trudge around waiting to be "challenged" along the way.

The Unseelie Queen flashed him a sharp smile. "That's right. Any other questions?"

Talina fidgeted with her fingers. "How long will it take?" she asked.

"That entirely depends," Kalimea said.

"How long does it take, on average?"

"It varies."

Talina huffed. "How long did it take the last person to do this?"

"I don't know," Kalimea said. "Go and see for yourself."

Sirius interjected with, "What can you tell us, then?"

She gestured, opening a portal for them. "It's cold in the Outer Reaches, especially as you climb further into the mountains. Dress warmly." Her face was set into a bland poker face. There had to be more she wasn't saying, but her burning eyes dared him to demand what it was.

Instead of trying to shake her down, he took a deep breath, letting go of some of his hot anger. *I'm not mad at her,* he told himself, releasing the tension lining his back. "Thank you for your guidance," he said. "And thank you for all of your help. I literally wouldn't be alive without it."

A little smile touched her lips. "Too true. Consider my debt to you paid."

"Debt?" Talina asked quietly, glancing up at him for some explanation.

"Oh, yes. Your man is very human and tried to play it off." Kalimea clasped her hands behind her back. "But he served the Unseelie Court while I was incapacitated and saved many lives while the gates to Ironhold were closed." She tilted her chin up, regal pride marking every line of her body. "All good fae pay their debts. Remember that, Sirius."

He nodded, remembering a discussion with her after he'd fought off Lucia's beasts attacking the fae of Cloman's Own outside Ironhold. At the time, he'd said he hadn't done it to earn any repayment with a queen he'd never met, but she'd gotten angry at that response. Debt was something deeply fae. Kalimea must've been relieved for repaying what she saw as the weight of debt for many of her peoples' lives.

He stepped aside to clasp forearms with Neala, warrior to warrior. "Farewell." At least this time, he could say a proper goodbye to his sister in arms.

"Until we meet again." Her grip on him tightened as he tried to pull away. She murmured in his ear, "Gwendolyn's dying. The least you could do is give her a chance to speak with you."

He growled. "That's not your business."

"Sure it is. She's family." She patted his shoulder, leaving it at that. This time, he didn't engage like she'd baited him, even though his inner beast whispered that she had.

Instead, he turned to Cedric, who startled back a half step at something in his expression. He offered the half-fae a handshake, knowing he must look quite serious. "I mean it about that song," he said.

Cedric blinked, then grinned, shaking his hand enthusiastically. "The best song, of course, but I won't sing it in front of your brother. I'll have no part in this sibling rivalry."

"That means I'll end up with the better song," Sirius said with a laugh.

"Too true, my man. Just throw me a bone here. If he's a dragon, what are you?"

He hardly had to consider it. "A beast." Had Cedric been paying attention?

"I guess that's the shapeshifter way." Cedric twittered like a songbird, his own shifter side. Gem alighted on his lute and sang back wordlessly, giving Sirius a smug look in the process. He fluttered away when Sirius raised his hand.

Cedric struck a melodic chord. "Hmm, no, too pretty..."

"I'll leave you to it," Sirius said, his gaze turning to Ash.

She rolled her eyes. "I love goodbyes. Miss you already," she said sarcastically.

"And I love figuring out what you mean," he responded in the same tone.

"Go die out there."

"Thanks, I will."

Ash sighed. "I mean good luck, okay?"

He patted her shoulder, offering a genuine smile. "I know. I think I've figured out Unseelie speak by now."

"That took forever," she replied. Her annoyed resting face lifted. It was the closest she'd come to smiling at him, so he took it.

Goodbyes said, he headed through the portal to whatever destiny awaited them. The ground sloped upward on the path before him, a rough-cut dirt road. Mountains stabbed into the air in the near distance, and he could make out small villages and roads cutting through the greenery lining the ones closest to him. Though the air was chilly, the plant life thrived. Rich grass marked every available space and hugged the road. Sparse ever-green trees joined them, and the air was sweet with harvest scents as the wind blew from the south. Ten yards ahead was an archway hewn artificially from a massive hunk of stone. He had no doubt this was the starting point Kalimea mentioned.

Yet the far mountains were dusted with white rock and a thick blanket of snow. At some point, they wouldn't be able to rely on their elks either. Kalimea had supplied everyone with one, so he imagined this entire expedition had been quite expensive for the queen. She'd paid him generously for her perceived debt to him, unless her charity stemmed from somewhere else. She did seem fond of Talina.

He smelled her wind-touched scent as she came through the portal next. Drawing her aside for a brief kiss, he held her like he'd been aching to since seeing her shocked face at the end of his duel. "I want you to have this," he said without preamble, pushing the Combat Key into her hand. "We can get you a weapon along the way, unless Korin brought extras."

She balked and nearly dropped it. "W-what? I'm not a fight-er," she protested.

"For your protection." He saw her as the only defenseless one amongst them. Even Cossette possessed an Ancient's strength and speed if she cared to use it. If they were attacked, it would do wonders for his peace of mind to know she was wearing the Key. "I'm not asking you to look for a fight. Just wear it for yourself. Please."

She turned the silvery band over, a crease forming between her brows. The storm clouds were rolling in as she shook her head, trying to pass it back. "I can't. It's part of my..." she slung the traveling pack off her back, rummaging within and producing the leather-bound journal he'd heard so much about.

Was she really referencing that silly thing? He frowned as she opened it and pointed to a line within. "The circle of swords is not meant for you," he said aloud. "But what happened to your journal?"

He took both the ring and the journal, recognizing Izell's handwriting on the page. She'd crossed out and amended certain lines, turning Talina's meticulous notes into a mess.

"When did you meet Izell?" he asked, puzzled.

Talina pressed her lips together. "I didn't. Apparently, this person came in and took my journal, wrote all over it, and put it back."

"Oh. Of course she did," he murmured. He opened up a two-page map with three distinct lines crossing south-to-north based off of a compass rose doodled in the corner.

"Your trial shall feature three:" was written at the top.

There were place names and the vague outline of mountain passes. A map of their three possible paths, he realized. At the very top of the page was a drawing of a bird-like creature with its wings open, but instead of a beak, it had a razor-lined muzzle of sharp teeth. Lightning bolts haloed it. Maybe it was meant to be Zalice, who had taken a dragon form that was similar.

Clues were peppered along the map, but he didn't know what he was looking at. "There's my village," Talina offered, pointing to a mark along the right-side path.

The clue next to her finger read, "Tempest in a teacup."

She touched the writing and sighed. "That's another line in

Lord Zalice's instructions. Actually, that one too. It went like this: Tempest in a teacup, djinni out the bottle. Great things look small to smaller minds."

"It suits you." Maybe she was the tempest in a teacup. She was certainly small and adorable if anyone asked him.

The nearby portal expelled their elks, plus Korin, Gwendolyn, Gabriel, and Collins. Once the drably dressed man was through, the magic disappeared, stranding them together. He didn't really want the extra company, but c'est la vie. Gabriel in particular would make Lucia think twice before attacking again.

"Maybe these hints mean something about the challenges we'd face. If we went this path..." She traced the right-most one, giving a shudder. "I would have a hard time if we passed through my old village."

He kissed her forehead. "Then we won't go there," he murmured.

Gabriel came over as they deliberated over the other two options. "Lord Gabriel," he said, nodding respectfully and introducing Talina. "We're just deciding which path to take to our destination."

"If it helps, Gwendolyn and I came because I could sense a demonic presence here. The feeling has gotten much stronger since we stepped through the portal," he said, straight to business. Just like the Gabriel he used to know.

He bit back a sarcastic comment. "Lucia is here," he answered. "Can you sense which direction would take us to her?"

They all squared their feet toward the north. Gabriel's eyes glowed faintly with angelic magic. "Is this our map? I would say she is fairly close." He indicated the leftmost path.

Sirius read the clues there, puzzling over what Izell was trying to tell them. If "Tempest in a teacup" meant Talina, then the other lines must also relate to someone. The three clues lined up to read:

Sinner on the rise.

Snake in a suit.

Djinni out the bottle.

He guessed they would figure it out as they went. It was

unhelpful and vague until then, though. "Considering how I don't recognize any of these clues, perhaps we should pick this route," he said. "If there's anything I've learned, it's that I need to pick the most difficult path to walk."

Talina hesitated before nodding in agreement. He flipped through her journal, realizing that Izell had re-written Zalice's words, undoubtedly into a real prophecy.

You have found each other at last
Walk your path with pride
No new words shall be whispered
A lonely god awaits his kin
Your tasks, three
Shall you save her?
Choose wisely.

"Of course I'm going to save her," he muttered, passing the prophecy to Talina when he noticed her craning her neck to read it too.

"Of course. She's going to get saved," she echoed.

For some reason, Sirius had the feeling they were talking about different people. They exchanged a glance, and she shrugged.

Chapter 31
Talina

"You won't be able to keep Raenith's blessing if you don't talk to her," she told Sirius a few days later. It was a fresh morning, a cool breeze on her face as they continued along the trade road gently winding around the mouth of the Outer Reaches. Villages dotted their path, guaranteeing they had a place to sleep each night.

"It hasn't faded yet. Nothing can be easy for Gwendolyn, else she'll use us for her own purposes again," Sirius muttered. His jaw was set stubbornly as he fixed his gaze ahead.

"But you forgave Adrius." In the wee hours before morning, he'd woken her to try to seal their bond again. Sadly, nothing yet, though she felt the moment was getting closer. His defenses fell after the mind-blowing pleasure they shared, enough that he admitted the Goddess of Fire had managed to pull him into one of Adrius's dreams so they could chat and find a new equilibrium.

Sirius played with shadows now, letting them dance and whirl between his fingers. He was starting small, as his brother had taught him, seeing how the magic would respond to a new owner. Forgiving his brother was the easy part, she thought. She knew Sirius had to love his brother greatly to have given up so much for him.

But Gwendolyn? He avoided her, and she avoided him, meaning Talina had barely said more than a "nice to meet you" to the elderly nephilim riding side-saddle between Gabriel and Collins. Every day that passed, the tension amongst them grew as they fractured into two uneven halves. Only Korin and Cossette floated between either group.

"That was different," Sirius said, echoing her thoughts. "I'll work up to it. Promise."

She nodded, hoping it was soon. She tugged on her elk's reins a few minutes later, idling until she could ride alongside the other group. The road was wide enough for three-abreast, so Gabriel noticed what she was doing and rode ahead to join Sirius and have a quiet discussion with him.

"Good morning. Talina, was it?" Gwendolyn offered a smile. "Have you met Bryant yet?"

She glanced past her to the vampire, who lifted his head. "I know of you more than anything," she admitted.

"There's not much to know," he answered quietly. "Bryant Collins, Ancient-aged vampire. My hubris led to the deaths of my wife and our whole coven, so I serve Lord Gabriel as his squire for penance."

Her eyes softened in sympathy. "I'm sorry for your loss."

He glanced away, clearing his throat. "So am I."

Gwendolyn's nod toward him seemed approving. "What can we do for you, Talina?" she asked.

Now that she was closer to this woman, she tried to push out Sirius's biases and focus on what she saw before her. She hadn't met many human-born, and most she'd run across were immortal vampires who never gained a wrinkle as time advanced. To see someone wizened by time was a curiosity. It was a reminder that humans aged and eventually passed away, like many species of lesser fae.

"I know of you as well," Talina said slowly. "Sirius is not very complimentary. I was wondering if, maybe, you'd tell me your side of the story."

Gwendolyn raised a brow. "You want to know why he hates me. If you're thinking of playing peacemaker, don't. I think we've both come to terms with what's broken between us."

"Maybe not," Talina murmured.

"I did my duty to the world," Gwendolyn continued, her golden eyes hazy with memories. "It was a sacrifice that needed to be made. Are you familiar with Fell Madness? Did he tell you about it?"

Talina nodded, her hands tightening on her elk's reins. She hoped there was some glimmer of hope here, something Sirius had misunderstood and blown out of proportion.

"All vampires have some Fell Madness in them. Humans turn into vampires by taking a bit of the curse, after all. For the Fell Hunters—Adrius, Sirius, Neala, and the rest—the level of Fell within them was very high. They drank directly from the monsters' veins to build up the power to fight them and survive.

"Talina, you have to understand the times. We were terrified of the Madness. Sane people turned into fiends with one drop too much of Fell blood in their system. It was nearly irreversible. The only thing that *could* do something about it was a potion made from the blood of my daughter, Nyah." Her thin lips pressed together, catching on something she didn't want to say aloud.

"But you all thought Nyah was dead because of Lucia," Talina supplied, earning a look of gratitude.

"That's right. For over a thousand years, I thought my little girl was gone," she sighed. "And in her absence, we had no way to tame the Fell Madness. I learned that the level of magical power within a vampire corresponds to how corrupted they are on the inside. And the former Fell Hunters were very powerful indeed. All of them were on short fuses, one spike of high emotion away from snapping and murdering everyone around them."

"Like Sirius tried to avoid with Adrius," Talina said mostly to herself.

Gwendolyn nodded quietly in agreement. "So, I did what I had to. I waited until an event which brought most of vampire kind together and trapped them on a sinking Nyixa by poisoning them all with a sleeping draught. My main target was Lucia..." The light in her eyes dimmed. "I admit it was a mistake not to kill her directly, but I wanted her to suffer for what she'd done to me. She ended up in the same room with the Blood Princes and Adrius and cast a spell over the room to give them air to breathe while they slept. Fell Madness was contained for a thousand years."

She thought about it quietly, piecing apart the nephilim's words for something she could use to help Sirius. "You meant to kill everyone, Sirius included," she noted. *A huge betrayal.*

"I did." Gwendolyn's lips trembled. "I thought for a very long time that I'd murdered what was left of my family. It was better that way, that they were dead rather than human-killing monsters. As penance, I've made sure other vampires who've grown too old, powerful, and corrupted disappear for one reason or another."

Talina shook her head slowly. "Why not find another way?"

Grim shadows lined Gwendolyn's wrinkled face. "There was no other way at the time. For a thousand years, I have contemplated the 'what ifs' and the 'what abouts' in search of what I could've done better. It's a miracle Nyah survived and we were able to reconnect with her. That's the only thing, I truly believe, that has us on the right path once more."

She heard the older woman's faith for her daughter. It softened the harsh reality Gwendolyn had to face...the terrible choice she'd had to make. "Sirius took your betrayal personally," she said, realizing where the disconnect was between the two of them.

"Of course he did." Gwendolyn's tone was neutral, though her eyes gleamed with unshed tears. "Though the other Blood Princes have found it in themselves to understand my choice and forgive me, Sirius has not. I imagine he never will."

"It sounded like you two were pretty close once," Talina ventured.

The nephilim pressed her hand to her mouth.

"Perhaps a conversation for another time," Collins interjected, glancing over with concern.

Gwendolyn waved his worries away. "No, no, it's quite all right. I can admit it." She dropped her voice to keep it between the three of them. "Sirius was like a son to me. Always volunteering to help and caring for me when I needed it. If I could've saved him from his fate, I would've. But I knew the corruption was strong within him." She swiped at her face and gave Talina a shaky smile. "He's come a long way since he first woke up. I imagine he has you to thank for that."

Talina's brows drew together, thoughtful. "He still has farther to go. It's going to work out, just you wait."

"I hope you're right, young lady. Aren't you sweet to come over and hear me out? Maybe you can convince him to do the same." Talina nodded, thinking that was the only way he would have a chance to forgive her and keep Raenith's blessing.

Chapter 32
Jaromir

Jaromir caved and allowed Sondus to assist him with his research after a few days of reading alongside him. The fae was more resourceful than he could ever be, accessing the restricted sections thanks to his wife's connections.

"I'm fairly sure you've been given an impossible task," Sondus said over the edge of *Greatest Work Spells*, a thin book without a translation spell on the inside, thus limited to his fae eyes. "No one's written down King Oberon's spell. I don't think anyone's alive who was there that day."

"One person is," Jaromir murmured, though he didn't dare say her name. He avoided mentioning Izell just like she avoided him. At this point, he was fairly sure she'd abandoned him to flounder here in this library. Out of sight, out of mind.

For God's sake, she'd been chewing on an herb to keep a demonic spirit contained. It had to be Jazrach's spark, which meant she was in incredible danger now that she'd given away her lifeline to controlling it. In a matter of months, it'd bent Lucia's mind into madness a thousand years ago. How quickly would it hook into Izell's powerful magic and start twisting her thoughts?

"Even if it was written down, you won't be able to diagram a new spell on your own. Advanced spellcasting is something greater fae study all their lives," Sondus continued, frowning. "And nothing is more complicated than a greatest work spell."

"Does it grow more complex with thirteen people?" One for each Fell Key.

"Thirteen times more so," Sondus sighed, placing his book aside. "Look, you need a fae doing this research. Someone who already understands advanced foci and line parallels and everything else that goes into creating a new spell."

Jaromir chuckled without humor. "I have you, don't I?"

"I'm about as useful to you as any other lesser fae. If you want to know a secret...I have almost no magic." Sondus waved away an illusion on his back, showing that he was wingless. Alaku glanced up from the book he was scanning, freezing with huge owl eyes at the sight.

"My disability prevented me from accessing formal training in high magic functions," Sondus sighed.

"I would offer to heal you, but I, too, have a disability," Jaromir said. He felt for the other man, knowing what it felt like to be disconnected from his potential. Finally, he admitted that he probably wasn't going to be able to help Izell with the task she'd given him. He could leave this library and try to petition King Orin for an audience instead. The King of Faerie held the Mending Key, a prize that would give Jaromir the one thing he wanted more than anything...his Gift returned.

Sitting back, he told Sondus and Alaku about the attack of Fell Mad in New York. Though it felt like years ago, it had only been months at the most since he'd pushed Sorsha out of the way of an attack and gotten bitten and afflicted by a version of the Madness that spread via infected saliva.

"If she were bitten, she would transform into a Fell. It was a sacrifice I was glad to make." Though, he delivered these words stiffly. A Fell with Sorsha's Archfae-level magic would've decimated New York. He would push her out of the way again in a heartbeat. But he still wasn't complete without the magic that had abandoned him from his brush with dark insanity.

Sondus stared, his face flickering with rapid thoughts. "Sorsha Shadestone is one of my good friends," he said, pensive. "It sounds like she was unable to fulfill her debt to you."

Jaromir frowned. "She doesn't owe me a debt."

The fae shook his head dismissively. "She definitely does. You saved her from a fate worse than death and lost your only magic in the process. I cannot in good faith allow you to continue sitting here, reading day and night, without making an attempt to assist you." Sondus shot to his feet, brushing off his tunic. "Stay right here."

He exchanged a glance with Alaku, who shrugged. The teen held Sofia the pup, playing with her fur as he took the lull as an excuse to close his book as well. "Does this mean you're done here, Prince Jaromir?" he asked, fidgeting with Sofia's floppy ears while she panted happily from the attention.

If Jaromir called it quits, he knew Alaku would be reassigned to help someone else with their research projects. He considered the pile of books they'd amassed and frowned.

Did he truly believe Izell would bend the truth to keep him here?

It was an ugly thought, which he pushed away. No, there had to be some other reason she hadn't trusted him enough to share. Izell asked for a great deal of faith and trust, perhaps too much. But everything she wanted, she wanted for a specific reason, and he knew if he was patient, he would probably learn it.

"I don't think we're done quite yet," he assured Alaku, continuing to read for a while until another young research assistant ran a message to him.

It was an invitation to go to lunch with Sondus and "someone with the ability to help you" at a local café.

What was there to lose? "I'm going to take a lunch break," he told Alaku. "Why don't you take Sofia for a walk?" The teen popped a bright smile.

WHEN JAROMIR THOUGHT OF A FAE WHO COULD HELP HIM, he envisioned that Sondus had somehow pulled strings to get him a private audience with King Orin. That was impossible, though. The man was busy with the Light Eye of Worlds and was visiting with no one, not even his most trusted advisors.

So, who else could it be? He hoped there was another recourse to a Fell Key anyway. Something more permanent, akin to the spelled potion which had granted Neala a second voice. Surely there was another such draught for a second Gift, even if the Gift was a purely vampire-owned classification of magic.

Sondus had picked a café only a couple blocks from the Library of Faerie, so Jaromir wasn't left with much time to ponder and worry. The cheery shop was painted light red, with an awning covering a front patio. It stood in the corner between two streets, broadcasting the scent of baked goods and coffee to those who walked by. "Over here!" Sondus waved from a circular table on the patio, sitting across from another man who looked distinctively human, with suntanned skin and a plain robe. He turned and smiled warmly, like greeting an old friend.

As soon as Jaromir sat with them, Sondus introduced him as Soren. An angel. It felt like his eyes were about to pop right from his head. "No kidding, an angel?" he asked, then felt terribly rude. If his former commander, Gabriel Legion, could come back as an angel, surely others could as well.

He'd even heard this man's name before, but they hadn't crossed paths until now. "No kidding," Soren said. He continued smiling rather than taking any offense. "I'd offer to show you my magic, but the light would hurt you. Sondus was just telling me a bit about you. Is it true you sacrificed your magic for someone else?"

"Yes," Jaromir sighed. It didn't sit right that most in Faerie knew him through this fault of his being.

A gentle light seemed to shine from the angel's smile. "Is there anything more beautiful than a sacrifice such as yours? Yet you are unhappy."

"I'm not worth much without my magic," he replied. It was obvious he was left behind while his companions traveled Faerie.

Soren looked thoughtful, steepling his fingers. "And did you feel fulfilled when you had it?"

Jaromir frowned. "That's a loaded question." The answer stung his tongue like a thousand tiny needles. It still wasn't any of this man's business.

A server interrupted to take Jaromir's drink order. Once he had an ice water before him, he considered his company anew. How would this angel be able to help him when Gabriel couldn't?

"Did you know there has been a devoted study of former vampires in Heaven?" Soren said, as if sensing the direction of his thoughts. "Ordinary humans..." He waved a hand with a shrug. "No magic. No immortality. Those things disrupt the process of souls being sorted to their final resting places."

"Hmm." Jaromir lifted a brow. He hoped this man wasn't going to try talking him out of seeking his Gift back.

For a moment, Soren seemed troubled. His luminous smile hid like clouds passing before the sun. "Most vampiric abilities come from the darker side of fae magic. Mind control, glamor, enhanced speed and strength, all designed for hunting human beings. We had to make new rules for vampires so we didn't judge them immediately to Hell for craving the taste of blood. There is one power that we approve of, and that is the Gift. Do you know what causes the Gift in vampires, Jaromir?"

"It's random," he answered. "Even amongst families. Take a pair of children with Gifted parents. One may end up Gifted too, the other an ordinary vampire."

Soren let the sun shine again through his expression. "We discovered that it is a latent thing, through the bloodlines of angels. Very, very dilute drops of nephilim blood in ordinary people."

Jaromir's jaw dropped. "How could you know that for sure?"

"We have records, dear man. There are no people forgotten in our annals, not even those who went on to be the most vile of demon kind. So, I can say with surety, the tiny part of you that was nephilim was sacrificed for the greater good. Perhaps...we can get it back."

Sitting back, Jaromir kept himself grounded while the world reeled. He would've never guessed that he had even a fraction of the abilities Gwendolyn or Nyah wielded. "It makes a lot of sense," he said, sounding distant to his own ears, "that it comes from angels. The Gift leaves if it's used to take lives."

Soren nodded. "Being a healer is only meant to serve good."

It was difficult to wrangle his desire into a polite question. Usually, Jaromir didn't struggle with the urge to jump across a table at someone in desperation, but he realized this angel really might be able to fulfill what he wanted so badly. "And you can give it back to me? My Gift?"

"I can't make promises, but if you can gain fae abilities with a taste of their blood, why couldn't an angel's blood do the same for you?" Soren glanced to Sondus, who listened to the side with a keen, bright gaze. "Do you have something sharp?"

Sondus patted his pockets before producing a wicked-looking dagger from his boot. Jaromir blinked in surprise. "Just in case." The fae winked.

"Do you want to give it a try?" Soren asked.

Again, he held his eagerness close as he eyed the sharp edge so close to the angel's wrist. "What could it hurt?" he asked.

Soren nodded, pricking his skin with the tip to gather a bead of blood. It caught the light, gleaming like a drop of pure white light, before he tipped the blade and let it fall into Jaromir's ice water. "I freely give you my power," he said as it happened.

Well, maybe it could hurt him, Jaromir reflected. He stirred the water with the handle of a fork, feeling the glass grow warmer and slick with condensation. It didn't burn him, but the threat was there as the drink seemed to glow.

"It won't burn you since it's freely given," Soren said. He leaned forward expectantly as Jaromir nodded, taking a cautious sip just in case.

The water was still cool and crisp, layered with a citrusy bite. It called to him to take another sip. His fangs descended so quickly his gums ached as his body recognized there was blood on offer. He ended up knocking the rest back, drinking with his throat and fangs alike and crunching on the ice for any remnants of angel blood.

He flexed his fingers, waiting for the familiar tingle of energy to return. His attention was so focused on his pale fingertips that he didn't notice the pressure mounting in his chest. It emerged with a bubble of heat, traveling up his throat to get stuck on the edge of a hiccup. He struck his chest, trying to dislodge it.

"Are you in pain?" Sondus asked. He sounded far away.

Pain? It felt like his body was aflame. His skin reddened as every nerve ending chafed. At first, he'd likened it to the touch of Faerie's pleasant sunshine, but it swiftly increased until he boiled from within.

"Jaromir?" someone shouted from a distance.

He tipped out of his chair, and the ground slapped his cheek. His ears rang with static.

"Damn you, you said you could help him," Sondus hissed, his voice barely a whisper as dark spots closed in on Jaromir's vision.

His hands blossomed with heat while his palms wavered between feeling numb and raw. Light spun from his fingertips in fractals, burning and mending. *Fascinating,* was his last thought before the darkness took him.

Chapter 33
Sirius

They slept out under the stars that night, before coming across a sprawling town covering the tallest hill for miles. Talina leaned up in her saddle, gasping as she gazed across endless grassy fields and forests, tilted and raised like a guiding hand hadn't finished smoothing out the wrinkles in this part of Faerie. The air was cool and crisp, drawing earthy smells through Sirius's nostrils and making his beast sigh in contentment.

It would be a perfect day, if Gabriel wasn't galloping up to join him and Talina where they rode at the head of their group. Gabriel wasn't so bad, he reminded himself. He obviously didn't approve of Sirius's decision to avoid his wife, but that translated to curt discussions rather than lectures.

"She's here," Gabriel greeted him.

He uttered a soft growl, his hands clenching on the reins. "How close?" he demanded.

Gabriel jerked his chin ahead, where they could see the front gates to the largest settlement they'd come across in the Outer Reaches. "Very close. I can take you right to her," the angel said.

Sirius motioned for him to take the lead and turned to Talina. "Why don't you hang back? For your protection." Her wonder at the view was gone, replaced with a scattering of clouds across her eyes.

Still, she lifted her chin. "I have my lightning. If we really take her by surprise..." She flexed her fingertips, displaying several bright arcs of electricity between them.

"Sure. But let us go first, okay?" He gave her a tender look, not intending to let her get close to Lucia again. He, Korin, and Gabriel would handle her, the latter of which would need to deliver the finishing blow to destroy Lucia's demonic spirit at last.

His beast stirred with eagerness to finally have a chance to sink teeth and talons into the woman who'd caused them so much pain. She'd probably tried to turn the fae in this town against them, expecting Sirius and Talina alone instead of their bolstered traveling group. For the first time, he was glad they hadn't undertaken this challenge alone.

Talina rode right behind him as they slowed to a more casual-looking canter along the cobblestone road cutting through the town's center. The afternoon sun shone cheery light over clusters of fae going about their tasks. He noticed most fae were either the Wind-aligned greater fae or lesser creatures with wings or ethereal bodies. Curious smiles and friendly waves followed their group's progress.

He sure hoped Lucia hadn't poisoned these peoples' minds. It was nice to get a warm welcome for once.

Gabriel held up his fist, dismounting from his elk. Cries of alarm sounded as he drew his sword, and Talina's breath caught at the sight of it. It was beautifully crafted, gleaming with golden runes and bright, angelic magic. "Show yourself, fiend," he announced, pointing the sharp tip straight at a terran fae woman laden with a stack of laundry.

She froze, her pink hair fluttering around her as a blast of magic stilled her form. Shirts and underwear scattered on the cobblestones. The woman's hands flexed, and she jerked like a fish on a line. The glamor layered over her true form started to peel away, and Sirius's vicious grin faded in confusion as, rather than wearing teal scales, her body was glowing and otherworldly.

Instead of legs, she had a trailing column of smoke which extended from her waist into a tapered funnel of air. A long tunic covered her modesty and was belted around the waist as the ends blew around from a personal wind, just like the sheet of her raven-black hair. Her skin glowed a bright red, and her long, lovely face was screwed up with deep ire. The bangles around her wrists clanked as she clapped her hands.

Sirius felt the breath in his lungs seize as his body was forced to still. Talina uttered a soft gasp of dismay. And Gabriel was frozen as a statue, his sword tip still wicking the sunlight.

"How very *rude*," the revealed demon huffed, crossing her arms and meeting the gaze of one of the fae around her. "Can you believe it?"

"Incredibly so," the fae agreed.

"Invited into our town, welcomed with open arms, just to assault me with magic," she grumbled, turning her dark gaze toward Gabriel's trembling form. She pointed back at him, and he stumbled, rubbing his arm as he lowered the sword. "Explain yourself."

"We are on the hunt for a demon, and I sensed you. You may not be the demon we're looking for, but—" As he took a step forward with intent, she clapped her hands again, freezing him.

She pointed at Talina. "You look more reasonable."

"I'm sorry, please don't hurt us," Talina said, her voice a frightened squeak. Sirius tried to ball his fingers into a fist, ready to put them through this demon's face for scaring his mate.

"Why do you think I'm going to hurt you?" the other woman sighed. "You lot are the ones who assaulted me. Lord Zalice told me you were coming, but I didn't expect it to be like this." Her gaze drifted from Talina to Sirius. "My name is Saniya, the first and perhaps only free wishmaker djinni. I am to administer your first challenge."

She clapped her hands, and Sirius felt his muscles start to respond again. He took a deep gasp of air, exchanging a look of disbelief with Talina. Obviously, the challenge was not to kill this woman, not that he wanted to. Even Gabriel sheathed his sword upon feeling the hostility of the crowd of fae around them.

He saluted her crisply. "I apologize, lady djinni."

"As you should," she said, nose lifting.

"You have no affiliation with Hell?"

"Why would I serve the same demons that bottled me up and

forced me to serve a family of wicked souls? Now come, I welcome you into my home, despite your worst intentions." She clapped her hands again, and her clothes were stacked neatly in her arms within a blink. She floated wordlessly toward a small manor in the corner of town, big enough to be an inn. The wood siding was painted in a cheerful swirl of colors, and the few fae they passed had respectful nods and smiles for her.

Sirius fought the guilty feeling rumbling in his stomach as some of the same fae turned distrustful looks at his group while they helped whisk their elks away. How were they to know that there was a secret demon hiding in Faerie? He certainly hoped Gabriel could turn his faulty demon sensing abilities toward the right demon, else he would be useless in pinpointing Lucia.

"You are welcome to spend the night here while the challenge is ongoing," Saniya said, opening the front door for them.

Her home rolled with heat from an extra-large hearth. What caught his attention was how she'd hung colorful pictures and scenic portraits everywhere, covering plain walls and surrounding herself with vivid images. For someone who could magically have most anything—as he assumed her magic worked—she had modestly furnished rooms otherwise. While she pointed everyone else upstairs to settle for the afternoon, she drew him and Talina into a sitting room with a porcelain tea set and her scowling self as she rested her undulating column of smoke in a rocking chair.

"I'm really sorry we thought you were an evil demon," Talina said, accepting a cup of steaming tea.

Saniya lifted a shoulder, drinking from a boiling-hot cup without so much as a flinch. "I suppose you should've had more of a warning than 'djinni out the bottle'," she replied. "Which, if you haven't guessed yet, refers to me."

"No kidding," Sirius muttered.

She lifted an eyebrow at him. "Which of you will undertake my challenge?"

"I will," he said automatically.

"Very well. That means the next challenge shall belong to you, dear." She smiled over at Talina. "And the last, of course, will be split between you both. I cannot offer you any hints of what is to come, but Lord Zalice is eager to meet with you both. Should you fail my challenge or the second one, he may allow you to continue on rather than restarting on a different path."

Sirius's brow drew into a hard scowl. "If he is so eager, why play games with these 'challenges' in the first place?"

Saniya's full lips spread. "Why indeed? That is the way of Faerie. You accepted three boons, with some of the debt shouldered by Talina. Now, you must both prove yourselves through three challenges."

He cast an uncertain glance to Talina, who was nodding in agreement. If it made sense to her, he wouldn't protest too hard, but...he still hated the fact that she'd had to repay any kind of debt for his sake. "Fine. What is your challenge?" he asked.

"Go get cozy upstairs. I'll visit with you soon," she said to Talina instead.

He shifted uncomfortably to be alone with this woman. Despite her claims, she'd neutralized the group of them with two claps of her hands. What would stop her from killing the lot of them now that they were under her roof?

"Relax," she sighed, reading his expression. "Today is a joyful day for one of your friends, and you get to pick which one. My challenge is fairly straightforward. I'm going to ask everyone for what wish would make them happiest. Now, you have to understand that not everything is within my power to grant. I cannot bring anyone back from the dead or influence actions that happened in the past."

"Right," he said slowly.

"Your challenge is to select which person I should grant their wish to. If it's within my power, I shall grant it, but your task is also to select the most meaningful wish to the person who asked for it."

"Without knowing what they wished for?"

She gave a thumbs-up. "That's right. How well do you know your group? Which wish will benefit the world best?" She swirled out of her chair, floating up to him and leaning in. "If you could have anything right now, what would you wish for, Sirius Raphael Fabron?"

His voice emerged in a low rumble. "How do you know my name?"

"I know many things," she responded, her dark eyes glimmering. "My power is only second to the gods of this land, who tolerate my presence here as long as I am beneficent. So...what is your wish?"

If that was supposed to impress him, she'd fallen short. He loosed a soft chuff. "If you are so powerful, why not grant all of our wishes at once?"

Multicolored glimmers danced through her gaze. "Who says I have to be *that* beneficent when your leader's first instinct was to kill me? Consider yourself lucky that I will fulfill one wish, you selfish man."

He stilled, his breath catching. *Selfish.* The accusation rang differently from a stranger's lungs, especially one who definitely knew more than she should.

"I don't have a wish," he muttered, turning his head away from her knowing stare. "I am not selfish enough to ask you to fulfill a wish that I make."

"Right answer." She stood straight, floating from the room while he turned his attention to the tea still steaming in his hand. He took a sip, enjoying the crisp warmth of the mint as he waited.

He could do this, even though he wished he could run after her and demand what his heart truly desired: that she make it possible for him and Talina to complete their mating bond. Even as he thought it, he knew there would be better wishes uttered by the rest of his group.

But if he could only choose one, he would have to analyze everything he knew about his group. Gabriel and Collins were huge blanks. What would an angel even want? He would return to Heaven once his duty to kill a demon was finished. And Collins...

Sirius twisted his lips. He should've at least talked to the man by now and asked what his purpose was. Now, Sirius could only guess what he wanted, except perhaps for his wife's life back.

"Are you ready to play, Sirius?" Saniya was back before he knew it, floating into her rocking chair after pouring a new cup of tea. The liquid boiled automatically at her touch, and she drank it down still bubbling. "You cannot speak to any of them, but I will confirm if you guess what they wished for correctly."

"And from there, you want me to select the most meaningful. How do you define that?" He frowned, feeling the pressure of expectation settling on his shoulders.

"A wish that I can grant that will do the most good going forward," she responded.

"All right. Talina wished for her ankle to be permanently fixed," he guessed, and she shook her head. "She...wished to finish the connection between us?"

"That's right," the djinni said. Oh, how tempting it was to stop there, but he gritted his teeth against the urge even as his chest filled with warmth. He knew with time, they'd figure out how to complete the mating bond without anyone else's help.

"Korin wanted the blood of the fae Lucia's controlling so he can track her," he continued.

"That's right."

"Collins wanted his wife back?"

She nodded in acknowledgement.

He stroked his jaw, thinking of Gwendolyn. What would she truly want? He didn't think she'd ever wish for something for herself. She was like that. Selfless, sacrificing. Even if she tried to sacrifice things that didn't belong to her, such as his life.

"Gwendolyn wished for another Dark Eye to be constructed," he said, sparing a little smile when she nodded again. "But that's not within your power to grant, is it?"

"Alas, no," she sighed. "Wouldn't it be nice to wish away such a big problem, though?"

That ruled Gwendolyn's wish out, at least, and Collins's too, since she couldn't bring a person back from the grave.

"I have no idea what Gabriel wished for," he admitted. "Did he want to know Lucia's whereabouts as well?"

She chuckled quietly. "No."

"Did he wish for me to be smitten with holy fire?"

"If you are truly so clueless to his inner thoughts, perhaps you should focus on your last friend," she remarked.

He sucked in a breath, because he'd truly forgotten about Cossette for a moment. *I'm your guide,* she'd said. *Izell promised I'd get what I came here for if I helped you.*

The answer was so obvious he smacked himself in the face. "I want you to fulfill Cossette's wish," he said.

A smile tugged at her lips. "No guesses as to what she wished for first?"

"No. This game's over. Fulfill her wish," he demanded.

She clapped twice. "As you wish."

High-pitched screaming sounded from upstairs a moment later.

Chapter 34
Talina

She looked out the window as she waited, hoping Sirius picked her wish. How nice would it be to feel the permanent bond snapping into place between them? She knew just what she'd say when they had another moment alone: *I wished for you. I love you.*

So, when someone else started screaming a room away, she startled in surprise. Had he picked a different wish? She scrambled and forced open the door to Cossette's room, witnessing how the girl had tumbled off her bed, her fingers grasping her head as her body changed and her dress strained to contain her.

Talina didn't know what was going on, but she whirled as she felt a large presence at her back. "Out," she demanded of Korin, seeing Gabriel was right behind him. She pushed at the stunned vampire, getting him to back up a step as he stared over her shoulder. She closed the door after him.

Bones popped and fabric shredded as Talina rushed to kneel at Cossette's side. She gasped for breath as she lay out, no longer screaming as her cloudy, red gaze stared at the ceiling. Tears pricked the corners of her eyes.

"He picked me," she whispered. "I saw so many futures where he didn't."

Lying before Talina wasn't a girl, but a fully grown human-born woman with Cossette's features, covered in scraps of her child-sized dress. She wore a disbelieving smile instead as she wept, clasping Talina's hands. "After nine hundred years," she hiccupped.

She couldn't help but share the newly aged woman's tears. Within a split second, she knew Sirius had made the right decision and given Cossette an otherwise impossible gift. "Let me get you something to wear," she said with a giddy laugh. Cossette struggled to stand, so Talina helped, realizing that she was nearly Sirius's height of six feet but lean like a bird with nearly no curves to speak of. Still, her clothes probably wouldn't fit the vampiress well.

She turned to go back to her room anyway, only to find Saniya floating at the door with some of her laundry in hand. "For the lady," she said, flashing a brilliant smile as she offered it forward. They stepped into the hall to give Cossette a moment to change.

"Your man has passed his challenge," Saniya murmured. She cast Gabriel a dirty look as he peeked out of his room.

"Everything's okay! Cossette's a woman now," Talina called for his benefit, since it was obvious the djinni wouldn't be talking to him.

His eyes widened in surprise, and he ducked back to speak with Gwendolyn. There were guest rooms all along this hallway, and they'd filled most of them, with Gabriel and Gwendolyn sharing their space and Talina assuming she was doing the same with Sirius.

"He guessed correctly as to what you all wished for, except for his wish," Saniya confided. "Gabriel wished to bring his wife back to good health."

"He hasn't really spoke with them," Talina whispered back.

"That will change. Raenith is not the most patient of the Four." The djinni shrugged, then smiled behind her. "Ready to make your debut?" she asked of Cossette.

The woman wore a tunic a size too baggy for her frame, though the pale lime color was reminiscent of the pastels she favored. "I must be," she said, her voice a soft lilt. Her curls came to her chin, framing an oval face with pale features. Her eyelashes had grown out and were two white fans shielding wet, albino-red eyes as she continued to weep at this change in her fortune.

She rushed forward and hugged the djinni and Talina together. "This is the best day of my life," she whispered. "I've scried it so many times, and now it's here."

"It is a beautiful day, indeed." Saniya cupped her face. "I hope you make the most of your new start."

"*Oui*. Of course." Cossette sniffed and wiped at her eyes. "First, there's something I must do."

The djinni nodded and floated to the side. Talina followed curiously as Cossette went downstairs, flinging her tearful self into Sirius's arms.

"Thank you! Thank you so much," she said, giving him the kind of hug that would crush an ordinary person. "This is the best gift."

He met Talina's gaze briefly, his ruby gaze shining with emotion. "I'm glad it worked—let me get a look at you." Cossette dutifully took a step back, smiling broadly. "You're still an albino."

"Of course, I am just an adult now. No change in anything else, right?" she directed to Saniya.

"Correct. You shall still need to overcome your child side's urges."

"But I am not expected to be a child anymore." Cossette tittered with glee. "Thank you again, Dad."

Sirius stirred in surprise. "Wait—"

"My father sold me to the man who broke me," she said, offering him a shaky smile. "It would be an honor if I could still call you..." A soft blush lit her cheeks. "...I mean, if it's not too uncomfortable."

Sirius beckoned to Talina. As she came to his side, she realized the rest of their group had snuck up behind her, all lined up on the staircase witnessing this moment. Gwendolyn held her hands to her face, weeping openly to see this gift for the former girl-Ancient. Gabriel supported her with an arm around her shoulders, whispering something in her ear. Even Collins, who seemed stony and distant, smiled broadly. Korin stared at Cossette, his brow lightly furrowed.

Talina put her hand in Sirius's. "What do you think?" he murmured. "Do you want a daughter? It doesn't feel right to make this decision without you."

She put a hand to her chest, a giddy feeling dancing within. For him to be asking meant that he saw only a future with her. He wouldn't be the only one adopting Cossette very soon, once they were properly bonded as mates. "Of course," she said, smiling broadly. "She deserves a better family alongside her new start."

The three of them embraced together. "Life can't be too bad if someone wants to join my family," Sirius murmured.

"Two someones," Talina reminded with a playful wink.

Cossette laughed, sniffing as she wiped away another fall of happy tears. "Life's great. Things are really looking up."

By the time they parted, the others had come forward to meet this new version of Cossette. Talina gave Sirius's hand a squeeze, so proud of his choice even if it meant their mating had to wait. "I'd best go help her shop for new clothes," she said.

"She will need a sword as well."

She blinked in surprise. "Why?"

He flashed the Combat Key between two fingers. "If I can't put this on your finger, maybe she'll take an extra level of protection."

THE TOWNSPEOPLE WERE WARM WITH THEIR NEW LITTLE family when they ventured out to buy supplies. It seemed the only one who would continue to receive a cold reception was Gabriel after so boldly challenging Saniya in broad daylight.

Talina enjoyed dolling up Cossette so much more now that her form reflected the woman within her. She used up some of their traveling money to make sure she was ready again for travel with several changes of clothing and a set of light armor.

Cossette left them to stroll alone as the sun set. Sirius shared that he'd ordered the sword, to be presented to the newly made woman tomorrow. Talina held her reservations, knowing Cossette needed an opportunity to learn how to defend herself.

"Well, should we return to the djinni's home?" Talina suggested.

He shook his head. "I have a better idea."

They walked hand in hand outside the walls of the town, where the long grass started and extended into rolling fields. As the sun set, the distant hills and forests lit with shades of amethyst and sapphire. The sight caught her breath and made her want to wander and fly above the land to see if it was just an optical illusion.

Sirius parted from her to bow, extending his hand in an invitation. It felt like an eternity since they'd taken some alone time for this, so she let him lead her into a slow dance. Their foreheads touched as they rocked together.

"I wished for us to have a complete bond," she whispered.

"I know. I want it too," he murmured, his warm gaze on her as the last trickles of sunshine lit his face. "We have time to try again."

"I know," she echoed. Nerves tickled her throat as she considered the very words she wanted to say if he'd picked her wish. "I love you, Sirius."

His nostrils flared on a soft gasp, which she muffled with a stolen kiss. "What you did for Cossette was just...so amazing. I don't think you give yourself enough credit," she continued. "You have such a good heart within you."

"I'm glad you think so. You have more faith in me than most," he murmured, tracing her cheek with a gentle thumb.

"Because I've seen the true Sirius," she said. The kind of man who continued to give, even after giving so much of himself in the past. Who persevered when an ordinary man would break or walk away. "Maybe someday, you'll open up and let others in again."

"Maybe," he agreed. "Maybe this old beast can learn to start again."

"Didn't you say you're fifty-something?"

He laughed. "On the inside!"

"Then you're not an old beast," she said, giggling.

His mirth faded quickly as he cradled her jaw, pressing a tender kiss to her lips. "I love you too," he said. She soaked in the moment. Time and familiarity had made his human-born features precious to her, from the not-quite-perfect texture of his skin to the quirk in the bridge of his nose. His eyes were like glimmering rubies, a pure and beautiful red.

"Is it time to try again?" she asked, eager to see the rest of him once more.

He twirled her, and she laughed at the sudden motion. "And we just got started with this," he said in a teasing tone. "I've been practicing something."

They danced their way down the hill, laying in the soft grass out of observation distance. Sirius twitched his hand, drawing the darkness of his cape-like wings around them in an inky barrier. It was only the two of them in this bubble, impossible to spot without the illumination of daytime.

They made love until the stars shone, feeling closer than ever even without a sustained mating bond. Something about the Outer Reaches' air and the cold glitter of starshine made her think they would eventually figure out how to complete it without any help. By then, it would be more of a happy blessing than a necessity, as Sirius had already found a secure place in her heart.

Chapter 35
Sirius

In the wee hours of morning, they dressed and snuck back into town, bedding down in the room Saniya provided. Sirius left Talina in a warm cocoon of blankets at sunrise and went to retrieve the sword finished by the local blacksmith. It was made of a non-iron metal with an unpronounceable name but was as sturdy as the ancient blade he carried around. Unlike his relic, Cossette's new sword gleamed like white gold.

She was already waiting for him outside Saniya's home, her white hair scraped back into a short ponytail and albino-red eyes full of understanding. "Do you already know what I'm going to say?" he asked.

A hint of a younger woman's mischief crossed her face. "There are three possibilities. I'm waiting for the one you choose."

He offered her her sword's wrapped package, and she accepted it with both hands in a grateful bow. "The world changed for you overnight because you became a woman. I want to teach you to thrive, like a father should," he said.

"Like you will," she said, smiling as she unwrapped the gleaming hilt of her weapon.

He nodded. Because of the unusual circumstances, she was new to the world again. She needed a mentor, and he was glad to serve that role for her. "First things first, you have to be able to defend yourself. That's not just learning how to swing a sword. You need solid food and a strength regimen."

Sirius knew modern vampires fought with bullets instead of blades, but other things remained the same for them. Without solid food, a vampire could live, but they would appear as thin as Cossette was. Her transformation had made her practically frail. They'd just be starting her training on the road.

"I understand," she said.

"At least you can cheat." He flicked her the Combat Key.

She admired the iron-colored stone in the light, a small laugh bubbling from her lips. "Thank you. This will make things easier. I can learn by doing, and you can practice your shadow magic." He stilled at her words. "That was your plan, right? I see four distinctive futures where you spar with me using only your shadows."

"How strong is your future sight?" he asked in disbelief.

"Stronger than it used to be. Which may not be a gift when it fractures into possibilities and chance perspectives moments before a decision is made." She frowned down at her hands.

"We'll train it." He was sure he was looking at someone who would be a better pseudo-Blade than him one day. The ability to predict an opponent's moves would be critical for her.

They started with the basics, the Combat Key helping perfect her form. By the time they had an audience, she was sweating from physical exertion, while he was from concentration.

His shadows were coming along nicely, but using them was like training a brand-new muscle. He could draw shadows from their surroundings or use his wings. The mist along his back was still forming into individual tendrils of impenetrable darkness that he could raise and bend at shoulder height. They interlocked into a wing shape—like a bird's wings, not a butterfly's. His "part fae" side may have made them possible, but he figured he would look more like a dark angel if they ever grew solid enough for flight.

"We're done," he said, turning to the curious faces watching their practice. Gabriel and Collins were there, as was Talina. The moment he went to her, Talina reached out to touch a portion of his wing. Tingles of sensation covered the whole of his back, radiating from the heat of her palm. He growled softly with interest.

"Oh!" She giggled, taking her hand back. "You can feel that."

He pressed closer, his voice a mere rumble. "I would love it if you'd explore more."

She giggled harder. "I would, but you're all sweaty!"

His gaze flashed to the other men, who had their backs to them while speaking to Cossette. Smirking, he whispered in her ear, "That didn't stop you last night." He stole a kiss from her surprised gasp before heading off for a quick shower.

Saniya's rooms had enchanted, running water, a mimicry of human innovation created with magic. The djinni was in her fae form, sipping tea in her sitting room and watching him come inside over the rim of her cup.

She didn't stir until he was washed and changed, coming her way to pay his respects for her hospitality. "Here." She held a letter out to him when he was within arm's reach.

"Trader" marked the envelope in Izell's handwriting. His gaze immediately narrowed.

"If you want to make your mate's life easier, give this to her," she said.

"Was Izell here?" He turned the envelope to the sun, making out more of the Archfae's handwriting. His brow puckered. What was she even doing? He hadn't seen her in weeks, but she was still influencing events around him.

It reminded him unpleasantly of Gwendolyn, whose politics had landed him with a thousand-year-long coma as she manipulated events behind his back.

"She was, briefly," Saniya answered.

"What game is she playing?" He didn't demand, not with her. She could do a lot of terrible things to him with a clap of her hands if he earned her ire.

Still, she gave him a stony look. "I didn't realize your quest for Lord Zalice is a game to you. Maybe she shouldn't be trying to help."

"Know what's helpful?" he grumbled. "Giving answers. Being here, helping."

"Being straightforward?" She barked a laugh. "Fae of her time aren't direct. Just know that she's helping you and fulfilling her promises."

He grunted, burning with frustration, man and beast alike. The letter crackled in his fingers. "You need to go," Saniya continued, giving him a pointed look. "Things will work out because Izell has guided you to the right path."

"It's just a hard one," he said, seeing the surprise flicker over her face.

"That's right." She smiled broadly. "Go and face your destiny, Sirius Raphael Fabron. The Lord of Storms calls your name."

He put on his best courtly mask, bowing elegantly like a prince, with the respect she deserved. "Thank you, Lady Saniya." Still, he wished she would give him more answers. Something he could sink his fangs into.

"Good luck," she said, clapping twice. He glanced around, but nothing had changed. He didn't feel any different, either. "You'll see for yourself. Go!" She laughed, and he did as she suggested.

The others were already astride their elks when he returned to the group. "This is for you, for later," he said, passing the letter up to Talina.

She glanced up from studying her journal, startled. "And this is for you...I think."

The first few pages of her journal were still her handwriting, plus Izell's additions. Flipping past that, the pages changed to soft, well-worn parchment, like a whole different book had been pasted to the back.

In bold, the title page of this new book read: "**A Compendium of Shadow Magic.**"

He blinked in astonishment, flipping through page after page of spells and applications, from the hand gestures to more practical uses.

Part of him knew Saniya had given this because he'd tamed his beast's anger and bowed to her mere minutes ago. He smiled and shook his head. "Well, looks like I have something to study."

However, books could wait. He closed it as he nudged his

mount next to Collins's hours into their ride. "Good morning," the other man said quietly.

Sirius really looked at him for the first time. The sight of him close-shaven and gaunt was a surprising enough change, but underneath, there was silent misery that he bore in a stoic mantle. He didn't make eye contact with Sirius, too busy gazing into the distance as they followed the gentle rise of the trade road.

"Why are you really here?" Sirius asked.

This startled Collins into turning toward him. "I am Lord Gabriel's squire. I go where he goes," he murmured.

"And did he require you make yourself as unassuming as possible?"

"No, this is all me. I gave everything else away," he sighed. "I must apologize to you, Prince Sirius. I worked with Lucia, and despite the false pretenses she set up for me, I still acted against you. I ask for your forgiveness so I may take another step toward forgiving myself."

Sirius's tongue traced the edge of a fang, making an unimpressed chuff. "You already made it up to me."

"I...did?"

Sirius grinned. "I heard you shanked Lucia. Closer than the rest of us have come to killing the bitch."

The other man did the exact opposite to what he expected, shrinking further on his mount. He resembled a kicked dog more than an Ancient vampire with a mountain of experience wielding one of the Fell Keys. The smile fell from his face as Collins muttered, "I only did it because she killed my wife and people. It was reactionary. I was ready to die for my mistake."

"You wished for her back. Your wife." Sirius didn't flinch from the raw pain he saw in Collins.

"That's right. The djinni even told me she couldn't fulfill my wish, but it is still the only thing I want. She couldn't patch over the past, either. I realize now that I was...misguided. I thought I was a paragon of faith, but in the end, I was literally serving demons." His hands clenched as his eyes watered. "There's nothing left for me in New York. I must atone some way for my sins—"

"Sinner on the rise," Sirius muttered.

"—Pardon?" Collins paused for a moment until Sirius shook his head. He stuttered back into his monologue with less fire. "So, I am here, hoping that Lord Gabriel gives me a chance to kill Lucia for what she's done to my people." Something dark stirred in his gaze, a deep blackness that Sirius recognized immediately with a cold thrill of fear. Collins's teeth sharpened, then retracted. The emotion that tickled a hint of Fell Madness sank back into him, and he slumped, defeated once more. "It's better than dying."

"Know what's also better?" he asked, turning to Gwendolyn for the first time, meeting her gaze. She glanced around, as if wondering if he was focusing on someone behind her. At his request, she stopped her elk and dug in a saddlebag, revealing a golden purification potion. He figured she handed it over so easily because she assumed it was for him.

Instead, he shoved it into Collins's grip and made sure he drank every drop. The other man gasped in pain as it scoured the darkness from his veins. "She bit you too, hmm," Sirius murmured to himself. She'd spread her version of Fell Madness through saliva upon coming to New York, looking for new people to victimize into her living shields. Through Collins, those victims had become his coven, all down to the last man, the coven master himself.

"Those never get any easier to drink," Collins muttered.

Chapter 36
Sirius

Days later, in the wee hours of morning, Sirius sat propped against a boulder with what used to be Talina's journal. He was in the middle of the textbook addition, scanning the diagrams in search for anything he could use.

He'd learned quickly that his old discipline to focus on a task to perfection was addled by Talina's presence. She was snoozing a few yards away in a warm bedroll, which he longed to return to. They spent most of the day together, either riding or sitting with each other, and she was far more interesting than a musty book.

However, that same musty book contained the secrets he needed to control his new shadow magic. The magic answered him when he performed the fae hand gestures detailed in the textbook, though many were too complicated to suit his needs in a combat situation. Still, he committed to memorizing basic commands.

This morning, he was determined to figure out how to change the size of certain spells. It was relating to intent, he read.

He grumbled to himself. The dozen or so tendrils that made up his "wings" were all engaged with a simple lasso spell, holding pebbles and feathers. He needed to figure out how to use them together to restrain something much bigger, like another person.

"How's it going, Dad?" an unexpected voice whispered.

Cossette dropped down next to him, nearly soundless. She

peered over his arm to the page he was studying before poking a pebble he held suspended behind him. It dropped to the ground.

"This is more complicated than I thought," he grumbled. "Maybe I shouldn't have grabbed Adrius's shadows."

She gave an exaggerated shrug. "Do you need someone to practice on?"

"Yes. Do you mind?" he asked. After she nodded, he aimed a lasso spell at her. It was just a quick circular flick of his index finger, summoning a tendril of shadow to shoot out of his fingertip and wrap around her wrist.

She lifted her arm, inspecting his handiwork curiously, before tugging out of the loop of shadow. "It's not very strong," he muttered. "It *could* have a lot of uses."

"Olivia had this problem too," she confided. He raised a brow, recalling that the bubbly, young Alchemyst was the current keeper of the Shadow Key. Cossette's gaze was clouded over, her lips slack. It was a common enough sight over the last few days; she was scrying for information either in the past or future.

He dropped his other mini lassos, waiting patiently for whatever she found. Cossette's seer abilities were invaluable now that she had the right headspace to wield pinpoint control. *Thank God she's on our side,* he thought.

Cossette gave herself a shake five minutes later. "She found that the magic is easy to wield but hard to master," she said. "Like with that spell, you tell it to grab my wrist. But you communicate other factors to it at the same time. How strong to grip, how many loops, how big you want the tendril to be..."

"So, practice?"

"Lots and lots of practice."

He let his head fall back with a low chuff. "This is what I get. Almost everyone I know truly excels at one thing. You have your seer magic, Talina has her wind, Neala her illusions, my shapeshifting, and here I am trying to add something else."

He wondered what other magic Lady Getana would've offered him had he actually stopped to listen to the options. He could've picked something simpler rather than *needing* the magic

Adrius was once so good at. What did he think he was going to prove?

Cossette offered a smile. "We have plenty of traveling to do. You're going to be fine. Plus, it's nearly time to duel."

Nodding, he figured that was why she'd woken so early. She'd already gotten his lecture on how a motivated soldier always gave their best early in the morning to train and improve. It was how he'd spent his early years as a Fell Hunter, the habit deeply engrained.

"Let's duel, then," he said, standing and offering her a hand up.

They walked far enough from the group that Sirius was fairly sure they wouldn't wake anyone up. He drew his sword, flipping its familiar weight through his hands. Every morning, he used it less in favor of training his shadows. Even with the Combat Key, Cossette was still learning and wouldn't hurt him anyway.

Today, he started the duel with a parry and then slipped a shadowy lasso around her ankle, tripping her.

She bounced back to her feet with a little laugh. "Not so hard, right?"

He grunted. "Lucky first try."

By the time they finished, he was sheened in sweat from pure concentration, but something had clicked the moment she swung her sword at him. All he needed was more focus so he could use his shadows with the purpose he required.

He resigned himself to many long hours of practice.

Cold wind blustered as Sirius, again, got up early. Talina flipped over with a wordless murmur, smiling in her sleep when he pressed a kiss to her forehead.

She didn't mind him lassoing her randomly during their day's riding, but the moment he experimented with sharp edges, he sensed her unease. While honing his magic to cut with shadowy blades, he had no one to use them on but himself.

He was close to a turning point with his magic as he sought

out that perfect blend of control, intent, and execution. If it distressed his mate-to-be to see him testing his shadowy blades on himself, he just wouldn't make her watch.

Unless...

He shook his head at the thought but went to the grassy ridge where the elks were resting for the night. Their saddlebags lay in an orderly pile, ready for the next day's round of riding. Sirius hoped for another village with a warm inn, growing tired of resting outside.

Spoiled, he chastised himself. But he couldn't refute it. He missed his modern tent and the warm sleeping bag Cloman had stolen and sold. The nights were growing too cold to be sleeping outside.

He bent down and dug deep in his saddlebags, retrieving the half-finished duck he'd started to carve weeks ago, back when his biggest worry was keeping his beast contained rather than committing to a long journey into the mountains on the whims of a god.

Talina's mercy had saved the silly thing, because Sirius had cut its bill too short. Now that he inspected it again, he realized its bottom was a little lopsided too. The wood was still good. Precious, even. He would have to go far out of his way to find a tree to scavenge more.

"Let's see how this goes, friend," he murmured, sitting in the grass with it. He shaped one tendril of shadow like a whittling knife and began working.

He told himself that, if he could make this work, he probably had the control to try more difficult spells in combat. He'd practiced and improved so much already.

Hours later, he was pleased. His shadows were better than any woodworking kit, morphing to his exact specifications. Tucking the finished duck under his arm, he snuck back into camp, nodding hello to Gabriel, who was still on watch as the camp stirred. The angel raised a curious brow, trying to see what Sirius held, but he'd wrapped a bit of shadow around it to obscure it.

Sirius went straight to Talina, who rested with one arm

extended to the side. He laid the finished carving in her palm, which was enough to prompt her eyes cracking open.

"Good morning, sweetheart," he said lightly.

"What's this?" she murmured, sitting up and rubbing the sleep from her eyes.

Now that morning light caressed its wooden side, he admitted he'd pulled out every trick he could remember to make it as perfect and lifelike as possible. She held his best likeness to a female mallard, except the bottom was perfectly flat.

Talina's face lit up as she realized what it was. He drank in her reaction, especially when she flipped it over and burst out laughing. "I didn't say that," she protested mid-giggle.

He grinned. "That was exactly what you said."

"'It's good to finish things.' –Talina" was etched on its underside, between two webbed outlines of duck feet.

"You didn't forget the feets, either." She covered her mouth, struggling to hold on to her composure.

"How could I forget the feets?" he asked like it was perfectly rational.

She wiggled out of the bedroll, flinging herself into his arms for an enthusiastic kiss. "Thank you, I love it," she said.

Her eyes glimmered with pure blue skies, the kind he could get lost in for days. "You're welcome," he replied. "I made it with shadows. I'm getting the hang of them at last."

Now to practice fighting with them until Lucia didn't recognize the force of beastly shadows he'd become.

Chapter 37
Talina

"I miss flying," Talina said to Gem days later as they watched Sirius train his shadow magic while fighting both Cossette and Korin at the same time. They sat together on a flat rock, overlooking the treacherous slate the three used as a stage for their duel.

The passing days blurred together, but the toll of constant travel was starting to wear at her. Things started to change the moment they realized the villages were no longer just one day's worth of riding apart. They bedded down in some uncomfortably rocky places and endured less sleep after Gabriel announced one day that he could sense a distant demonic presence in the direction they were heading. There was a nightly watch from then on out.

They started spotting groups of knights and bounty hunters, some of whom stopped to warn them away from further travel north. These fae shared reports of animals many times their natural sizes attacking travelers. Sirius had known immediately what that meant. "Lucia," he'd spat. "Her blood mutates regular animals into killing beasts."

"She knows where we're going," Talina had said mostly to herself. Their path was set, and the second challenge had to be close. She still had the letter for the "Trader" in her personal items.

Gem's twittering brought her back to herself. He had a sense of impatience, like he'd said something and she hadn't heard. "Sorry. Just worried," she murmured.

"I was saying, I would miss flying too, if I were you." He turned up his beak, the portrait of a smug bird. Managing a small smile, she tipped him off her arm with a fingertip, so he had to catch himself and flutter back up.

The wind chose that moment to blow past them. It was getting more vicious without the protective screen of trees. *"Come to me,"* it whispered. The only thing it said anymore.

"Give me my flight back, and I'll see you even faster," she muttered, assuming the Lord of Storms wasn't listening. She was an aether fae, and he, the God of Wind. Surely he should want her to fly to his mountaintop home?

The wind stilled abruptly, then reversed direction. She didn't think much of it until a shadow crossed overhead. Her jaw dropped while Gem flittered away with an alarmed screech. Even the three dueling vampires stopped, shading their eyes, as a massive shape dropped rapidly out of the sky.

Talina stood, hoping it wasn't about to whip out its talons and carry her off. It landed a few yards away on a different outcropping of rock, wings forming a wide vee before folding neatly to its sides. She released an awed murmur to be so close to a skyrider. The wind dragons were said to roost only in the highest mountaintops, and despite spending her youth in an Outer Reaches village, Talina had never seen one outside of the bird-shaped silhouette of their wings in the distance. They were an even rarer sight than fire dragons or sea serpents, both of which required trips to the other most extreme points of Faerie's biomes to spot.

Now, one walked toward her, navigating over the uneven terrain with ease. Its muzzle was beak-shaped and leathery. Within its relaxed mouth, she could make out the sharp points of a top set of teeth. It regarded her with canary yellow eyes, bright in the grays of its scales and feathers. The top of its head was a full crest of feathers ranging from the darkest of storm clouds to the silver of flashing lightning. Those feathers continued down its long neck and made for a beautiful set of plumage finishing the graceful, closed sweep of its wings and the closed fan of its tail.

The rest of its body was rugged scales, mostly its belly and the underside of its wings. Static danced over it even grounded. Skyriders could generate their own lightning bolts, powerful enough to fry the hardiest of creatures. Considering how this one loomed over her, twice her height, she doubted it needed anything other than its claws and fangs if it were hostile to her.

No one moved as the dragon stopped and swept its wings out, head bowing low. A deep voice rumbled from its—his—throat. "Greetings, sky sister."

"Um..." She glanced toward motion in the corner of her eye. Sirius was trying to get to her, but Cossette stood in the way, shaking her head. The skyrider stayed in the submissive position, waiting for her to say something. "Hello?"

"The Lord of Storms sent me. It is time for your next challenge." He watched her with a keen, yellow eye. "You are to take only what you need as the rest of your group continues to ride."

She nodded before rushing to get the letter. A deep growl lifted the hair on the back of her neck. Turning, she witnessed Sirius nearly face to muzzle with the skyrider, stabbing a finger in his direction. "I will be coming with her," he was saying.

"You will not." The dragon growled, visible arcs of electricity flashing over his neck and between his fangs.

Talina breathed a frightened cry and rushed to place herself between them. "It's okay. He says it's for my challenge. You did the first one alone...so I'm doing this one alone. Right?" She shook the letter to show that she wasn't completely on her own at least. Saniya had said it would make her task a lot easier.

Sirius had his teeth bared with lingering anger. "You should not be going anywhere alone," he said, putting his hands on her shoulders and leaning down until their gazes were level. "We know Lucia and her animals are somewhere in this area. She could easily capitalize on us being separated."

"Talina will be protected," the skyrider growled. "The Lord of Storms makes no mistakes with his timing, nor with the messenger he has sent."

"That's my mate, bird," Sirius snapped.

"She's going," he stated flatly. "Unless you want your boon revoked here and now?"

This seemed to strike some chord with him, though he didn't relax more than a fraction until Talina kissed him. "I'll be okay," she promised. "You've never heard of skyriders, but they're terrifying. He can scare away a few beasts."

"He won't scare this one," Sirius muttered but turned away, his fists clenched. "If you must go for the challenge, then I have to allow it."

The dragon turned away from him with a chuff. "Come, sky sister. Let us be off."

"See you soon," she whispered to Sirius, kissing him farewell. He deepened it, stealing her breath away and reminding her why she wanted to get this challenge over with as quickly as possible.

The skyrider encouraged her to sit on his shoulders, where she could feel his muscles flexing as he turned and spread his wings. Her traveling companions lifted their hands in farewell, still looking stunned to see a dragon carrying her away. She waved back before clutching at the dragon's neck when he took off down the road at a run. They left the ground with a hard jolt, smoothing out as soon as he caught the wind and soared.

A joyful laugh escaped her lips as she enjoyed the breeze whipping through her hair. The skyrider carried her higher and higher still until her ears popped and the world below was as small as a child's playset. "This is too high for me!" she called. Her mother always warned about flying into the real aether—at some point, even Wind-aligned fae would find it impossible to breathe. But as the dragon canted his head, glancing back at her, she realized she had no such problem yet.

"Are you sure?" he asked. "Have you ever skimmed the clouds, sky sister?"

She shook her head no.

"That's a pity."

He tucked his head straight, hurtling them through the sky faster. The logical part of her brain screamed to duck and hang on for dear life, but she didn't. The wind didn't sting her eyes, much as it brushed past her body and extended her wings into impossibly thin trails. She felt more alive up here than she had in weeks, stuck riding rather than flying as her nature intended.

"The Lord of Storms welcomes you home," the dragon said in her mind, like a familiar. She startled back to herself, wondering how quickly they'd reach their destination on the speed of his wings. *"He cannot speak to you right now, so I am to be his voice. I am known as Parax."*

She could feel the magic radiating off of Parax just from the brush of his mind. *"And I'm Talina."*

"I know, sky sister. Father told me of your journey."

"You are related to the Lord of Storms?"

His laughter rose like a deep-throated caw. *"All skyriders know him as our father. That makes us kin,"* he said. *"I know you must have many questions, but I am not permitted to tell you too much. However, I can show you something."*

They continued to rise, and now, she grew alarmed, scrabbling at his neck as the wind lifted her hair. It carried words, so many words, Lord Zalice's instructions smearing into a meaningless jumble that haloed her all the same. *"You will not be harmed,"* the skyrider promised, arrowing them through a cloud while she considered if she had enough control of the wind to catch herself should she choose to jump from this distance.

Nothing happened. She didn't freeze, or run out of breath, or feel any undue pressure on her skull. Up above the low-hanging clouds was an endless dome of blue sky and harsh light, reflected off the fluffy layer of water vapor below them. *"Why? You could've killed me,"* she protested.

"You must know what's at stake...and what you're capable of." He angled his wings just right. When she spotted it, her heart leapt into her throat. A distant cluster of peaks pierced the cloud cover, haloed by a vicious storm that spewed constant streaks of lightning. She blinked rapidly, dismissing the spots from her eyes until they ran together like spider webs.

"I thought I wasn't to see the destination until we'd completed all the challenges," she said, even her mental voice stained with awe.

"Things have changed, sky sister. Someone else has beaten you to the summit."

Cold thrilled up her spine. *"Who?"* she asked with a sinking feeling. *"How? I thought it was impossible to find."*

Parax bowed his head briefly. *"A demon has invaded the body of one of the only fae that knows how to reach the Lord of Storms directly."*

That chill turned to a sick cramp in the base of her stomach. Lucia had exploited Lyana's knowledge while they traveled toward Lord Zalice the hard way. They'd all but handed her the perfect head start to set up traps aimed toward killing Sirius and stealing away his soul. Feeling incredibly foolish, her hands clenched in the dragon's feathery mantle.

"Do not despair, sky sister. He has seen your path since before you were born. He will not repeat the mistakes of your predecessors."

"What?" she asked, wishing she understood his hints. There was some mystery afoot, and sometimes, it felt like everyone understood it but her.

"Before you ascend, you must complete your challenge, and your fatecross must also complete Raenith's boon. The Lord of Storms will crush this demon if she attempts to face him directly." Though his tone was reassuring, she shook her head.

"She doesn't face anyone directly."

"Then you must be hasty, yes?"

She nodded in quiet agreement, realizing she was no longer enjoying this ride above the clouds. It was a relief when Parax tilted his wings, cutting downward through the clouds and wheeling them toward her next destination.

Chapter 38
Talina

Parax landed within minutes, perching on the wall of a larger settlement. Fae of all kinds stopped to gawk at the sight of a skyrider. Talina felt herself flush, thinking they were staring at her too as she dismounted with shaky legs.

"Good luck, sky sister." He nuzzled into her hair like an over-large, affectionate bird. "I will be right here when you are done."

She patted his neck with gratitude. Maybe if she hurried, he could fly her back to Sirius and the others. He would be worried and, knowing him, dwelling on how he hadn't taken on a light-ning-spewing dragon twice her size to keep her safe.

"Need help getting down? Father is cruel to clip your wings," the dragon mused. He grabbed the top of her cloak in his jaws and lowered her off the wall while she scrabbled, flapping her wings like it would help. The magic of the Path of Imagination made them heavy and useless on her back, so she landed on her rump instead of something more graceful when Parax released her clothes.

She rubbed her backside and wandered into town, wondering who she even needed to talk to. "Trader" was a broad profession.

Asking around, she earned laughs and side-eyed looks when she asked about the town's trading hub. Eventually, she found a younger aether fae who was willing to take her there, straight in the middle of everything. A broad, one-story building squatted at the apex of a traffic circle, its sign simply reading "Goods" with the s slightly tilted.

"Good luck," her guide giggled.

Talina opened the door before rubbing her palms on her riding pants. She wasn't nervous when face to face with a skyrider or even when said dragon took her to impossibly high altitudes. But the unknown of this challenge had her heart stuttering in her chest.

"Ah! Customer!"

She twisted around with a startled squeak. Above the door, the wall was...moving? The grain of the wood shifted irregularly until she scrubbed her eyes and identified what she was seeing. A lizard-like man crawled down and peeled off the wall, turning a pleasant green color from snout to tail tip. He wore no clothing, not even a loincloth, but his form was straight, with no visible genitals to worry about covering.

She had no doubt this was the person to lead her second challenge. Despite being naked, he was the "snake in a suit." Her throat clicked as she dry swallowed.

"Hello, new customer. New face. Not from here?" he said rapid-fire, looking her up and down with a narrowing of his reptilian eyes. She inspected him back, thinking he looked just like how she'd imagine an oversized gecko, except he had a thumb as one of his four digits.

Her gaze darted to the cuckoo clock behind him, which popped out a tiny bird to screech the exact time: thirteen past thirteen.

"Ssssshut up," the lizard-man hissed toward it. It stopped crowing abruptly. He pasted back on a smile that extended too wide across his muzzle. "What do you fancy? I have anything you might need."

He swished around her, tugging at her clothes. "These seem new. Maybe you want to make a trade? I'm not known as the Trader for no reason," he said, winking. "Rules are on the wall." A tail tip pointed her gaze in the right direction as she tried to keep up with his mile-a-minute manner.

The Trader, she realized, ran a pawn shop. There was no

other way to categorize this shop full of any item she could imagine being sold. Near-endless rows had food next to occult tomes, untapped occultari next to children's toys. She imagined getting lost looking for something specific...probably by design.

"...Maybe a nice puppy for the lady?" The Trader was still talking, she realized, tugging her cloak absently. She read the wall with the rules, which was straight to the back of the shop.

1. All trades final.

2. Surprises are unrefundable.

She stopped there, turning to the Trader, who was now babbling about engagement rings. "You misspelled 'nonrefundable,'" she pointed out.

"Oh, are you more interested in the surprises? I love them, myself. Right this way, right this way!"

She decided to follow him, suppressing a giggle as he skittered to the counter in front of the rules board. Beneath the glass glittered a veritable hoard of gems and other small, fine items. The Trader ducked underneath, placing a few black boxes on the counter before her. Each was of a different size, from ring box to jumbo present, but was otherwise unmarked.

"Ssso," the lizard-man lisped, turning an expectant shade of lighter green as he threaded his fingers together. "What do you want to trade?"

She reached into her jacket and retrieved the letter, smoothing out some of its rumples before handing it to him. His scales shaded into blue tones, which she watched with fascination as they turned teal, then sapphire, and finally a bright, electric blue as he scanned the letter.

"Izell! You're with Izell?" he practically squealed. Speckles of white crossed his hide. "Who are you?"

"I'm Talina," she responded. Her Seelie tongue stopped the lie before she could say she knew Izell.

"Oh! Oh my gods," he said, fretting with his fingers as he looked around rapidly. "I'm supposed to test you! I'm supposed to challenge you! You're—" He cut off abruptly as he turned pure white, holding his throat as he thumped to the ground.

Gasping, she rushed behind the counter to discover him

sprawled in a full faint. She glanced around, confirming that no one else was in the store. Easing the Trader on his back, she checked his pulse. Seemed he just had a fright, so she wasn't too worried yet. She worked the letter out of his hand and skimmed it quickly.

Dear Trader,

I hope this letter finds you well. I so dearly miss my future sight and hope you are not using it to grift hapless travelers.

Who am I kidding? That's what you do.

The aether fae delivering this letter is here to collect my debt. You will give her your prototype without expectation of compensation.

She should also be on a Path of Imagination challenge, which means Lord Zalice will expect you to play along. Just take a good look at her face. You can figure out the rest.

Signed,

Archfae Izell Firebrand

PS: Talina, it is time. Lucidiar.

"What does that mean?" she murmured, reeling as she placed the letter back into the Trader's hand. "*Lucidiar?*" Pain shot through her skull as she repeated the word of power. She screamed, falling to her side as she clutched her head.

She must've blacked out, as she had a vision that she was the wind, whirling through the sky and above the clouds. Faster than a skyrider, free. Whispers filled the area around her, but they didn't belong to Zalice. They felt like thoughts and conversations, but nothing interested her until she heard Sirius's voice.

She wheeled downward, spotting the elks as dark blotches against the snaking road. She became a cool murmur of wind, lingering and watching Gwendolyn and Sirius mid-conversation. He reached out and took her hand in both of his, emotion brimming in his ruby eyes.

Curiously, she saw more of them both than just the physical. They had outlines. Auras, perhaps. Gwendolyn was limned in golden light, which Talina reached out to touch with fingers of wind. She felt a lot in that moment, everything that was the essence of the elderly nephilim. A person who was flawed but brimming with faith. A woman who would always choose the greater good.

Talina pulled back, overwhelmed and feeling invasive. She'd merely scratched the surface of understanding what was going on. A sense at the back of her head tickled, suggesting she didn't have much time. She turned to touch Sirius's shoulder, watching his hair ruffle.

His aura was darker and, in places, broken. She had a sense that it'd recently been much worse, before great change had helped him. Was that change her? She hoped she had made such a big difference.

"I forgive you," he said. Talina gasped, and the wind responded, picking up speed to whistle by and steal Gwendolyn's response. It wasn't just the words he uttered, but what it meant for him. His aura mended further, stitching back together under her phantom hand.

Her sense of him faded like wind petering out. She woke up wondering what kind of strange fever dream she'd just had. Pushing to her knees, she saw that little time must've passed. The Trader was still lying on the ground.

She hoped he was okay since she was next to useless at first aid. Reaching out to check his pulse again, she realized he had an aura now as well, and touching him was like sinking her fingers in a psychic mire. He felt like greed given form, clever and vicious.

"No customers behind the counter," he murmured, his eyes flickering open. They recoiled at the same time.

"Are you all right?" she asked.

"Yes, yes, of course." He glanced to the letter in his hand and tossed it away with a yelp. "So, what were we trading?"

"You were going to give me a challenge." She wished she had a towel to wipe away the lingering feeling of his aura on her fingertips.

"Yes, but you're coming to get something for Izell. What are you trading for it?" he asked, slowly transitioning back to his usual, green self as he stood.

He started wondering aloud about her money and clothes. Eyes narrowing, she backed away before he could take the cloak from her back. She realized his game now as he gave her a sparkly-eyed, winning smile.

"Izell has already paid. I want the item," she replied, watching his jaw snap shut.

"You're right. Let me just...go get that." He turned a dejected gray as he headed into the next room, shielded from the eye by strings of beads. His snout popped back out a moment later. "Don't touch anything!"

She crossed her arms and waited, hoping she recognized "the prototype" so he didn't try giving her a fake. He skittered back in on all fours with a box under his chin, popping up before her and placing it on the counter.

"Thisss is the prototype Izell ordered," he sighed. "She wanted a magic absorption device that was also an occultarus, so that's what it is. It hasn't been tested, so it's not my fault if it blows up or anything. No refunds." He stuck his snout in the air.

Lifting the lid, she inspected the item nestled in black velvet. It was the prettiest occultarus she'd ever seen, shining like a pure gold pearl nearly the size of her head.

"How does it work?" she asked. If Izell wanted her to retrieve it, maybe she expected her to use it too.

"Instead of magnifying magic, it absorbs it. Cast something at it," he said with an impatient gesture.

She held her fingers out, intending to flick static over it. What came out was a blast of ions that made even the Trader back away with a fearful pallor over his scales. But the golden orb sucked it all into a funnel, the lightning disappearing down to the last tiny arc. Its surface gave a single shimmer once it was all gone.

"Wow," she murmured, viewing her wide-eyed expression in its reflection. She already had ideas for what to use it for.

"As for the matter of your challenge"—the Trader sidled back up to her as she replaced the lid and tucked the box to her side—"the Lord of Storms wanted you to have one item in this store. If you can find it and bring it back to me, you can keep it. If you pick something else, you pay for it. Okay?"

She frowned, wondering how she could ever find a specific thing like that here. "Okay," she said. "But I want you to stay over here." His constant stream of conversation could easily distract her.

He huffed. "Fine."

She swept into the shop and wondered how she was going to do this. What would a God of Wind want her to have anyway? Izell's letter was supposed to make this easier, but as she inspected stacks of books and rows of boxed fruits, it seemed like a wash to her. It wasn't until she touched the corner of a book that she realized some of these items glowed faintly with auras of their own.

She nearly recoiled when encountering the first strong aura, which lingered with the stench of despair on a faded cloak. Taking a deep breath, she closed her eyes and somehow knew a mother of two had traded it away days ago for the money to feed her children just a bit longer.

Tears pricked her eyes. Whatever spell *lucidiar* was hurt her heart. She hoped it faded the moment she touched the item she was meant to have. The walls of the shop seemed to close in on her as she touched everything and soaked in the tenor of poverty lingering in the shop.

She knew she'd found her item when she spotted an aura of sparks around a glass vial resting in a rack. Lifting it gingerly, she expected a surge of magic and instead was surprised by a warm feeling in her chest. It felt like...love. Strong and protective. She held the vial to her chest and soaked in it for the minute it lasted.

Had the Lord of Storms held this vial? She wondered who had planted such a pleasant vibe in this lizard's nest. She tilted the contents in the glass, which was an ashy powder that sifted like fine flour.

"Is this it?" she asked, returning to the Trader. His eyes nearly bugged out of his head.

Whipping his head around, he gave an uneasy laugh. A family of lesser fae was browsing now as well, watching this exchange with curious, deer-like faces.

"Yes," he muttered. "Congrats, I guess. You passed your challenge."

Her heart did a somersault in her chest. "Can you tell me what it is?"

The Trader glanced around again before beckoning to her. She bent down to hear him whisper, "It's eletaria powder."

She glared and hissed, "The drug?" Eletaria powder was a highly illegal substance. Whole alchemy operations were shut down to eradicate the knowledge of how to produce it.

He nodded, holding up his hands. "It has a use. You should use it." He tapped the space between his brows. "I've seen the future. You want to do this to get answers."

"You mean, die and ask the Lord of Storms what the plan was in my afterlife?" She frowned down at the powder. Its high was magically enhanced to create literal out-of-body experiences by briefly allowing a soul to leave its body and explore the next plane of existence. A small percentage of those who took it never came back.

"I don't know what he intended. Don't try to drag me into some liability about it," he huffed. "If you don't use it, the big and angry man in your life is going to need it. But the Lord of Storms wanted you to have it, so..." He waved his hand dismissively. "Take it and go."

"Fine. Thanks..." She turned away and muttered, "I guess."

She stopped short as the door closed behind her. It was full night. Mouth open, she turned to look at the shop, just to see a "closed" sign posted at the window. *Surreal*, she thought.

Chapter 39
Sirius

THE NIGHT BEFORE A SKYRIDER SWOOPED OFF WITH TALINA, Sirius had a nightmare. As he and the rest of his group committed to a day of hard riding to catch up with wherever she was flown to, he dwelled on fading tatters of memory.

I won't concern myself with you anymore. Next time you see me, I will have the power of a goddess. Lucia. She'd managed to wiggle into his mind's space again. Raenith's flame must've guttered in his chest at last, as he felt extra cold from the slicing wind passing overhead.

He suspected she hadn't stayed long in his mind, knowing it was a hostile place. Gwendolyn's muffled screams had woken him, after all. The nephilim was extra pale and bundled double, her face turned from the breeze while Gabriel guided her elk on a lead rein.

Whatever had happened in her dreams, it was his fault. Raenith's boon was a blessing to protect everyone around him, and he was the one to lose it. Maybe it wasn't too late. This could be the day he'd be able to look her in the eyes and understand her past decisions.

He urged his mount alongside hers, feeling his mouth dry. "You are unwell," he said in a low rumble.

There was deep resignation in her tone. She didn't open her eyes. "It will not prevent us from getting to our destination."

"We can slow down. I think that would be okay."

Her face clenched. "I thought you wanted to catch up to Talina as soon as possible."

If it were any other day, they'd leave it at that. She was stubborn, and he didn't care. Except...today, things were different. "Did Lucia haunt your dreams last night?"

Her golden eyes flashed toward him. Bright with her faith, they distracted from the wrinkles and graying skin around them.

"I had a nightmare. Whether it was Lucia's doing is up to interpretation. If it happens again, obviously some blood-covered specter has arrived to test me," she sighed.

She tucked her scarf more firmly, glancing away like she expected the conversation to be over. It should've been. They both seemed to accept that there was a new status quo here that rendered them strangers rather than family. The gulf between them was a thousand years too deep.

"What did you do without us?" he asked, hoping that when he stepped over that gulf, he would find a bridge rather than a fall into an abyss. He'd barely considered what life had been like after her "sacrifice," too caught up being the unwitting one to her machinations.

"I traveled. I became an urban legend." She chuckled without humor. "Surely one of the Coven Rehnquist vampires told you about The Curator."

"A mysterious figure that removed the oldest vampires when they grew too corrupt. Was that you?"

"It was."

"That was a job. What about friends, companionship?"

Her face grew stark. "I gave those things up. Sorsha and Keegan helped me remove the most difficult vampires, but I spent most of my time alone."

For a thousand years. Could he forgive her when she'd suffered alone with her ghosts for company? She didn't talk like she wanted acknowledgement of her burdens.

As he hesitated, Sirius realized he wanted amends from her. But Gwendolyn had nothing left. Now that she had lost her vampire side...she really was dying. Not only that, she'd spent some of the last weeks of her life traveling, exposed to the elements. No wonder Gabriel would barely talk to him.

"What would it take for you to forgive me?" she asked in a quiet voice.

"I don't know," he said honestly. "It's the same thing with Adrius. You took something I can never get back. My time."

Her head bowed in defeat.

"But you didn't do it because you hated me." She seemed surprised as he tried to see from her side. "I've been submerged in the 'what ifs,' but I'm still alive and aware enough to feel them." That was why it seemed like everyone else had already left the past behind. Death hadn't come for them, despite the intentions behind Nyixa's sinking.

"That is true," Gwendolyn said cautiously. She watched him like any sane person would observe a dangerous beast. It was the face of someone waiting for him to strike.

He pinched the bridge of his nose, speaking his thoughts aloud. "Why is this so hard?" he asked his palm. "Talina makes it look so easy. Did you know she used to be a ballerina? A competitor's mother broke her ankle, and magic can no longer fix the damage. She holds no grudge even though she had to leave that life behind."

"Sometimes unexpected adversity brings welcome change."

"Sometimes. But then, I was addled by Lucia's magic and struck at her. She forgave me, too," he said, knowing Gwendolyn had to have heard all about that by now. She nodded slowly. "I don't know how she does it, except she must be a better person than I. Maybe... that's why we haven't been able to complete a mating bond..."

He hadn't expected to own up to his demons so openly, but there it was. His secret fear that Talina's all-powerful gods had taken a second look at their relationship and sabotaged the fate-cross so it couldn't unite them permanently. That he was part of a mistake, a glitch in their perfect godly system that'd matched a vampire and a fae by accident.

"I sincerely doubt that," Gwendolyn said, tilting her head up at him. "You may have buried it deep, but you are still the same hero that helped saved Earth a thousand years ago. You deserve to be remembered that way." She cleared her throat as emotion crept into the words. "Time has a way of tarnishing champions and ideals. Adrius toed the line very closely of becoming just like the creatures he hunted—"

"I know," he said grimly.

"—And so have you. You were right to seek an answer to your rage, and I am glad you found it in a woman's heart."

His vision stung, which he could blame on the breeze if her words didn't reaffirm his whole journey to this point. "Thank you for your wisdom," he said.

She smiled like she used to when he was younger, which usually accompanied her calling him "her respectful boy" since Adrius used to be the more exasperating brother. He reached out, taking her hand between both of his. "I forgive you. Let's move on to better things and kinder words."

A sudden sharp wind passed by, ruffling his hair. It smelled a little like Talina, wild and electric, and he lifted his nose to inhale deeply. Warmth crept back into his chest, like the slow ignition of a candle's flame. He'd done it—he'd saved Raenith's boon, hopefully forever.

Gwendolyn hiccupped, a single tear rolling down her weathered cheek. "You have no idea what this means to me," she whispered, dabbing at her face with the edge of her sleeve.

"Sure I do. It means we're family again."

He hadn't realized it until now, but those who rode with him were mostly family. He wasn't nearly as alone as he'd once thought. Gwendolyn smiled through her tears. "To family."

"To family," he agreed, hearing that sentiment echoed by Gabriel. He wasn't the only one listening in, though, as a pink blur fluttered over, landing on Sirius's saddle. "Missing Talina, hmm?"

When he held his hand out to Gem, the little bird moved to nestle in his palm. He held in a gasp, smiling broadly to finally touch Talina's elusive familiar. Ever so carefully, he rubbed Gem head to tail feathers with a fingertip.

"You're not so bad," the hummingbird twittered, settling in for a nap.

FOR ONCE, THE LONG RIDE PASSED AS A BLUR AS THE WHOLE group chatted and carried on together, divisions mended the moment the tension between him and Gwendolyn dissolved. The next town came into view with the first scattering of stars, and Sirius knew they'd found the right place from the massive bird-shaped shadows perched along the wall. The skyrider who'd whisked Talina off had found three friends, and they were lined up like silent sentinels.

He sensed that they were watched as the town's guards let in their group. But the skyriders didn't swoop down to address them, so Sirius ignored them in turn as he let Korin take his elk. With Gem in hand, he took a deep breath, filtering through layers of scent until he pinpointed a hint of Talina. He followed it to the center of town, finding her standing before a building. She was scratching her head and inspecting it.

He crept up behind her, sneaking his free hand around her waist. She jumped and yelped, giving him a solid shock in the process. Gem woke up and twittered joyfully, swooping around her. "Sirius? Gods above, you scared me," she said, laughing as she spun with Gem, catching her familiar and fluttering her wings until she was at face level with Sirius, stealing a kiss in the process.

"What's wrong?" she asked, her expression creasing with concern a moment later.

Glancing down, he saw her feet hovering a solid foot above the ground. "Oh. I can fly?" she flapped and shot skyward, spinning elegantly into a pirouette.

"Did you finish your challenge?" The results were pretty obvious, and he caught her laughter as she drifted downward into his arms. He pressed his forehead to hers, taking in her face like it'd been weeks rather than hours since he saw her last.

A hint of trouble rocked through her smile. "I did. There's a lot you should know. Where are the others?"

He carried her back toward the town gates, picking up Korin's scent and following it to an inn. It wasn't difficult to gather everyone into one room, squeezing in together despite a claustrophobically low ceiling. They'd surrendered the two chairs to Gwendolyn and Cossette, everyone else sitting while Talina paced.

She shared her entire experience in the Trader's shop. An easy challenge because of some new magic she'd unlocked. It turned out that *had* been Talina he'd smelled on the breeze, witnessing the moment he and Gwendolyn made up.

"Maybe the skyrider you flew with knows more," Gabriel suggested, since her talk of auras and breezes was otherwise baffling.

"About that..." she said, sighing. "Our challenges are getting cut short. I think the Lord of Storms needs us right away." She shared Parax's warning and described the raging storm over Zalice's peak.

The heat in his chest threatened to hit a rolling boil. So, this was what Lucia meant. She wanted to steal a god's magic for herself... but he ended up barking a laugh, interrupting Talina mid-word. "This is ridiculous." He glanced around at the baffled faces around him. "Lucia may be powerful, but she is no match for a god."

After an uncomfortable pause, Cossette murmured, "I wouldn't be so sure."

"We set out for the peak at first light." Gabriel nodded in agreement.

Talina swallowed nervously. "Not sooner?"

Both Gabriel and Sirius shook their heads. "It's late," the angel said. "If things go as I suspect and we are flown there by skyriders, we will be face to face with Lucia very soon. It's best to rest before a fight so important."

There was a general murmur of agreement, the group dispersing to their individual rooms soon after. Talina plopped into one of the seats with a sigh, as this was their shared accommodations for the night. "There's one more thing," she said, pressing her fingertip to his lips when he leaned in to distract her.

She produced a vial of ashy powder, holding it like it was liable to explode. "This is what the Lord of Storms wanted us to have. It's a drug called eletaria powder, and the Trader suggested that you should have it since I'm not going to use it."

"I come willingly, sweetheart. You don't have to drug me," he teased, though he held his hand out for it.

"Don't open it. It's really dangerous," she warned, slipping it into his palm. "It temporarily severs your soul's connection to your body so you can have the ultimate out-of-body experience. I've heard it's the most incredible thing, but...there's always a chance it kills you."

He whistled low, giving the powder a shake. That was powerful magic, but he saw why she was hesitant. "Maybe it can help my soul give Lucia the slip if she comes close to killing me," he said, placing it in his pocket as she paled.

"You're not going to die."

"And neither are you." He stood, carrying her to the threadbare cot in the corner of their room. Their lips locked, hands roaming, squeezing. He shook his head, catching her wrists with a soft sound of denial. "No sex before battle," he whispered.

She blinked up at him owlishly. "Why not?"

He flashed a wink. "Encouragement."

"Well, if that isn't the most frustrating, baffling, and annoying thing," she grumped, crossing her arms.

Chapter 40
Talina

The others dressed for battle, giving Talina a fright as she recognized the armor on Sirius, Korin, and Gabriel as what they were wearing in Getana's glimpse of the future. "We're going to fight today," she told herself, feeling underdressed as they walked to where Parax waited with three more skyriders. All four great beasts joined them once they left the town's walls, flapping into the empty area by the roadside.

They angled their heads her way and bowed before Parax said, "We are to carry you to the Lord of Storms. Are you prepared?"

"Will there be more skyriders coming?" she asked.

"No."

She wasn't the only one turning to Gwendolyn first, who put her hands up. "If it involves Lucia, I am going," she said.

Talina edged closer to Parax, which startled Gem from her shoulder, sending him fluttering off with a squeak of alarm. The dragon lowered his head and pressed his muzzle into her hair. "Couldn't you carry more than one person?" She tried to tune out the growing argument behind her as the elderly nephilim started to raise her voice.

His warm breath gusted over her scalp. "Perhaps, sky sister. You do not weigh much."

"We only want to keep you out of the elements," Sirius was

beseeching. He spoke to Gwendolyn with respect, which filled her chest with pride in just how far he'd come. "Talina said the summit is above the clouds."

"Should we mention that Lord Zalice's magic will protect them?" a female skyrider asked Parax quietly. She was a study in white, her feathers fluffy, making her body seem rounder than Parax's sleek shape.

"Let them discover it for themselves," he responded.

Rolling her eyes, Talina ventured back to the group to share the information herself. She'd dressed as heavily as possible, expecting to freeze on the way there despite her earlier flight with Parax. "I will stay behind as well," Cossette was saying, smiling when Sirius immediately scowled. "I'll just get in the way right now, Dad. The rest of you know how to fight, and the biggest dragon can carry two."

"So, it's decided," Gabriel said. He offered his arm to Gwendolyn, who let him lead her to the town's gates. They shared a gentle kiss farewell before he allowed Cossette to take her back to safety.

Sirius and Parax shared a brief stare down, which she interrupted by stepping in between them. "We're ready to go," she said for him.

"Aren't you a pretty bird...thing," Korin was saying to the white skyrider as he settled on her shoulders. Amusement flashed in her silvery eyes. He'd tucked the golden occultarus into a bag slung around his shoulder, just in case they needed its magic absorption capabilities.

Talina ended up fluttering onto Parax's back in front of Sirius. He put an arm around her, the other anchoring into a fistful of the skyrider's neck feathers like holding a horse's mane.

"The Lord of Storms told me you learned one of his words of power yesterday," Parax said, turning his neck to look at her. After a rest, the auras *lucidiar* had summoned were gone. "He wants you to use it again when we are in the air."

"Why?" she asked with an edge to her tone. The God of Wind had also given her eletaria powder, so she finally had to wonder if he had her best interests in mind for this journey.

Instead of answering her, he clicked to the other skyriders and tilted his head as they clicked back. He rolled into motion, taking a running start before leaping skyward, wheeling them upward with a few mighty flaps of his wings. Sirius moved with Parax, holding her tight as they ascended rapidly from there.

"*Lucidiar,*" the wind whispered under the chilling roar of it resisting their speed. "*Lucidiar.*"

"Oh, now you're talking to me," she muttered.

"*Come to me,*" the wind answered.

She wondered if she could direct the spell toward Lord Zalice. Maybe he meant that he wanted her attention up on his peak. She'd cast the spell while holding on to worry for Sirius—so the magic had taken her to him, if only for a brief time.

Secure in Sirius's hold, she figured there was little harm in trying it. "*Lucidiar,*" she breathed.

Suddenly, she was wind, screaming through the feathers of the skyriders and lining every fiber on Gabriel's eyebrows with ice crystals. She shot forward, skimming the mountain far below them and rocketing up toward the peak. Rock turned to ice and impacted snow, untouched by all but a few brave fae. She passed the massive bowl of a skyrider nest, spotting the shadowed face of one of the creatures. It turned toward her, hostility in every line of its body and sparking over its scales.

She was past it too quickly to wonder if it'd known what she was doing. She didn't even know what she was doing, actually, carried along to the very top of this mountain, where a ring of black clouds produced a constant stream of dry lightning. The home of a god.

The air suspended there, giving her a moment to control its flow. She headed for the forms of two people. One was instantly recognizable by her *mort loci* scales, throwing massive waves of magic toward a figure standing behind a wall of wind. Behind her was a dark aura, which coalesced before Talina's eyes into the form of the same shadowy woman who'd whispered in Sirius's ear and incited him into such a rage.

"*Come...*" the wind whispered around her, pushing her toward the other person. She stuck to the wall of air he'd erected as he stood there calmly, watching Lucia throw everything she had at him.

Every nerve ending in her body lit miles away from this spot as her wind-formed consciousness beheld the true form of the Lord of Storms. He was an aether fae, with wings like storm-torn clouds on his back. They sparked and roiled, frothing with lightning. She barely noticed anything else as she looked him in the face and the sparks within herself buzzed like a thousand fireflies.

His lips curved into a smile. She'd seen a face much like his every day in the mirror, though his delicate features held a masculine slant and his sky-touched eyes rolled with pure power.

The moment I saw her face, I knew, Queen Kalimea had said.

Just take a good look at her face. You can figure out the rest, Izell had written.

The secret hiding from her, yet obvious to these two powerful women who'd met Lord Zalice before.

"Daughter," he said in a voice crackling with static. "We meet again at last."

The magic that'd brought her here threatened to wane as her body was seized by heat just from the sound of his voice. His eyes slanted, concern touching his features. "Your ascension is here. Do not lose control of your power." He made a dismissing gesture, blowing away the wall of wind as well as her magic. The moment before she opened her physical eyes, she spotted a tendril of shadow wrapping around his neck and dragging him forward into an onslaught of magic.

She screamed, knowing any injuries he sustained would be her own fault. "Talina? Talina!" Sirius cut into her awareness, his hand against her forehead as she twitched. Electricity danced over her whole body, building in her chest in a burning lasso of power.

She hadn't been imagining it—meeting Lord Zalice had changed something in her. Tilting her head back to tell Sirius the amazing truth, that her mysterious father was actually a living god, she spotted something else swooping down for them. Her finger lifted with another raspy cry.

The aura of the skyrider preceded it, black like shadowy ink.

It screeched, turning midair and extending its talons to strike Parax's wing. Feathers exploded everywhere, and Parax released a deep-throated roar of pain as he spun out of control, his broken wing hanging uselessly.

Sirius curled his body around her as the mountainside came into view far too quickly. She extended a hand to control the wind, creating a cushion to push back against their crash landing, but the impact still sent the three of them flying in different directions. She knocked her head against a jutting rock.

The world went black.

Chapter 41
Sirius

Sirius landed on his feet, sending rocks pelting down the steep mountainside as he caught his bearings. He'd lost his grip on Talina, spotting her lying slumped below an overhang with blood dripping from a cut on her forehead. Several yards in the other direction, Parax dragged his ruined wing as he sought a stable place away from a drop to his death.

There was nearly no cover here. Sirius watched the dark skyrider wheel around, swooping for them. Lightning danced over its neck as its muzzle gaped wide, the air charging from the bolt it aimed straight at Parax.

Sirius didn't know if skyriders were immune to each other's breath, but it wasn't the time to find out the hard way. He rushed over and lifted under Parax's good wing, pulling him forward just in time for a blinding flash and deafening clap of thunder to strike behind them. He fought unpleasant heat in his legs as Parax's talons scraped a more stable shelf of rock and he shrugged Sirius off.

"I'll be okay," he said, both of them watching as the white skyrider rushed in and scared their assailant back. "The demon has corrupted that one."

Sirius nodded and left him there, getting away as Parax started charging his own lightning. A huge scorch mark burned where they'd nearly been fried. Sirius leapt over it as he fixed his attention on the corrupted skyrider. Gabriel had taken flight from his mount, spreading wings of pure light. His weapons and armor gleamed.

Deciding they could handle the corrupted dragon for a moment, he rushed to Talina, checking her pulse despite the shock of electricity that flowed from her skin. Her eyes cracked open, and she offered a shaky smile upon seeing him.

"Behind you!" Korin bellowed. Sirius turned, shocked to see a massive serpentine form rearing back to strike at him. A corrupted snake, just like the one that had crippled Neala with paralytic poison. He caught the back of its head, twisting to break its neck.

More of Lucia's creatures poured off the mountainside. Created with a few drops of her blood and supposedly loyal to her, he imagined she'd amassed quite the patchwork army in anticipation of this moment. His jaw set as he helped Talina to her feet. "Stay here. I'll protect you," he whispered.

With that said, he whirled into motion, shadows and blade moving in concert to end the lives of his enemy's newest minions. She'd thrown away every ally she had in such a way—starting with the Fell Mad she'd created in New York—until the only things she had fighting on her side were poor animals she'd forced into her service. He felt bad but knew they were all made deadly with new toxins, sharper claws, or impossible strength. None of them could get close to Talina.

Lightning lanced from Parax, striking the corrupted skyrider. It twitched from the force as Sirius and others cringed from the deafening blast of sound. His sensitive ears rang so much that he missed Talina slipping in next to him, fighting with her own lightning and cutting blasts of wind. Tears streamed down her face.

She turned and exchanged a look with him. He knew she wouldn't stay out of fighting, and she likely understood that he didn't need any help. Kicking off from the ground, she sped into the sky to strike the tide of scales and fur from above.

He glanced up, seeing Gabriel in the corrupted skyrider's talons. Light built from the other man, building into a glimmering ball. Sirius turned back to his work, hoping the majestic creature could be saved and that the angel's light could sweep over the rest of the beast army to help them as well.

"Help!" someone called. Either they were far away, or Sirius could barely hear anymore. He turned to see Collins overwhelmed on all sides by a pride of lions covered in spikes all the way down their spines.

Sirius made his way over, leaping over precarious stone. How had the other vampire gotten out this far? His skyrider was elsewhere, so maybe it'd dropped him off far from the group.

His boot slipped and he banged his knee against rock. He hissed in pain, scrabbling as he felt how unstable the footing beneath him was. Out of instinct, the shadowy wings on his back flared and he tried flapping them, shocked when his weight lifted. He didn't kid himself about being able to fly, but anything that helped him crawl over the rock face was welcome.

"Where's your weapon?" he shouted, even though it came out muffled to his ringing ears. Collins was pinned and defenseless, already covered in countless lacerations. Sirius didn't wait for a reply, killing the creatures aiming for a fatal bite on the other man.

"I dropped it over there." Collins pointed to a distant snowbank, where the dark handle of a gun poked out like a black root. Sirius shot him a look of disbelief. "S-sorry. We were still in the air."

Sighing, he said, "I'll cover you." This far up, he saw that they were starting to win this fight. The corrupted skyrider was nowhere to be seen—purified, he hoped—and the sky darkened overhead as Talina wielded lightning and wind like a miniature storm herself. He smiled with pride for her, knowing it couldn't be easy for her to turn her magic against creatures fighting only because of Lucia's will.

Unfortunately, reinforcements flowed over him and Collins first, coming down the mountain in seemingly endless waves. There had to be a portal somewhere north of them, he thought, fighting while Collins dove for his gun. With only three skyriders to make the flight the rest of the way up the mountain, he didn't know how they'd disengage from this fight without finishing off all of the corrupted creatures.

He glanced aside only to confirm Collins had his gun in hand, hearing the *pop pop pop* of gunfire after his body jerked. Grunting in shock, he touched the blood marring his chest as he went down heavily, pain radiating from his legs and torso. Claws and teeth raked his skin the moment he showed the smallest hint of weakness, pain like fire coursing through his veins from the bite of more than one creature.

He slashed out blindly with his shadows, having dropped his sword. It rolled down the slope, useless now. Heavy, limp weight pinned his legs, making the struggle to rise and escape the seething horde of beasts that much harder. They only abated as Collins rushed for him, striking him square in the forehead with the butt of his weapon.

"Back," he heard Collins say as the man's hand closed around his collar. He could barely move as the fire in his veins turned to a pins-and-needles sensation.

"The...fuck?" he managed to say, too heavy to do anything but get dragged past the corrupted creatures. They parted like water for Collins, who turned to look at him with sorrow marking every feature.

That wasn't the only thing his face held. Lines of black blood ringed his eyes, which had filled in dark as pitch. His parted lips showed sharpened teeth, the change still twisting his features into that of a full Fell Mad. How? Sirius had witnessed him drinking a purification potion.

"She still had her fingers in me. I'm sorry," Collins choked out. "I saw her...in my dreams..."

Sirius muttered more curses. Of course he had. She'd walked right through his mind when he'd lost Raenith's boon, attacking Gwendolyn and Collins both while they were at their most vulnerable. Lucia could've re-planted her corruptive seeds within him, letting them germinate for just the right moment. Now.

"Resist..." Sirius ordered, knowing it was falling on deaf ears. If Collins had the twisted features, he'd already lost his will to the demoness.

He sent out a mental call for help, feeling it connect to Korin. There was no way anyone else would reach them in time, as Collins dragged him straight to a portal nestled between two jutting outcroppings of rock. They went through, immediately buffeted by a cold, screaming gale. The change of air pressure popped his ears. He witnessed clouds of pure black throwing endless bolts of silent lightning through the sky.

He thought quickly. Even though his limbs had stopped responding and breathing was a challenge, he could feel his shadows moving underneath him. This could work. The vial of the dangerous drug Talina had given him was still nestled in his pocket. He worked it free with a careful jiggle of a tendril of shadow as Collins slid to a stop, kowtowing to a figure walking toward them.

"I knew you'd come in handy someday." Lucia's malicious voice came from a different set of vocal cords. She smiled hatefully at Sirius, her face looming over him upside-down. "The snakes are my favorite. Look at what their venom can do to the proud Sirius Fabron," she said with faux sweetness.

She gestured, and Collins hopped to his feet, dragging Sirius's limp body up what felt like countless bumping stairs. He seethed within, feeling just like his beast, helpless and frozen within his body, screaming and spitting, going mad with the desire to inflict violence. Lucia was just feet away, smirking and sashaying with another victory won over him through her underhanded ways.

"Sit him upright," she ordered. Collins positioned Sirius like a doll so he could see the half-formed pentagram scraped into the stone before him. He knew he was sitting in a vast, open space.

"I'm tired of taking orders, Sirius. I realize it will never end, even if I give my master the soul he craves. So, I'm using your soul for something new," she informed him while she started cutting into the rock with focused blasts of water magic to finish her handiwork. "You see, Hell left behind some interesting literature in Faerie, and I came across a scholar quite eager to tell me about this ritual in exchange for his pitiful life."

Sirius's brows formed an angry "v" as he struggled for breath. He whispered a vile curse at her as his shadows lifted the vial of eletaria powder. Neither Lucia nor her pet noticed the subtle motions within his wings as he drew it out and jiggled at the cork firmly sealing it closed.

"My demonic master cannot control me if I have a god's power," she continued. A cackle left her lips as she looked up. "So, I got myself a god. With your help, your soul will strip away his life and you will *both* go to Hell, while I become the new Lady of Storms."

If only Sirius's face could communicate how terrible he thought her plan was. She was etching unfamiliar runes around the pentagram now, creating a circle of tiny markings that flared hellfire red. He was running out of time, and Collins was standing there like a puppet at attention, ready to fulfill her every whim.

He forced a tendril of shadow to form a sharp edge and jammed it into the vial's cork, finally removing it with a sharp *pop*. Lucia looked up, glancing around with a snarl. "Figure out what that was," she snapped at Collins. Sirius threw the vial's contents as the other vampire kneeled down, dosing them both with a big lungful of powder as the wind changed, blowing it back at them.

Sirius went limp, his body slumping to the ground. He could see a humanoid figure several yards away, forced into a bow and chained around the arms and neck with shackles of dark magic. The man was an aether fae, his face half in shadow, but he wore a vicious smile as Sirius felt cold blackness weave around his consciousness.

Chapter 42
Talina

Gabriel's purifying light turned the tide of battle, even with the arrival of countless reinforcements. Beasts of the land and air alike were forced at them, but the moment they were healed by a blast of light, they scurried or ran away. Still, the mountainside ran red with blood, and the sheer loss of so much life filled her with horror.

The sight reminded her that they were fighting against pure evil, the kind that needlessly slaughtered anything it could control. When it was obvious nothing else was going to slither out to attack them, she landed next to Parax, who stood in a semi-circle of death despite his hanging wing. "They thought I was weakened, sky sister," he said in a thick voice.

"What can we do for you?" she asked, her stomach twisting at the sight of his wing. That would require a talented healer.

He bent his head, licking away the trails of tears on her face. "You are a demigoddess, and I am of your element. Heal me."

The power coiled up and buzzing in her chest needed little reminder. It'd felt like such a relief to unleash her magic, but now, it was building to uncomfortable levels and sending static skittering over her skin. "How do I do that?" she asked in a small voice.

"Father did not teach you any more words of power?" Parax

tilted his head and sighed. "Hold my injury, and run a current through it. That should work."

She did so gingerly, cringing as she felt the wetness soaking through his feathers. Closing her eyes, she let her power filter through her fingertips, becoming a buzzing thread of electricity that flowed into him. Her senses became aware of the lines of his skeleton, seeing where it was broken and where the muscle and sinew had ripped. At the same time, her power turned inward, making her see her old ankle injury.

"More, Talina. You will not hurt me," Parax murmured. She forced more energy into him and felt it bounce back to her, burning around her ankle. Her bone popped at the same time Parax's wing shifted under her hand, mending and flowing together.

He trilled in gratitude, nuzzling her cheek. "Thank you. I wish—" he said, shaking his head abruptly. "You must go to the Lord of Storms before it is too late. I can feel your power increasing."

A man's voice took up a shout, rocks scrabbling as Korin moved at a sprint up the rock face. "What do you mean?" Talina asked, getting onto Parax's back as he effortlessly glided into the air.

"I will let Father explain," he sighed. Korin had stopped dead, his head tilted and mouth open in horror.

She fluttered off the skyrider's back. "What's wrong?" she asked. The rest of their group closed in as he looked to the sky.

"Sirius. His location suddenly jumped..." He pointed upward. "I believe he is at the peak. If I tap into my blood tracking, it feels straight up."

Curses sounded from Gabriel. She blinked in surprise, thinking the angel wasn't capable of such crass language. "Lucia's doing. And where is Collins?" he demanded.

Talina's stomach sank like a stone. She felt herself breathing more heavily as she imagined what would happen if Lucia had either man in her clutches. She wanted Sirius's soul so desperately, after all. How had she snatched him away right under Talina's nose?

Parax nudged her. "Go," he whispered.

She nodded, breathing, "*Lucidiar*," and throwing her magic up the mountain once more, in search of any hint of Sirius. Her magic swooped to the peak, focusing on the form of a cluster of movement. Lucia was clutching at her hair and screaming, but that didn't matter much.

Lord Zalice was chained a few yards away, forced to kneel despite his godly power. He glanced up as Talina's wind settled over the scene and she focused on Sirius. He was curled on the ground, motionless, next to a strange, star-shaped symbol carved into the rock face. Collins, his face marked with black veins, was also lying on the ground, sprawled like a discarded doll.

Talina floated there, feeling numb for a moment as she waited to see if Sirius's chest would rise and fall. It didn't. Blood dripped from his nose and mouth, cutting small furrows through a gray dust that remained on his face.

Eletaria powder.

Her whole self gave a sick lurch.

Sirius was *dead*. The powder didn't stop its user from breathing unless they died during their high.

Zalice yelled a word of power, its magic wrapping around her. She popped into form only yards away from Lucia, who turned her vicious teal gaze toward her in shock at her sudden appearance.

The circle of storms flashed bright white as lightning streaked multiple fingers through the sky, in cue with Talina's clenched fists. Electricity danced through her wings, turning them as dark as a thunderhead to match her mood as she took a step forward, stabbing a finger toward Lucia. "You!" she screamed. "You killed him!"

"He killed himself," Lucia replied. Her hands raised and started forming a spell.

Talina put up her palm, blowing the sea serpent *mort loci* over with a huge gust of wind. Her face twisted with a bloom of grief as she realized this was real. She'd just lost Sirius before they could finish the Path of Imagination trial together. Before they could get answers from Zalice—her *father*. Her heart splintered, knowing she would never hold his mating bond in her chest.

And the woman before her was the cause of it all. Lucia's shadowy form loomed behind the body she'd stolen, forcing it to rise with animosity brimming in the depths of her face.

If she hated Talina, she held a mere candle compared to the blaze in the young demigoddess. Her power continued to boil up, lifting her feet off the ground with the sheer power of wind flowing through her. Hanging suspended three feet up, Talina's hair whipped around to her own personal breeze as the storm above swirled faster at her command.

"You will pay for everything you've done. I will make you repent myself!" she roared, and the heavens answered, flooding the mountainside with bolt after bolt of pure electricity. Talina pointed, and the storm obliged, hurling lightning straight at Lucia.

The demon's smug hatred erased into a look of pure fear, and she vanished through a portal, appearing several yards away to avoid electrocution.

"He was my mate!" The wind carried her voice as she threw another bolt after the woman. Talina floated behind her as inexorably as a storm rolling in, chasing her across the wide peak of Zalice's mountain home. It was pure white rock, perfect to spot a scurrying demon on.

"How dare you take him from me!" She finally struck, watching the woman's body bend back and dance with static. More lightning struck the mountain, not bidden by her. As she screamed and cried, her hold on her magic slipped through her fingers and filled the sky with a cyclone spewing lightning from its core. She was at its center, floating in the eye even as her power fed the tower of death to grow taller and taller.

Electricity ran up and down her insides, leaving behind branching lashes of pain. She coughed droplets of blood. She couldn't stop the flow of power out of her, spinning up to the circle of storms overhead and connecting. Her storm grew and mounted, looming past the mountain and streaking the sky with electricity just like her face streamed with tears.

Her grief mingled with agony, pushing and pulling and

tearing at her body until her skin started to split so more power could escape her quicker. Every scream from her throat was matched by the rumbling of her storm.

"*Hold on, Talina,*" the wind whispered to her in her bubble of peace, there in the storm's eye.

"He's dead," she cried. Her body cracked head to toe as it stretched, contorting to the whims of the storm. "What is there to hold on for?"

Howling gales were her answer, screaming with her. Time slowed to a trickle. She didn't know how much longer she could sustain this nightmare before she fell apart.

"*...Just a moment longer.*" The whisper sounded, impossibly, like Sirius's voice.

Chapter 43
Sirius

Sirius and Collins arrived at a place that made little sense at first. Sirius's boots sank into a cottony cloud, standing on a small ledge right before an overhang of open, bottomless sky. A foot away, Collins stood on a brick walkway with the same drop behind him and a gold-inlaid fence preventing him from accessing a building constructed of glimmering blocks on the other side.

"You fucker," he snarled, launching himself at Collins and socking the other man in the jaw. Collins jerked back, raising his hands as Sirius pinned him against the fence.

"Look, I had no control over..." he wheezed, bending double from Sirius's next strike. "I'm sorry, I'm sorry!"

"As you should be, bastard." Sirius locked his into a headlock, twisting off his air just like he'd wanted to do before freeing their souls with the eletaria powder. "You didn't say a damn thing about Lucia. When did you notice her trying to take control of you?"

"A while... I thought I had it...handled," Collins gasped.

"Handled, my ass!"

That was how the angel found them, Sirius trying to choke the unlife out of Collins while he struggled and slowly turned purple. The shining figure stopped short and stared. Despite his rage, Sirius recognized the newcomer instantly, releasing one man to round on another. "You! What are you doing here?"

"If you didn't notice, I died," drawled the very last angel he wanted to see. Elandros, former Blood Prince Legion, stood there with his brows raised. He wore shining, angelic armor rather than the suit and cravat he'd preferred in life, his aquiline nose even more pronounced without a vampire's glamor to smooth over the flaw. His dark hair was cropped military short.

Collins pushed to his knees, still gasping for air. "Did we die... too?" he asked in a small voice.

Grimly, Elandros nodded.

"How?" Collins turned his gaze up at Sirius, who, in turn, rounded on him with renewed fury blazing in his chest.

"I had to use a fae drug to drag our souls out of our bodies. There was always a chance it'd kill us," he said, clenching his fists. It'd been his choice to use the powder, but he'd gone into the fight thinking that there was no way it'd *really* harm him with his powerful vampire blood.

"So, this is actually your fault," Collins ventured. He flinched backward as Sirius advanced a step. Despite his inner beast being absent in death, he still snarled.

A strong hand seized his shoulder, stopping him from striking out again. "As amusing as this is, you're both in this particular part of Heaven for a reason," Elandros said.

"Let me at least push him off the edge," Sirius muttered.

The angel sighed. "Neither of you has wings. What do you think will happen?"

"Why don't we find out?" he said through gritted teeth.

"I'm here to speak with him. You need to go over to the Faerie side to wait for your advocate." Elandros's hold on him tightened until he nodded reluctantly. He had to pass by Collins to go back to that side, but knowing that it belonged to Faerie had him moving without causing any more trouble.

The cloud under his feet drifted away from Heaven, taking him deeper into the endless sky. Winged shapes cavorted in the air far above him.

He could still hear Elandros and Collins conversing. "This is the end of your life, Bryant Collins. You may come forward to face judgment, but another path is open to you," Elandros said, drawing himself up formally to deliver this pronouncement.

Sirius huffed. His cloud drifted back their way, like it was stuck on a loop. "My superiors have said your path will take you to Heaven. You have repented for your deeds and been wronged by a demon. It is the same way I earned acceptance despite my actions in life," Elandros continued. "However..."

There was a longer pause. Collins shuffled nervously. "However what?" he asked.

"The Council is aware of a large group of vampires..." His voice drifted to an inaudible whisper as he cupped his hand over his lips, giving Sirius a distrustful look as he came back to stand quite close.

Collins gasped at whatever Elandros had imparted. "I need to go to them. My wife, especially." He met Sirius's gaze, squaring up. "This is farewell, then."

"Where are you going?" Sirius asked, raising a brow.

"It is time I righted my wrongs. My former coven is stuck in the place between Heaven and Hell...because of the misguided path I placed them on." He rubbed his hands on his legs, shifting with obvious nerves. "There is no guarantee that we will get to Heaven, but I will not go there without them."

Collins barked a short laugh. "It's funny. I've feared this moment for my whole life, wondering what would finally get me. But now it's here, and I still have a purpose. I get to see everyone again. My only regret is that I never got to apologize to Alex Rehnquist. Hopefully, he reads between the lines of my will."

Sirius saw a hint of something in him for the first time. The man was made anew by the goal in front of him and the chance to be with the people he'd mourned. "Good luck. I hope you all make it," he said, meaning it.

"A sinner may yet rise," Collins responded, turning to nod to Elandros. The angel motioned, and then both of them took a dive off the edge of Heaven. Down to where he'd be joining his coven, Sirius presumed, watching them disappear as tiny specks in the endless sky.

Sinner on the rise, the final clue for the third challenge. Sirius had suspected his last challenge would involve Collins, but not to this degree. And as he stood on his lonesome, he knew he'd failed it. He'd never see Talina again. He wished Collins was still here to punch him again, take out the aggression that bubbled right under his skin. But ultimately, that rage was meant for him for being too hasty and dying right when he was on the cusp of living.

They were going to ask the Lord of Storms together about their mating bond and why it was so elusive. The moment they solidified it, he was going to get down on one knee and propose. He didn't want her for anything less than eternity. Yet the eternity he'd promised her was already over. His head bowed in defeat. He hoped Talina could forgive him for going out in such a way—to prevent Lucia from getting her claws in his soul. The only death he would accept was one that spited that woman.

Wings approached, cutting directly toward him as he inspected the abyss below. He did a double take when he realized just what was coming—a towering skyrider made entirely of storm clouds. It was Zalice's original form during the Convocation, though at least double Parax's height, with a wingspan that stretched across the horizon. As he reached Sirius, Zalice beat his wings to check his momentum and transformed midair, gaining a fae's shape as he sank gracefully. His talons transformed to feet as they touched down on a cloud that appeared before Sirius.

The wings were the last thing to change, retracting from huge storms into the back of the aether fae that regarded Sirius with a face he instantly recognized.

"Congratulations, Sirius. You made it," Zalice said, his real voice a crackle of power. "You have brought Bryant Collins to Heaven and come face to face with me. The first half of your challenge is complete."

"You look so much like Talina." Sirius was hit with a twist of pain at the resemblance. This wasn't Talina, though. His mate was still alive and well.

Zalice nodded. "She is my daughter."

"What—?"

He held up a hand, stealing the words away with a puff of

wind. "Let us discuss what comes next. Your true challenge awaits in a simple yes or no question. Talina needs you."

"Yes," Sirius answered immediately.

A scowl twisted Zalice's seemly familiar face into something terrifying as lightning danced in his eyes, promising just a hint of his storms. "I am not Getana, to humor your decisions before you hear their weight. Let me speak."

"Apologies," Sirius muttered.

"Talina is my fifth child. It has...hurt to try again," Zalice sighed, and the air sighed too, a gentle wind eddying off of him. "All of my children suffer from an excess of power. My firstborn ascended when he was six, and his little body could not contain the essence of the wind. I have watched the same thing play out three more times, no matter how carefully I have acted and guided them...because I was still a part of their lives, the essence of my power encouraging theirs to blossom.

"The same thing has happened to Talina, but I made sure she had something my other children did not." He tilted his head, peering at Sirius as keenly as any skyrider. "A powerful mate that can shoulder some of her burden."

Sirius chafed to point out that he was dead, but Zalice spoke like he was still of use. Maybe, as an all-powerful God of Faerie, he could provide another miracle. "I tried very hard to become her mate," he answered instead.

The Lord of Storms inclined his chin. "There is a trigger that you two don't know, that completes a fatecrossed bond. Talina was supposed to use the eletaria powder. I would've been able to tell her how to complete your mating bond, but this is an emergency, so I will give you the knowledge instead. You both bear a mark on your hand, the fatecross marks from my domain. She is the Tempest, and you are the Fury.

"It is ancient tradition that a god picks the mates of their children. I picked you, Sirius Raphael Fabron, from millions of males that could've crossed her path in the thirty years she has lived away from my home. You required an intervention and some polish, but you will suffice."

Sirius scratched the back of his head, fairly sure that was the politest snub he'd ever heard.

"That is, if you make the right decision," Zalice continued. Power rolled off of him, crackling through his wings. "Talina requires a place for her excess magic to go. Otherwise, it will rip her apart. You have experience carrying more magic than any human-born should. Do you accept Talina as your mate, knowing all this?"

"Yes," Sirius said without a beat's pause. "What, do you want me to be insulted? You had Getana remove most of my burdens so I could carry Talina's, didn't you?"

"That is correct," Zalice said. Neither of them flinched from this truth, as Sirius realized the gods had probably intervened on him specifically for this moment. So he could be useful to Talina. He was, in fact, hand selected to do so.

"You were really desperate to pick me," Sirius murmured.

A hint of mirth danced in the god's eyes. "Are all human-born so refreshingly self-deprecating?" He shook his head and held out a hand. A leather bag flew out of nowhere to land in his palm. "You will need this..." He dropped a ring with a citrine stone inside. The Light Key? Surely it was still on Collins's corpse.

"And this..." He flexed his palm, and the golden occultarus that Korin was carrying flashed into his hand next. He dropped it into the bag, ballooning it out into a sphere shape.

He tossed a second ring at Sirius, who fumbled it on when he realized it was the Flight Key, a clear gemstone set in a silvery band. "This trinket too. Never let Talina wear it."

"I won't. How do I finish the bond?" he asked. He slipped the Flight Key onto his finger.

"You put your marked hand over hers. I made the trigger her true name." As Zalice spoke, he gestured over the abyss. Sirius's sword appeared, the blade quivering as the god closed his hand around the hilt. "It's a mouthful. Talina Evenfall Stormcaller, Daughter of the Wind. She has to desire your bond for it to work."

Sirius nodded. That, at least, wasn't a hardship. "I'm ready."

"Not without these things." Zalice handed over the bag and sword.

"Okay, now I'm ready," he said, simmering with impatience. "Bring me back to life."

"Who said *I* was bringing you back?" His laugh was like the distant rumble of thunder. "Did you know that Getana was unable to remove all the invasive magic from you? She described one trait as having a will of its own and a desire to protect you."

Sure would've been nice if she'd told me, Sirius thought, scowling.

"So, she left it. It brought you back when you died during the Convocation, and it waits to do the same now. You owe your brother thanks for his Shield."

Sirius had a split second to gasp in shock. The Lord of Storms held up his palm and summoned a wind that blew his feet clear out of the clouds and into a freefall.

Next thing Sirius knew, he was hitting the ground, if the ground was actually his body. The impact jolted his whole self and jumpstarted his heart, his eyes peeling open to behold an unholy monster of a storm swirling overhead. He sat up, marveling at how he'd "slept" the venom off, only his joints stiff with protest at any sudden movements.

It was a miracle, Shield magic bringing him back from the dead. He had no doubt some essence of his brother had made it stick to him for just this purpose.

Lying close by was his sword and the spherical bag. He sheathed the weapon and fumbled the drawstrings of the bag onto his belt as he drew out the occultarus. Judging by the cyclone guarded by constant, jagged teeth of lightning, he would need some kind of protection to get to Talina.

He stood, noticing a new heft to his wings. The ring on his hand warmed as he flexed the tendrils of smoky shadow, which interconnected to give him the facsimile of angelic wings. He flapped them, taking to the sky and hurtling toward the cyclone faster than he expected. Lightning arced around him to hit the occultarus, which absorbed every impact.

Determination hardened in his gut as he caught a glimpse of a figure within the cyclone's dark winds. His wings wobbled from shaky turbulence as he struggled to stay steady with storm gales tearing at him from all directions. He would get one chance to clear the wall of wind and lightning before the cyclone would toss him about like a ragdoll.

The very air around him shrieked as he closed in, matching the screaming of his mate within as her magic fueled this force of nature. "Hold on, Talina. Just a moment longer," he murmured, reaching out for her as the wind grew sharp enough to cut. Lacerations opened up and down his torso and blew away the golden occultarus from the shaky grip of one hand. It was worth it the moment his hand closed around Talina's.

There in the eye of the storm, pure electricity flowed out of several open wounds over her exposed skin, her wings storm dark. Between her screams came babbled words soaked in pain. "I can't...I can't wait... It's too much."

Her electrical power flowed into him, giving just a taste of her pain.

Chapter 44
Talina

In the midst of this ordeal, she began hallucinating. She imagined Sirius's touch, the warm rumble of his voice at her back.

"Talina. Look at me."

Her swollen eyes were a struggle to open. Sirius's ghost was here in the eye of the storm—hopefully to take her away before the agony overwhelmed her. She whimpered. She'd always thought herself a pushover when it came to pain, yet she'd survived so much before succumbing.

Sirius flapped his wings, pulling her into his embrace. "Talina. Sweetheart," he said. "Let me help you."

If it were really him, any joy was short-lived as the skin on her arm split, uniting two separate wounds into a free fountain of electrical energy. She howled, back arching as dark spots threatened to overtake her vision.

"S-stay with me," Sirius said in the midst of this. His claws scraped across her skin as he secured her fingers through his, holding her closer despite the way she threatened to explode into a storm to end all storms. She forced her gaze back on him, noting how he took the current stoically, only squinting and gritting his jaw as the smell of burning skin filled her nostrils.

"Be my mate, Talina Evenfall Stormcaller," he said, stuttering to take a breath. "Daughter of the Wind."

For the first time, the offer of his bond came not in a moment of passion, but didn't retract as her mind reached for it, clinging to it like a raft at sea. "Yes," she whispered. Just like that, it clicked into place. Weeks of trying, and finally, it was there, right before she died.

Yet something else happened as she felt Sirius as a mate should for the first time. Her magic rerouted, siphoning into him rather than the storm around them. Without a constant stream of power, it started to die down. Chunks of rock rained from the sky, returning to the ground the wind had ripped them from.

The lightning reverted to the more placid circle of storms, striking through the sky soundlessly. She and Sirius fell a few yards to the ground, but he took the impact since she tumbled into him, limp and broken.

"You're alive," she whispered into his chest. And somehow, she was too, though her whole body throbbed from its close call.

His response was clipped by a hail of sarcastic applause. "My, wasn't that something," Lucia said, having approached under the cover of the dying cyclone. A lightning-shaped wound crept around the back of her neck, splashing over her exposed cleavage. The silver-eyed demon shadow behind her stolen body looked pleased and smug once more.

Sirius snarled and put Talina behind him. For the first time, she felt the pulsing hatred he held for the other woman, a strong echo amongst the weakness in her body. It was all she could do to stay upright.

But she didn't forget for a moment that she'd promised Getana that she'd try to save Lyana, the woman whose body Lucia controlled. She hadn't expected to be one stiff breeze from collapsing upon being presented with the chance, however.

"You should've escaped while you could," Sirius growled. He drew his sword and advanced. Static rained down his legs, released by even the most minute of movements. His pain mirrored Talina's own, but there was a new ring on his finger, glimmering brightly even with the storm overhead. Maybe it was helping him.

Lucia scoffed and hitched a thumb over her shoulder. A massive skyrider made of the elements flew by, leaving a trail of gray magic in its wake. "Your precious wind god wants to see us fight to the death. So be it."

Her hands flashed through a quick spell as Sirius rushed at her, thrusting his sword forward. Water wove through her fingers, freezing into a complicated lattice that caught his blade. Ice snuck up the metal as they tugged it back and forth.

"I can see you there. Hiding in this poor woman's body," he said, glaring directly at Lucia's leering shadow.

Talina blinked in surprise. Maybe their mating bond gave him the same senses as her. "That's all you've ever been good at," Sirius continued. "Hiding." He let the sword's hilt go, sending Lucia collapsing backward with the metal tip just centimeters from piercing her throat. She threw it and the ice lattice to the side.

Talina raised a shaking hand, taking aim at the shadow. There had to be something she could do to make the demon release her hold on this person. She unleashed a bolt of lightning, groaning as static danced in her wounds and forced her to sway.

The moment static crackled over Lucia's spirit, Talina noticed her floating away from Lyana. She and Lyana moved independently. Lyana flexed her fingers, and Lucia shook her head. Before anything else could happen, the shadow stretched its control over her chosen body again.

"What will you do when you free me from this body and I possess you precious mate instead?" she leered.

"Did you see that?" Sirius asked her privately over their bond, stepping in front of her protectively. He spun several thick tendrils of shadow, knocking a hail of icicles off course. *"I think we can save the woman she's possessing."*

Talina's heart soared with pride for him. The man she'd first met wouldn't hesitate to thrust his sword through Lyana's heart if it could spite Lucia, but now, they were in sync for the same goal. *"I saw it. Can you hold her still?"*

Sirius turned and raised a brow, flashing a confident smile. He rushed at Lucia again, lashing a tendril of shadow out to grab his sword and return it to his hand. Lucia dodged and ducked the edge of his blade, just to have a single tendril catch her around the wrist.

Rage flickered over Lucia's face. She took a breath between her sharpened teeth and exhaled a cloud of freezing mist, which solidified into a sheet of ice over Sirius's torso. "Do you think you'll kill me with mere party tricks?" she laughed.

Cracks appeared in the ice immediately as Sirius struggled. But she took the moment's reprieve to turn to Talina, raising her hands. "Behold the power of a sea serpent shifter!" She flung a storm of icy shards toward Talina, who threw herself to the ground. Agony flashed through her whole body as sharp ice skewered her wings, tearing the magic to wisps. If she'd reacted any slower, that would have been her body instead.

"Get away from her!" Sirius roared. Blood flew in an arc as his sword slashed across Lucia's back.

Pain and rage marked her face. She flicked her wrist, summoning a lance of ice and whipping it into his face. It happened so quick that Talina blinked and missed it, only witnessing Sirius stumbling back with his head snapped to the side. Lucia used the weapon to keep him at bay, dodging sharp-edged tendrils of shadow as they circled each other.

Talina knew she needed to stand. Every fiber of her being screamed for her to stay on the cool, stable ground, but she couldn't. Sirius needed her help. Her trembling fingers hooked into the rock beneath her, pushing with all the effort left in her. Bitter cold flowed over her face, the blowback from a spell Lucia had used to snare Sirius's feet in place.

Lucia thrust her lance toward his heart.

"*No!*" Talina screamed. Wind burst from her extended palm, cutting the ice weapon in two jagged pieces. The sharpened tip dropped to the ground and shattered.

Lucia's rage blazed from Lyana's teal eyes. She raised her hands over her head, summoning a frigid gale. The wind was laden with snow and mist, throwing the world into shades of white. Sirius and Lucia disappeared.

Talina glanced around uncertainly, feeling her heartbeat throb in her every wound. "Talina!" she heard Sirius call.

"Over here!"

A massive icicle pierced the haze, flying straight for her forehead. She ducked, feeling her hair snag and rip in the projectile's wake. *Gods above*, she thought, stumbling into the mist.

Sirius's hand shot out of nowhere. His face was drawn in a snarl, covered in several slashing wounds still in the regenerating process with his vampiric healing. *"Stay with me,"* he said over their mating bond, posturing in front of her as the mist started to eddy away.

Ice crackled. Sirius saw it before she did, grabbing her as a massive icicle formed right above them and slammed down hard enough to fracture the earth. Its top exploded into several smaller shards, embedding in his back as he shielded her from the onslaught.

Sirius gritted out a curse.

"You know, I expected more," Lucia said from the depths of the mist.

"Hold very still," Sirius murmured. She could feel that he had some sort of plan brewing.

"But I guess you really are weak, Sirius. That mate of yours has so much magic, but you? Pathetic." The voice was coming closer, bolstering with confidence.

He shifted his posture, gently releasing Talina so she could totter on her own two feet. His sword's leather hilt creaked from a tightening grip.

"How does it feel to know death is near?" Lucia hissed. "Can you feel its cold breath on your neck?"

Sirius whipped around, lifting his sword up in a lightning-fast arc. His wing folded around him like a shield, catching a coating of ice meant to slow him down.

His blade smacked the side of her skull, ringing with the force of the blow. Lucia crumpled to the rock, unconscious. With the sound of her fall, the lingering cold mist disappeared.

Talina shuffled forward, elation starting to rise in her chest. They'd done it. They had time to sever Lucia from Lyana's body, sparing the sea serpent shifter that was Cyranos's only kin.

She realized their mistake too late. Lyana was the unconscious one, while the demon within her was still fully aware. Sirius was still catching his breath and staring down at her in distaste when her form detached from Lyana and flew straight into him.

Chapter 45
Sirius

Pain dropped Sirius to his knees. He cursed letting his guard down when he realized what'd happened. Lucia's icy talons dug into his muscles, scrabbling for control.

Sirius hadn't been present when Elandros had been possessed by Jazrach, but he'd heard about the body-bending contortions that had ultimately killed him and made him the perfect puppet for the demon.

God. What if this was folly? Lyana could've been dead this whole time. He'd held back thinking they could somehow save her.

Now, he struggled on the ground, kicking and writhing as he fought for control of his body.

"Weakling," Lucia's voice hissed in his mind. *"It took me two days to gain control of Lyana. But I can feel you breaking already."*

He snarled in denial, froth dripping from his mouth as he called on his inner beast to repel her. His body contorted and changed, taking on the strengths of different animals, like he could physically fight her off.

"Get out of my head!" he roared.

"Don't worry so much. You're just a stepping stone," she cooed. She tried forcing him to stand, throwing him onto his back.

Into Talina, he realized grimly. That would be so much worse than killing him and harvesting his soul. She couldn't be allowed to control his mate's body or her demigoddess power.

Lucia's laughter echoed in his mind as she fought to make him stand. His whole body trembled, split between two opposite orders. Lucia forced him to focus on Talina standing only a couple yards away.

Talina watched, wavering on her feet, her expression etched with horror. "Ta...lina...hit...me..." he gritted out. She shook her head, shoulders hunching.

"Look how cute she is. Even scuffed up." With a burst of psychic influence, his fallen sword flew back into his grip. He sensed the intent in her control now, screaming in denial as she forced him to take a dragging step forward. *"That's right. You're going to take her life. Just like you were meant to before."*

He spat a curse, determined to do anything to stop her.

The reluctance was obvious in Talina's face as electricity ran up her arms, leaking from the wounds in her shoulders as she gritted her teeth in pain. Sirius worked the Flight Key off his finger, knowing this would hurt without its protection.

It looked like his mate wasn't about to launch her charged bolt, but then Lucia forced him to lunge at her. Eyes widening, she lifted her hand and aimed, sending a bolt of pure power straight into him. And it was agony, electricity shaking him down to the bone and burning on impact.

He went down again, his vampiric healing struggling to keep him alive. His muscles danced, but Lucia's hold on him faded for only a moment before returning stronger than ever.

Lucia forced him to stand again. It felt like she'd keep making him move until his body was broken and incapable. *"Your soul will be mine very soon,"* she purred. *"I came and took it, just like you wanted."*

"Fuck you," he snarled.

His lips moved without his consent. "Poor, broken girl." It was his voice but Lucia's inflection, and she dragged him forward. Talina looked moments from fainting, her color sickly pale. That may have been the last lightning she could provide.

"Run, Talina," he gritted, forcing his body to a halt. Static quivered in his muscles as he locked them down.

Talina managed to retreat a few steps. "Help!" she called, waving her hands to the sky. She called to her godly father, who watched the battle with a reptilian eye as he circled the mountaintop. Sirius knew it was futile, much as the God of Wind had arranged this moment.

Lucia forced her laugh through his vocal cords. He took another unwilling step, his wings unfurling into several sharp-edged tendrils without the aid of the Flight Key. "You're all alone, little girl."

"T-that's not true." Talina's hands curled into fists. "If Lord Zalice won't help, I'll get you out of Sirius myself!"

She unleashed a gale-force wind, and Sirius worked with it, shifting his lower body into an invertebrate's long enough for the blow to bowl him over like a felled tree. His ears rang on impact with the ground, sight swimming with pained tears. This was the way. If she stood any chance, she'd need to disable him and then extract the demon.

Pain lanced his head as Lucia forced him to get up again. Another fall like that, and he figured he'd crack his skull.

"One problem, girl," Lucia said.

This time, she managed to keep Sirius upright as Talina threw another harsh wind.

A grin split his face. "You don't know how to remove me, or kill me once you have," she purred.

Lucia moved him forward a step, just for them to lurch backward. Some invisible force closed around his body like the tightening of a fist. It wasn't Talina's doing, though her storm-torn eyes widened at whatever she saw behind him.

"She doesn't, but I do," came a roughened woman's voice. Realization seized him as a magical force ripped Lucia out of his body. The agony of her control lifted, and he breathed a sigh of relief. He whirled around, shocked to see Lyana's eyes open, her arm extended and glowing with teal magic. She breathed a word of power, forming icy chains around the shadowy, silver-eyed apparition floating next to him.

Lucia's mouth opened soundlessly to scream, her fangs backlit by a flash of crimson hellfire. She writhed like a fish on a line, barely contained by the links crisscrossing her form.

"Magic," the sea serpent shifter gasped, turning her gaze toward Sirius. "Only magic...can kill her."

He made a circular motion with his index finger, lassoing the Flight Key and putting it back on. Its power thrummed through him, making his flesh numb to the pain of lingering electricity.

"On three," Talina said, coming to his side. Her fingers crackled with electricity coming painfully slow.

"One," he said, bristling with sharp tendrils of shadow.

"Two," Talina murmured, her right hand filling with a humming burst of electrical energy.

Neither of them spoke the last number, instead unleashing their powers together on the shadowy creature. Lucia screamed soundlessly as her body was torn, electrocuted, and crushed by Lyana's constricting chains. Her floating form fell to pieces, strewn across the rocks in front of them.

Through his bond to Talina, he saw every detail of her death. Her body didn't dissolve like he expected. Instead, a glowing hole opened below her torso, showing the lick of real flame over its edges. Lucia's pieces were sucked into it until all that remained was a single hand reaching for them, digits flexed in supplication.

While her demise was soundless, he swore he heard someone else's voice as she disappeared completely. *"You've failed me for the final time..."* It was a soft hiss of sound, just on the edge of his awareness. Talina didn't seem to notice it, so maybe it was his imagination.

Sirius watched with a sneer until the hole into Hell closed, gone in a blink. "Where she belongs," he muttered. Lucia's body was ash, and now, her soul was in shambles—at least, that's what he assumed he'd just seen. Hopefully, she never recovered from it.

Talina swayed into his side, her eyes rolling back. He caught her, laying her battered form down with trembling hands.

Let a miracle come, he thought, noting that Lyana was unconscious again too. In the silence that followed, he watched the Lord of Storm circle in for a landing. A portal opened nearby.

Chapter 46
Talina

THE NEXT TIME SHE OPENED HER EYES, SHE DIDN'T recognize the person bent over her. Casting a spell over her was a beautiful terran fae with white hair to offset her cocoa-brown skin. Her smile came in and out of focus, but from her magic flowed the most welcoming feeling. Tendrils of plants wove around Talina's body, smelling of lavender and honeysuckle. Their cool touch probed at her wounds, mending them with the brush of healing sap. A patient set of hands coaxed a warm honey draught down her throat.

Talina closed her eyes, warring with deep fatigue the moment her pain left. "You won't want to miss this, dear," the woman said in a gentle voice like rustling leaves. Getana laughed when Talina went upright abruptly, taking a closer look at her.

The only hint of the goddess's life and death motif were her wings, which were formed of tiny pine trees and vines as sinew, all stained white like winter ornaments. She wore a rich, silk gown of emerald green, matching her druidic-green eyes. "I thought I would indulge your desire to see me in a form you could hug. Niece." She held her arms out, and Talina hugged her without hesitation.

"I still can't believe it," she admitted, drawing back to look Getana over again. This must be the goddess's true form. Maybe all four gods were secretly incredibly powerful fae. With a little glamor and a leash on her power, it would be nearly impossible to guess who she was.

"Your father has moved the world itself to keep you alive, child. You should go to him," Getana said.

Talina nodded, a bundle of nerves buzzing in her throat. "What about Sirius? Is he okay?"

"He insisted I see to you first." She stood and left Talina with a smile.

She got to her feet too, flaring her wings to balance as her knees wobbled. Sirius wasn't too far away, murmuring to Gabriel as Getana joined them, giving him a cup of medicine to drink. The flat mountaintop had more movement still, as skyriders swooped and played in the circle of storms overhead. Korin carried an unconscious Lyana to Getana.

Several yards away, a fae man stood over a carving in the rock next to a sprawled figure. She walked that way, wondering what she'd even say to her father. Like many orphans, she'd dreamt of who he could be and what kind of heroic business had called him away from looking after his little girl. Her imagination paled to the reality in front of her. He was a god. And not only that—he'd had thousands of opportunities to tell her the truth but had let her discover it in the most shocking way possible.

Zalice turned when she was closer, gesturing her over. He wore fine material, much like Getana, a royal blue tunic and pants covered in silvery filigree. But his feet were bare on the stone, as ordinary and fae-shaped as her own. "You must have questions."

"Why did you pretend to be bound by Lucia?" she blurted. It stuck in her mind most immediately. He'd let Talina see Lucia closing a shackle around his neck, but by the end of the fighting, he was the one keeping her contained to the mountaintop.

"Ah. Did you know skyriders maim prey for their young to catch?" The more he spoke, the less his voice crackled with power. It was familiar on some subconscious level. "She was making a nuisance of herself and overstepped, thinking she could come into my domain and overpower me. Tradition dictates that the heirs to a god prove that they are worthy. So, I set the trap and allowed you to crush her like the insect she was."

She rubbed goosebumps from her arms. "She took over Sirius's body. She nearly killed me!"

"I put no challenges before you that you weren't capable of overcoming." He abandoned his inspection of the pentagram, holding Talina's cheeks with both hands. "You have ascended safely, the first of my children to survive the transition. I am so proud of you," he said gently.

She felt herself start to melt under his warm regard. "There is so much you should know," he continued. "First and foremost, I am sorry I could not be there for you personally while you were growing up. You and your mother had to leave my home when you were a mere four years old. The power in my voice and person was starting to trigger your ascension."

"The same one I just went through?" she asked, her throat clicking on a dry swallow.

"Indeed. Four have come before you, and they all died in the same way." His jaw clenched, and he turned away, gesturing toward the pentagram. A sheer wind cut into the stone, leaving a deep groove he repeated three more times. He lifted the square slab of stone with Lucia's markings upon it, dropping it down to shatter into a thousand little pieces and scattering any demonic magic that remained within.

She saw the grief he tried to hide from her. "You were more careful with me, then," she said quietly.

"I sent you as much guidance as I could. The wind is fickle, even with me," he sighed. "I also sent you a mate to hold your excess magic. Does he fulfill your needs?"

A touch of purple shaded over her cheeks as she thought of Sirius.

"If he does not, I will find you another," he said quickly.

"No, no!" she exclaimed. "He's perfect."

They relaxed again at the same time. She closed the gap between them, pulling him into a hug. "Thank you for everything, Father. I hope we can get to know each other better."

The Lord of Storms held her tightly. "I've missed you so

much," he murmured into her hair. "But it was worth it, to see you alive and whole. You won't be without your father for the rest of your life."

Tears pricked her eyes as she nodded. "Thank you for making sure I'd live."

"Of course. I love you, little cirrus cloud." It sounded like a nickname to her, something that tickled the back of her mind, just out of reach of her memories.

Still, she smiled under the warm regard of her godly father. If she didn't end up remembering her early childhood, they had time to make new memories as family. "I should go to my mate for now. See you soon?" she asked.

Zalice held her a few moments longer, sighing. "Very well. I shall be opening a portal to my home shortly."

"This isn't your home?" she asked in surprise.

He lifted a brow. "It's a flat, uninhabitable rock. Once I leave, the magic does too, and anyone left behind freezes." He cast a glance to the body still lying on the rock. "I shall give him a proper burial here. Go for now. I'm sure my other siblings have arrived."

She turned away just in time to see him using wind magic to cut the hole in the rock into a cross shape. Just as he'd suggested, there were new figures mingling with the old. Both Raenith and Cyranos were immediately identifiable. The Goddess of Fire was literally made of flames even as a fae, having little definition past her limbs when she was flowing white flame everywhere except her wings and other extremities.

Sirius was edging aside as a portal was still in use, releasing a sea serpent still wet from his ocean home. Cyranos transformed into an astral fae, unbothered by the way water made his hair and clothes cling to his frame. He scowled askance at the vampire.

"Feeling better, sweetheart?" Sirius murmured, drawing Talina a step behind him as the God of Water went straight for Lyana's unconscious form.

"Like a whole different person." She wasn't even joking. The new current of magic within her, now that it had shrunk to bearable levels, lent her the kind of confidence she'd admired about him. He was strong and knew it. Now, she was the same in a slightly different way.

Cyranos lifted Lyana and cradled her close to his chest. He looked straight at Sirius, his features starting to revert to those of a sea serpent already, revealing a fanged muzzle and oceanic blue eyes. "Thank you. Perhaps you are welcome here after all." He tilted his head to peer at Talina. "And congratulations, Daughter of the Wind."

She nodded, a smile splitting her face once more as the old god nuzzled Lyana before carrying her back through the portal he'd come from. "Two of our number have regained their kin," Getana said, elbowing Raenith's fiery form. "Shall we celebrate?"

"I propose we raid Zalice's cellars," the other goddess responded. The two of them cackled together.

Talina turned to Sirius, flapping her wings to hover at eye level. They shared a kiss, but not just any. Sparks literally flew as she claimed her mate's lips for the first time since they'd bonded. His touch stirred her electricity, leaving tingles in the wake of his fingertips.

"You were dead. I saw you," she whispered against his lips as they lingered, foreheads brushing.

"I came back for you," he murmured. "Turns out death had no hold on me."

She sniffled, brushing at the moisture gathering in her eyes. "That's amazing."

Sirius's eyes shimmered with the same emotion. He kissed away what lingered on her skin. "You're amazing. You're a demigoddess," he said with a little, disbelieving laugh. "A dancer at a circus! Destined for so much more."

"Destined for you," she said, resting her head against his chest. What she wouldn't give to have this man alone, to remind him just how much he meant to her.

"Actually...I believe I was the one destined for you. Hand chosen by your father." She felt a little twinge of uncertainty from him. "Are you okay with that? Knowing it wasn't quite fate that brought us together?"

"Absolutely," she said without hesitation. "I don't care what led us here. Just that we *are* here."

He breathed out his tension, nosing into her hair with a content sigh. They stood like that for a long while, until Zalice came to open a new portal with an offhand gesture. "You all have viewed my new heir. Let's enjoy this reunion," he said, gesturing invitingly toward the oval of magic. Everyone filed through, even the skyriders. Talina held Sirius's hand as their turn to go through approached.

"You may experience some suppressed memories," Zalice warned.

He wasn't kidding. The moment her feet touched down, she recognized this place from her distant past. This was home. A placid lake surrounded by a bowl of grass, protected on all sides by the high walls of taller mountains. With few trees to speak of, the area was open to a chill breeze, rustling the gold-tinged plants all around them.

Home was also the cozy brick house everyone filed toward. There were wide, metal bars around for skyriders to perch on the roof or out by the front porch. She remembered the rocking chair out front, but back then, she would sit in her father's lap as he relaxed with her mother, sipping cold water and watching the sun set. That second rocking chair was gone now.

She hadn't realized she'd stopped there until Zalice's voice distracted her from the memory. "I miss her too," he said quietly. "Know that her spirit is at peace."

"Couldn't you have saved her?" she asked.

He shook his head. "It was her wish. We knew it was coming, but it was a surprise to see her return to my domain so soon."

She accepted that with a heavy heart. It sounded like her mother, joyful and independent as she was. Besides, she had more memories as soon as she smelled the mild incense he still used to make the home smell of sandalwood. "My room was on the second floor," she murmured. "I would always have... Wait..."

Sirius watched with concern as she broke their handhold and rushed back outside. "I had a friend back then," she told him as he followed. "A skyrider chick! Father gave him to me before I could even walk. I think we were meant to be something more. Like familiars."

Parax perched on a metal rod outside, waiting patiently for her. He still had the same canary-yellow eyes, but he'd grown from a tiny puffball into a huge dragon. "You remember me?" he asked hopefully.

"We got into a lot of mischief together here, didn't we?" she answered, laughing as he leaned forward and nuzzled her face.

"Father thought it was unwise for you to have a skyrider familiar before you ascended. It would bring up too many questions," he sighed. "I was an orphan, so he raised me when you left. I've missed you so much."

"Well, I'm back now." She scratched into his neck, giggling when he trilled in appreciation. "But I do have a familiar."

"Yes...the tiny bird." He turned his head, and so did she. Saniya had appeared in a blink and was clapping her hands, summoning up a portal. And from it shot Gem, who fluttered up to her and hovered anxiously.

"*I sensed your soul change. Are you okay?*" he asked.

She cupped him in one hand and continued rubbing Parax's neck with the other. "I'm great," she said, really meaning it. "If that was what Father was warning me of this whole time, then I'm glad it's done. My true name has changed, and now, I get to be a part of the most amazing family."

She turned toward Sirius, feeling her eyes sparkle, not a cloud in sight. "And so do you."

"*Gods above. Don't get mushy on me already,*" Gem complained, though he alighted on Sirius's shoulder just to be out of nibbling range of Parax.

"Can demigoddesses have more than one familiar?" she asked the skyrider.

"Maybe we should find out sometime," he said, giving her one last nuzzle before she returned to Sirius's side. "Bring me some wine, won't you? I love the lightning reserve."

"Never heard of that vintage before," Sirius murmured.

"That's because the Lord of Storms makes it himself. It's got a nice zing." Little arcs of electricity sparked over the dragon's neck.

"I think I've had enough electricity for one day." He chuckled, lifting a hand in greeting as Gwendolyn and Cossette came from Saniya's portal next, followed by the last person Talina expected to be interested in coming to this little get-together.

Queen Kalimea stopped and embraced the djinni before turning to the group milling about outside. "What are you waiting for? No party like a god's party," she called.

Chapter 47
Sirius

Turned out, Kalimea was right. All Zalice wanted to do was introduce her to the faces around the table before the wine was poured. Once they moved to the back patio, Lady Getana pulled out a violin and summoned up a few vines from the ground to complete her string quartet, playing upbeat melodies.

"You try this stuff? It'll put hair on your chest," Korin laughed, choking halfway into his second glass of lightning reserve.

Sirius took the bottle from him. "Maybe when I've forgotten what it's like to be nearly electrocuted," he said like he was joking.

"Yeah, you might have to get used to that." Korin grinned and glanced around. "If you haven't noticed, her family is special."

Raenith was dancing a few feet away, her fiery body obviously naked but otherwise formless. She had a bottle of wine in either fist, dancing more sinuously to her sister's music as the night wore on. Korin made for quite the enraptured audience.

"Be careful. That will definitely burn you," Sirius laughed.

As soon as Talina flittered around like her hummingbird, paying respects and speaking to everyone, he snagged her for a dance. "How about you and I find some alone time?" she suggested as they spun together, freestyling their movements together to the song playing.

"That's the best thing I've heard all night," he admitted. He'd done his duty, passing the Light Key to Gabriel, figuring a literal angel would be the best place for it with Collins's passing.

The other man had taken the news hard. "I didn't see the corruption in him," he'd sighed. "In truth, I have failed him, but it sounds like he's gone to the one place he'll be happy. Even if it's not quite Heaven."

"I'm sure he'll make it one day, with what you have taught him," Sirius had said.

Still, the exchange pulled down his mood too, until he'd gotten Talina back in his arms. It was impossible not to smile when he saw and felt how happy and fulfilled she was now that she'd discovered who she was meant to be.

He just wanted some of that sunny smile to himself. It seemed she was thinking along the same lines, as she led him away from her childhood home after they danced together to a few more songs.

"I'm not sure if Father has kept my old room, but it'd be too small for us anyway," she said, sneaking him toward the lake. Once they were at its shores, though, she hummed and looked around. "There's a nice place around here. I just have to remember..."

Snapping her fingers, she took him to a clearing where the grass was deceptively deep. With the help of his shadows, they were completely hidden. They took their time undressing, coming together tenderly. He wasn't quite sure what to expect from a coupling with his newly bonded mate, but it exceeded his every imagining. Her pleasure was his and vice versa, drawing them ever closer.

Their hearts beat to the same rhythm out under the stars. He drew little patterns on her belly afterward, content down to his very soul. They didn't need to say anything, not when his love for her was echoed back over the bond and made all the stronger for it.

"We have to stay here for a bit so I can learn how to use my power," she whispered.

He played with a lock of her hair. "That's fine." As long as they were here together, he saw no hardship in enjoying the little amenities of her godly father's isolated home. "I claim this little spot as ours, though."

She giggled, bundling closer as a cool breeze rustled the grass around them. "Have you thought about what you want to do afterward?" she asked.

"After we make the Dark Eye anew?" he mused aloud. "I didn't really think about an afterward. I didn't expect you, Talina. What do you want to do?"

She smiled wistfully. "Wouldn't it be fun to travel? Just you and me."

He closed his eyes, imagining it. "Earth or Faerie?" he asked.

"Both. It'll be fun." She turned a hopeful look toward him. "Don't you think? Maybe after that, we can settle down in the best place we find along the way."

"Sweetheart, anywhere by your side is the best place I can think of," he answered. "I'll build you a house to fill with a family, or we can travel until the end of time. Name it, and I will make it happen."

Sparkles danced over the open sky in her eyes. The joy and hope in her heart melted his. He really would move Heaven and Earth for this woman. She was the sky to hang his sun upon, the light to draw him ever onward into an immortal lifetime he could finally see himself living.

Her expression turned coy. "Right now, all I want is more of you."

And that, he was more than happy to oblige.

Chapter 48
Sondus

Weeks passed, and Jaromir didn't wake up. Sondus made sure he had the best round-the-clock care out of sight in Shifting Wood Manor. With a heart heavier with guilt, he assumed control of Jaromir's work and research while also borrowing the Blood Prince's identity.

His laboratory brewed the rare doppelgänger potion that would hide his true self under a thick coating of magic, stronger than any glamor. Someone with True Sight could reveal him, but they'd have to suspect something was wrong first.

Sondus had studied Jaromir's mannerisms in their short time together because it was second nature to a spymaster to know everyone around them inside and out. He hadn't intended any harm in inviting Soren to help him, and despite the angel's assurances, Sondus knew he was now in great debt to repair this newest trespass against the Blood Prince as his body healed from the blinding light he'd ingested.

However, his absence was an opportunity Sondus couldn't ignore. When Izell returned to speak with "Jaromir," he could finally bring her in for interrogation. In the meantime, he passed his spymaster work to his lieutenants and assumed the quiet, unassuming life of the Blood Prince.

Alaku was still sprawled on the floor with him, painstakingly reading *The Legacy of Primal Magic* while Sofia the dog stared distrustfully at Sondus. She'd growled the first time he'd retrieved her from Alaku's family, and the angry, raspy sound revealed that while she may look like a puppy now, she would be something much more wild and dangerous in a few years.

Sondus had a notebook full of diagrams at this point, and he added the finishing touch to another as the afternoon light waned to evening, splashing a triangle of light on the page. He had misled Jaromir; he understood advanced spellcasting quite well in theory, even without the magic and talent to put it into practice. After enlisting the help of a Sorcerer he had on staff, he knew he was getting closer to replicating King Oberon's greatest work spell and translating it to the modern situation, with thirteen people each holding one Key.

It was the culmination of weeks of deep cover. While he enjoyed the change of pace and the importance of the work, Sondus chafed to go home and kiss his wife and snuggle their young son. They understood that his job close to the royal family required time and sacrifice...but not the extent of it.

He was starting to wonder if Izell would ever come check on Jaromir just that morning, despairing that this could be a futile endeavor. But as he sighed and inspected his drawing, turning it this way and that as if it would reveal its viability to him, a flash of gold appeared out the corner of his eye.

The air charged briefly with the closing of a portal. No one could portal in and out of the Library of Faerie unless they had clearance, he thought, frowning to know Izell had tricked the standing wards. He stood slowly.

"Taking a break, Prince Jaromir?" Alaku asked sweetly.

Sondus flashed a fond smile. It wasn't hard to pretend with him, since he was so much like his youngest son. "Yes. Why don't you do the same?"

"I dunno. I just walked Sofia..." With his learning disability, Alaku needed more breaks from the page. Sondus insisted he stop more often than Jaromir had.

However, he shrugged now, too full of adrenaline to argue. "Suit yourself." He headed into the stacks, coming face to face with an unglamored Izell. Heart skittering, he put on a hesitant smile and forced himself to wait for her to speak first.

It took her a few seconds. She inspected him like she knew something was off before breathing the kind of high-pitched laugh that set his teeth on edge. "Hello, Jaromir, hello. Not excited to see me? I'm sorry how we left off."

She tried to tug the journal from his hand. "Izell. I need you to explain." He tightened his grip on it as he spoke with Jaromir's quiet intensity. She'd left the man confused and floundering with a bag of demon suppressing herbs in his hand. He would want some answers.

"I will. Very soon. Just tell me you did what I asked." She tugged again, and he released it this time, watching warily as she flipped through it. The smile that spread across her face revealed sharp teeth, stretching too wide to be natural. Goosebumps broke out over his arms.

"This is it," she said, tucking it under her arm. "You've done it! I saw you would before I struck out my future sight. While some things have gone wrong, one thing is steady..." Her hand curled through his, and she tugged him as she took a step back. "You are my rock, Jaromir. Studying this long, keeping your faith in me."

Sondus bit the inside of his cheek and kept a neutral expression, while on the inside, he wanted to laugh. Jaromir hadn't figured out anything—but her glimpse of the future didn't show that someone else wearing Jaromir's face would crack the code on the spell she desired.

"And I want to reward you," she continued, opening a portal behind her. She pulled him toward it as she backpedaled.

"Where are we going?" he asked in a low voice. With a smile like that, he was half afraid it would be a dark room with no exits so she could unleash her demon's hunger on him.

Instead of answering, she jerked him through with a flash of her dragon side's strength. They emerged into a sunlit clearing, over-bright to his eyes after hours of studying and reading. Magic hung thick in the air, sparkling in rainbow fragments.

Sondus scrubbed his face, turning in awe as he beheld the

river valley sloping down from where they stood. "Welcome to the Sanctum of Faerie. Where all good little fae souls go, under the watch of the goddess Getana," Izell said, heading down without hesitation and stopping at the nearly transparent barrier that had prevented her from portaling directly into the beating heart of Faerie's most sacred place.

If Izell had any negative intentions toward the Sanctum, that barrier would burn her to death the moment she tried to pass it. And if she had no business here, it would repel her. She stopped short of it and turned, shooting him an impatient look. "We don't have much time," she growled, waving him forward.

Saving his dubious thoughts, he came forward and watched as she passed through the barrier without issue. He tried to follow, shuddering as the magic ran over his skin like thick gelatin, but they were both in, and she hadn't died horribly. He really was about to get some answers.

"Since when do you wear jewelry?" she asked, pointing out the ring on his right index finger.

He'd been hoping she wouldn't notice it. "It was a gift," he said simply.

Shrugging, she led him further into the Sanctum. Knee-high grass waved around them from a gentle breeze, while thicker fragments of magic congealed into sparkling crystals floating and sparkling through the air. "I really am sorry," she said, casting a glance over her shoulder. "Things have to be done a certain way in order for us all to survive."

"Is that why you've been taking herbs to suppress demonic influence?" He couldn't help the sharper tone, and her eyebrows lifted fractionally.

"Yes. I see you looked up what they were. You had to hold onto them for me because...I didn't want to stop taking them."

Izell wrapped her arms around herself, stopping under a curlicue of crystallized magic. He'd never seen a vulnerable moment in her, deeply shook as she curled inward with lines of fear marking her every feature.

"I'm going to die, Jaromir," she whispered. This powerful

woman held herself, because she'd permitted no one else to hear these words. He realized he'd gotten her intentions wrong. Like a fool, seeing only the hints and not the whole.

She was going to sacrifice herself to power the spell, like her grandfather before her. "If you have a demon's spark..."

"I do." She wiped at her cheeks as he came in, pulling her to his chest. She hid her face in his shoulder and wept soundlessly, great heaving sobs. "I have to give him some control so he is powerful enough to go back into the new Eye of Worlds," she hiccupped.

"Izell, no," he said in quiet horror.

She shook her head. "But if he's still weak, he will die for the final time on the transition. It has to be done right."

"This will not work," he murmured. Her view of the future already had huge holes, himself being the case in point. The demon she carried could easily overwhelm her while she thought she was still in control.

It had to go. He just had to figure out the specifics. He was already twisting the ring behind her back, exposing a hidden needle full of enough tranquilizer to drop a fully grown dragon. One swift poke in the neck, and they could make a better plan together. A plan that didn't require her to be a martyr.

Izell had been his mentor, saving him when he'd needed her most. He would do the same for her.

He paused when an otherworldly sound rent the air. Izell tore away from him and dried her eyes, thankfully looking away as he hid the needle and glanced around. It sounded again, closer, the call of a creature mingled with shimmering magic.

"He's here," she said, breathing a sigh of relief. The crystal-lized magic began to ring on a low frequency as light shimmered, coalescing into the form of a majestic white stag. Sondus counted over twenty points in his rack as his hooves stepped with delicate intent toward Izell. The dragon shifter turned back to him, her cloudy eyes still shimmering with tears. "It's my grandfather."

Sondus watched in stunned silence as she embraced the stag's massive head. *You smell of Jazrach.* The spirit of King Oberon spoke in their minds, a gentle and commanding voice to match his new stature.

"I saw it was the only way to summon you back from the beyond," she answered. Sondus reached up to shut his jaw.

Fae spirits never returned from the beyond. They joined the land, enriching the elements and keeping the company of the gods. Eternity was supposedly quite blissful. Why would anyone want to return?

"*His presence is a stain on our history.*" The stag's liquid-black eyes inspected Izell closely. "*He was supposed to be dead for all this time. But I see I did not quite finish the job.*"

"A lot has happened, Grandfather. Perhaps you can stay to listen and share your wisdom." She clasped her hands, holding her breath as he considered.

"*Perhaps. Tell me of your troubles.*"

They wandered further into the Sanctum. Izell threaded her arm through Sondus's and spoke in depth of everything...things Sondus wished he knew. He listened just as keenly as Oberon as she talked about the dawn of the Fell and how a chunk of Faerie was sunken into the sea and turned into a place of exile for them. Unluckily, the Dark Eye of Worlds was part of that land and ended up powering a ritual that allowed Fell to head to Earth.

She spoke of human heroes turned to vampires by Fell blood. How they defeated the creatures...but Jazrach's spark found a host in Lucia, who exiled the true Queen of Vampires to the Fell Lands. Queen Nyah had turned the dark land into a utopia with the help of the familiar bonds between Fell and their deceased familiars, creating a world where *mort loci* were the norm.

She spread her hands, tipped in dragon talons. "I was the first to discover that the Fell curse could not stick to a shifter. So, we were all cured."

"*Fascinating,*" Oberon murmured. "*Go on.*"

She nodded, summarizing three thousand years of advising and waiting to be freed from exile. How, on Earth, the Dark Eye had been destroyed and Jazrach freed. "I saw a future where demons would soon return to Faerie after we were allowed back into the sun. So, I have scried and scried, forming over those thousands of years a specific path we all must follow if we are to survive the Everlasting War briefly brushing past the Veil. We seek to create a new Dark Eye to replace the one destroyed."

She took a deep breath, a mantle of resignation falling over her. "There was one thing I couldn't scry, and that was the spell itself. My good friend here has been studying the spell and created a diagram that may work...but I need you to teach me the words of power you used. Please, Grandfather. It is for the good of Faerie."

She showed him the notebook as Oberon acknowledged Sondus with a dip of his head. *"Good friend, hmm?"*

Sondus felt a chill down his spine. The spirit probably saw right through his disguise. Izell gave Sondus a look both fond and wistful. "It could've been more, had we had more time."

He cleared his throat and nodded. "I understand," he responded quietly.

Thankfully, Oberon turned his attention back to Izell. *"I can give you the words right now. Write them down, for you will need to practice the pronunciation. It is primal magic."* He tilted his rack with a low sigh. *"You may be the last primal fae alive, granddaughter. Faerie itself will mourn your loss."*

"Faerie has to survive long enough to mourn," she replied. Izell drew her arm from his, writing down the spell as Oberon dictated it. He critiqued Sondus's diagram, making minor adjustments to add a fourteenth person—a spell caster who wouldn't be holding a Fell Key. Sondus grunted, irritated with himself for missing such an important detail.

"A word of caution. I know why Jazrach didn't perish when he was placed in his prison," Oberon sighed. *"The gods disapproved of my choice. He was a Greater Demon, not as powerful as Archangel Cerindra, who sacrificed herself for the Light Eye. The gods knew I chose Jazrach out of pride, to punish him for what he did to ruin my daughter."*

Izell exchanged a glance with Sondus, who frowned. He'd never read about this in any history book. "I was little more than a child when he performed the spell," she whispered to him. "But I heard later that—"

"Jazrach was my lover. Before he fell and succumbed to his new nature, he was the most beautiful being I'd ever met." At least Sondus knew some context to this—Oberon had had several lovers and family lines, in addition to his royal wife. Times were different back then.

"But upon shedding his angelic grace, he became the monster to convince my daughter to pledge her forces to demon kind. She went on to become the first Unseelie Queen..."

He stared into the distance, lost in memory. Izell turned away with a sigh. "He may need some time," she said.

"Of course. This must be traumatic for him." Besides, Sondus knew the rest. Some fae aligned with demons, others with angels, and they fought bitterly down their divided lines, urged on by their new leaders and masters. Oberon had created the Veil and the Eyes of Worlds because he was sick of seeing his people die and the demon-allied fae twist to human-hunting monsters. And in his dying breath, he'd cursed Unseelie with their backward tongues, binding them to the lies they'd believed, while Seelie fared slightly better as eternal truth tellers.

Sondus had to ask one thing, though. This opportunity would never arise again, to speak with ancient history face to face. "Is it true that Unseelie will be released from your curse if they prove that they are friends to humanity?"

Oberon sighed, taking a slow blink. *"That's right,"* he whispered. *"To do so, they must work closely with the Seelie. That is what I wanted to see.*

"The gods revoked their blessing over me the moment I chose Jazrach for selfish reasons and split the greater fae people forever. That is why Jazrach lived through the ritual—I was weakened at the last moment, and my magic could not fully consume him. That is the last link you need to gain, granddaughter, if you want to succeed where I have failed. You must gain the backing of all four gods if you want your new Dark Eye to stand forever."

Izell nodded, her expression troubled. "I was not expecting this. The gods forsook Adrun. They must despise *mort loci.*"

"I suspect your well-scried plan has more holes in it than you would expect." Oberon was looking at him again. Sondus hid a dry swallow with a little cough. *"I suggest you trust your allies with your ideas. It is possible that there is more than one path to success."*

"No, Grandfather. I have seen thousands of possibilities. Only one leads to us succeeding," she responded.

Oberon dipped his head in acknowledgement. Light dropped from his horns, turning to brilliant floating particles. *"Very well. You have what you need...so I rest once more."*

"Farewell," she breathed, drawing her hands through the glimmers of light as he dissolved into nothing more than air. Her scaled hand formed a fist to hold on to him just a little bit longer.

"Do you understand now, Jaromir? Why I couldn't tell anyone?" she whispered. "But I trust you. I just wish we had more time."

"There's still some time, right?" He sighed, feeling like the biggest ass to witness this confession. She really must have caught feelings, so he would need to proceed cautiously.

At the same time, he knew he couldn't let her plan proceed without the backing of the Crown. There was no way there was only one right answer to what she was trying to do.

"Not much," she murmured. Still, she crossed to him, her hands caressing up his chest. He knew she was moments from planting a kiss on his lips.

He put his arms around her. She leaned in, face softening with tenderness. The moment would be immortalized in his memory forever, because he'd never see something like this again.

He twisted his ring in a swift motion and pricked her neck with the hidden needle.

She gasped, her eyelids already drooping. *"Trucaris,"* she breathed, casting the Spell of True Sight over him. The doppelgänger potion melted away as she swayed into his arms. *"Sondus..."*

"I'm sorry," he murmured.

"What have you done...?"

She slumped into his hold, unconscious. With a sigh, he lifted her and turned to leave the Sanctum of Faerie. They would smash the demon spark within her and find another way.

The apocalypse is nearly here. Can Izell still save the day? Don't miss...
Rule the Night: Blood Legacy Series Book 6

Also by Elise Hennessy
Altare World

Are you ready for a high-flying adventure on gryphon-back? Join Sivana as she becomes the first female cadet at the highly competitive Gryphon Rider Academy after the blind gryphon Arimus chooses her as his new rider.

Dragon Riders of Pern meets Song of the Lioness in this YA fantasy series in which a pair of underdogs rewrite what's possible in a formerly all-boys military academy.

- See Gryphon Rider Academy on Amazon -

Also by Elise Hennessy

Join an unlikely crew of five misfits and a mouse as they strive to become one of Altare's newest elite spy teams. Heists and adventures await!

The Gilded Wolves meets Six of Crows in this YA fantasy series in which a former thief uses her skills to become a spy. If you like clever heroines, strong friendships, and found family, then you'll love Royal Spy Institute!

- See Royal Spy Institute on Amazon -

About the Author

Elise Hennessy is an author of young adult fantasy full of adventure and found family. She holds a master's degree in journalism and enjoys crafting unique stories. When Elise is not busy writing, she's trying to reduce her prodigious TBR list. She lives in Texas with her family and is owned by two cats.

Find out more about her books at: www.elisehennessy.com

Glossary

Adrun: A section of Faerie submerged under the ocean and shrouded in magic to make it impenetrable. Formerly a prison for the cursed Fell. Queen Nyah renamed it from "The Fell Lands" when she and her shifters reclaimed it and eliminated the Fell curse. It is a place of complete darkness that sustains life through druidic magic.

Alchemyst: An incredibly rare sub-distinction of vampire with golden blood. They can create powerful tonics and potions with one drop of their life essence. They are immortal, but lack the superhuman aspects of vampirism and the bloodlust.

Angel: A being of pure light and a denizen of Heaven. All angels are called to uphold and spread a grace, or positive emotion/trait. Can only be permanently killed by another angel or demonic magic.

Blade: A fae skilled with martial magic and a weapon of choice, usually a sword. Traditionally they serve as bodyguards to Sorcerers.

Blood Prince: A title given to the few Fell Hunters that survived the Fell Crisis. They are the first vampires and each started their own unique bloodlines.

The Crossing: Seelie fae can cross The Veil and travel between Earth and Faerie or vice versa during midsummer in a magical process called The Crossing. The only way to otherwise cross between the two worlds is through one of a handful of well-hidden portals.

Demon: A being of pure darkness and a denizen of Hell. The most common demons represent one of the seven sins, though it's possible to find a demon that represents any negative emotion. Can only be permanently killed by another demon or angelic magic.

Deveaux Accords: A set of laws created by the major covens of New York City and enforced by Ancient vampiress Cossette Deveaux. Covens are required to police their members to keep mortals safe.

Dhampir: A half-human, half-vampire by birth.

Drasonii: Literally "dragon-blessed." Members of a fae orchestra with instruments blessed by the four dragon gods of Faerie. The instruments are peerless and capable of conveying the emotions of a song to a listening crowd.

Druid: A fae or shifter that has manifested the virtue of druidism. They maintain the balance of nature through husbandry and control of the elements. It is possible to be both a Sorcerer and have druidism, but a fae or shifter that has both gifts is considered a druid exclusively. A druid in Faerie serves the four gods and the balance of the elements, while a shifter druid in Adrun keeps the land alive in the absence of sunlight.

The Everlasting War: The conflict between angels and

demons. The Veil was created to keep this eternal war away from Earth and Faerie.

Eyes of Worlds: A pair of giant tools that anchor The Veil into place. One was created by the willing sacrifice of an Archangel—it is the Light Eye located in Faerie. The other was created from an unwilling greater demon and became its prison—it was destroyed during the events of *Dream Walker*.

Faerie: A separate world magically linked to Earth. The place of origin for all magic and mythical creatures.

Fell: A fae afflicted with a curse of eternal hunger. The curse was spread from Fell to fae via a bite and was considered incurable. Fell are twisted creatures known for squat, frog-like legs, sharp and interconnected teeth like a bear trap, black veins, and pitch-black eyes. All Fell were banished from Faerie to The Fell Lands (see Adrun). The Fell Crisis or Fell War occurred when the Fell learned they could create portals to Earth during the Dark Ages and began consuming man and beast alike like a black tide of locusts. After their defeat, all records of the Fell were expunged from mortal record to hide the existence of vampires.

Fell Hunter: The first vampires. Soldiers exposed to Fell blood became strong and fast enough to fight Fell in the service to humanity. Though the first Fell Hunters were turned by accident, many were turned on purpose after the phenomenon was studied. In those days, being a vampire was considered a sacrifice for the greater good. Most Fell Hunters died fighting monsters.

Fell Keys: Thirteen in total, referring to a set of rings with gemstones of pure magic. Each one represents one of the schools of fae magic and grants the wearer great power.

Fell Madness: The boogeyman of vampirism. First manifested in Fell Hunters when they consumed too much Fell blood. Fell

Glossary

Madness gives vampires black veins, a mouthful of sharp teeth, and endless hunger for blood. Very little is known about the affliction because those that manifested it were swiftly executed. In modern day, the affliction can be cured by an Alchemyst's potion.

The Gift: Some vampires manifest the Gift rather than the abilities of their bloodline. They are capable of healing others from even the worst of mortal wounds. The Gift leaves if a vampire uses it to harm or kill others.

Heartsong: The fae version of a lifemate (see below). Every fae has a unique melody that they create when they come of age, which they refer to as a heart's song. Two fae with harmonizing heart's songs are destined to be mates.

Heaven-Hell Accords: A set of rules agreed on between angels and demons as it concerns their interaction with Earth. As the Everlasting War is based off of balance, if a demon is summoned to Earth, an angel is allowed through The Veil to hunt it down. Resurrections of newly created angels or demons is strictly forbidden. Hell attacks, Heaven defends. Demons historically have bent these rules to the breaking point.

Lifemate: A perfect match to a vampire. It is possible to identify a lifemate on sight and many vampires describe the sensation as being as subtle as a punch to the gut. A lifemate is usually a vampire's perfect opposite. It is possible for a vampire to have more than one lifemate, but the phenomenon is exceedingly rare as most vampires don't survive to an advanced age if they lose their first lifemate.

Mort Loci: Translated to "death speaker." A derogatory term for a person with the soul of an animal inside of them. The fae consider such people possessed or cursed. (See shifter below.)

Nephilim: A person with angel parentage, who is capable of wielding light magic. Nephilim are considered extinct in modern day due to The Veil and the Heaven-Hell Accords.

Nyixa Island: A chunk of The Fell Lands that the Fell managed to drag to Earth. It is a relatively large island with the Dark Eye at its center. After the Fell were defeated, vampires made it their seat of power before it was sunk to the bottom of the ocean in a bid to eradicate Fell Madness. It has only resurfaced recently in modern times and is considered inhabitable.

Occultarus: A tool used by Sorcerers to concentrate their magic. Instead of using complicated gestures to summon magic, a Sorcerer can hold an occultarus and cast spells more quickly. An occultarus is a sphere of glass forged by dragon fire and contains concentrated magic within. The Eyes of Worlds were modeled after occultari and are giant versions of them.

Primordial Fae: The very first denizens of Faerie. They were powerful, but unstable, and evolved into the four sub-races of greater fae, split into the four elements of earth, fire, water, and wind. King Oberon is the most notable Primordial.

Seelie Fae: Greater fae who aligned with angels before The Veil separated Faerie from Heaven and Hell. Their tongues are cursed to utter only the truth. While Faerie is at peace now, Seelie and Unseelie have historically been at war along the same lines as their patrons. Their sub-races are terran fae (earth), solar fae (fire), astral fae (water), and aether fae (wind).

Shifter: A fae or human with the soul of an animal within them. While the fae will refer to a shifter as *mort loci* in a derogatory manner, the denizens of Adrun all became shifters as the Fell curse cannot take root in a body with two souls within it. The creation of a shifter is a partnership and the resulting person can appear fully humanoid or gain physical characteristics of their animal side. Some shifters fully give in to the whims of their animal and never return to humanoid form.

Glossary

Spark: A piece of a demon's soul that can be given to a "willing" person. A spark will slowly corrupt the person's soul until it resembles the same level of darkness as the original demon, twisting their personality in the process. A spark can out-live a demon if they are killed. Powerful demons can "resurrect" by taking over the body of a humanoid afflicted by their spark.

Spellbreaker: A fae skilled in reflecting or mitigating magic. A highly trained Spellbreaker can render a Sorcerer's magic useless.

Sorcerer: Originally a distinction for the rare fae who can control all thirteen schools of magic, this title is also awarded to the sub-class of vampire that has silver blood and the ability to control every school of fae magic. Sorcerers are highly trained and often manifest extra rare abilities called virtues. The five virtues are: true sight, future sight, empathy, druidism, and mediumship.

Unseelie Fae: Greater fae who aligned with demons before The Veil separated Faerie from Heaven and Hell. Their tongues are cursed to utter only lies. While Faerie is at peace now, Seelie and Unseelie have historically been at war along the same lines as their patrons. Their sub-races are curse fae (earth), destruction fae (fire), death fae (water), and blight fae (wind).

Vampire: Descendants of the original Fell Hunters, spread by their cursed blood. The existence of vampires has become a myth to modern mortals as the purpose of vampires has tarnished from war heroes into former mortals trying to avoid their mortal coil. Contrary to popular myth, vampires are not walking corpses; they eat, breathe, and reproduce, though the chance of conception narrows as a vampire ages. Young vampires act a lot like humans with a taste for blood, though as they age they grow more powerful and inhuman. Vampires manifest an aura, which communicate to each other how old and powerful they are.

The Veil: A magical barrier that separates Earth and Faerie from the realms of Heaven and Hell. Anchored in place by the Eyes of Worlds, it's been in place for over a thousand Earth years and prevented the worlds from coming to ruin by being battle-grounds for angels and demons.

Cast of Characters

Modern Day Vampires

Residents of New York City's covens.

Alexander Rehnquist

A vampire nearing his five hundredth year. Master of Coven Rehnquist and skilled shapeshifter. He is bitter rivals with Bryant Collins and lost his first lifemate due to the conflict between their covens. Fate crossed him one night and he ended up partnered with a second lifemate, Violet Reynolds.

Violet Reynolds

Formerly a mortal zookeeper, Violet was exposed to vampirism after Lucia secretly turned her into a kind of vampire that hadn't been seen in a thousand years. She became a silver-blooded Sorceress, learned how to master her magic, and captured Alex's love.

Julian Fairfax

One of the officers of Coven Rehnquist. The only vampire who mysteriously manifests an icy cold aura. He searched for his lifemate for hundreds of years until they were united via Lucia's machinations. He was viciously hunted by Lucia due to him killing her obsession. Possesses the Winter Key.

Olivia Cooper

A struggling mortal actress who was kidnapped to New York. She knows of the vampire world due to her best friend, Charlotte, but was quickly over her head after taking in Violet's blood and turning into an Alchemyst. She developed magical empathy and used it to save her Ancient allies from Jazrach's corruption. Due to her blood and quick thinking, she transformed a portal manifesting a connection between Earth and Hell into one that linked Earth to Adrun instead. Possesses the Shadow Key.

Charlotte Smith

Olivia's best friend and the only dhampir around. She is loyal and protective of her friend, joining Coven Rehnquist when Olivia did. She joins the supernatural police and becomes Armando's patrol partner when Julian retires.

Armando Nizzola

Julian's cousin and a member of the supernatural police. He is Charlotte's lifemate and earns her affection in the Christmas special *Dhampir's Wish*.

Bryant Collins

A bitter rival to Alex and Coven Rehnquist. He owns the telecommunications company Haven and thus members of his coven are referred to as Haveners. He is an Ancient and a religious zealot, believing the Light Key is his by his faith. He allied with Lucia thinking he could finally crush Coven Rehnquist with her might and magic, instead realizing his mistake too late after she got his entire coven killed and sacrificed his wife's heart to power a portal. He now seeks repentance for his misguided ideals.

Kim Cox

Bryant Collins's wife, known for her sadistic personality and enjoyment of torturing others. She is deceased as of *The Winter Key*.

Cast of Characters

Cossette Deveaux

The Ancient leader of the most powerful coven in New York City. She is an albino and a rare vampire who possesses future sight. She is stuck in the body of a little girl due to the twisted ideals of her vampire master. Due to her unique circumstances, her mind is damaged. She usually acts like a cheerful and sweet girl, but sometimes shows hints of her age as she delivers prophecies of the future.

Ancients

Surviving Fell Hunters whose bloodlines have shaped the vampire world in their absence.

Adrius

King of Adrun

Strongest Fell Hunter and owner of the Shield Key. He fell into a deep pit of depression to be separated from his lifemate, Nyah. Possessed every vampiric ability until he became a shifter by bonding to the spirit of the dragon Zerenth.

Lucia

The first vampire Sorceress. She inherited Jazrach's spark and was slowly driven insane. Nyixa was sunk partially to contain her evil. Upon dying in *Queen's Return,* she was reincarnated as a demon of corruption and now terrorizes her peers as she tries to capture a powerful soul to fulfill the debt of her escape from Hell. Was briefly Queen of Vampires in *Blood Curse*.

Gwendolyn Firetree

A nephilim who represents the grace of duty. Conspired to sink Nyixa in *Blood Curse* to contain Fell Madness and Lucia. She has committed her immortal existence to curbing the damage of old vampires on the brink of Fell Madness by making them mysteriously "disappear."

Sirius

Blood Prince Sirius, the Dawn
Adrius's second-in-command and brother. Was once a kind and giving man, but emerged from his thousand-year rest bitter, angry, and unable to fully control the whims of his inner beast. He is a shapeshifter and possesses the ability to walk in daylight without harm.

Korin

Blood Prince Korin, the Bane
The gentle giant of the Ancients, a steady and quiet personality. He is a blood tracker.

Neala

Blood Princess Neala, the Wraith
A mute orphan raised by Gabriel and Gwendolyn. She defied the odds and survived the Fell Crisis, though she sustained several terrible wounds that scarred her face and chest. Despite being an illusionist, she refuses to hide her scars or make herself more attractive and feminine. Loved and lost her first mate, Marcus Hartson, to Lucia's machinations.

Elandros

Blood Prince Elandros, the Legion
Squire to Gabriel Legion and also his murderer due to unfortunate circumstances. Possessed the ability to make minor illnesses and blights. After being blackmailed for the rest of his life by Lucia, he confessed his crime to Gwendolyn and was forgiven. Deceased as of *The Winter Key*. His soul was delivered to Heaven in *Queen's Return*.

Jaromir

Blood Prince Jaromir, the Mender
The doctor of the surviving Ancients. He was in possession of the Gift until he was briefly afflicted with Fell Madness in *The Winter Key*. He believes himself incomplete without his Gift.

Cast of Characters

Qin

Blood Prince Qin, the Ascended

He is considered a greedy coward by his peers, as he took a payment from Lucia and went into hiding, never to be seen again.

Taryn

Blood Prince Taryn, the Blade

Lucia's bodyguard due to taking a stage three love potion and being enslaved by his emotions. While he was immediately driven to Fell Madness upon being released from her control, he found his peace and center by becoming a druid as of *Queen's Return*.

Marcus Hartson

A close friend to the Ancients and Neala's former mate. After his mating bond was severed by Lucia, he was poisoned by her cursed blood and grew increasingly insane as the years passed. Died in an honorable duel with his son Julian after he drove the family to the brink of ruin from countless wars with other vampires. Deceased as of *Blood Curse*.

Adrun

A land of shifters and eternal darkness, full of life despite the odds.

Nyah

Queen of Adrun

Banished to the Fell Lands in *Blood Curse* due to Lucia's machinations for her throne. Instead of dying in the desolate land, Nyah used her Alchemyst blood to cure the Fell around her one at a time and establish life with the help of the Spring and Autumn Keys. Once her people discovered they could become shifters to permanently stave off the Fell curse, she was crowned Queen of Adrun and ruled with an empty throne beside her until she was reunited with her lifemate, Adrius. She is a shifter bonded to the greater wolf spirit Night's Howl.

Celeste

Princess of Adrun

A shy druid accustomed to taking the form of her beast, the greater fox spirit Swift Spirit. Raised believing her father was a great hero, she helped push him out of his depression so he could achieve his destiny and win back her mother's affections.

Izell Firebrand

Considered to be the oldest fae alive. She is King Oberon's grand-daughter and the first Archfae of the astral fae people. She's been through a lot and has learned to keep her true thoughts hidden under a thick layer of cynicism. Bonded to the spirit of her familiar in life, the golden dragon Queldian. She's a distant ancestor to Keegan Firetree, much to his chagrin.

Cedric Applewhite

A half-fae, half-human born in Adrun. He inherited an enchanted lute from his grandfather and became a self-taught musician. He is known for his energy and enthusiasm.

Chandra

Blood Princess Chandra, the Dreamer

The only Ancient locked into the Fell Lands alongside Nyah. She shed her vampirism and bonded to an earth spirit, becoming the head druid of Adrun. She now believes in peace, love, and parties, and gladly helped Taryn escape the grip of his rage.

Caladorn Nightweaver

An astral fae Blade who lost his wife tragically when they were both afflicted by the Fell curse. He surrendered his newborn daughter, Sorsha, to Neala and promised to repay the favor one day. He serves Nyah as her general and has developed an icy façade to endure his immortality alone.

Calinhes Nightweaver

An incredibly powerful Sorcerer who was afflicted with the Fell curse while defending an academy full of fae children. He became the leader of the Fell, crowned the Fell Emperor, and became the reason the Fell came to Earth due to his keen mind and magical prowess surviving the transition. His familiar was Zerenth and the dragon mourned Calinhes's death for an eternity, refusing to believe his master turned into a monster until confronted by the facts. Deceased as of *Blood Curse*.

Faerie

The mythical residents of a secret world.

Orin Lux

King of Faerie

A solar fae who cemented the peace of Faerie by marrying the Unseelie Queen, Kalimea Dread.

Kalimea Dread

Queen of Faerie

A destruction fae said to be soft for an Unseelie due to her efforts to curb homelessness and creation of social welfare programs. She is a forward-thinker amongst a people used to cruelty and callousness from the royals that preceded her.

Talina Evenfall

A circus performer and aether fae who has caught Sirius's eye as a potential lifemate. She is a ballerina who can defy gravity with powerful wind magic. Her familiar is the iridescent pink hummingbird, Gem.

Sorsha Shadestone

An astral fae Sorceress with the true sight ability. She was born in the Fell Lands, but her father gave her to Neala to raise, who adopted her alongside her brother-by-circumstance, Keegan. She is petite, sweet, and still sometimes acts like a teenager when she lets her guard down. Otherwise, she's a diplomat and advisor to King Orin from her position as an Archfae.

Keegan Firetree

An astral fae Blade who comes off tight-lipped and reserved. He was adopted by Neala alongside Sorsha and took on his adoptive mother's warrior persona. He is considered to be very powerful due to bonding with a fire dragon as his familiar.

Ashaela Dread

Unseelie Princess

Queen Kalimea's destruction fae half-sister. She is a Spellbreaker and trained assassin who relies heavily on her shadow magic. She is cagy and sarcastic, preferring not to be identified by her titles as she does not want to be the heir to her sister's throne.

Theron Shadestone

A powerful terran fae druid who has earned the title of Archdruid due to his skill in training young druids. He is standing in for his mate, Sorsha, in her absence from Faerie. His honest and to-the-point personality is already rubbing the rest of the Archfae the wrong way.

Sondus Arus

A spymaster for the royal family. He lost his wings long ago as a punishment from the last Unseelie Queen and thus has very little magic. His quick mind and photographic memory serve him well in his chosen profession.

Lyana Wavecaller

A guardian of one of the last known portals between Earth and Faerie. She is a sea serpent shifter, bonding to the soul of her familiar when he died. Fae society shunned her for her choice to become a *mort loci* and she was forced into a lonely underwater post.

The Trader

A reptilian lesser fae who runs a supernatural pawn shop.

Cast of Characters

Saniya

A wishmaker djinni, freed after millennia of servitude to the Unseelie royal family. Hides away in a remote village and rarely reveals herself.

King Oberon

A Primordial fae who served as the first King of Faerie. He originally welcomed both angels and demons to Faerie before they started infiltrating amongst his people and causing strife. He created The Veil and the Eye of Worlds in a powerful spell that was fueled by his life force. His sacrifice also cursed Seelie and Unseelie alike, but the way he worded the spell suggests that the Unseelie may one day break it by proving they are "friends to humanity."

Other

Soren

A humble man who is Adrius's guardian angel.

Gabriel Legion

In life, a vampire named for the amount of Fell he killed. In death, an angelic soldier whom has returned to Earth to hunt Jazrach. He was the original commander of the Fell Hunters before his untimely death.

Jazrach

A greater demon of corruption whom was unwillingly sacrificed to create the Dark Eye of Worlds. He plotted to escape his prison and eventually stole a living body to wreak havoc and spread his corruption. He is deceased as of *Queen's Return*, but his spark remains...

Getana

Fae goddess of earth.

Raenith

Fae goddess of fire.

Cyranos

Fae god of water.

Zalice

Fae god of wind.